NAYANA CURRIMBHOY grew up in India, where she attended an all-girls boarding school. She moved to the US in the early 1980s. Nayana lives in New York City with her husband and their teenage daughter. This is her first novel.

MISS TIMMINS' *School for Girls*

A NOVEL

Nayana Currimbhoy

HarperCollins *Publishers* India
a joint venture with
THE INDIA TODAY GROUP
New Delhi

First published in India in 2011 by
HarperCollins *Publishers* India
a joint venture with
The India Today Group

ISBN: 978-93-5029-073-6

2 4 6 8 10 9 7 5 3 1

HarperCollins *Publishers*
A-53, Sector 57, Noida 201301, India
77-85 Fulham Palace Road, London W6 8JB, United Kingdom
Hazelton Lanes, 55 Avenue Road, Suite 2900, Toronto, Ontario M5R 3L2
and 1995 Markham Road, Scarborough, Ontario M1B 5M8, Canada
25 Ryde Road, Pymble, Sydney, NSW 2073, Australia
31 View Road, Glenfield, Auckland 10, New Zealand
10 East 53rd Street, New York NY 10022, USA

Printed and bound at
Thomson Press (India) Ltd.

To my two true loves
Tarik & Sana

Acknowledgments

Special thanks to:

Carol Frederick, the book angel that every author of first fiction deserves.

Arshia Julian Mrugank and Rachel, my generous friends who waded through various half-baked versions over and over and over, over the five years it took to write this novel, and held my hand over the rough spots. And all the kind readers—too many to name—for their insights and encouragement.

My ever-beautiful mother and all my family and friends for the cushion of their love and support.

My valiant, wonderful agent, Dorian Karchmar; my brilliant editor, Claire Wachtel; and all at HarperCollins for making my story better, for giving it a chance to see the light.

And to the Ledig House writers' residency for the sweet writing spot.

MISS TIMMINS'
School for Girls

PROLOGUE

The Closet Room

Merch

TODAY CHARU CAME back to me, suddenly. On a summer morning, with the sunlight forming a sharp square on the balcony, she waltzed up the stairs to my room in Panchgani, above Dr. Desai's dispensary.

"What kind of idiot were you, Merch?" she asked, sitting on my bed, legs dangling. "Who were you in those days? Did you think you were that young man in *Crime and Punishment*? I can't remember his name. You know, that pale young man who lived in a cupboard and killed the old lady."

"Dimitri Dimitrovich," I said. "It's safe to call all Russian heroes Dimitri Dimitrovich."

"You know what I mean," she said. "Were you actually making devious plans in your closet room?" She lit herself a cigarette from the packet in her pocket and took a deep first drag. I recalled with a pang how she would fumble and look up at me to light it. I was her lighter in those days, and I loved it.

1974 was a forked tongue of a year, it spoke to me of murder and madness, and love and laughter in equal measure.

I did not answer her question directly. "I was obsessed with you in those days, Charu," I said. It was not the answer she was looking for, but it was the truth. I was obsessed with Charu in 1974, when we were all embroiled in the murder of Moira Prince, and I am obsessed with her now, though twelve years have passed.

"And who are you *these* days, Merch?" she might just as easily have asked—Charu, if she asks these days, is always forthright—and I would not have answered that, either, though I think about it constantly.

Today, when she walked into my room, all the surfaces turned glossy. She tilted her head to the side, she ran her fingers through her tousled hair, she stood, she sat, she smoked, she was a ball of nervous energy, she brought with her a heady whiff of the old days. I thought of the roses we crushed with our fingers and piled on a steel plate, our walks on rain-soaked nights. The mountains that framed my windows stopped being paper cutouts. I felt the current creep back into my hands.

"I just had to ask you in person. I rushed all the way from Bombay, dropped everything," she said. Charu was Atlas, holding up her world, caring for everyone. So sure, she had a lot to drop. I had picked up nothing all these years. I was as free as a vagrant and should have been content.

"You were seen on the cliff that night," she said, accusing. We both knew, of course, that she meant the night the rain stopped. The night the body of the British girl was found broken on the black rocks below the cliff.

"Why didn't you tell me, Merch?" she said. "All these years."

It is that kind of story. Though it lies sleeping, it can awake at any time. Facts and fictions are nearly one. They ripen and burst suddenly, without a warning.

"I forgot," I said, though I knew she could not possibly believe me. "Anyway, it's not exactly true," I said, and then added a third excuse for good measure, an extra pat of butter on a frying pan, "and we all had our secrets, didn't we?"

1974 was the year of the Great Panchgani Scandals.

Panchgani is not on the way to anywhere at all. It is a small town on a medium mountain reached only by one long and winding road. In the summer families come from the cities in the plains, children lurch through the bazaar on undernourished ponies, honeymoon couples climb up to Sydney Point to watch the sunset. But the monsoon settles long and hard in this region of the mountains. Nobody comes to Panchgani in the monsoons, except perhaps sturdy parents of small sick children. The retirees, TB patients, and hotel owners close their homes and their businesses and go off to live with their daughters in Poona. No one leaves Panchgani in the monsoons. The steep mountain slopes are slippery, and you can see trucks overturned in the valleys. The rain closes in around the town, and those who remain consider themselves the real people of Panchgani.

The eight boarding schools stay open, and all those that serve them. The teachers, the servants, the shopkeepers, the post office, the police station, Kaka's Bakery and Eatery, the Irani Café, and the old men who have nowhere to go. And me, Merch.

At the Irani Café in the rain, the old men played bridge while we drank endless cups of tea between joints, which we would smoke in the abandoned municipal park just outside the bazaar. We would watch the Timmins girls file past in their rubber raincoats. In the monsoons, the schoolgirls were lined up in twos and taken for long walks. There were only yellow, blue, and green raincoats that year, each of the ugliest shade possible. The line would stop to regroup just before the end of the bazaar, and the laggards would waddle across my vision like seals in hospital bed mats.

When I picture Panchgani in the monsoon of 1974, the line of schoolgirls turns into a line of ants. I see Panchgani as a circle of anthills rising out of the red mud, each with its own separate army of ants. The murder of the British girl smashed through the world order like a sharp rock thrown by a cruel boy. I remember the shock of it, the sheer insanity of it. White women and locals who lived in mountain hollows, schoolgirls, hippies, policemen, mad teachers, were all forced to rub up close against each other. Information jumped lines and became contaminated.

Then the scandals passed into memory and myth. Everyone went back to their anthills, regurgitating their own scraps of information. No one has the whole story, not even me.

I could have told Charu that she was at least half right. I *was* sitting in this very room and making dubious plans that year. Truth is, I have sat in the cocoon of closet rooms and made devious, dubious plans all my life. I could have told Charu that plans are nothing unless action follows. Or, I could show her.

I think I should, tonight. Twelve years is nothing.

BOOK ONE

Panchgani

Charu

ONE

High Upon the Mountains

IN 1974, JUST three weeks before my twenty-first birthday, I left my family and traveled halfway across India to teach English and literature at Miss Timmins' School for Girls. The school was in Panchgani, an eight-hour drive from Bombay in those days.

My father and I joined the school party at Poona Station. Two train carriages carrying the banners *Miss Timmins' School for Girls Traveling Party* had departed at dawn from Bombay and deposited the girls at Poona Station by noon. We had been instructed to meet them in the First Class Ladies' Waiting Room, where we found the girls in blue-checked dresses eating sandwiches and boiled eggs from brown paper bags. Their dresses were flared from the waist, like umbrellas. Bananas were being passed around. We were to go the rest of the way up the mountains by road. After lunch, the girls were lined up and stuffed into three red and yellow buses. Baba and I were told to get into the middle bus by a dark lady in a white sari, no doubt a teacher.

Baba was the only male on the bus. We sat apart, he and I, like lepers on the last, bumpy bench. The girls looked back curiously from time to time. The bus had a sullen air as it grunted and groaned up the foothills outside Poona. Some girls were sniffling. They seemed to be feeling as rough and as raw as I was.

As we went deeper and higher into the mountains, up the narrow winding road, the sunlight became slanted, and the air thin and clean. The girls revived and started singing. Baba and I sat quiet and erect, I near the window. Eventually the girls swung into their school song.

High upon the mountains
Away from city clamor
By graceful trees surrounded
There stands our own dear school

On the bench beside us sat two sisters with short brown hair, twins I thought. They sang loudly and soulfully, and completely out of tune. Baba looked at me and we exchanged a brief smile. We were both thinking of Ayi.

We revel in the leisure
The studies, sports, and fun
The beauty of the hillside
The breezes, rain, and sun

I knew the words by heart. I had spent a large part of that summer in my room with the school prospectus, imagining myself in its blurred black-and-white photos. A certain Miss Timmins had founded the school in 1901 for the daughters of British civil servants whose health was too delicate for the heat of the plains. In those days, the girls were carried up the mountains in chairs by natives, a journey that took two weeks. After the British left in 1947, the school had tottered for a time but then come into its own. Now the girls were Indian, and came from Bombay and Kerala and Aden and Africa and from sugar estates along the Deccan Plateau to get the right kind of English education.

The song lurched to its high finale with the girls swaying as the bus twisted up the last mountain.

So here's to Timmins
To dear old Ti-im-mins
May we be always true

I was close to tears. It just all seemed so silly. This was not a part of the dream. I wanted to be a Bombay girl, with bell-bottom pants and foreign perfume floating in the breeze behind me. I wanted to be a Bombay girl, with no stain on my face.

I had broached the idea the day I got my B.A. results. "I want to go to Bombay," I said at dinner, still basking in the glory of my First Class. "To teach in a college."

I had expected dismay and shock. Instead, a meaningful glance passed between my parents.

"Well, what's wrong with Indore? Why don't you teach here, in Indore?" said Ayi.

"For a little while," said Baba.

I saw then that they had spoken the truth between them, man and wife: It would be very difficult, perhaps even impossible, they had agreed, staring up at the whirring fan with their heads on identical hard pillows, to find a good boy for their only child. Charu should get a job. Be independent. But they had imagined me at home, with them. I soon convinced them they needed to let me go. They too must have known it deep down. It was time to let me go.

Bombay was out of the question. "We have no real relatives there," said Baba firmly, and Baba was not so often firm.

And so they settled upon a cloistered school where I could be tethered, and perhaps even tended. Miss Timmins' School for Girls, run by British missionaries. Indian teachers were allowed, but only Protestant Christians. The school was making an exception for me because cousins from the shiny branch of my family had studied in Timmins for many years. No doubt the missionaries had been assured that I was a conservative, well-brought-up girl. I myself could not dispute that.

It had seemed a good step. Closer to Bombay than my tight middle-class world. Now, though, I had the feeling I had veered in the wrong direction. I wanted to hold Baba's hand and say, "Let's run back home."

But Baba sat beside me impassive in his public face, his trousers creased, his back ramrod straight. I looked out of the window and let the wind unfurl my hair. Baba, the fountain of all facts, had told me that it rained over two hundred inches during the monsoons in Panchgani.

"You should expect the current soon, around the second of June. I will keep you informed of its progress," he assured me as the bus puffed past a yellow signboard that said *Welcome to Panchgani, the Kashmir of Maharashtra* alongside poorly painted mountain ranges.

The road to the school was a narrow one, lined with tall trees that shook silver leaves in the wind. "The British planted silver oaks in the early 1900s," said Baba. He always spurted more facts when he was uncomfortable. Ten minutes later, we turned in to the school.

I hold it in my mind still, the way I saw the school on that first day. A red castle with two towers, rising from red mud. The bus shuddered to a stop in a compound with a large banyan tree in the center. Girls pranced around the benches between the roots, chattering like birds.

"The iron in the water is very healthy. You will soon have rosy cheeks," said Baba, picking up a pinch of the dry red mud. Later, it was the water that we blamed for all the madness and chaos of that monsoon—water from deep old wells that dug into the gut of the ancient mountains.

The principal came towards us, smiling. "Ah, you must be Miss Charulata Apte. Welcome to Timmins," she said, her hands outstretched towards us.

Miss Nelson, a British woman with tight brown curls, wore a blue-and-red-striped dress and a two-string pearl necklace. She walked erect. Her smile was grave and her eyes were large and round through her thick glasses.

I am not sure if I even noticed the purse on that first day. But now, of course, it is impossible to imagine her without it. Miss Nelson always carried a flat white purse. No one had ever seen Miss Nelson without her purse. The girls claimed that she took it to the bathroom with her. They said she kept inside it photos of a lover who jilted her at the altar. In England, of course.

The outrageous Miss Prince, who delighted in shocking the staid school, claimed that the saintly principal collected pornographic pictures of young girls. "Every night, she prays to the Lord to help her burn them. But the next morning, she cannot. So she carries them around another day, afraid to die," she said in the staff room one day as all the teachers pretended not to hear her.

No one had ever seen Miss Nelson open the steel clasp of her purse.

Miss Nelson lifted a thick green curtain to a room lined with pink wicker sofas. "Do sit down and have a cup of tea in the staff room. I will greet the little ones and be back to show you around," she said. The little girls, some of them seemed to be four or five, were tumbling down from the last bus.

Then Miss Nelson turned to reveal the largest bottom I had ever seen. It started at the waist, just below the belt, and seemed to be strapped onto her like a shelf, like a pillow a clown might wear. It joggled and jiggled along quite unaware of her front, and completed a turn a split second after she did. When she walked towards you she was an ice queen, a model of decorum and dignity. But from behind, as she waddled around among the children like a mother hen, I could just see the feathers sticking out of her bottom.

I felt, suddenly, that she might understand me. I thought that she too might have spent hours agonizing about when to enter, and when to leave, a room. She was two-sided, like me. But she was the light, I thought. She could enter straight and strong.

I, I am the night. I prefer people to see me first from behind. My hair is rain. It is thick and black and long, and it swings on my hips like music. My hair is my own private beat as I walk to school, to college, to family dinners, as I walk behind my mother, carrying her vegetables and fish.

I often combed my hair drooping over my cheeks in one low plait. I hoped to cover the red blot on the right side of my face, even just a little. Specially at weddings and parties, when the old aunts gathered. "Oh, no, Shalini," they wailed as my mother's shining face closed up. "What happened to her? Oh, she was so fresh, like a cucumber, when she was small. Now how will you get the poor thing married?"

My mother always tried to shield me; she would give me a pat, or a pleading look, which hurt even more. I hurt for me, and for her, having to bear us both, her husband and her daughter, like weights upon her back. For we both had our blots, he and I.

My ayi rarely hugged me; we were not a hugging family. She put all her love into my hair. She massaged my scalp and oiled it with the special homemade coconut oil. She coiled it around her hand, shining in the sun like a serpent before she plaited it. She wove bright and beautiful ribbons into my hair, and tied them in big bows that I wore through the day like medals. She told me stories, mainly from her endless legend store. And she would weave it all into my hair.

"This mark makes you special. Now only those who can really see inside can know what a beautiful girl you are," she would say, tilting my chin up so she could get the parting straight down the middle. "It is your special mark, maybe from your last life. It is a signal for the right man. Now don't forget your Ayi-Baba when you go off to the palace with your prince," she teased, sending me out laughing to meet the world. Later, when I started wearing flowers instead of bows, Ayi paid the doorman's son five rupees a month to bring gajras and fresh flowers every morning at seven.

Miss Nelson put her purse arm comfortingly around me and assured my father that they would take good care of me. "We are a family here," she said.

The school was terraced down a hillside. Behind the stern gothic face, it fanned out into long low buildings with red tin roofs. Miss Nelson led us down wide covered corridors and staircases, through the school to the hospital building. I was hypnotized by her jiggling bottom.

"Most of our younger teachers are in Sunbeam, a separate house behind the bazaar, but we thought we would keep Charul-a-a-ta-a here with us," Miss Nelson told my father. Then she turned to me, and her eyes seemed to twinkle a little. "We can't have your parents worrying, now, can we?" she said.

She never got to calling me Charu, like everyone else. And until the end, she did not change the drawn-out *la-ata* with the very wrong *t*.

The hospital was at the bottom corner of the school, set at

right angles to the rest of the buildings. It contained about ten narrow beds with white counterpanes and painted white metal lockers. There were two smaller rooms for infectious cases. In the front was a dispensary. Out to the right, two rooms, one for the nurse, and the other, to my horror, was to be for me.

Baba, being a man, could not stay in the school, and had decided to go back to Poona right away. He looked at me longingly, passed his hand over my head, and left. We promised each other a letter every week. I went back to my room and sat on the narrow spring bed. The room had a desk, a lamp, an upright chair, and a small lumpy sofa covered in the same bright pink fabric as the staff room. There was one window facing some trees and dried bushes. It smelled of disinfectant. I felt dislocated from everything I had ever known. I did not have the strength to get up and unpack. I just sat on the bed, staring at the peeling wall, until it was time to go to dinner.

TWO

The Playing Fields of Eton

Miss Nelson had told me to come to the staff dining room for dinner at seven, and I walked in as stiff as a post. Only the three British missionaries had arrived. Besides Miss Nelson, there were Miss Manson and Miss Wilson, both with short curled hair, long dresses, and big red feet encased in sensible sandals.

I imagined how they must have come from picture postcard villages in England to this remote outpost in the hills of western India to do the Lord's work. They were here to convert the daughters of rich Bombay businessmen. They were known as the Holy Trinity. They sat at a table for four in the center of the room. Miss Nelson invited me to join them "while we wait for the others to arrive," she said.

"Indore, Miss Apte," said Miss Wilson. "It must be very hot at this time of the year." I was grateful to her for giving me such a solid opening line. Miss Wilson wore a straight orange skirt that reached just below her knees. I guessed her to be in her thirties. She was the youngest and most fashionable of the missionaries, though she was by no means beautiful. She had a long, hatchet-like face, stringy blond hair, and narrow brown eyes that twinkled when she smiled.

"Yes, we all drink sherbet and wait for the monsoons," I replied.

"You will find Panchgani most pleasant, Miss Apte," said Miss Manson, a thin, blue-eyed woman with big teeth. "Although the monsoons can get very heavy in these parts, and unfortunately, you have joined us in the monsoon term. The girls get very restless with the constant rains. This is why I introduced Scottish dancing last year; it keeps them active and busy. Perhaps you would like to join me in teaching the middles Scottish dancing this year," she added brightly. "I could do with some help."

I really knew nothing about the dancing habits of the Scottish. But I wanted to help. "I could teach them Indian folk dances," I offered, scrounging my mind for school dances in gaudy garments.

"Well, I'm not sure that they would be complex enough for competitions," she said. Pursing her lips, she blushed a dark, deep red. I knew I had said something wrong, but it took me a few days to understand the reason for Miss Manson's disapproval and discomfort. She blushed a beetroot red because I had unwittingly questioned the core belief of the school: British was Better.

The rest of the staff members came streaming in and saved me from the need to continue the conversation. Miss Nelson bowed her head, and said, "For what we are about to receive may the Lord make us truly thankful."

After grace, Miss Nelson took me around and introduced me to a blur of women, occasionally putting an arm around me in an encouraging manner. She pulled out an empty chair for me at a table made up of three brown ladies in curls and frocks.

"The last empty chair," she said, smiling at the ladies. "I am sure you will welcome young Miss Apte to your table."

Turned out that, in a room arranged, both at breakfast and at dinner, quite symmetrically by race, I was deposited at the Anglo Indian table because there was no empty chair at the Indian tables. The British table at the center, one Anglo Indian table to the right, and the rest, Indian. I had never in my little life met either a British missionary or an Anglo Indian. I learned soon enough that Anglo Indians were a small ethnic group of mixed race—progeny of British civil servants who had married native girls. They had adopted Western ways, and though most of them looked as brown as us, they wore dresses, and spoke English with a nearly British accent.

The food was awful. The mutton was chewy, the gravy watery and tasteless. I felt all choked up, thinking of myself every evening in this room, with all these strange women, eating nasty food and then going back to my hospital room. *Gird your loins*, I told myself firmly, *this is not the time to turn into jelly*, although jelly was what I longed to become. I stuffed the food in my mouth and answered in monosyllables.

As we got up to leave, one of the three Anglo Indian ladies, Miss Henderson, the middles matron, invited me to tea. Her room was in between Upper and Lower Rowson, the two dorms that were her domain. It was a large room, with runners and tablecloths with lace edges everywhere, and smiling photographs of family looking down from every wall. Miss Henderson, a brown woman with bowlegs and buckteeth, had been in Timmins, she told me, for fifteen years.

A tall and stately ayah bought in the tea tray, with an embroidered pink tea-cozy. Miss Henderson produced some delicious biscuits from a tin.

"I hear you are teaching the seniors. If you have any trouble with them, you come and talk to me," she said. "So many of them have passed through my hands. This is your first time teaching? The thing to do, my dear, is to be strict for the first month. After that you can relax."

"Are they difficult?" I asked, anxiously.

"Well, at this level, there are some troublemakers, but it's mostly just high spirits," she assured me.

After tea, she took up her knitting—she was halfway through a tan sweater for Frankie, her sister's son, who was soon to be going to college. She asked after my cousins who had been in Timmins.

"And you looked a little lost at dinner," she added, as I was leaving. "Don't worry. You will soon meet all the nice young teachers who live in Sunbeam, in town, and then you can go out with them. Not that there is anywhere to go, really, in Panchgani," she said with a sigh.

I left her room feeling much better.

Timmins was a small school, with less than two hundred girls, no more than fifteen in each class. It was set firmly in the pattern of British boarding schools. The girls were divided into three houses—green, yellow, and red—called Rowson, Clarens, and Willoughby. Miss Rowson and Miss Clarens, it appears, were former principals. No one knew who Willoughby was. The girls wore their house belts and badges at all times.

The prospectus and accompanying instructions had made it clear that each girl had her bed, her stool, her locker, her peg, her bath time, her place in the dining room, and her desk assigned. From the rising bell at 6:45 a.m., to the lights-out bell at 9 p.m., each moment in each day was regulated. Activity changes were signaled by bells, and each activity had a prescribed dress code down to shoes and knickers. Navy blue blazers emblazoned with "God My Leader" were worn in the winter term. Before entering the dining room, the prayer hall, or the church, the girls naturally fell into class lines in height order, and when they left the school, they formed a double line that was called the crocodile.

"The Battle of Waterloo," Miss Nelson often said without a trace of irony to a hall brimming with brown girls, "was won on the playing fields of Eton."

I had decided that I was going to stick to my dress code from college. Tight chudidars with A-line kurtas were in fashion. Even Bombay girls wore them when they were not wearing short dresses or bell-bottom pants. I had had ten "teaching sets" stitched, each of them with cotton dupattas in solid colors. I always wore them crisp and starched in Indore. I did have a sari moment when I saw all the Indian teachers wrapped up in them, but I had brought only two silk saris from Ayi's Bombay days. "Take them in case you have to attend a party or function," she said. They were not appropriate, and so I decided against it. I was the youngest teacher in the school, and kurtas were very long and decorous. Even conservative young girls in second-city colleges were wearing them—there was no doubt about that—and I would look most ridiculous in a frock, with my wide hips and thin stick legs.

Mornings started at 8:30 with prayers. The girls lined up by class and filed into the prayer hall to piano music, and then they stood up and launched into hymn number 328 from little bound hymn books.

Great is thy faithfulness.
All I have needed,
Thy hand has provided.
Great is thy faithfulness,
Lord unto me . . .

The prayer hall was a part of the school's main building. Light streamed in from large windows to the right. Through the front arches, I could see the net-ball field, and beyond, the school gate. The air was crisp, and quite cool for the month of May. The girls' sweet voices rose and fell, the gold frames of Miss Nelson's glasses glinted in the sharp sunlight. It was all from a novel I should have read.

In the drawing room in Indore, we had a glass paperweight with an Eiffel Tower inside it. I had spent years gazing into its magical depths. If you turned it upside down, snow drifted around the tower. I saw Miss Timmins' School inside the paperweight, sloshing in blue water. That morning in the clear mountain light, I stepped inside that paperweight. My life in our third-floor flat in Navjeevan Housing Society, my room overlooking the gulmohor tree, my days as an earnest student in Jeejeebai Wadia College seemed all wavy and distant, like a shore seen from the underbelly of a sunlit lake.

I'll give myself six months here, I thought. Then, with the money I collect from teaching, I will go to the best plastic surgeon in Bombay, get my blot removed, and then, and then, after glamorous adventures and maybe even a romance, I will go back to Indore without a blemish and marry a handsome boy from a good family. After that moment I did not feel homesick for a single instant. I simply felt that I had been dropped into another life.

THREE

Baba's Blot

THE WINDOW OF my room in the hospital looked out upon a few straggly bushes. I missed the moon from my balcony window in Indore, though there were nights there when I had hated everything, especially the cold hard moon. Those were the nights I blamed Baba for my blot. But in the morning when I saw him, puffs of graying hair above the newspaper and curling toes popped up on the footstool, I could not hate him. I could not love him, either. He was a man who had learned to be content with the pickings from the ground.

He began to teach me chess when I was seven years old. We had just moved to Indore under a cloud. My father was a good and patient teacher. "Think at least three moves ahead," he always said. He was proud when I beat him. "Look here, Shalini," he would shout to my mother in the kitchen across the hall. "Your daughter is getting smarter than us." He made me love the game. We played with the sounds and smells of my mother's cooking, the children shouting in the corridors, and echoes from the radios of neighboring flats. But I was at best a middling player, and we both knew it. Later, in college, when I had to study or preferred to read or go out, he began to play with Prashant, our neighbor's son. Prashant turned out to be a star student and became a state champion when he was ten. My father went with him to the championship games and beamed happily from the sidelines, his receding-hairline forehead shining under the tubelights.

Baba had been a rising star in the navy, a favorite of the Admiral. It was understood that he was being groomed for the big time in those heady years after Independence. I remember him coming home in the evenings, putting his white cap on the telephone table, and throwing me up in the air. I remember him rubbing his stubby evening chin against me till I cried. The father of my childhood was tall and broad-shouldered. He had a loud voice and a quick temper. We lived in a flat in Bombay facing the sea, and we had many parties in which women in chiffon saris and bright red lipstick leaned out into the sunset, their sari pallus billowing out like sails.

One hot afternoon in Indore, in my mother's steel Godrej cupboard, I found a family photograph from those days. I kept it in the top drawer of my desk at all times, until one late-night moment in Panchgani, when I shoved it into some safe spot from which it has not emerged. I know it will turn up smiling some day from some forgotten purse or shoe box. But in those days, even when I was not staring at it, I could see it, lying on top of my notebooks, taunting me, like a naughty child.

Waiting to pull me into a vortex of strawberry and cream dreams, and then return me, rigid, to my empty little life.

We were so full of promise then, the three of us. My father, lean and erect in his white uniform, looks sharp and arrogant, reaching for the world. My mother is pregnant, perhaps five months. She smiles straight past the camera into a future filled with laughing sons. It is a black-and-white photograph. I stand between them, six years old, wearing a white lace dress, my hair tied with a large bow. I am frowning because my mother has forced me to wear a stiff petticoat to hold out my frilly dress. I still remember how it poked that morning. There were times I would open the drawer and kiss the chubby, petulant little face in that picture. That face had inhabited another life, not mine. My skin was clean, soft, and smooth in that life.

But I remember also, from the flat by the sea, raised voices of my parents fighting late into the night, and my mother sobbing in the balcony. I remember once she shook me awake in the middle of the night, and said, "Get ready. We are going to visit your cousins." She dressed me up in a red dress with a white sash, made me sit in the living room, and went to pack our things. I fell asleep on the sofa and woke up the next morning in my red dress. She had lost her courage, or her resolve, and decided to stay on. The house was always filled with the glare of the sea, so that in the afternoons you had to squint around with half-closed eyes.

Two years later, we were a flat-tire family, the air sucked out of us. If a photograph had been taken of us then, it would be a Hindi movie parody of the first one. My father, his face gray, his shoulders stooped, his uniform gone. My mother, twenty pounds heavier, her face ten years older, her tall and strapping sons to live only in her dreams. During the nightmare of Baba's court-martial, she had lost her pregnancy in the eighth month. She barely escaped with her life and knew she could have no more children. And for me, just above my lip, on the right side of the face that grown-ups had always found so beautiful, the first signs of a vivid strawberry mark appeared. That was the last time anyone ever petted my head and said, "You will be beautiful, just like your mother."

But in the flat-tire photograph, I would have been smiling. The blot had made me conscious of how people looked at me, and I was always careful to put my best face forward. I was always smiling.

I did not know why my father was court-martialed, though I knew that the charges had finally been dropped. He had never been found guilty. I asked my mother once, many years later. "There were people who were jealous of him, very powerful people. Your father played big games in those days," she said, sighing. We were folding the washed clothes, stiff with starch. She kept rubbing down the same pajama leg, and I was afraid to ask again.

I did not want to jump into the deep unknown that swirled around our family island. I'd rather step into it slowly, testing the waters. But I would reinflate the family again one day, I promised myself that evening. I would go back to Bombay and discover the truth.

The dream blossomed in my mind and became a big, shady tree. The blot sometimes disappeared before I began the sleuthing, or sometimes it disappeared towards the denouement. But, always, beautiful and bold, I would lay the whole truth bare before the world, my glowing parents by my side.

I would be like Jhansi ki Rani.

In 1858, during the siege of Jhansi, the British soldiers wrapped their burning heads in wet towels, and, in the long hot hours, as they lay behind their sandbanks, they strained for a sight of the rebel queen. They wrote in their diaries how for hours, for days, they watched her, their rough uniforms sticking to their red bodies. It was said that the Rani, during battle, wore a long red tunic, red trousers, and a belt with a diamond-studded sword. In the cool of the evenings, the British strained their field glasses at the ramparts of the fort, hoping to catch a glimpse of her. Some claimed to have seen her, seated together with her female favorite—who never left her side and dressed just like her—drinking sherbet with four hundred troops of the Fifth Irregular Horse. Sometimes I dreamt that I was the Rani, charging on my white horse to save the world.

But in the mornings I would be the same smiling, tentative girl again, swinging her pigtails to school.

Baba was kind and careful now, very slow to anger or emotion. He was small and shrunken; he had closed in the canvas of space around him, this man who had once been waiting to paint in large, bold strokes. The first move he taught me in chess was castling. "The king is the core of your game. First protect the core," he said, "and then you can take your risks." The only time he was ever angry with my mistakes at chess was when I passed up the ideal castling opportunity and wanted to forge ahead instead.

The year of the court-martial for me was a year of whispers. At home, the adults were whispering behind closed doors at all hours of the day and night. At St. Anne's School, where I had been just one of many children, suddenly I was surrounded by whispers. I would find teachers whispering to each other and pointing to me. Bhavna, my best friend, came to me one day when I was drinking at the water fountain. She was with two other girls. "My father said that her father is a bad man. He took things from the government," said Gauri with the puffed chest and double chin of a child imparting important information. Bhavna did not look at me as I passed by them, and she stopped being my best friend.

I told Ayi what they had said as she was combing my hair one morning. She began to weep. My mother was a common crier. Tears came into her large green eyes, and they slid silently down her face for weddings, Hindi movies, and arguments with Baba. But that day she wept. It was the first time I felt that bottomless feeling in my stomach. We hugged each other and wept and wept and wept. I did not go to school that day. Soon after, we moved to Indore, and into the soothing arms of anonymity.

Over the years we built a life for ourselves, a small and simple life of rituals and habits. My parents turned their backs on the world and wove me into a little safety net. They created a snug little nest of a life for me. There were no raised voices, no fights, and few issues. No passions, no dreams. Baba got a job as a regional manager in Chitnis Transport, the large trucking company that belonged to my mother's family. He sat in a small air-conditioned office above the garage. He rarely missed a day of work. He left the house at 9:30, after his morning walk. He came back at seven, and then we played chess or read or listened to the radio.

He earned much less than he used to in Bombay, but it was enough for our new lives. We lived in a one-bedroom flat in a concrete-block colony of tiny flats with gray and green terrazzo floors. We lived on the third floor. My parents enclosed the bedroom balcony, built some cupboards, and put in a bed, and I had a cozy little balcony room. It overlooked a gulmohor tree, which played with every tiny breeze on hot afternoons, and swayed under the night sky. I had to go through their room to enter mine. In Bombay we had a cook, a cleaning boy, and an ayah just for me. In Indore, we had no servants except the maid who came to clean the bathrooms and sweep and mop the floor for one hour every day. Nobody ever came to dinner. Sometimes we went to family or community functions, and once or twice a year my mother took me to Kolhapur to visit her parents. The family gash was closed up, unlicked, unmourned.

And so it seeped into my face, red and angry. It started with a rash on the right side of my face, just above my lips.

At first, Dr. Dhavle decided it was an allergic reaction to food.

"It could well be a mango allergy. I have seen that very often in children. Starts suddenly," he said.

But the rash became a stain as large as an onion. When active it itched so furiously that I had to fight from rubbing and rubbing and rubbing till it grew red and sticky and white liquid would ooze out so that everyone would be afraid to look at me. When fallow it lay brown and round above my lip with a paper-thin patina over it. I became quiet and secretive. I called it the blot. It was the blot on my face, a blot on my world.

We went to see a skin specialist. "It is an eczema, a nervous condition caused by the recent changes," he said. Ayi tried homeopathy, she tried Ayurveda, and she took me to all sorts of astrologers and healers. I remember so many afternoons when she would come in a rickshaw to pick me up from school, and we would wait in crowded rooms and corridors, and even in a line that snaked down the steps of dark buildings, for some famous visiting savant. She always brought me lemonade in a flask and a chutney sandwich. Those afternoons, surrounded by people with improbable diseases being cured by outlandish procedures, were tinged with the aftertaste of those sandwiches.

All my life green chutney sandwiches have stood for hope.

The more bizarre schemes were the ones we expected the most of. They seemed more likely to produce miracles.

We disagree now on whether the cow-dung phase was after the cow-pee phase or concurrent with it. I clearly remember washing the blot with hot and foaming cow urine in the morning, and at night, tying a bandage of cow dung on it.

The cow-dung bandage was a big event. Ayi mixed the dung with some herbs and medicines, and then applied a thick paste of it to a bandage cut from soft cotton saris. The poultice had to stay in place over the blot, but not cover the mouth, a process that took hours. It would always be done in the back balcony where we hung our clothes to dry. Baba would patiently tie a sling over my left ear with his deft naval fingers, till all three of us felt it was just right.

The dung bandage would smell and prickle, and I could not sleep. Ayi often sat by my bed in the moonlight, singing old lullabies. I thought she had the sweetest voice. It was much later that I realized she sang completely out of tune. Every morning we would open the bandage breathlessly, wash my face, and examine the blot. Each morning, we felt it was fading, getting less angry, or getting marginally smaller. I remember this phase going on for at least half a year, though Ayi assures me it was just a little over a month. She also insists that the cow-dung phase was different from the cow-urine phase. "I can tell you because I remember going to get the urine from this old woman called Tanbai. At five every morning. It used to be dark, and she would come with the cow, holding the urine in a tin mug. It had to be the cow's first urine."

Another urine phase created a more lasting change. My mother became what she referred to delicately as a urine-therapy practicer, which actually meant, much to my disgust, that she drank her own urine.

It started with a dream seller who came to our house one mellow winter morning. He had an unkempt beard and a juicy, nasal voice. Slurping his tea from his saucer, he told us that he was confident that he could cure 90 percent of all diseases with two things: a buttermilk enema once a week—"Cleans your whole system out," he roared—and drinking a few sips of one's own urine every morning. "You can even apply your urine to cure skin diseases," he said. He assured my mother that my blot would be gone by puberty if I did this.

My mother wisely decided against the buttermilk enemas, but felt that the urine therapy was worth pursuing. Even Morarji Desai was doing it. "But he is at least sixty-two years old," I whined. "That's different."

I was twelve years old, and I just could not bring myself to drink my urine. I did pour it in a red plastic glass and try to bring it to my lips, but I could not. In order to set an example, my mother started doing it herself. She began to feel healthier almost immediately. "You know how my feet hurt at night? Now all gone," she would say. Or, "You know that burn I had on my right hand? I applied it for two days, in the morning, and see, it's gone." I was embarrassed and disgusted at the thought of my mother drinking pee, and I made her promise never to tell any of my friends. The first person I ever told was Merch, the Mystery Man, but he always made telling so easy, listening with those big, still eyes.

My mother had been a beauty. She was a small-town girl, from Kolhapur, but she was the daughter of the famous Chitnis clan, an upstanding and light-skinned Maharashtrian Brahmin family whose gaily colored trucks plied the roads as far north as New Delhi. She was a princess. She had large green eyes that lit up when she smiled, and an oval face with delicious dimples. She was vivacious and high-strung. Her match to a promising young naval officer from a much less stellar family had been quite controversial since there were already many offers for her hand from good families. My grandfather had met my father in Bombay at a dinner and was so impressed by this bright, graceful officer that, without even meeting his family, he had decided to marry his favorite daughter to this man. The young man would give her a big life, he had reckoned. Wisely, he cultivated him, followed the young man's career for two years while his daughter was finishing college. Then, a month after her B.A. exams, when Shalini was twenty-one, the couple had a grand wedding in Kolhapur. My father was ten years older than my mother. With his well-bred beauty by his side, he jumped a few steps up all sorts of ladders. I wonder still how she felt about it. Did her father ask her what she wanted?

The "tragedy" of Shalini's life always hung in the air during our visits to Kolhapur. I dreaded the visits. I felt apart from my cousins because I was marked. For the aunts, I was a part of their beloved Shalini's "big problem." I hated and feared the seven aunts. I slunk around the rambling house on hot afternoons as they sat gossiping, waiting to pick up clues about my mysterious past.

One day, I overheard Tai, the oldest sister, talking to a new young daughter-in-law of the house. "And that night, after the court-martial, she broke every bottle in the house," my aunt said with relish. "She took a stick and smashed the whole cupboard, bottle by bottle. Then she started cleaning up the mess. But she was crying so hard, and, just imagine, eight months pregnant, she was down on her hands and knees, picking up the glass. They found her passed out and scratched and bleeding. I tell you, she is a saint," she said, solemnly, adding in a whisper, "They said her sari was soaked in whisky."

Tai was the oldest, fattest, and most domineering of the aunts. The younger women called her Hitler. She was going through a long and sweaty menopause, and periodically had to wipe her fat and pitted face with a small towel she kept tucked into her sari waist. I remember the towel as always being shocking pink with white polka dots.

The episode she related brought alive an afternoon I had until then believed to be a dream: My mother is in hospital, and Baba has been sleeping there at night. My ayah Anandi bai and I are picking up pieces of glass in my parents' bedroom. It is hot in the room; the windows facing the sea are closed against the monsoons. Anandi bai has big patches of sweat on her pink sari blouse. I remember finding a large, thick piece of glass on the counterpane. Often, in my little balcony room in Indore, I awoke in the dead of night from a dream in which I was picking up large pieces of clinking glass off my bed. I would find myself sitting up, sweeping the quilt with my hands, my hair falling over my face.

Now I knew the central memory was true, and the dreams, ripples. The story filled out a whole corner of the jigsaw puzzle. My father's booming voice, the late night fights and tears, the long parties. My father was drinking in those days! And my mother had blamed that for all the troubles. She had passed out that night and lost her baby.

After that stolen conversation, the summer holiday in Kolhapur passed in a daze. I was fourteen years old. I was numb with shock. In all my years in Indore, I had never even met anyone who "drank." Sometimes a person was referred to as a "going to clubs and drinking sort of man," and I always imagined such men to be mysterious and brutal, smelling of aftershave. Not like us. I spent that holiday reading Barbara Cartland romances, novels set in nineteenth-century England. Every morning I would set out with one of the ayahs, walk to Kamal's Book House, and take out a romance. I read twelve Barbara Cartland books and a thick, fat hardbound romance called *Thelma* on that holiday. At night, I read with a torch under the mosquito net and listened to the dogs howling. There were nights when the dogs of the town seemed to be discussing the history of the entire universe.

"Shalini, what's with that daughter of yours?" the aunts would ask. "All day she lies around and reads. She should learn to cook. How will you get her married?"

How will you get her married? That was the refrain that always followed my mother and me like a tail on a dog. We had learned to ignore it. Ayi would smile and proudly say, "Our Charu is so clever, she wins so many prizes. English prize, chess prize, history prize. Charu, go get your report," she would order proudly.

As she sat gossiping with the women in the courtyard at the center of the house, I could see that she was apart from them all. Not only was she the most beautiful, I would think happily, she also had an inner grace. I do not know if it was the urine therapy, as she said, or if it was her sweetness and strength, but her skin had become more and more translucent over the years, and her face glowed with an inner light. Her soft green eyes were always ready to twinkle. I called them the Eveready batteries, because they were ever ready to light up with a smile.

She had grown over the years from a spoiled daughter of a transport magnate to a strong and grounded woman shepherding her wounded family. She was our shelter from the storm. My father became quiet and retiring, rarely venturing an opinion. She, in turn, became cheerful and optimistic. She did it at first to hold our fragile lives together. We could always trust her to see the brighter side of things. "When you marry, you are together rowing the same boat through life," she told me. "If one partner loses his oar, you just have to row harder; otherwise, the boat will sink."

She kept all her fancy saris, jewels, and purses from those

days locked in a separate Godrej cupboard. Some evenings I would open the cupboard, pull out the saris, and finger all the brocades, silks, and chiffons. A faint perfume always clung to the saris, petticoats, and neatly piled lace handkerchiefs—the perfume of the flat by the sea.

I got my period when I was thirteen. That night I heard my father firmly say, "Ata bus kar, Shalini." Now stop it all, Shalini.

Soon after, all the cures were terminated. My parents had always believed the blot would go away or at least fade a little after puberty. When it did not, my mother braced herself and set out to teach me to live with it. She taught me to be a stoic, to fold up my life and expect little, to live within the borders of my fate, to make my joy from small things, from incense and flowers and shining surfaces and delicately cooked food. I was raised to be happy in the graces of an orderly life.

Her words washed off with the first rain of Panchgani, because they were a lie. She told me to be content with my lot, but she was not content with hers. She taught me to follow her, but she did not know where she would go.

Because our life was a sham. Because while I lay in my room with my hair spread out on the pillow and dreamed of escape, I believed Baba behind his patient eyes was dreaming too. Of leaving us one morning, of walking out of Navjeevan Housing Society and turning the corner and becoming a man without a past.

It was not a life without passions as I had thought—hearing them snoring in the room next to mine as the seasons passed and I ate and slept and my body stretched and bulged—but an elaborate mask dance. We did have dreams, the three of us. We lived piled atop each other in six hundred square feet of space (including the balcony), inhabiting a hive of secret dreams and passions. We ate and slept and awoke each day, putting nothing into the family dream pool. We did not say we will go to the caves for a picnic this Sunday with Dhanu, we will go to Simla for holidays this summer, we will get Charu married with so much pomp we will bring in a band from Bombay. No. We did not dream together, we did not hope together. It had been a half-life, a life in the shadows.

But the glass, Ayi always said, look at the full side of the glass. And so, dutiful daughter that I am, I swirl my Indore life around again and see through the clear liquid.

I see that I did not scowl and glower at my parents at the dinner table. I did not say I am counting the days until I leave this place, I am waiting to go to Bombay. I passed the spinach demurely under the tubelight because I could not bear to hurt them.

I understood why Baba did not leave. Over the rim of his newspaper each morning he saw Ayi with her hair parted down the middle making his perfect cup of tea, he saw me with my starched school uniform and my spanking white socks and my satchel slung over my shoulder—and he knew he would have to come back so he could see us again. He bowed his head and manfully shouldered his yoke each day, only because he loved us.

And Ayi. Who knew what Ayi dreamt of as she smiled and sang and surrounded us in her net of love? The trajectory of our dreams did not include her. We did not know, we did not care to know, that her joy was as thin as tracing paper.

FOUR

Miss Nelson's Cross

LATER, WHEN THEY asked me how I, a conventional girl usually considered meek, had become so friendly—they would say "friendly" with a wink or a leering grin—with the scandalous and most salacious Miss Prince, I would sometimes say it all began with Shobha Rajbans.

Shobha Rajbans was in my ninth-standard class. She was one of the sparkling ones, those bold girls who make others laugh and cry. At fourteen, Shobha was already fully bloomed, tall and wide hipped, with respectable breasts bobbing inside her blue-checked uniform. She flashed her almond eyes, she tossed her short wavy hair, and she knew that the world was hers. She had dimples and wonderful, loud laughter that could be heard echoing in the hallways.

Shobha intimidated me from the start. She was bright, she was confident, she was rich, and she was so, so superior. She also had the right accent. She had the urban-upper-class-right-school English accent, and although I knew more of the literature of that little island than she ever would, my accent was what the girls called vernacular. And that gave them the permission to turn me into a caricature.

I was teaching the ninth-standard English, English literature, and the British Raj in Indian history. I taught them for at least two and sometimes three periods a day. And until I was able to raise my voice against her, the classes with Shobha could dissolve into hell at any time. I got to being thick-skinned about it once it occurred to me that there was no need to take it personally. It was merely a part of the girls' great ongoing war against authority. And Shobha was a natural warrior.

The first day, after prayers, I had her class for English. I made them all stand up in turns and tell me their names and their hobbies. But that was a mistake. Hobbies were for ten-year-olds, not thirteen- and fourteen-year-olds. The "good" girls said reading, sports, and music. The rebellious ones said things like seeing movies and meeting boys, watching my face for a reaction. Shobha, sitting at the back of the class, stood up with a disdainful flick of her hair and said, "My two best hobbies are drying Mahrukh Tunty's bras on the sigri in the monsoons, and rotary swinging."

I did not understand, of course. But I did know that it was a part of their insular humor.

I forgot Miss Henderson's biscuit-tasting advice and flashed Shobha a friendly smile. I was sure I was going to win them over by just being friendly. I couldn't really go wrong, I thought; I was almost their age. "Maybe you will explain them to me after school today," I said.

"The explaining of this would indeed be terrific, Miss Apte," she replied in a very vernacular accent, at which point the already giggling girls convulsed in laughter. I thought they laughed at my accent. I vowed to speak like them.

"Please write a three- to five-page essay, 'How I Spent My Summer Holidays,'" I said before I swung out, pigtail and dupatta flying.

The next night, I slipped up at dinner duty and said "Eat your vegetable" to Amla Sanghvi, pronouncing it "vagitable." Shobha imitated me all evening. Every time I passed her table, she would loudly say, "Can I have more va-gi-ta-ble, please?" or "The vagitable is so good today, no?" The girls would then burst out into giggles all over again, until little Amla had to be taken out to the dormitory because she choked on her food.

It was the second-worst evening of my entire stay in Timmins. The noise grew in bursts, bouncing around the room like a ball. Girls began to squeal and shout from one table to another, and soon started throwing bread and even cutlets across the room. I thought I glimpsed a girl on her hands and knees scurrying under the table. Butlers in red turbans passed along the periphery of my vision, carrying large steel trays. I knew my humiliation to be complete.

I had long ago devised a trick for dealing with all those patronizing aunts, all those nudging girls and staring strangers, living as I did, with a blot by my side. I could take my soul out of my body, or perhaps it shrank and became transparent inside me like a boiled onion. Anyway, I could be looking down on myself from above the room. And I would keep telling myself in a firm but kind voice, "This is not happening to you. Not happening to you." I had never cried in public, not even when I had been punished for kicking that little girl in a pink nylon dress at Baba's office Diwali puja. I had not cried when Baba shouted at me right in the middle of the prayer ceremony, and so I knew how to keep the tears from my eyes.

Two days later, I came upon Shobha's essay in the staff room. The staff room was between the gym and the piano room. It faced the upper netball field, where the senior girls wandered around during their breaks. In the afternoons, the sounds of chopsticks and Brahms wafted into the room. There was usually some tepid tea in a large brown teapot covered with a tea cozy embroidered in a green and red rose design, in chain stitch, which looked most certainly like the handiwork of Miss Henderson.

I was sitting in the staff room. It was a hot, quiet afternoon, pregnant with the promise of the monsoon. When I came upon Shobha's essay, I couldn't help laughing out loud. I had just met Miss Malti Innis, small and smiley, in a printed cotton sari, sitting on a creaky sofa nearby. "Call me Malti," she said. She was the class teacher for standard five and was mainly involved with the juniors. "You must come to Sunbeam for dinner soon."

I showed her the essay. She arched a neat little eyebrow and started reading it aloud.

> In the summer holidays, parents are Apt to spoil the child. In Timmins, we are Apt to get food that the village goats discard. So, after the terrible, terrible food of the past three months at school, all my favorite dishes were Apt to be cooked every day. Deoka, our cook, who has been with us

since I was a child, was Apt to ask me every morning what I wanted, and spent most of the day making it. I was Apt to eat too much. All the girls are Apt to eat too much, like camels, storing up for the desert ahead. It is Apt to be hot in Bombay in May, and I was Apt to eat ice cream and go to the club for a swim everyday.

I saw four movies this holiday, three English and one Hindi. I am Apt to like English movies better than Hindi movies, and my favorite movie was "Guess Who's Coming to Dinner," with Sidney Poitier. I went to see it with my cousin Bubli, who studies in Bombay. But she is Apt to like Hindi movies better, and preferred "Bobby" starring Dimple Kapadia.

Summer holidays are Apt to go by too fast. Soon, three weeks were over. Now we are back in school, not tired, certainly not happy, and Apt to be angry when asked to write retarded essays for English class. As Hurree Jamset Ram Singh, the Nabob of Bhanipur, would say, "The unfairfullness of this is terrible."

Moira Prince strode into the room around the second sentence. I had heard of her. They always said her name in lowered voices and stopped short. She was one of the two British teachers in the school who were not missionaries. I had not seen her because she never came to lunch in the staff dining room, itself quite a scandal, since it was a quickly conveyed if unwritten rule that all teachers must come to lunch.

She poured herself a cup of tea, stood with her legs apart, and stared at me long and hard. Her green eyes reminded me of glass marbles. Most adults look at me, flinch a little, look away briefly, compose their eyes, and then look again at me. Some studiously avoid looking at the blot, others take it in their stride and treat it naturally. It is my Rorschach blot; I had a whole science of judging character by the way people first looked at me in those days. But the Prince deliberately moved her cat eyes slowly around me, stopping, always, at the blot. It was an insolent look, I thought. I hadn't come across anything like this before, and I froze into a clear cube of ice, a pasted grin on my face.

When Malti finished reading the essay, Prince put down her teacup with a decisive thump. "That Shobha girl needs to be brought down a peg or two," she said. "I would love to put her across my knees and spank her bottom until she cries." She spoke in a soft, slow drawl, in an accent I had not heard before.

She had a compact, muscular body, a freckled face, and reddish brown hair, cropped short. Large jowls and a button mouth with soft pouty lips lent her a slightly bulldoggish air. She wore khaki jodhpurs that puffed out at the thighs and then became tight from the knees down, and brown tall boots that stopped just below the knees. She seemed to have stepped out of some other universe, and I was quite completely flustered. For some reason, I had a flash of Phileas Fogg striding around the world in eighty days.

The Hindi teacher, Miss Raswani, a vigorous white-haired woman who wore her sari an inch above her ankles, had been sitting at the back correcting her papers. Miss Raswani was a crusty old bird. The girls were terrified of her, and the teachers just left her alone. No one ever sat at "her" desk in the staff room, no one spoke to her, and she never entered conversations. She sat at the desk backing the room, slashing at notebooks with a red pencil.

Suddenly, she banged her books on the table, pursed her lips, straightened her sari, and strode out of the room muttering "wicked, wicked, wicked" in a hoarse voice. She did not look at any of us. I wasn't sure whether she was referring to Shobha's essay or to Miss Prince. I suspected it was Miss Prince.

Malti flashed a conspiratorial smile. She had her back to Miss Prince and did not turn around to look at her. The bell rang, and, stowing our books in our respective shelves, we both left to face our classrooms.

"Shobha's last line is a reference to the Nabob of Bhanipur," Malti explained to me on the way out. "He is an Indian character in the Billy Bunter books. He always says only one line in any conversation, and it always goes like this: 'The telling of this would indeed be terrible,'" she said, shaking her head from side to side in the Indian version of the British version of the Indian speaking English.

"The nines and tens were speaking like him all last term. They said that this is how the British expect the brown race to speak. It was very funny at first, though I must say it is getting a bit tedious now," she added. She did not bring up Shobha's cheeky manipulation of my name. She must have sensed that I would need to digest this on my own, and I liked her immediately for that.

Shobha had passed the essay around the class before she handed it to me. It went down as the Apt Essay. In Timmins, I will always be called Apt behind my back. It could have been worse, I figured. Most teachers had a "behind their back name."

I could so easily have been christened by one of the more spiteful girls and ended up with a meaner name. They called Miss Debabushnam, the fleshy-faced junior art teacher, "Gaylord," after a Punjabi restaurant in Bombay.

I wanted to know about Moira Prince. I wanted to know who this scandalous white woman with a strange accent was, and what she was doing in this small backwater school. I brought it up that evening with Miss Henderson while having tea and Shrewsbury biscuits in her cozy pink room.

"Moira Prince is Miss Nelson's cross," Miss Henderson said. "You wouldn't think it to look at her, my dear, but Moira's parents were missionaries. They were in Nasik with Miss Nelson, and very dear friends. It appears that Miss Nelson promised Moira's mother on her deathbed to look after her."

"How did they die?"

"It was a big news story. A bus overturned just outside Nasik. It was mostly full of locals, I think ten people died. They were coming back from a prayer meeting in another town. Her father, Reverend Prince—we knew him, he held such wonderful meetings here with us—died instantly, but her mother was in critical condition in hospital for some days. It was all so sudden and tragic. She called Moira and Miss Nelson to her deathbed, joined their hands, and said, "She will be a good mother to you."

"Poor thing. How old was she when her parents died?" I asked, imagining the Prince as a tomboy of ten, the day she became Miss Nelson's cross.

"Oh, my, I can't say for sure. Let's see, she must be twenty-seven or twenty-eight, maybe twenty-nine now. She's not thirty, I can always tell thirty. So she must have been at least twenty-five when her parents passed away. It was in the monsoons, in August, I think, two years ago. Miss Nelson had to rush down by taxi it was raining so hard. And Moira was teaching in Pelham Girls School in Mussoorie—you know, in the north, in the Himalayas."

She was already older than me when her parents died. "So why did she need to be looked after at that age?" I asked.

"Moira will always need to be looked after," said Miss Henderson with a sigh and a shake of the head. "Mothers know these things."

Miss Henderson always got her tea piping hot, because, as she pointed out, she was closest to the kitchen, and also because she and Mrs. Cummings, the mistress of the kitchen, were the best of friends.

Miss Prince, I was told, had saintly parents. She was an only child, and a bad seed. Started out teaching in Bombay, in Queen Mary School for Girls, but had left under a cloud. In Mussoorie, she had been asked to leave Pelham.

"My sister Rosie is the kitchen matron there, and she told me this," said Miss Henderson with relish.

"But what was she thrown out for?" I asked, all agog.

"Lord only knows," sighed Miss Henderson, wiping her lips with her lace-edged handkerchief, which she kept tucked in the sleeve of her flowered shift. "It happened soon after the parents died, in the middle of the winter term. Miss Nelson called some of us to the drawing room and told us that Miss Prince had had a difficult time, and that we were going to look after her a little. She said she was confident that our Timmins was such a good place that Miss Prince would get along just fine here. Miss Nelson always believes the best of everyone, you know. And Miss Prince has been given very few responsibilities here, less chance to get into trouble."

Although Moira had taught various subjects in her other teaching jobs, she had been given a more marginal role as sports teacher to the middles and seniors in Timmins. She worked closely under the watchful eyes of Miss Manson, who was the sports mistress.

"And has she?" I asked. "I mean, has she got along fine here?"

"Well, there has been some trouble, here and there, and it could have turned into a scandal, I tell you," she started, lowering her voice, and then paused to do some complex maneuver with her knitting needles.

When she looked back up at me, she changed the subject. She had decided not to tell the story. She's too young and raw, and she'll find out soon enough in this place, she might have thought. Miss Henderson was absolutely right. I did find out, though the knowledge did not come to me in quite the way she might have imagined as she sat there knitting her cable design sweater.

So far, Miss Henderson had emerged as my best guide in this dense and opaque world. She was a homely, maternal woman with bowed legs and thin brown hair that was always composed in neat rows of tight little ringlets. Her room was on my way down to the hospital after classes, and I had made it almost a habit to stop by for tea. Miss Henderson always seemed glad to see me. The girls would have gone down for evening games, their shouts floating up from the hockey field and lower garden. She was usually free at that time. She would put down an extra plate and bring out her tin. The Shrewsbury biscuits were thick, butter-laden, and not too sweet, and they crumbled deliciously in tea. Miss Henderson always took only one biscuit, but she always urged me to have two, which I always did, though I did it with the guilty feeling that I should really be more well-bred and take only one, and I never enjoyed the second quite as much as the first. Those early, innocent days always taste of Shrewsbury biscuits.

"These are the famous Poona biscuits. Kayani's Bakery is not far from our house there. I always make everyone who comes bring me a tin," said Miss Henderson. The Hendersons were a large and close-knit Anglo Indian clan with good English names. There were four Anglo Indian staff members in our school. Miss Henderson, Sister Richards, Mrs. Cummings, and Miss DeYoung, who all ran the home section of the school. They were all descendants of British railway clerks who had married Indians many generations ago, and were proud of their blood. Anglo Indians married each other, held on to their British names, and identified with the whites, not the Indians.

Miss Henderson was the crossroads matron. The girls got their periods in her dorm, they became boy crazed, had crushes on their prefects and teachers. They turned high-strung, cheeky, and delinquent. But Miss Henderson was a simple woman of good instincts, and she managed to herd them through those difficult years without too much trauma. Unlike the missionaries and most of the teachers, who kept their worlds quite shuttered from the girls, Miss Henderson could often be seen at the center of a blue-checked crowd, listening to eagerly told anecdotes from home. And she shared her life with them. She discussed her father's railway job, her mother's asthma, her widowed sister's only son, Frankie. Even I remember how her brother's daughter got third-degree burns and was forever scarred.

Miss Henderson was carrying a large pot of boiling water with a towel into the bathroom of the family home in Poona. Little Joan, naked and ready for the bath, was to have been sitting on the stool near the cold water tap. But Joan thought of hiding behind the door, and as Miss Henderson kicked the door wide open with her left leg, Joan burst out from behind to say boo. "Oh, how much I wept," she would say, shaking her head. "And to think nothing happened to me. Just one or two small burns."

But Hendy, as the girls called her, had a legendary temper. It could erupt at any moment, sometimes quite unexpectedly. There were times when I heard her high-pitched shouts all the way in the hospital. She kept the naughty ones in a small dorm next to her room. Shobha had been in that room the year before.

Her advice on Shobha was pitch-perfect, and I was still humbly holding on to good advice.

"You must give her detention," she said firmly.

"But it is a funny essay, and I have hardly started teaching," I protested.

"Believe me, you will never get any good work out of her; she'll get more and more cheeky. You have to take the upper hand right away," said Miss Henderson.

That is just what I did. I gave her detention in as firm and unwavering a voice as I could muster, and though the upper hand did not come so quickly, my detention forged the first link in the chain of events that bound me to the Prince.

DETENTION WAS ON Saturday mornings, after dormitory inspection and tuck shop, during the girls' precious free time. In the true British boarding school tradition, the young minds and bodies were kept busy at all times, given very little time to be the devil's workshop.

The Prince was on detention duty that day, and she caught Shobha reading *Rosemary's Baby.* Miss Prince had one of her famous fits of "bad behavior." From snatches and whispers and teachers' gossip, I learned that the whole school waited for Miss Prince's periodic outbursts of inappropriate behavior. Last term she had slapped a senior girl across the face so hard that she left red finger marks across her cheeks, and had been called into Miss Nelson's hushed office and made to apologize right then and there. The term before, she taught the middles a dirty marching song to the tune of "Colonel Bogey March."

While pacing up and down the detention room, the Prince had noticed Shobha reading a book. She strode back to the teacher's desk in front of the class.

In a voice chilled twenty degrees below zero, she said, "Shobha Rajbans, bring that book to me." She examined *Rosemary's Baby* and looked from Shobha to the book and back at Shobha with an unnerving glare that would have sliced through almost anyone.

"This is Miss Apte's detention," she said, with a sneer. "That was a nasty thing you did to a new young teacher. Think you are the smartest thing, don't you now? Bring me the essay you were supposed to write."

Shobha tossed her hair, returned to her desk, and swaggered back up with her finished detention assignment. Miss Prince glanced at it fleetingly. "Since you have obviously finished your work, you can go back to your desk and remain standing," she said.

Shobha strode back, head high, and stood and stood and stood. Detention ended, the girls walked out. Miss Prince remained seated at her teacher's desk in front of the classroom, reading *Rosemary's Baby*. She did not look up. Shobha remained standing. At first, the girls buzzed around outside the classroom, but they had to leave when the lunch bell rang. Shobha did not go down for lunch; she remained standing until two o'clock, when the rest bell rang.

News of the incident spread through the senior and middle school. Miss Henderson heard the girls discussing it around her dorm in excited clusters.

When Shobha was not on her bed ten minutes after rest bell, Miss Henderson was seen going to Miss Nelson's room. Soon, Miss Nelson was observed trotting past Upper Willoughby on her way up to the classrooms. Shobha had stood for two and a half hours, and had had no lunch.

Shobha became the heroine of the moment. At teatime, girls from other classes offered her condensed milk, Kraft cheese, and other snacks from home to make up for her lost lunch. This was one of the more rare and selfless acts of boarding school life, since food from home was the highest rung of heaven. Even the standard-eleven prefects called for her during the evening walk and asked her to tell the story again.

Miss Nelson gave Shobha an order mark, the highest punishment that Timmins conferred. Nelly, as the girls called her, announced the order marks after prayers on Friday mornings. She announced them with a sad and solemn air. The guilty girls would have to stand up and hang their heads, suitably ashamed. For the more serious offenses, Nelly would pause and give the offending girl a piercing stare, dripping with disappointment. The worse the offense was considered, the longer the pause. On very rare occasions, she even added a reproving word after the pause. The entire prayer hall looked on with frowning faces.

"There is enough evil in the world," she said that day after a very long pause, "without adding to it." For Miss Nelson, I think the larger sin had been reading a book about the devil. She confiscated *Rosemary's Baby*, and the girls imagined that her purse was thicker after that.

The Prince had expected an apology as she kept Shobha standing. "It was like waiting for a bus," she said to me sheepishly later, in one of her mellower moods. "The longer I sat there waiting for that wretched girl to say sorry, the harder it became to get up and call it off. I was quite relieved when the old goat came and got me out of it."

FIVE

Dinner with the Woggles

"ARE YOU GOING to the bazaar, Miss Apte?" called the nurse, Sister Richards, as I stepped out of my hospital room one evening a couple of days later, all dressed up in my peacock-blue chudidar kurta. "I am going to the general store to buy supplies for the dispensary. I can show you our shortcut to the bazaar if you wait just a few minutes while I lock up."

I was glad to have company, and we set out walking down a small footpath that came out in five minutes to Oak Lane, which ran parallel to the bazaar.

"This way, you don't have to walk all the way to the top of the school to the main gate. You can come and go as you like," muttered Sister Richards. She had a grumpy air, and at first I was a little intimidated by her. I soon realized that it was her general anger at getting old, losing her looks, and finding herself in her sixties as a nurse in a girls' boarding school.

Sister Richards was fair and stout. She had very fine, translucent skin, now sagging in clusters around her mouth and gray eyes. She may have remained beautiful well into her forties. She always wore her nurse's uniform, a belted white dress with the stiff nurse cap, and she wound her white hair into a small netted bun at the back. She had about five safety pins stuck onto her right breast, like a badge.

She always made it quite clear that she was not like the "rest of them"—the bunch of spinsters, she did not say, but indicated, with a smart sniff. She had been an army nurse in World War II, and she had seen a thing or two. She had been stationed in Burma. "You know that song 'The Road to Mandalay'?" she would ask. "It was practically written in my barrack." Nobody had ever heard of that song.

Panchgani Stores took up one whole corner of the bazaar. It was the largest store in Panchgani, and it sold almost everything one might need. There was a display counter running across its length containing soaps, talcum powder, Pond's cream, Himalaya face snow, hair oils, and shampoos. The store sold biscuits and tea and homemade jams and honey, lanterns and Duckback raincoats.

We waited at the counter, Sister Richards and I, but no one came to attend to us.

There was a grumbling woman already waiting at the counter. I recognized her by her shock of white hair as Miss Raswani, the Hindi teacher who had run out of the staff room crying "wicked, wicked, wicked." I gave her a weak smile. She ignored me, glared with a kind of venomous anger at Sister Richards for a short while, and then turned her face away from us and walked out of the store. "What kind of shopkeepers are these?" I heard her muttering as she went past me.

"This is very strange," said Sister, and I thought she meant the strange behavior of the Hindi teacher, and so I nodded yes, because it had been most strange indeed; but no, it was the service at Panchgani Stores she referred to. "Very strange. Either the owner or his wife or at least the peon is always here. I think we should go in the back and see if there is any trouble," she said, and lifted up the wooden slat of the counter. We could hear large snorts billowing out from the back.

We walked through the shelves and cupboards and hanging umbrellas to the office at the back where, around a desk piled high with dusty files and papers, there sat a policeman with a pendulous paunch, and a very thin and small man and woman who looked, against the light, like a doll couple. They were all convulsed with laughter. "Oh, Sister, good to see you, come and have a cup of tea, oh so funny this story is," the thin man said with a giggle. The peon, who was also hovering around and quite merry, set out chairs and brought in the best masala chai I have tasted to this day.

"You tell," said the wife with a smirk. She had a loud, hoarse voice that burst forcefully out of her small frame.

"Well, you see, if you had come just ten minutes ago, Sister, you would have seen me in handcuffs, being dragged out by Inspector Wagle," said the man, who seemed to be in his thirties. He was as thin as a stick, and a bit stooped. But his lips were full and sensuous. He licked them slowly, between words. I found it hard to take my eyes off them.

"Come now, Mr. Sheth," said the nurse. "A more law-abiding person I have yet to see."

"No, it is true. My friend Inspector Wagle came here to arrest me," he said. His laughs were like a series of backward hiccups.

"You know, Jitubhai, I would always hear your side first," protested the inspector, his big belly shaking as he laughed.

The story unfolded gradually. Jitubhai, the biggest merchant in town, had successfully been making his own jam from his own strawberries and raspberries. The jam was now beginning to sell quite well in Poona, and there had even been an offer from a Bombay store. Ever the entrepreneur, Jitubhai decided to begin making honey too.

Since he knew nothing about making or selling honey, he wanted to get the best information about making honey from abroad. "In America, they write books and magazines about everything, so I thought I will order from there," said the astute one, who was wearing that day a brown-and-white-checked bush-shirt. Poring over catalogs from America late at night, he said he came upon the right magazine: *Honey.*

It was no easy matter to get a magazine subscription from foreign lands, he assured us. Since you were not allowed to own any foreign exchange, you had to buy postal-stamp certificates and then carry on a correspondence with the magazine to convince them that postal stamps from India were actual currency. Every letter took ten days to get across. Finally, the magazine came by sea mail, taking a month or two. The whole process had spanned eight months, and Jitubhai had waited patiently, dreaming of his factory in which prolific American-trained bees would churn out rivers of honey.

Today, Inspector Wagle had come in with the magazine in his hands.

Inspector Wagle now related his side of the story. He spoke English with a Marathi overlay. "This afternoon Postmaster Gaikwad came to my office with this magazine in his hand," said the inspector, merrily slurping his tea. "He himself was quite embarrassed. 'Sir,' he said, 'I have a puzzling matter on my hands. I thought it best to bring it to your attention.' 'Just wait till I clear it up,' I told the postmaster. I would be forced to arrest Jitubhai under the Suppression of Obscenities Act, you know. I had to get to the bottom of the matter immediately."

The inspector was telling this story for the first time, and he could not contain himself. Tears streamed down his face. "The sheer terror on Jitubhai's face when he saw the cover of the magazine he had ordered," he gasped. "It was not about beehives or bottles of honey, not at all."

"How was I to know that in America they call these kinds of loose women honey?" asked Jitubhai, looking at us for support. "Now I have to start again to get information about honey."

"You better make sure it's not another funny magazine before you order it," said Inspector Wagle, and that sent us all into another round of laughter.

Inspector Wagle started up a conversation with me in Marathi about my caste and subcaste. The laughter had warmed the air between us, and he smiled and said, "Come and have dinner with my family. Come next week. I will send my hawaldar to bring you to our house on Tuesday. Janaki's food will remind you of your mother's."

"Oh, my Lord," Sister said with a chuckle as we walked back. "To think of little Jitubhai and that dirty magazine."

She told me Jitubhai had moved to Panchgani from Bombay many years ago, when he had been diagnosed with the dreaded TB. This was before streptomycin, and Panchgani with its dry mountain air was known to be good for the lungs. He and his wife had come to the town, thinking he had but a few years to live, as an invalid. He started the store with his share of the family money and now was industriously running the best store in town.

"Good night, my girl," said Sister as we parted. "I don't suppose you will go to Inspector Wagle's?"

"Why not? He seemed like a nice family man," I blurted out, surprised. He seemed like a homebody in this alien place. He actually reminded me of an uncle from Dharwar.

"It's just that they don't like you mixing with bazaar people here," said Sister. Clearly, I had still not picked up all the snobberies of my position, of being a teacher in a white school.

In my outside life, I would never have dared to go after that; I needed so much to be the good girl. But then, hadn't I decreed that my Panchgani life was to be an inside life, and I was to float free for six months? A giggle of delight welled up deep inside my stomach and rose up to my throat. I thought, I might as well go. It will be fun, eating dinner with the Wagles.

I don't think Sister was waiting for my answer. She was just advising me about school protocol. "Good night, Sister," I said chastely, and walked into my room through the back door.

IN INDORE WE waited for the rains through the long summers when the sun pressed its back hard and tight upon our heads. My gulmohor tree turned to flame in May, and mothers in the compound collected the fallen orange petals to bathe their babies. It soothed their angry red skins. My mother fed me fridge-cold buttermilk in a tall steel glass when I came home from school.

Baba would track the progress of the monsoon current across the Arabian Sea. As with everything, he had his own private observations to go by. When the sparrows dug their beaks into the dry earth, he said, the monsoon was less than two weeks away. He was usually right.

It was Tuesday, the day of my dinner with the Wagles, when the sky broke open in Panchgani. The girls were at tea in the dining room, gorging away on pickle and Ferradol syrup and other improbable snacks. The clouds had been gathering over the mountains since noon, and the winds were high. We could hear thunder in the distance. The school was electric. The girls' hair burst through their black ribbons, and their dresses billowed around their belts like checked balloons, ready to float them up into the blue light.

It was dark in the dining room, the tubelights were on and humming when the rain came crashing down. The middle and senior dormitories were low, sprawling buildings with verandas and walkways wrapped around the upper garden. The girls spilled into the veranda; the missionaries, having tea in Miss Nelson's private drawing room as was their custom, came out onto their balcony; and I, on my way down to my room after classes, without a thought, I rushed into the rain, arms outstretched.

In school, in college, at home, when the first drops fell, we always rushed out to drink the rain, the young mothers with their children in their arms.

In Indore the first rain came as a teaser, a few big hot drops releasing the heady smell of first wet earth. Today the cold rain came down hard and thick, with the force of buckets of wet paint at Holi. The musky scent of the earth wound itself around me like a satin sheet, promising bright green paddy fields and the fragrance of white flowers, of mogras and jasmine and raat ki rani, and of bunches of sontaka sold on the streets in the evenings. It was only after I opened out my wet hair and tucked a fallen flame-red shoe-flower behind my ear that I realized I was the only one out in the rain.

The rain was pouring down over the sloping tin roof in a great big gushing tap. Girls and teachers were lined up in the verandas, behind the curtain of water. Every eye was on me. I felt the hard green eyes of Miss Prince. My skin prickled. The moment seemed to hold forever. I was a tragic actress in a stadium. I lifted my hair up, wound it around my hand, and tied it in a bun. Should I bow, should I wave, shouldn't they clap? I could feel my blot begin to prick. I knew it would soon turn sore and angry. I felt ugly all over again. I wrapped my wet green dupatta around my shoulders and forced my feet not to run. My bun came undone as I turned. Back straight up, my wet hair live like snakes upon my back, I made my way with measured steps to my room. I did not look back. I was my father's daughter; I knew there was an art to retreat.

The lights went out as I was peeling off my clothes. "The

wretched lights always go off with the rain," grumbled Sister as she brought in a lantern for me. The hot water I had ordered for my evening bath had turned tepid; the mali had probably dumped it into my bucket hours ago. But I was too dazed to care. I lit five candles around the bathroom and quickly threw a few mugs of the water over each shoulder.

In the mirror, my eyes flashed black and quick, and my face glowed. The blot looked pink, like a nipple. I might just be a creature of the night, I thought, feeling strange and elated. I made one long shining braid with my still wet hair. I wore a bloodred kurta to match the hibiscus in my still-wet hair, and was screwing on my silver dangle earrings when I heard Shobha's voice in the dispensary.

"Sister Richards, can you please tell Miss Apte that there is a policeman upstairs asking for her," she called above the rain, her voice sharp and curious.

"Please tell him I will be up right away," I shouted. To walk up with her would have been to talk to her. Let her wonder.

It was seven o'clock, the dinner bell had just rung, and the girls were lining up ready to file into the dining room. Their whispers and nudges followed me as I walked past them. "She's being arrested," I heard them say. But I was learning to live in the fishbowl and did not even look at them.

The hawaldar, a wiry mountain man with bowed legs, was waiting outside the pantry. Bearers in white uniforms were pumping hissing pressure lamps to light the dining room. The hawaldar was dressed in khaki shorts and carried a large black government-issue umbrella. He sprang up when I arrived and opened the umbrella like a sail over our heads as we launched into the churning night. I knew at once that I should have worn gum boots.

We sloshed through the lantern-dim bazaar and turned right just before the municipal park. The Woggles, as the girls called Inspector Wagle and his wife, lived in a pink and white house behind the bazaar on the way up to a plateau called table-land, past the cemetery, but before the big fallen boulder that was said to have crushed a marriage party many years ago.

The Woggle came beaming up. He had on his uniform pants, but had changed into a blue bush-shirt and worn rubber slippers. There was a kerosene lamp on the dining table. A dark, fat boy with bad skin was sitting beside it, poring over a thick book. He did not look up. "This is my youngest, Kushal," said the Woggle. "He is almost sixteen, goes to Sanjeevan School. My older two girls are twins. Yellow and Pinkie. They are in college in Poona." I could smell the fish frying in the kitchen.

A sofa set with plastic covers on the back to keep off oil stains, a glass showcase cupboard with figurines and photographs, a gleaming white fridge standing proud in the dining room. Their home was my home. I slipped into the role of being the good Maharashtrian girl as into a soft slipper. I neatly presented them with the cushioned version of my life. My father was from Dharwar, he worked with Chitnis Transport. No naval references.

Mrs. Woggle had graying hair, which she tied in a low bun. Tendrils of curly hair escaped the bun and framed her face. A coarse gray hair curled out of a wart on her chin. She brought out our plates with green chutney fish and kokum curry with rice. We ate slowly, talking as the food dried on our hands.

"The twins, they were so alike, absolutely, so I always dressed them in yellow and pink. So it was simple, Yellow and Pinkie," she said. She ate delicately, resting her fingers, fanned out like a flower, on her steel plate between bites. You just had to weep for poor Yellow.

The rain thundered around us, the lanterns flickered in the wind, and the evening had a special glow. The Woggle, it transpired, had been the head inspector in Panchgani for eighteen years, the only policeman in long pants since 1956. His children had grown up here. "It is a quiet place," he said. "We don't even have a jail. We keep them in lockup in the police station overnight, and then drive them down to Vai in a jeep. Just the petty criminal classes, you understand. Never a murder, or anything, in all these years." He spoke proudly, taking a measure of responsibility for Panchgani's good conduct.

After dinner, the tubelight blinked on, though the rain kept its steady pace. "Come as often as you want, you are like our Pinkie and Yellow," said the Woggles, screwing up their eyes in the sudden brightness as they saw me to the door. The hawaldar had been smoking a bidi on the bench in the veranda. He jumped to attention and obligingly, under the watchful eye of the Woggles, ferried me across the puddles in their compound. Just after we turned the corner to the park, I realized that I had left my little red purse behind. And so we had to trudge back. The hawaldar muttered under his breath, but gamely held the umbrella up.

The pink house was blazing. Even above the pouring rain, I heard the scream of "Kill me! Kill me now and be done with it!" It was a banshee scream, torn from the soul. I saw the tense torso of Mrs. Wagle silhouetted in the window, her hands over her ears.

The inspector came scowling to the door, but smoothed his features into a smile. The wife scurried into the bedroom, and I collected my purse and left.

Were deep dark secrets lodged in the laps of all middle-class Maharashtrian families? Was there no soft, smooth place on this earth? I glanced at the hawaldar, wondering if I should try to get some information from him, but decided against it.

The lights-off bell rang as I walked into school through the back gate, and the dorms snapped dark as I went back to my room.

"CAN I HAVE a word with you, Miss Apte?" called Miss Nelson as I walked past her office the next morning after prayers. The room was cool and quiet. It had a hushed and dignified air.

"Do sit down, Miss Apte. So how are you adjusting to your new life?" she asked, her grave eyes large.

"Please, call me Charu," I said.

She seemed not to have heard, and continued, "You are barely older than the girls, and away from home for the first time. Hmm, that can take some time. But you must remember, now, that in the school you are not Charulata, you are Miss Apte. The girls need to look up to you, to respect you and to obey you. These young and impressionable minds have been given to us for safekeeping. We do the Lord's work. We lead by example. Now, of course it is fun to get wet in the rain"—she paused, and smiled briefly—"but I cannot afford to have two hundred wet girls on my hands, now, can I?"

I agreed and was duly chastised.

"Don't worry, my dear," said Miss Nelson, rubbing her hands. "You will soon get used to it." She smiled, and her eyes softened. "At first, this change can be a bit puzzling. But we are all here to help you."

She said she had heard I was having some trouble with Shobha Rajbans. "She is going through a difficult phase," she explained. "Her father has warned me to expect some trouble this term. You see, he is planning to marry again, and she is not happy about it at all."

"So what should I do?" I asked. "I am finding her very hard to control."

"You must create a bit of steel inside yourself," she said. "Only then will they see it, and learn to respect you.

"And, er, Miss Apte," she added, flushing a deep shade of red. "I hear you had dinner in the bazaar last night, with a policeman. Now, of course I want you to go out and have a good time. You will soon get to know the nice young teachers from Sunbeam." She was trying, I suppose, to find a subtle way of explaining the not so subtle superiority of the white school.

"We call it the memsahib school," the Woggle had said at dinner. "Those mames are so stiff. Your father should have put you into Sanjeevan; it is a nice Maharashtrian school."

I was about to roll over and say, "Yes, Miss Nelson, it will not happen again," when I was interrupted by an inspiration. "I had dinner with the inspector and his family," I said, meekly. "Inspector Wagle is a childhood friend of my uncle's, and my father has asked him to be my local guardian."

"Well, then, I suppose you must go," said Miss Nelson,

grudgingly. "But don't let it interfere with your other activities," she said. "But don't let them contaminate you" is what I really think she was trying to say. Perhaps she was regretting—despite the Chitnis connection—opening her doors to a Hindu teacher.

I turned smartly on my heels and left, almost bumping into an earnest bunch of girls as I turned. "So *sorry*, Miss Apte," they chorused. Miss Nelson's office opened at a slant to the wide corridor that led through the prayer hall to the classrooms, so you could never tell if someone was waiting outside.

It was some girls from standard ten, the senior-most class I taught in Timmins. I had them for history and literature, so sometimes it was twice a day for the arts girls. They were a smart class, much less aggressive than Shobha's ninth. I was somewhat embarrassed at the thought that they might have heard parts of my conversation with Miss Nelson. The girls poked their heads into the office.

"Excuse us, Miss Nelson, may we please come in for a minute?" said Nandita, a portly girl who sat at the back of the class.

Miss Nelson had an open-office policy; anyone was free to go in with grievances. Grievances were taken to the principal only under extreme circumstances, and Nandita should have been as nervous as the rest of the girls. But she was not. She turned her head and gave me a smile as she walked in. It was a small and measured smile, but for some reason I felt it was the first real smile I had received in that bristling school. It was appraising, but it was frank. I walked on feeling somewhat better.

Flamboyant Shobha and prosaic, portly Nandita, they became

my two pillars of the schoolroom. I thought of them as my two stances—resistance and assistance. Throughout my time in Panchgani, while Shobha mocked and strutted, I felt that Nandita had my back. I felt that when the girls gossiped about me, Nandita took my side, and later, when she saw I was in trouble, she leaped without looking.

SIX

Lifting Latches

LATER, I UNDERSTOOD that we were so drawn to each other, Merch, the Prince, and I, because we were the outsiders. Merch, who was called the Mystery Man, was a watcher. He was a tall gangly man of quiet brilliance. He was a Panchgani character, a recluse who lived in two rooms above Dr. Desai's dispensary. Merch rarely spoke to anyone, and so, when we stayed up and talked all night, his unused voice sometimes dipped and swirled without pitch.

I see the three of us on a beach. I am walking at the water's edge, getting my toes wet. The wind curls my hair and tickles my body. I long to go in, but I am waiting for a miracle to transport me. Merch, the wise man, sits at the shore, gleaning the world's wisdom from the sea. He is averse to action, and will not go in. And the Prince, our surfer, waits only for the excitement of the next wave. She plunges in and is transported back to the shore, to fall at our feet, angry, or laughing, or bruised.

She is reckless and giving. And for that, we love her, we fear her, we fear for her.

But I know now that we were the shallow ones. There was no deep-sea person among us, not a swimmer, a fisher, or a diver.

I had been in Panchgani for three weeks, or forever. We became friends, the three of us, starting on the night of my twenty-first birthday. It was the fourteenth of June.

Word of my passage into adulthood had been passed along among the teachers, who sang "Happy Birthday" to me at lunchtime. I received a card from my mother with "To Our Darling Daughter" in curly gold letters, and Miss Henderson gave me an embroidered tea cozy. It was Friday, and the Sunbeam teachers had invited me for dinner. They said they were going to cook. I heard they had ordered a cake from Lucky's Bakery. I was excited. I wore a pink silk kurta, made a luxurious, loose plait, and tied four small silver bells into the end of it.

The monsoon had weakened, and we had had no rain for four days. But the air was soft and sweet, and my hair tinkled along as I walked under the rows of swishing silver oaks and saw through them an orange sunset. The bazaar loudspeaker was playing an obscure Hindi song, which now echoes often in my head. It was the first time I felt happy to be in Panchgani.

There were five teachers in Sunbeam: the ever-smiling Malti Innis whom I had met that first day in the staff room; her childhood friend Beena Keval; the Misses Mathews and Jacobs; and Miss Prince. Malti and Beena, both twenty-four years old, were friends from Allahabad. They were going out with two young Anglo Indian teachers from St. Paul's School, and their romances were imagined in graphic detail by the girls. Two years later, they both married their young men and moved to Australia. They were nice girls, ready to have a good time, but both were grounded quite firmly in reason and responsibility.

Miss Mathews and Miss Jacobs were Syrian Christians from South India, very conservative and pious. They had an innocent air about them; I presumed they read only romance novels and never saw movies.

Their first names were Jacinta and Susan. Jacinta was a waif of a woman who, but for her face, could pass for a girl of twelve, playing house with her mother's sari wrapped loosely around her. She would be reduced to paroxysms of coyness when Miss Nelson addressed her. Miss Nelson would continue the conversation, smiling faintly and condescendingly as Jacinta shook her shoulders and her head and fluttered and giggled to an extent that I was moved to feel sorry for her naïveté. Jacinta taught science to the seniors and was said to be brilliant.

Susan Jacobs was older, a poised woman who mostly wore starched white saris. She held her head high, and moved in a calm and dignified manner. She conducted her life as an ambassador for the Syrian Christians. "We are a very small community of South Indian Brahmins, converted by St. Thomas the Apostle," she told me.

"You mean St. Thomas as in the Bible?" I asked, trying not to sound incredulous.

"Yes, the very one," she said with a quiet pride. "He landed in South India, in 52 A.D., and is buried in Kerala itself."

There were quite a few Syrian Christians in Timmins, both teachers and students, and if any of them failed to behave with decorum and dignity, Susan Jacobs took it quite personally. Her dark face was pitted with pockmarks, and one presumed that she was consigned to spinsterhood because of this. She talked softly and had a generally sad air about her, though she did have quite a pleasant smile when she could muster one, showing a small set of gleaming white teeth.

The four of them gathered around me when I arrived and ushered me into their drawing room. There was no sign of Miss Prince. I had not seen her since the day I ran into the rain and looked up and saw her eyes boring into me. I had heard of the debacle with Shobha secondhand and had been imagining my next encounter with her in blurry outlines. I was quite relieved not to have it happen quite so soon.

Sunbeam was a comfortable house halfway up the Panchgani hill, a twenty-minute walk from the bazaar. A long, enclosed veranda worked as the drawing and dining room. The side tables, piled high with papers and books, were draped in dark green tablecloths. All the teachers' rooms opened out into the veranda. The last room was closed, though I could see the light on through the painted glass panes. I presumed that was the room belonging to the wayward Miss Prince.

The teachers were determined to show me a merry time, and I was happy for that. We got into gossiping about the girls. I learned that night that Shobha had many boyfriends—her father even let her meet them during the holidays—and that Bindu Mathais' mother had been sent to an insane asylum. In the staff room the teachers talked of the girls, and in the classrooms the girls talked about the teachers. It was the safest and most satisfying of topics.

The only teacher who was fair game for both was Miss Raswani, the Hindi teacher. Miss Raswani walked straight as a ramrod, her sari always severely pinned and pleated, her thick white hair pulled back in a tight bun. Her pupils had a white rim around them. She had a loud, hoarse voice that terrorized the whole entire school. She had formed no alliances and had no champion but Miss Nelson. She sat in corners, looked at the floor when she walked, and never had conversations. If you ever taught in a class next to her, you could hear her hoarse voice roaring, reading aloud, or grinding down some poor victim. I had never spoken directly with her. She always looked determinedly past me.

Beena informed me that Miss Raswani had a set sari for every day of the week.

"Yes, we know it's Tuesday when she wears her mustard-colored sari," added Susan.

Before sitting down to dinner, Susan turned her head towards the last, lit room, and called, "Moira, come join us," but when she did not come, Susan shrugged and said grace. The dinner, baked spaghetti with capsicum and tomatoes, and dry chicken masala with chilies, was tasty after the regimen of water curries and leather chapatis, though not really very good. The Sunbeamers, as they called themselves, ate school food through the week, but always cooked at least one of the weekend dinners. Before the end of the evening, I had been persuaded to be the chief chef the following Friday. "Bring some new food into our world," begged Malti.

After dinner, Susan emerged from the kitchen, beaming, holding up a frosted layer cake. Malti lit the candles and switched off the lights. They all crowded around me, and, in the middle of the "Happy birthday, dear Charu," I heard a deeper voice join the chorus. I realized that the Prince had arrived. I realized that the whole giggly dinner conversation had taken place under the shadow of the Prince.

The lights were turned on, and we sat around the living room eating cake. I hated birthday cakes, but I ate dutifully with a cheesy smile. The Prince, barely looking up, wolfed it down. She wore a white cotton kurta pajama, like the ones my uncles in Kolhapur wore in the house. The kurta, made of thin voile, was transparent, and I saw the dark purple patches of her nipples across the room. Though she lounged in her chair, lazy, unaware, limbs outstretched, she had shot a bolt of lightning across the room. No one talked. She finished her cake, came to my chair, and gave me a peck on the cheek. "Happy birthday," she said in a husky whisper. I had a clear view of her breasts as she bent towards me.

I had just turned twenty-one and had never seen anyone's breasts but my own. My breasts were small and pert, like apples on a board, with a little cherry sitting on top, I thought. Through the translucent fabric, the Prince's breasts looked as big as ripe mangoes, with large plum-red nipples stretched wide. I wanted to brush my shoulder against them. But the moment passed me by. The Prince stalked off to her room without a backward glance.

No one had much to say after that performance. There was no way for them to talk about her in the veranda, because she could hear every word. But I wondered what they made of her and how they lived with her.

Dinner was over, and I guessed that it was time for me to leave. I got up to go. While I was saying thank you and goodbye, vigorously nodding my head like a new adult, Miss Prince emerged from her room. She was wearing her jodhpurs and gum boots, and a white man's shirt made of thick khadi through which no breasts were visible. "I am going to the bazaar to buy some cigarettes," she said, reaching for her raincoat without looking directly at me. "Would you like to walk with me?"

"Should we take the back road?" she asked as we stepped out into the night. For some reason I was a little tremulous.

"Yes," I said. "I did not know there was a back road." My voice came out a simper in the yellow lamplight. We fell into step with each other and walked quietly through the empty street. The night was cloudy and close. The Prince did not look at me. She had on a blue raincoat, which she threw over her shoulders, top button closed at the neck, like a cape. I kept mine chastely folded and tucked under my bent arm.

The road was a narrow one, lined with little homes. It wound itself out onto the lane beside Panchgani Stores, just outside the first pan-bidi stall, before the Timmins end of the bazaar. The Prince bought a packet of Charminars. I wanted a pan, but found myself too shy to ask for it. This twenty-first was turning out to be a first in so many ways. First time actually seeing breasts, and first time buying cigarettes. I had never seen a woman who smoked. But of course, she was white and did not have to go by our rules.

Then she said, looking up and straight at me for the first time, "Would you like to come with me to a friend's place just here? I'll have a smoke, and then we'll go." When I hesitated, she smiled and said, "How about it? I'll walk you home after." How could she know, I wondered, that I was afraid to walk home alone at night?

When she said "friend," I had imagined a woman, British or perhaps Anglo Indian. Not an Indian man. And certainly not the slightly seedy, stalk-like man I had seen slouching through the bazaar a couple of times.

"This is Merch," said the Prince, sounding somehow bashful. "We call him our Mystery Man."

Merch lived in two dimly lit rooms. Bookshelves lined one wall. The shelves had speakers mounted on them, and a table in the center held his music system. A bed and one cupboard with a hazy mirror occupied the back wall. A lumpy flowered armchair from some prior generation was next to a table, and a large mattress against the other wall made up the rest of the room. A door on the left opened onto a balcony, and another, across the room to a kitchen. Filled ashtrays were to be seen everywhere. I felt stiff and awkward, in an alien environment. I sat on the edge of the chair. There was an open chess game on the carpet. "It's your move," said Merch to Prince, lighting her Charminar and one for himself. His fingers were brown with nicotine. The air had an odd, sweet smell.

Prince sat cross-legged, and stared intensely at the game for a long time before moving her knight to check the king. I had thought of two better moves, but I kept them to myself. Merch did not say a word to me that night. "You looked so scared, I was afraid you would fly away if I even looked at you," he said later. Prince lost the game in a few moves. "Anon," she said to him at the door as we left.

I judged Prince to be a poor chess player by that game, but learned later that she was just erratic. She would stare blankly at the board for long periods and make such daft moves that you could not help underestimating her. But then, suddenly, in a flash, she could bring you to your knees with two brilliant moves.

It was a short distance down Oak Lane to my hospital. "Good-bye, Miss Charulata," she said, and she brushed my blot with the back of her hand. She said the last syllables of my name—*lata*—short and clipped, the sound of a horse trotting on a tar road. I fell into bed in a stupor.

SEVEN

Lemon Dal

THE NEXT FRIDAY, I cooked my first dinner at Sunbeam. It was a resounding success, mainly due to Mrs. Woggle. I had gone up to the inspector's pink house a few days earlier. We were still in the dry pause between the rains; the red mud in the ditches had begun to harden, and the air was heavy. I caught up with Mrs. Woggle as she was turning up the path from the park, carrying an orange cloth bag plump with vegetables. I had not seen the house in daylight before. The pink had the tinge of cheap cake icing, and the doors and windows were a freshly painted bright green. It was called the Nest.

She was very enthusiastic about my dinner plans and happily offered me fresh-ground flour, sweet yogurt, and her own homemade ghee and pickle. I was going to make the perfect Marathi vegetarian meal. "You are just like my Pinkie," she said, patting my back. "Everything you want to do well. I will send a hawaldar to Sunbeam with all the items on Friday evening. You can return the vessels and the bag later." I looked for her unhappy soul but could see only the calm and serene fish-fryer.

The next evening we went to buy vegetables together. She wore a blue nylon sari and was a master vegetable buyer who could pick out a pile of juicy red tomatoes from a heap that looked near death. As we bought piles of rain-green methi bunches, I wondered how my ayi was shopping without me. I usually walked behind her with the bags, lost in my own thoughts. I had written about my dinner with the Woggles, because I was sure she would approve of them.

That Friday, Malti was in Sunbeam when I got there after school. She tucked her sari pallu to her waist and helped me wash and chop. "I never went into the kitchen in Allahabad," she said, gingerly holding a tomato under a running tap. Susan laid the table. She set a place for Miss Prince. We sort of smirked at each other in school now, the Prince and I, when our paths crossed, but it was not that often. The Prince did not hang around the school during her free periods like the rest of us. Jacinta informed me with a giggle that Moira often went to meet her friend—"that strange man they call Merch," she said, wrinkling her nose. It was, of course, considered scandalous, as was everything the Prince did.

I wondered if they were having an affair and imagined how they would look together, she with the white full body. Merch, angular and unclothed, I could not quite imagine. He was a clothed kind of man. That I had not ever seen a naked man was another reason. I did not think she would deign to come to our dinner.

But she did come. She walked in wearing shiny, knee-length gum boots, even though the air was turning torrid. Miss Jacobs had finished grace, and I was dashing around with hot bhakris. She popped a large smile and said, "Oh, can I join you, please?" Her eyes grew bright when she smiled, and her mouth spread wide and generous across her face. It was a smile that you could follow. She infected us all with her high spirits that night. She went into her room, turned on some music that I did not know, and returned with feet clad in elaborate embroidered slippers, her hair shining, slicked back. She was carrying two fat red candles. "Mood, ladies, we must have mood," she announced. "This is our Charu's first solo performance: surely a river-crossing on the path to adulthood." I was not sure if she was mocking me, but I felt happy.

The food, the music, and the flickering light of the candles made us all expand, and soon Susan's pitted face relaxed and began to look like a schoolgirl's. "I used to have hair like yours, Charu," she said, smiling shyly. She told us how her mother used to wash her curly hair every day, and comb and oil it in the sun while it was still wet, and how she walked to school along the water in her village in Kerala.

Beena and Malti were meeting their bright young Anglo Indian teachers from St. Paul's and left soon after dinner, both with raincoats and torches and shawls over their arms. Jacinta and Susan said their good-nights and went into their rooms.

All of a sudden, we found ourselves alone in the dim dining room, the Prince and I. I sat around for an awkward moment, and then I got up to go. "I have to mark a history test," I mumbled.

"Come sit in my room a while, please, Miss Charulata," said

the Prince softly. I wished she would not address me as Miss Charulata, because she made me feel like a middle-class Maharashtrian girl crossed with a Timmins teacher.

And so I entered her room. I realized then that you could live in the world for a full twenty-one years, imagining always that everyone except movie stars lived like you, in stuffed and brightly lit places with scrubbed kitchens, only to find out that you were completely free to decorate your room anyway you wanted.

Her room was red. Two lamps on two low stools were draped with thin deep-red cloth, casting a soft red glow around the room. There were mattresses lined with colorful cushions on the floor. It was the kind of room I imagined in lush harems. There was even a hookah in the corner. There was no sign of school-issue furniture, except for a large cupboard with an oval mirror on one door and a bookshelf in the corner. She sat me down on the mattress and, with increasing urgency, began rummaging around in drawers. "Damn. No cigarettes again. We'll just have to go to Merch's, won't we?" she said with an impish grin. And so we trotted off to Merch's again, the same silent walk, but now I knew the road and was much more comfortable. I was sure I could even talk to her, and there were a lot of questions I wanted to ask her, but I could not frame any of them.

If I said, "What are you doing here?" she would have to make a reference to her infamous record.

Should I say, "When did you come here?" she would surely think I knew she was thrown out of two schools

I wanted to know if she had ever been to England, but if I

asked her that, she might think I was in awe of England, like so many of the teachers.

"Did you grow up in India?" Yes, I could ask that. She spoke to the servants in fluent Marathi, and her accent was different from the missionaries. But then again I started thinking that perhaps it was too intimate a question to ask an Englishwoman you hardly knew.

And so the road that had seemed so long on that first night came to an end, and I said nothing at all.

That night the rain started up again when we were with Merch. First the wind began to blow in gusts so that curtains flapped and doors and windows snapped around the town. We stood on Merch's balcony until the rain crashed down like a wall upon us, and then we ran in, laughing.

"How about a game of chess, Charu?" said Merch. He guessed that I played the game, although I had not said anything that first night. He gave me a thin graying towel to wipe my hair, but I couldn't bring myself to use it. He had just set up the game, and I'd made the first move, when friends dropped in. They were a couple of rich kids from Bombay who had rented a windy house called Aeolia at the outer edge of the town. They had come, they said, to "soak up the monsoon." I concluded in awe that they were hippies, though I had seen the likes of them only in *Life* magazine. The boy was tall and lean, with long curly hair he tied in a small low ponytail. The girl was wraithlike in a long and flowing dress, and moved gracefully, like water. They wore orange clothes. No one explained anything to me that night.

"Let's go for a drive to Mahabaleshwar," they said. They had a beige Fiat, and the three of us squeezed into the back, the Prince in the middle. We left the car windows half open, so the rain sprayed our faces and the wind tore our hair. Mahabaleshwar, straddled on another hill, was famous because it had the second-highest rainfall in the world. All of us on the third ghat felt a little more important at having our little corner recognized by the whole wide world. We were sometimes mentioned in geography textbooks.

As long as I will remember it, they were playing the Doors song "Riders on the Storm" that night in the car. The mist was as thick as whitewash; it flung our headlights back at us. We could see almost nothing. Shabir, as the boy was called, made his girlfriend, Raisa, wipe the inside of the windshield from time to time. They all seemed to inhabit some cryptic, and very funny, imaginary world. "Should we wake up the farmers?" said Shabir as he turned the corner out of Panchgani. "Place problem in the car, boss," said Merch. The farmers were another couple of just-married Bombay hippies, who had started a halfhearted strawberry farm on the road between Mahabaleshwar and Panchgani, but no one bothered to tell me anything. My new friends left me to sink or swim. It was dark and close in the car, but my blot was calm. I was so shy and quiet with all these new people, but, surprisingly, I did not feel at all self-conscious. They were all inventing themselves as they went along, and I felt oddly at peace among them. They did not even try to draw me into the conversation.

We had a series of blurry adventures that night, but I do not really know if that was the night we went madly hunting around the shuttered town searching for tea, or if that was the night the car got flooded and water came gushing out of the backseat, or if that was the night we went to Kate's Point and parked the car at the top of the hill. I remember we all got out and stood with our bodies plastered against the car. The wind from the valley sucked our breath, our clothes became wet and heavy. I remember a filtered moonlight, which made our teeth glow white.

I know it was the night when we sat shivering and wet in the backseat that she squeezed my hand as our car went slithering and sliding down the Kate's Point hill, and the girlfriend hung her head out with a torch to check if the wheels were slipping off the mountain edge. But I do not remember if it was on that first night of the long rain that the Prince held my hand in the car, or if it was deeper in the heart of the monsoon. We locked our hands, tight and sweaty, as the car lurched and slithered most dubiously down the hill, and then unlocked them, quite naturally, when we reached the road.

I lived for the weekends. They began with dinner at Sunbeam and then stretched out into nights of pot and music and deep discussions, mostly in Merch's room.

The excitement began on Friday evening, after school. The Sunbeamers also waxed enthusiastic. Jacinta summoned delicious homemade fish pickle from deep Kerala, and Malti showed us how to make the only thing she knew, her Tibetan ayah's dumpling soup. In the small kitchen, where it took at least four damp matches to light the gas stove, sometimes by lantern light, we stuffed parathas and made chutney fish wrapped in banana leaves; carrots with grated coconut and coriander; and, once, chicken with cardamom and crushed cashews.

Like me, the Sunbeamers were just getting to know Moira Prince. They had lived with her for almost two years, but at a distance. She kept to herself. They were wary of her. She was white, she was moody, and she had a dark and scandalous past.

I began to call her Pin. I learned the order of names from Merch.

"She hates being called Moira. The girls call her Miss Prince. Her friends call her Pin," he warned me one night as we talked in his room while she sat in a corner with eyes closed, lost in some song.

"Why, what's wrong with Moira?" I asked.

"She told me she herself would never associate with anyone called Moira. Can't blame her. It's a kind of a prissy name, don't you think?" It was true, the name did not suit her. I began to notice how she flinched when Miss Nelson and the teachers called her Moira.

She talked of the Sunbeamers with disdain. "Eager little twits," she called them.

But she always came for the Friday night dinners. She would emerge from her room in a fresh white khadi shirt and jodhpurs, smelling of Cinthol soap, her hair combed back and shining wet.

She told her share of stories. "In Singapore I ate a monkey brain," she said. "After midnight, in the streets, they cook monkey brain, and they have this hollowed-out table where they put the monkey, live and wriggling underneath, between the plates. And then they slice the skull like a coconut so that you flip it open and eat the brain."

"What did it taste like?" I asked, though I wasn't sure how much of this I should be believing.

I remember she put down her fork and spoon, looked up at me very gravely, and said, "Balls. It tastes like balls," and then she continued to eat. Everyone looked down at their plates. Malti cleared her throat and got up to fetch more rice from the kitchen. With Pin you never knew when she would go too far, when she would take a moment over the edge.

It was Pin who gave us lemon dal. One Friday she sauntered in early while we were cooking, leaving the door of her room ajar so that we could have music as we chopped and stirred. She wasn't about to cook, but she was a good taster. There was a half-lemon lying near the stove, where dal was being boiled. "Why don't you throw it in the dal, just like that, with the rind, and let it boil?" she said.

"Everyone knows you only put in lemon after the food is cooked. It turns bitter when boiled," we protested. "And that too, with the rind in it."

Nobody in the room had ever heard of such a thing. And we had grown up on three different cuisines, spread far across the land.

I threw the green lemon in anyway, as an act of faith. The dal turned out bewitching, with a lime-bitter fillip I had never tasted in anything before. We called it the Sunbeam Special. And I know in my gut that of all the things we cooked together, every one of us will always make lemon dal. And when we eat it, we always will be back in that breathless monsoon. The evening when we made it first, the dal was a lovely yellow; it slipped down the throat and warmed your stomach like a new world opening.

Soon after dinner, we would disband. The Allahabad girls

were off to their dates, the Christian ladies went chastely to bed, and Pin and I walked down to Merch's room.

They taught me many things in the rain, the Prince and the Mystery Man. They taught me that sitting in Merch's room at night, we could well be in Switzerland.

They convinced me of this by presenting an array of facts. Panchgani, they pointed out, was the Kashmir of Maharashtra, since it said so on the sign when you entered the town from the Sandy Banks side. And Kashmir, every child knew, was the Switzerland of India. All we needed, they said firmly, was the right kind of music. And they had the right music. I learned slowly to love Bob Dylan, and the Rolling Stones, and Lindesfarne, and the Doors, but most of all, that monsoon, it was the White Album we listened to. I thought of myself as Dear Prudence, afraid to go out and play.

They told me I was heaven-sent, because with my rich knowledge of Marathi and English, I could add to their compendium of words and phrases that were common to the two. They had extracted phrases such as "hey bug" and "neat bus," "far white luggage" and "what lovely," but were searching, they said, for a sentence that would make sense in both languages. I never did come up with anything, and they soon moved on to French and Marathi, though they were hampered by the fact, which Merch admitted, that neither of them really knew French. They did manage to come up with "à la mode" and "tout le monde," which in Marathi mean "here comes a turn" and "head has broken," respectively.

They had a world of private jokes and word games that they pursued with relish. I had not before seen humor used with such sincerity, so that it became a screen from the world, and I was enchanted.

They could turn without a warning into Freny and Cyrus, a retired Parsi couple with a retarded son and a servant called Somu, whom they were always sending off on impossible missions. Late, in Merch's room, with the rain thundering down around us, we would send Somu out for cigarettes and sweet spiced chai, and while he was at it, could he go to Kaka's and get hot, hot kheema pau, and five plates of dal fry, and also wake up Dhondu, the Panchgani Stores' peon, who slept behind the store, and ask him to take out two choco bars from the only kerosene freezer in town? "And also, Somu, could you run off to England for a jar of that marmalade I love?" Freny would call.

"English this and English that." Merch's face would become craggy, and his shoulders curled close to his neck. He sometimes let a glint of a shy smile escape from his eyes just before delivering an exceptional line. "And who will change Tempton's diapers, I ask you, when Somu is not back in the morning?"

Freny and Cyrus had the worst marriage. They would blame each other for everything, especially their son.

"It is because of you that Tempton wears diapers," Merch said one night, his voice thick, his accent pitch-perfect. "I told you to start training him at least when he was six. I begged you on his tenth birthday. But no. Now he is twenty-two. I ask you, is this any way to bring up a child?"

"Not that you have ever bothered to change a single one of those diapers," retorted Pin. She did attempt a slight imitation of a Parsi accent, but she sounded mostly like herself, her Indian accent with a British undertow almost intact. She would burst out laughing in the middle of a sentence, and we would have to wait for her to recover before she delivered it.

Merch would pace around the room, he would go and loom over Pin as she sat on the floor with her knees drawn up to her chin, he would wave his arms and shout, becoming the Unmerch.

That night—Shabir, his girlfriend Raisa, their friend Samar, and I were there—we laughed so hard we had to bend and gasp. No one in the room ever entered those exchanges. No one dared, I suppose, because they were so perfect. The skits, though short and sudden, would develop a history. After the performance that night, Tempton was always twenty-two and always wore diapers.

When I still thought they were lovers, I imagined that perhaps they had a practiced repertoire of jokes and skits. I imagined them laughing as they made them up, and I was jealous.

Later I realized that they just had the same quirky humor, and could build quickly off each other. But I was still jealous.

EIGHT

Scottish Dancing

IN 1974 THERE were eight boarding schools in Panchgani, representing almost every religion of India. There was Sanjeevan, the Hindu school near Sandy Banks; the Anjuman Islam School for boys; the Parsi girls' school; the Parsi boys' school; the three Christian schools; and a Bahai School on the way to the valley. The schools stayed in session during the monsoons. The students played indoor games and went for long walks to dissipate their energy.

In Timmins we had Scottish dancing. It had been raining constantly for ten days. We talked louder, and our laughter was high-pitched, pouring into thin spaces between the drumming water. The girls were often in the gym, bobbing up and down, while bagpipes played on an ancient record player donated by young Miss Wilson's twin sister, who lived in America. Miss Manson, during a furlough to England, had brought back Scottish dancing manuals, and now had divided the girls into groups of eight, lined them up, and had them doing padoba kuppes.

My weekends were still quite secret, and at school I was good little Charu, smiling and scraping and trying to get the girls in hand. I would sit with Miss Henderson in the evenings, when she had kilt fittings with the girls, her mouth full of pins. Her knitting basket overflowed with red, blue, and green balls of wool, because the girls wore pom-poms in their house colors sewn onto their navy-blue church berets for the Scottish Dancing Competition.

Miss Manson, Miss Henderson, and the girls were busy scrounging for kilts and plaid scarves. Miss McCall, the piano teacher, a soulful Scottish woman who was not a missionary but for some reason was languishing in Panchgani in a flat little house behind the bazaar where she kept parrots, could be counted on to come up with three kilts; Miss Manson of the Holy Trinity was good for two; and the rest were a challenge. Shobha Rajbans' mother, who was on a European tour, had sent her a red-checked pleated skirt that bobbed just above her knees as she danced.

The Scottish Dancing Competition was also known as the mid-monsoon dance. It was on July 10, almost a month after my first dinner at Sunbeam. The school was in a fever pitch of excitement on the evening of the competition. The top tier of Panchgani residents trooped in wearing just-pressed jackets and saris. The senior boys from St. Paul's, in long locks and red blazers, filled the gym with the smell of their sweaty socks. The convent girls sat next to them, blushing and giggling. The big news at the back of the gym, where the dancing girls were lined up in their formations, was that Shobha had a new boyfriend, and he was sitting in the front row. The gym served also as our auditorium and had a good-sized stage at the far end. The Scottish dancing, however, took place on the gym floor, with the audience seated in rows on the edges of the floor, and on the stage. At the front of the stage sat the three judges: a nun from St. Mary's Convent, an Anglo Indian master from St. Paul's, and Mr. Billimoria, principal of the Parsi school, whose culture was considered more attuned to the finer, Western arts and music.

It was when the girls bobbed in, their toes perfectly pointed and their chests puffed out like Scottish Highlanders, that it struck me just how bizarre the school was. No wonder I felt I was swimming underwater. Not only had the missionaries created a British boarding school in this corner of India, they had even managed to create the Victorian boarding school of their own childhoods.

I saw Pin sitting with Merch at the back of the stage. In Indore, when I pored over *Femina* and *Eve's Weekly*, dreaming of the lives of the models that lounged across those pages, it was their sophistication I yearned for. And though Merch and Pin were too eccentric and ungainly to be glamorous, this same sophistication glowed around them, pulling me into their orbit.

I was intrigued by Pin's past. I had pieced it together by now, from scraps dropped by Merch, Hendy, and Sister Richards. I had assembled the skeleton of her life. Her parents had been traveling missionaries. They went around the country holding prayer meetings in schools and camps run by the same Presbyterian mission. Her father was a very persuasive preacher, and the prayer meetings often turned into teary, emotionally fraught conversion marathons. Moira grew up in Nasik, attending the mission school there. At fourteen, she was sent to boarding school in England.

"That's where she must have learned all her bad habits," said Hendy with a suggestive sniff, though she did not deign to specify the habits.

Every time I heard something new about her, the dark side beckoned.

I was learning to decipher her many moods. It was her mood that always drove our evenings. Merch was the harbor. I had no idea what he did with his days and nights—Sister Richards told me that he wrote for the district newspaper and was a stringer for the *Poona Herald*, though he said the last story he wrote was in 1968, when two Irani boys had kidnapped a girl from St. Mary's Convent—but I imagined him, always, in his room, ready to draw us into his special world.

Pin had times when she carried a dark cloud on her head, those nights when she smoked silently in the corner with her eyes glazed, and we played chess or talked softly in a glow, Merch and I, of books and exotic places we would visit in our lives. There were some nights, though, when she was just plain angry. On those nights, it was target practice. Anyone was fair game. She slashed everyone. Raswani, the Hindi teacher who had pronounced her to be wicked that day in the staff room, was a spying, conniving psychopath. Malti and Beena were silly blind mice. Jacinta was an empty little potlet, Susan a frustrated cow, and all the teachers "fucking spinsters." But on those angry nights, it was mostly Miss Nelson she ranted against. "That saintly bitch," she would say, her eyes small slits of venom. "Biggest hypocrite on this planet."

I was unsettled by the profanity and anger. "Who has wronged her?" I asked Merch once, when we found ourselves alone.

"It's all about the parents," he said. I could not buy that package. Many people lost parents. It was tragic, no doubt, and it must be terrible. But she was already a grown-up then, so why this intense hatred for her guardian?

"Her parents were strange creatures."

"So?" I asked.

He laughed, "OK, all parents are strange creatures, I'll grant you that. But she feels they hated her, all three of them, her parents and Miss Nelson."

"Never heard of parents hating their children. And if Nelson hates her, why would she keep her in the school in the first place?" I asked.

Merch shrugged. "Yes, there is that," he said, and changed the subject.

I knew there was a secret, and Merch was its keeper. I tried to work it out of Pin. I would pry in small corners, but everything she said made her more mysterious. In the beginning, I took her with a pinch of salt. It was a touch of paranoia, I reasoned, and I felt somewhat sorry for Miss Nelson having to keep her in line.

"She is a wounded one. Sometimes you just have to wrap her in cotton wool," offered Merch, following my thoughts, and suddenly, instead of recoiling, I wanted to hold her in my arms and shield her poor naïve heart against the hard world.

And then there were those other nights, when she was quicksilver. Her eyes would turn large and liquid, and she would say small funny things unexpectedly, in the middle of conversations. There was a sparkle around her. The hippies and the farmers would often be there, and we would sit around Merch's room. The nights were redolent with music, laughter, and dreams that stretched thin and clear into the future. It felt like we were all in a cozy little spaceship, spinning around the universe.

With Merch I felt light and graceful. With her, it was butterflies. My stomach turned somersaults when she looked at me. I thought about her a lot. I constructed conversations in my head with her, but I rarely had them. In my hospital room, with the rain drumming on my temples, I would stay up and think of ways I could have answered her sudden swirls of tenderness and humor. When we walked from Sunbeam to Merch's at night, she had this way of striding along deep in conversation, and then stopping suddenly to deliver her punch line. I would have to look back at her to hear her. Walking up alone to classes, I would often catch myself nodding and saying a word out loud, looking back for her tousled head behind my shoulder. She often kept her hood down, even in the pouring rain, and rivulets of water poured down from her curls.

Some sort of Shiva, I thought.

She waved to me as we were all leaving the gym after the Scottish dancing, and was waiting for me outside under a dripping eave. She was in a good mood, bouncing with laughter and enthusiasm.

"Brown girls bowing in kilts," she said with sparkling eyes.

"This is *absolutely* my reason for being here." We both laughed out loud. I was thinking then only of the colonial implications of this neat turn of phase. Later that night, it came as a complete revelation to me that there was also a further meaning embedded in that line, and she had hoped that I would guess it. If I'd known, I'm not sure that I would have walked up to table-land with her that night.

We walked out together, I thought, perhaps to buy cigarettes around the corner. She did not stop at the bidi stall, however, and we walked on. I did not ask where. The rain had slowed to a fine drizzle, but the world was still encased in water. The wind tugged at my raincoat hood as we turned the corner and saw the land rise up to the clouds.

In Marathi, Panchgani means five volcanoes, the "panch ganis" that surround the village. The nearest of the volcanoes was a long plateau called table-land. During the day, table-land filled the horizon to the right of the bazaar like a resting lion, its back parallel to the sky. That night, it became a giant cake, with the clouds hovering like white icing on the top.

I guessed she'd had a miserable childhood. But so, I figured, had I. As we walked past the Muslim cemetery on the way to table-land, I asked her what was the best memory of her childhood.

"My skates," she said warmly. "Every evening in Nasik, in the mission compound, I would sail through the air. I went fast, I could swoop and swirl and whiz. People from the mission would often sit around and watch me. I think I did that for two whole years.

"The skates were great," she said, in a rush of remembering. "We went back to England for furlough when I was seven. I learnt to skate there, and they bought the best pair of skates in the shop just before we came back to India." She usually referred to her parents as "they."

"And when did you stop?" I asked, wanting to hold that memory complete.

"Well, you see, I started sneaking out of the compound."

She would. "It was more fun on the road," she said, shaking her head ruefully, her lips turned up in a cheeky smile.

"Did they yell at you?"

"They were quite sorrowful. They thought I was being deceitful. And then of course I had an accident, and broke a hand and a foot."

"And then?" You had to pry it out of her; she never volunteered too much.

"After that I started cycling," she said, matter-of-factly.

As we walked up to table-land that night, Pin darted suddenly through a gap in the hedge into the Woggles' garden. I stood outside, too timid to breach a property line at night. She came back a few minutes later with a handful of the jasmine that grew on the creeper behind the garden gate. She held the flowers in her cupped hands, and we walked slowly up the winding road, burying our heads in their fragrance.

This was my first time on table-land at night. It was easy to walk in the dark, because the ground was hard and smooth. Its top felt like it had been sliced with a sharp knife. The wind churned the drizzle and spat it at us in angry bursts. We kept our raincoats on and sat on some rocks beside the pond. "Why is Merch called the Mystery Man?" I asked her. She threw a few aimless pebbles into the pond. "Now you see him, now you don't," she said. She turned to me and brushed back the hair scurrying around my face. Then, without a warning, she pulled me to her and kissed me on the lips.

She pulled back, smiled at me, and started kissing again, her tongue slowly massaging mine. I had read in some faceless love story that a girl is never completely surprised by her first kiss. It can be sooner than she expected. Not ever unexpected. But for me, that kiss on table-land was a bolt of lightning flashing down on from the sky.

In my dreams, I saw always, my clear dewlike face, being held in the moonlight by a lean man, usually called Rahul. Kissing another woman on a wet night, kissing the Prince on table-land, no. The kiss was unexpected and completely undreamt. But the plunging in my stomach was the same as in the kisses of my dreams. Her tongue coaxed mine out, and slowly my lips, my tongue started dueling and dancing along with hers. We broke apart, and she kissed the rain off my face, licked my blot with a flat tongue, and then went back, again into my mouth. I cannot say how long I stayed. I remember licking a raindrop from the tip of her nose.

But then the devil of confusion and panic possessed me, and I tore myself away and ran and ran and ran all the way down the slope and through the bazaar and down to my room. I did not look back, but I knew she did not follow me that night. The hard rain started up again, the fireflies I had seen on the way up had closed themselves up, the edge of my gum boots rubbed raw against my calves, and my pink silk kurta was plastered to my breasts. I rubbed the thin towel hard against my skin, and jumped, naked, into my damp bed. All night I drifted in and out of strange half-finished dreams of childhood dread, turning ice-cold one minute, and then, when the kiss came back to haunt me, I would grow hot and flushed.

The next morning my blot was red and angry, and my face swollen. I could do nothing with my hair but tie it in a knot above my head. I felt naked, I felt that anyone who looked at me would know my deep dark secret.

I missed breakfast and slunk into the prayer hall from the back, just as the girls stood up and launched into "Jesus loves me, this I know, for the Bible tells me so . . ." My hands were clammy with sweat, strange strips of excitement and dread ran down my spine. I stood next to Miss Raswani, who glared sternly at me, her lips pursed in disapproval. I remember I was holding on to the back of the pew in front of me, clutching for safer ground. I saw the certainty in the faces of the missionaries, and I toyed in a third-person kind of way with the idea of letting Jesus into my heart. But there, in front of me, stood Miss Raswani, Our Lady of the Pursed Lips, her white-rimmed eyes raking me with scorn and disgust, as though she had seen that very kiss.

No wild thoughts, I told myself firmly. I will be brave, like my sweet Ayi. "Ayi, I had my first kiss yesterday. With a girl," I imagined telling her. I quickly brushed Ayi under the carpet. I walked out of the prayer hall and went in to teach *Macbeth* to the standard-ten girls.

I remember that lesson, because it was the day the tenth-standard girls turned to me, suddenly. Like a school of small silverfish.

"Had he not resembled my father as he slept, I'd have done it," I read. "Why do you think she would say that?"

"Shakespeare sees her as weak because she is a woman," said Nandita. "He's a chauvinist. She's evil and weak." Nandita Bhansali was short and plump and had a thick fringe of black hair, which, by midterm, hung raggedly over her square black plastic glasses like eaves. Literature was her favorite subject.

The whole school—teachers, girls, and I imagined even the British missionaries—was in awe of standard ten. They had all been together in Timmins since a very young age and had flowered together into a bouquet. They moved as a whole, and they looked after their own. You could not pry them apart and find a spoiler. At the quiet center was Nandita.

Nandita was one of those girls you would not notice at first, but once you did, you never forgot that she was there. You wanted to know what she was thinking. I thought of her as bobbing through the class, earnest and wise, keeping everything good and aboveboard. She made me teach at a higher level.

Shobha had turned my ninth-standard classes into a circus. She was a drama queen. The tens, on the other hand, gave me a chance. They waited, poised, hanging in the tank with waving fins, until that day when they came towards me, flashing their silver tails. I could feel the whoosh of Nandita's tail turning.

"But as a character within this play, would you say that Lady Macbeth is a coward?" I asked.

"Yes," said Nandita, not missing a beat.

"She's also manipulative. She can't plunge the knife herself, but puts her husband up to it," said Akhila Bahadur, an impertinent and squirmy little girl who usually played for laughs in class.

"So that means in the end it's all her fault. Her husband turns out to be the lesser villain. All these male writers, they always blame the women," announced Nandita, folding her hands as if to say, "Your honor, I rest my case."

"Perhaps, yes. Shakespeare was grounded in his time, in terms of male and female roles," I replied. "But these are the big moments of life. You do not know your own weakness until you are tested. You cannot know how you will act till you are actually in that moment." I said this with feeling. I, who had rarely dreamt of anything but a love marriage, I, who had just arrived from hatching with my parents in a small town, I had been kissed by a woman. To have been kissed by a woman on a windy mountaintop was one thing. But for that kiss to have opened up my body like a fault line was another.

Fie, my lord, fie, a soldier and afeared? I told myself, becoming both Lord and Lady Macbeth, the adviser and the advised, at once. It is only the shock of a first tongue kiss that I feel, nothing more and nothing less. This was the first and last time. It was an accident. It would never happen again.

I made the class play it out. "Let's put ourselves there. It's dark and rainy. The castle is large and echoing. You are Lady Macbeth. You're going to do this. It will be easy. And then your weak husband will be king. You have always guided him. It will be easy for you, you think. You can do anything. Your husband is too high-strung. You enter the king's chamber. You adjust your eyes to the dark. You hold the dagger up with both hands, practice how you will plunge it. Then, a flash of lightning. You see this old man, his mouth slack. Maybe he is snoring, like your father. You think of the strength it will take to plunge the knife. You don't know where to plunge it; the rib cage looms large beneath your knife."

"OK, so she realizes that murder is a big thing. Then why is she so ruthless with her husband?" asked Nandita. "Shakespeare is a chauvinistic pig, that's why."

"Because Lady Macbeth has a weak imagination," I said. I don't know from where that came. "She still sees it as a simple act. It's only after the deed is done that she feels the enormity of it, and feels remorse.

"I think Shakespeare is great because he gave her remorse," I said, feeling I had just understood a universal truth. Surely it was remorse I felt, the shivers and the guilt, the flush on my cheeks when I thought of her tongue circling my blot. In truth, I knew nothing of the depths of remorse on that day. That came later.

"That will be your homework question this week," I continued, flashing brilliance and strength. "Examine Lady Macbeth's role in the light of the women's liberation movement of our time."

"Can we please have a choice, Miss?" asked Daksha Trivedi, dolefully. Daksha sat in the front row with grumpy determination and always worked very hard. But she usually didn't get it.

"How about, would Lady Macbeth have really killed the king if he had not resembled her father?" said Nandita.

"Very good," I said. "Do either." The day after my first kiss was also the day I first began to like teaching.

NINE

Monsoon Swimming

ON MY THIRD day in Timmins, when I saw the green inland form with my mother's little curled letters, my heart turned a half-circle: I had never gotten a letter from my own mother. We had never been apart, my ayi and I. She filled the inland with marching sentences in neat Marathi script.

> I have now started going out for walks with your father in the evening. Anita got engaged to a boy from Lucknow, very handsome boy. Auntiji sent us mithai, and Anita came herself and gave it. She said to tell you. The house feels empty without you. I have made chakri and your favorite pickle. I will send it to you in a parcel tomorrow. Baba says that Panchgani is very pretty. He feels you will be happy there. I am knitting you a green and red sweater. I have made fresh sandalwood paste for your face [read blot] and will send it in the same parcel.

I saw our home without me. What would they say to each other, my ayi and baba, across the table? It was I who made them anxious, I who made them laugh.

I wrote long letters to fill the void. At first it was Marathi with Ayi and English with Baba. But soon I just wrote to them together in English. I wrote about the missionaries, marching through the school like onward Christian soldiers, each pursuing her pet mission.

Take Miss Manson. She does spot-checks on the girls' bloomers. The other day I was climbing up the steps to class, when suddenly Miss Manson sprang past me, taking two steps at a time, and ominously patted some poor girls from behind. "Nandita and Akhila," she said, her big blue eyes awaiting a sinner, "let me hear your elastic."

The girls live in terror of this. They are to snap the elastic on each leg to prove their bloomers are firmly in place. Luckily, that day, Nandita and Akhila both produced resounding snaps.

She used to give them detention for bad elastic.

But soon, the standard-ten girls went into Miss Nelson's office to complain. "It's not fair, Miss," said Nandita, the spokesperson. "Detentions are for study-related issues. Miss Manson gives us detention and makes us sew name tapes on our black ribbons." "It's just not fair," said the chorus of girls around her.

"Yes, you are quite right, Nandita. This is not an academic issue," pronounced Miss Nelson after due consideration. I can imagine that she must have paused and looked gravely around—all these white women, Baba, they quell people with a grave look. And once you say "fairness," they have to listen. But Miss Nelson is a master. I am trying to be like her, at least when I am teaching.

"It is not an academic issue," she continued. "It is a behavioral issue. Miss Manson is a sports teacher and is in charge of you after school. If you disobey her, then the punishment for that need not be a detention." Some of the girls might have already been fidgeting with excitement at the victory, so Miss Nelson probably waited a moment. "It will be an order mark," she said, looking at them with a bland smile. You have to hand it to her. The girls retreated in defeat, because an order mark is a punishment of a much higher magnitude; it is on record against you and your house the whole year, and counts in getting some prize or other, some "Best House" cup or something that they seem to all be working towards.

I tried to write funny letters. I knew they needed to laugh. I began to enjoy writing them, and every time I saw something new, it played along in my mind until it turned funny. I would think of how I could present it. It was like combing my hair. Move a pin, put a pin in, take a pin out. A deft knot, a small twist, and a turn in the mirror.

Sometimes I think that like you, Baba, I am on a ship on high seas. A sealed place with its own set of intricate

> rules. But a female version, of course, which makes it as different as night and day, I am sure. In this case, as far as I can tell, at least half the "officers" are hysterical. The Hindi teacher, I think, is the worst. Her name is Miss Raswani. First she would purse her lips every time she passed me. Recently she has begun to sniff like a bull about to charge before turning her face away. I spoke to two other young teachers, and they said she does the same to them. They say that laughter makes Miss Raswani's blood boil. Specially if it sounds carefree. These women have no life but the school.

I, of course, made it clear that I was not like "these women" because I met with people outside the school. I wrote home of my evenings, which I had set up in an orderly succession, like a slide show. There was Shrewsbury with Miss Henderson, and spicy peanuts at the Nest with Mr. Woggle drinking beer and the black steep rocks of table-land rising through the mist.

And then, there were the bazaar evenings. I bought ribbons and cold cream and chocolates from Panchgani Stores, repaired slippers, stopped in at the post office to buy stamps and inland forms, and sometimes even booked an "urgent" call home. If it went through, all of us would give a few shouts of "Hello, is everything all right?" to each other through whistling wires.

I almost always went into the Irani Café to buy their famous gootli-pau, the meat cutlets served hot between fresh baked bread. The owner, Mr. Blind Irani, was usually at the cash counter. He took his time, figuring the change, sizing the notes, and weighing the coins in his beefy pink palms. He was a straight-backed dignified man with silver hair, and he talked to everyone while he sorted out the money in his five note drawers and five coin bowls. He put everything in its place first, and then carefully went back in and counted out the change. When no one was buying, he counted the money. "I never write it down," he said. "I always know how much there is." He wore thick dark glasses and kept his red-tipped cane hooked behind his seat. He turned his ear towards you when you talked and spoke in the unmirrored way of the blind, face and lips twisting and twitching. He did not accept notes over twenty rupees.

I was very shy with him, and so he spoke to me rarely. I, who had always wanted to fade into the furniture, I thought it would be a release, being invisible. But it wasn't so, and I didn't know why. I doubted if he knew about my facial imperfection. I was not a topic of conversation in those days. He knew I always bought gootli-pau, and he knew I was a Timmins teacher. And yet, I was shy.

The old man had a clear channel to the Letters to the Editor section of the *Poona Herald*. He always kept a cutting of his latest letter at his side, passing it around proudly to his regulars. He was our very own Ved Mehta. He commented on corruption in high places, the conditions of the ghat roads, the need to grow silver oaks in all the hill stations of India. Through all his letters there was a definite undertone of "The British Did It Better."

One of his pet subjects was the sliding morals of youth.

> Even at twenty, these young men are wandering around with long sideburns, trying to play Romeos. In my day,

> they would be supporting families. They are given too much money by lax parents, too intent on their own pleasures. Little wonder, then, that the young men have no moral fiber.

Merch had been Mr. Irani's conduit into the *Poona Herald*. He had also been the conduit for the old man's antagonist, Mr. Dubash, who lived in Dalwich House, a vast, ramshackle building that the girls said was haunted. We passed it on the way to Parsi Point when I took them for walks.

> My worthy opponent talks of the moral fiber of our youth. But I would like to ask him where he was in those days when this humble writer donned a khadi cap and fought beside the finest of our brethren in the freedom movement. Where was he, I ask you. Where were these much-touted ideals when we were exposing ourselves, nay, even risking our lives, chanting "Quit India" on the streets of Bombay? He was not there; oh, no, he was busy sailing boats with young women of dubious character.

The two old men wrote letters, back and forth, like a game of badminton. Lengthy, cantankerous rebuttals and counter-rebuttals written in courteous colonial English, all thuses and therefores and thereabouts. They still played bridge together on Tuesday afternoons, but otherwise did not speak to each other.

Merch would grin and claim to be quite neutral in the matter of the Dueling Parsi Gents of Panchgani. But since he was Mr. Blind Irani's main reader and writer, he was considered to be in Mr. Blind Irani's camp.

I always bought the gootli-pau for two rupees and left. Sitting down alone in a bazaar restaurant would have been risqué. Sometimes, the Prince and Merch would be lounging at Irani's. On those days, I walked past with a tight bazaar smile, the taste of uneaten bread cutlets in my mouth. I hated running into them together in the bazaar. If I passed Merch, I usually more or less ignored him. I knew he understood quite perfectly and did not take it personally. But with Prince, who could tell? She might just wave her arms and shout, "Charu, Charu, come and join us," and then I would have to go and be seen lounging in the bazaar with hippies during the day, when teachers or girls in uniforms going for evening walks might see me.

I was still trying to keep my two worlds apart.

The first week after the kiss, I did not even look at Pin in school. I was glad she was barely there. I will pretend it never happened, I told myself, and through the Friday dinner at Sunbeam I looked away and spoke to Jacinta or went into the kitchen to stir. Then after dinner, as soon as we turned the corner from Sunbeam, she pulled me to her by the raincoat and we kissed each other like two penguins, water dripping down our hair and cold in our mouths. And then we pulled apart and trotted off to Merch's room without another word.

I was one of those who sat straight-backed in corners and read at breaks. I rubbed my blot furtively at the corners of playing fields. I was a dreamer, and now I delegated it to dreamtime, the rush and sparkle when our eyes would lock and our hands would brush in Merch's room, or our thighs would rub against each other in the backseat of the beige Fiat. The kisses were few and stolen, and only when we were alone. Pin would dart at me behind the bushes as we walked in the rain, and I would kiss her back for a while and then turn my face, or pull away. We did not talk about it.

The Sunbeam dinner was the loosening of the stays. Our eyes would slide around the room and lock with a click.

"I'd rather be mellow," muttered the Prince as she passed me the puris on the night the lemon dal turned out bitter. She always managed to sit beside me at the Sunbeam table, and would rub her leg against mine, just a little longer than accidentally. Her eyes were chameleon eyes. I had seen them as slits of venom, but they could also grow and fill a whole room with light. And turn so tenderly, to me. I thought of the walk in the rain to Merch's after dinner, and of how she would kiss me on the back road and we would let our hands wander through the gaps in each other's raincoats.

Our fingers brushed static as she handed me the plate. She looked beautiful. I took a plump hot puri and turned to pass the plate to Jacinta. It was a white dinner plate with scalloped edges. She was sitting at the head of the table, and I thought she had grasped it quite firmly. But then she dropped it on the floor between us. I think she threw it. She made a sort of mewing sound and tumbled into her room, her pallu trailing on the puri-strewn floor behind her. Sobs followed. After a few minutes, Susan took Jacinta's plate to her in her room. She could be heard muttering soothingly to her in Malayalam, though we still heard sporadic sobs above the steady rain.

Jacinta talked to me often in the staff room, mostly about

herself. Jacinta had an oval, elfin face, limpid eyes, and enormous lashes that she used like Japanese fans. I judged her emotional maturity to be that of an eight-year-old.

I was fascinated because her parents were teachers in Ethiopia. She had been sent to boarding school in India when she was ten and went home only once every other year, for the two-month winter holidays. She seemed to have had a stern childhood with a difficult mother who loved the sons better. "Jacinta is an unusual name for a Syrian Christian. My mother got my name from a gravestone. Shows how much she must have loved me," she said. She had been sent to Panchgani to wait for marriage prospects. Her parents were looking for boys, she told me, fluttering her eyes coyly.

She must have seen us flirting, Pin and I, seen our eyes dancing. She must hate the Prince. She must hate me too. She had felt akin to me during those long chats in the staff room, she had confided in me, only to find that I had turned depraved, making eyes at the strange foreign woman. And now she was mewing like a tormented kitten in the bedroom.

"I'll clean up the mess, don't worry, just keep eating," I said perhaps too loudly, and dashed to the kitchen. I had goose bumps from tip to toe. I splashed some cold water on my blot and took a long time finding the broom and bucket.

I knelt to clean the floor. I kept cleaning, long slow strokes. I could not sit across from Malti and Beena and show them my shocked and guilty face. I could not risk them confirming what they might only have guessed. The Prince kept eating, though she did not touch the dal. She heaped large amounts of rice and curry onto each spoonful—as always, she ate quickly and with purpose—and then reached for more. From time to time, she shook her head ruefully. She seemed unaware of everyone else. Malti and Beena swallowed their food with some nervous chatter and raised eyebrows. From my vantage point crouching on the floor—that is how servants must see us, I thought with a start: from the floor, looking up—I saw that Malti and Beena did not look directly at her, but were aware of her every move. They were in awe of her. And then, I thought, so am I. I watch her every move.

That night was the first Friday that I did not go to Merch's. I left quietly without saying good-bye as soon as I finished cleaning, and walked back to my room alone. It was all just innocent flirting, I told myself. I will stop it straightaway. It means nothing to me. I sat in my room and wrote a long letter home to calm myself. I forgot to send it. On Monday, Shankar, the school handyman, gravely handed me a telegram from my mother as I was sitting in the staff room correcting essays with my red and blue pencil. *Going to Kolhapur stop will come and see you soon stop letter follows stop.*

It was the beginning of August, and we had about a month to go before the end of the monsoon term. All through this time, Ayi's letters came as regularly as the rain. I read them in a minute and tucked them away.

All the years of growing up, I hid only my dreams and fears from them—my actions were as clear as glass. I went to school, I studied, I played chess, I had two friends who were as mousy and as middle-class as I was. In college, I wore bright dupattas and hugged my books to my chest like all the girls. I saw Hindi movies and hummed the popular songs. I did not talk to the boys, and the phone in our house hardly ever rang.

As I stepped deeper into this swirling world, it was not my dreams, but my actions I now hid from the world. I could think of very little to write. The long nights I had spent composing my letters I now spent dreaming, or reading the new books that Merch gave me. As if in response, Ayi's letters grew shorter, sometimes only five tight lines on the top of the green inland letter. But they came in like clockwork, twice a week, and I did not pause to think about them.

I was living in some kind of trance. I had been thinking of it as a hemlock trance ever since I taught the poem to standard nine.

My heart aches, and a drowsy numbness pains
My sense, as though of hemlock I had drunk,
Or emptied some dull opiate to the drains . . .

"Anyway, Miss, we should be allowed to try hemlock. Otherwise how are we expected to understand the poem?"

"Keats says *as though* of hemlock I had drunk," I shot back. "For you, Shobha Rajbans, it will be sufficient to be able to dispel the dullness of the senses." I had understood by now that a quick retort—even if flawed—was the best way to move onward in the classroom.

The telegram jerked me out of the trance. I was left gasping and blinking in the harsh light of reality. I went to the post office that evening to make a call home and sat in the dimly lit trunk-call section for two hours. "No connection, Miss, due to rain," said the trunk clerk. So I spent two days in a dither. But Ayi Baba are fine, I reasoned. Otherwise, I would know. On the third day, a letter followed. Ayi had written the letter the day she left. It seemed she had made a sudden decision to go to Kolhapur, but did not explain.

> It has not rained much in Indore this year, and it is still very hot. I have decided to go to Kolhapur for some time. Please write to me there. I will come and see you soon.
>
> Yours,
>
> Ayi

That was all.

Mostly, Ayi wrote form letters. Every letter always had two or three lines about Baba.

> Your Baba is keeping good health. He has gone to the regional chess tournament with Prashant.
>
> Your Baba has developed a bad cough and has been laid up in bed for a few days.

But this time, nothing. She did not ask about me, or my Sunbeam dinner of the week, either. She did not say why she was going to Kolhapur, though there could have been a hundred reasons. Things happened at a hectic pace in the Kolhapur branch. Every year, marriages, babies, scandals, sickness, deaths. And every so often, without a reason, a gathering of the sisters from all their mofussil districts. She did not mention any of these things. Just, *I am going to Kolhapur.* But I simply folded and tucked the little worries, and went back to my exciting new world.

Merch had casually handed me *One Hundred Years of Solitude* one gray evening while we were deep in the arms of the big rain. "You might like it, after a while," he muttered, rubbing his stubbly chin. I started it that very night. I followed Ursula, followed the whispering of her stiff, starched petticoats through the labyrinthine novel, and fell in love again.

"Macondo is Panchgani," I wrote in a note to Merch when I returned the book via the hospital ayah, who scuttled medicines and notes between the nurse and Dr. Desai's dispensary.

We had always been a reading family. Baba was a science and history reader, and knew everything about a lot of things, especially the Second World War. "Why read about things that did not happen when there is so much to know?" he would always ask, shaking his head as Ayi and I devoured fiction. Ayi and I read many of the same books. We read all the popular fiction of the time, the murder mysteries, the sexy romances. Secretly, I read *Valley of the Dolls* and *Peyton Place*, and I thought I was daring. When I came to Panchgani, I had reached the tumultuous period romances. My favorite books were *Gone with the Wind* and *Frenchman's Creek*.

But *One Hundred Years of Solitude* wove a spell that is still with me.

"Everything else I have read has paled," I wrote to Merch.

"It is because we have been reading the novels of the pale," he wrote back. He had a small and spidery handwriting that was almost illegible. With that note he sent me *The Book of Imagi-*

nary Beings by Jorge Luis Borges. Merch only made comments after I finished a book. I knew he revered Borges. I read a few intriguing lines from a story and put it down meaning to pick it up again, but I could not sustain interest in it. I felt somehow inadequate, but Merch refrained from comment. I did read *Invisible Cities* by Italo Calvino and loved it, as he did. All those cities of the mind seemed to have been conjured up for a man just like Merch.

Merch held the view that the only reality was fiction. "This includes, of course, movies and music," he assured me, just in case books might leave me wanting.

TEN

The Comma

ONE EVENING A few days later, I was walking out through the main gate, going to the bazaar—to Panchgani Stores, I remember, with the main intention of buying toothpaste—when I saw a white Ambassador car shudder into the school. The girls gathered around to look at this unscheduled arrival. Out popped my immaculate cousin Padmaja, her uniformed driver opening an umbrella over her head. Padmaja, one of the Timmins cousins, was four years older than me. She had been a sporty girl, and I saw her name on an unbeaten high-jump record from 1964. She did not see me, but walked straight into Miss Nelson's office, the pallu of her sky-blue sari neatly pulled over her head to keep her hair dry. She floated in like a cloud. I ran behind her, the blood pounding in my brain.

"Padmaja, my dear, you look well," beamed Nelly, striding out from behind her desk. "I hope everything is fine back home," she added, as she saw my anxious face bobbing into her office.

"Your mother is in Kolhapur and wants to see you," Padmaja turned to me and said. I knew something was wrong; I knew Ayi had been counting the days to come and see my school. *"You can show me all the places you go to,"* she had written in so many of her letters, adding always, *"I look forward to meeting the Wagles."*

I looked at Padmaja, frightened, raising my eyebrows. "Oh, she's just a little tired from her journey," said Padmaja. "Miss Nelson, can I please take Charu from you for two or three days?" she pleaded, smiling up at Nelly with confidence. Padmaja the perfect. She was bright, popular, and pretty. Everyone liked her. "She has the family looks," the aunts would coo. "Looks so much like Shalini. Could be her daughter." I hated her. At least she didn't have the Chitnis green eyes. Ayi's green eyes were a family heirloom. They missed a generation and were only passed down through the daughter. "Charu's daughter will have green eyes," the aunts would say, and I would feel a sad wind passing through them. "And who knows if that girl will even get married" rode on the tailwind. "Best to do it early," I had heard them tell my mother. "Girls look their best at sixteen. Get her engaged straight after school, and then let her study for a few years before getting her married."

It was Thursday evening, and so we agreed that I would be back on Monday morning for school. I packed my bag and consigned a note through hospital post to Merch explaining the reason for my absence from the weekend's festivities. I felt quivery and nervous as I left, but instead of thinking of my mother, I was praying I would run into Pin while going up, so I could at least smile at her and see if she smiled back. Yesterday, she had walked away from me in a huff and had not even looked back. It had been our very first terrible moment, and I wanted to make it up before I left. But no such luck.

In the car, Padmaja explained that my mother had not really gotten out of bed since she had come to Kolhapur a week ago. She lay facing the wall and cried all day.

My ayi, not getting out of bed? My ayi, who never lounged and was always dressed in fresh saris with the pallu pulled firmly back? My ayi, who was always bathed and oiled and fragrant before anyone else in the house was up?

"Do you know why?" I asked, thinking that perhaps something of the dark past had reared its head and snapped.

Padmaja shook her head. "We called in Tai," she said. My mother's oldest sister thundered in and seized all matters in her fat, capable hands. She went straight into the last room, the visiting daughters' room, where Ayi lay with her face to the wall, and closed the door. She emerged an hour later. "Menopause," she announced to the huddle of women in the courtyard. "Let her cry a little," she decreed. "She has been through too much. And she has kept it all in, all these years."

They began to encourage her to go up to Panchgani to visit me, but she just shook her head. Sometimes she wept loudly, so that her sobs could be heard through the house. Yesterday, Tai had gone in to confer with their father. It had been decided to get Charu to Kolhapur.

"That will cheer her up. We all know you are everything to her," added Padmaja. She was reassuring and quite kind. Actually, she had always been quite kind in the offhand, unimaginative way of the favored. When I came to Kolhapur in the winters, Padmaja the glamour girl would be there on holidays from Timmins. She had a generally superior air, which I now recognized in the girls at the school. In the evenings, the driver would be summoned to take her to the club, where she played tennis. At twenty-one she had married the right boy from the right family and now had two children, in the right order. Milind and Malini. First boy, then girl. Her path was always straight and sure, and I always held that against her.

For the first time, I was grateful for Padmaja's shallow kindness, her lack of curiosity about me. I was glad she left me alone the rest of the car ride. I wanted my ayi back. It was a physical pain, deep inside my stomach, that grew and filled my whole body so I could hardly breathe.

"I wanted to tell you everything before, so you could compose yourself," said Padmaja, adding softly, "You must be strong in front of her."

Kolhapur was close, only a three-hour drive from Panchgani. Dinner was just over when we reached the house. Tai waddled in, her sharp breasts preceding her. "Oh, Charu, you have become so thin, like a stick," she said, and clasped me to her bosom, the points of her 48D cups digging into my chest like sabers. "Come, she is waiting for you."

But my ayi walked out to me, looking ten years older in the dim corridor light. The fumes and the fragrance of the dhoop hung in the air. Her cotton sari was crumpled, her hair stood out of her bun in white wisps, she walked with a stoop. "Charu," she said. "Charu," my name, was swaddled in love and sadness. She hugged me, hugged me hard. We were Maharashtrian Brahmins, reared to be aloof, self-contained. We did not draw comfort from our hugs. For the first time, I held her tight. She felt soft and crumbly in my arms, like a Shrewsbury biscuit, I remember thinking, though the Timmins life was already a world away. We are the same height, my ayi and I. Both five feet three inches. But she had always felt taller to me. That day, I was taller; I could feel the bones in her thin shoulders.

We ate a dinner of bhakris and potatoes in the bright white dining room, Padmaja and I, while Tai and Ayi sat and watched. And for the first time, in that house that had been so forbidding, it was I who told the stories while Tai and Ayi and, yes, even Padmaja listened. For the benefit of Tai, who believed that in good food lay the foundation of a good childhood, I told of what we ate for breakfast, lunch, and dinner, those dead vegetables and water-curry chunks of chewy meat and rotis—which they called chapatti—so thick and leathery that the girls said they should be better used for making shoes.

"Yes," Padmaja laughed, "we used to say our food was first put in front of a goat, and if the goat did not eat it, it was given to us."

I did not directly look at Ayi. I felt we would both burst into tears. But I was speaking to her, I wanted to make her smile. Tai looked on fondly, seeing the light come back into her young sister's eyes. Their own mother was a thin, quiet woman ground down from childbirth and the demands of her dominating husband. Tai was the oldest of seven children, and she was the family mother and matriarch. It was always Tai who went into grave discussions with her father—Dada, as the old man was called by everyone, including the servants—on all family matters. They would sit in the garden in the evenings, Dada with his pipe, his majestic Dalmatian at his feet, and later, Tai would relay the decision to the women as she saw fit. She lived in a pleasant house not too far away with a fair and pudgy husband, and one fair and pudgy son, both of whom were largely inconsequential.

"Come in, Dada is waiting for you," Tai said to me after dinner. Though I imagined him always tall and erect, he too looked shrunk and bent that evening, as did the room around him. He was sitting on the sofa near the bookshelf in his white starched pajama kurta. He pulled out a large handkerchief from his kurta pocket and blew a loud honk into it. I realized with awe that he had been crying.

"Come here, Charu, beta," he said, and I went to him, for once, without clenching my fists.

"Oh, she had the world at her feet when she was your age," he said with sorrow. It hurt, as it always did, when we were cited for dragging her down, the husband with the blemished record and the child with a blemished face. And a girl, at that. They could not understand why god had given her this heavy burden.

But for once I did not cringe. "Her life hasn't been so bad, Dada," I said, though timidly. I was speaking also for Baba. After all, we both loved her, we both needed her. He looked at me, he really looked at me, blot and all, for the first time, and nodded gravely. He was one of those who never looked at me. I do not know from where I got the courage, that day, not to flinch. Everything was different, even the house, smaller.

"It will be best if you take off from your job for a few months and look after her," Dada said gruffly. "I will have Manohar speak to that principal of yours." Manohar, a portly man with salt-and-pepper hair, was Dada's oldest son, Padmaja's father. His three daughters had gone to Timmins.

Ayi was in the visiting daughters' room with only the bedside lamp burning. She had taken off her sari, and was in her white blouse and petticoat. I had seen her so often oiling her thinning hair and then tying it into a tight little knot for the night. "Come, I'll oil your hair, beta," she said with a catch in her voice.

She rubbed my scalp while the tears were tap-dancing around the dim room. Her hands on my hair. That was our umbilical cord. I had not even realized how I missed them. She too, she did everything slowly, she seemed to be remembering every stroke. We were walking down our lives together. I know we both went back to the day when it all started, the day we both wept in Bombay in the flat by the sea, before we left for Indore. Maybe it was all ending now, I thought wildly. I was so afraid, imagining all the horrible things that might befall our little family boat. But the knot that tied it to the shore had already been cut, the string was unfurling as I closed my eyes. She smoothed my hair into a shiny snake, and then wound it into a knot around her arm.

"I think I'll stay here with you for a few weeks," I said.

"You will?" she said. I turned to face her, and I saw a spark of light in her transparent eyes. But she was too quick for me that night. She saw that I was not ready to do it, even before I did. The light in her eyes snapped shut.

"Sleep well," she said in a flat voice as she opened the flap of her mosquito net and turned off the light. All my life, I have blamed myself for this, I have felt that this was the moment when I failed her. She needed me, but I wasn't big enough inside to help her then.

The dogs barked on, stretching out the night. My bed, cozy beneath its mosquito net, was at the other corner of the large room. In Kolhapur, the nights had always been sexy and long. I read *Gone with the Wind* in Kolhapur, lying in bed all day and late into the night, emerging in a daze for meals and outings, my mind pegged to the book. And then, awake, encased in dreams, watching the moon move against the net.

Although my ayi was suffering at the other end of the room, that night I understood that I was in love with Pin. But it's just a game, I assured myself once more, I am not like her. "Sometimes," she had once said, "I feel I was put into this world to seduce straight women," and she smiled with one side of her mouth.

Yes, she seduced me. She brushed her lips against mine in sudden tight corners, she threw me insolent smiles across a crowded room, she pulled my hair as I passed her in the staff room. I should be feeling shame and guilt and worse, dreaming so wild with a depressed mother in the room beside me. But I held a pillow to my stomach and longed for her, the air around her.

I wanted to go back and sit beside her on Merch's steps and run my hand through her hair. It was just yesterday, although it had drifted quite far away already.

I had sat beside Pin on the step, contrite. The stone was damp from all the rain, I could feel it through the thick cotton of my salwar. "I'm sorry," I said.

She did not look up. Her eyes were red-rimmed. I could see

she had been crying. She was angry with me, and she had every right to be.

I had coaxed and cajoled her into coming to the staff dining room for lunch. All sorts of business, such as announcements, plans, and duty-swaps were conducted at this time, and all teachers, including the day teachers, were supposed to attend. Pin never did. As I spent more time with her, I realized that she avoided Nelson.

I had been working on her for weeks, in subtle and not so subtle ways, trying to get her to come for lunch. In my grand plan, this was the first step towards social rehabilitation. I did it because I thought that if she calmed down and saw how easy it was to stick to the rules and be accepted, she would be less angry at the world. I thought, naïvely, that it was all as simple as that. And if I am honest with myself, I must admit that I thought it would earn me a brownie point. Miss Nelson would know I was a "good influence" on the wayward Miss Moira Prince.

In the end, Pin came to lunch to make me happy. Protocol was more relaxed at lunch, teachers straggled in and sat wherever they liked. I was about to sit down at the table on the far right with Pin when Miss Nelson walked in. I sensed Pin stiffen in anticipation of what she might say. Nelson walked towards our table, rubbing her hands. "Ah, Moira! Well, good afternoon, Moira," she said with what I imagined to be a welcoming stress on the "good," and a pleased expression on her wide face. I sensed Pin straighten up, fill out. I felt vindicated.

And then, Nelson turned to me. "Charulata, I need to discuss taking over some of Miss Debabushnam's classes with you," she said, putting a hand on my shoulder, ignoring the Prince. "She is going to be away next week. She has a family situation. Why don't you sit with me, and we can go over the details," she said, guiding me to her table.

Nelly sat at her fixed place at her table, which for dinner was the Superior White Table. At lunch it was like the captain's table, by invitation only.

I shrugged my shoulders regretfully at Pin and followed Nelson like a little lamb, my fleece as white as snow.

The teachers came in and distributed themselves around the room. I was backing Pin, but I turned to see that not one teacher deigned to sit at her table for four. Even the Sunbeam teachers stayed away. I sat across from Miss Nelson as tensely as at a birthday party with a bunch of rowdy boys—dreading the loud pop of a burst balloon behind my ear.

It happened ten minutes into the meal. "Mallu," she called to the bearer, and said in her perfect Marathi, "take away my plate. The dal is raw." She slapped her napkin on the table. "Bring me the fruit," she said, scraping her chair back with a screech that hurt your heart. She picked an orange from the tray and strode out of the room.

"I do not know how all of you can eat this rubbish day in and day out," she called over her shoulder to the entire room. There was a minute of cowed silence before we put our spoons into our mouths.

Thank god they can't see me flush, I thought. Thank god my blot is not raw these days. After lunch, I grabbed my raincoat and ran down Oak Lane to Merch's, because it seemed the first logical place to look for her. Sunbeam was too far, and I knew she would not be lounging in the staff room. I found

Merch's room locked and Pin sitting on the top step. I sat down next to her, my thigh running along hers.

She was drawing letters with a stick on the stone step below her, her chin resting on her knees, the soft white nape of her neck exposed. A drop of rain slid off the angled eave and fell plop upon her head. I wanted to reach out and brush it off, but a perky little five-year-old was staring up at us from the dispensary window, and I kept my hands to myself.

"I'm sorry," I said again. "You know, I don't think she meant to hurt you. She was quite welcoming, in fact."

Pin ignored me for a few minutes. Then she stood up. "OK, Miss Tinker Bell, if that is how you see it," she said without looking at me and ran down the stairs. I caught up with her, but she turned towards the bazaar and I had to go back to school for class. She did not say good-bye, just walked on with a stony face.

I had not seen her since.

Ayi moaned. It was one soft sigh, but it brought me back to my senses. I must be the good daughter. It was the first time my mother needed me, and I would stay with her. I would cheer her up. The monsoon term ended on the ninth of September. Three more weeks of class, then three weeks of holidays. Ayi would get stronger, and I would go back to school. I would go back to Timmins for the winter term.

As soon as I made up my mind to stay, and decided that it was really not bad at all, the six weeks without Pin began to stretch out for a lifetime. I wanted to run back to tell her that she was right.

"I don't go because Nelson can't eat if I am in the same

room," Pin had said to me when I first asked her why she never came to the staff lunch. I had thought her paranoid or, at best, flippant. But I believed her now. Nelson had humiliated her. It was a public lashing. She had ensured that Pin would never come to lunch again. The two of them must have a tangled past, and Pin was right. I was Tinker Bell to think I could just come in and wave a small wand.

But I wanted to hug her to me. "I believe you now," I wanted to say. "Nelson *is* twisted." I wanted to protect her. Anything could happen in six weeks. No, I could not wait so long. I would go back on Sunday to get my things. Kolhapur was close enough; I could take a bus. I would go back every weekend. Yes, I thought, happily ordering the world, I would go back for the weekends and spend the weekdays with Ayi. Maybe Merch could teach in my place. Although the missionaries rarely allowed men into the hallowed halls, except for servants and priests, they had, for some unknown reason, allowed the Mystery Man access to the outer sanctum. He filled in at times for suddenly sick or called-away teachers. But of course he never strayed from the upper level, where the classrooms were. He said he had never even seen the staff dining room. So I slept in peace, and woke up deep into the night and had a sweet private little orgasm.

My ayi was up before me. She was sitting erect on her bed, meditating. She had started this a few years ago, said it made her feel much stronger. I watched her, pretending to be asleep. Her shoulders were straight, which I felt was a good sign. She got out of bed and went out to the bathroom. She walked with purpose, as usual. She was up. She was going to be strong, for me. I thought this was an excellent first step. I would cheer her up. I would patch her up and soon send her back to Baba, I thought, for I was still intent on stuffing it all back into the box.

"Let's go shopping. I want to buy a Maharashtrian sari, with a border," I said to Ayi as we sat with our morning tea. It was a way to draw her out, and I really did want a cotton sari. I was fed up with wearing my teaching outfits from Indore; I felt that they were tight and badly cut. Samar's wife, a quiet girl who sometimes joined the group, wore traditional cotton border saris of different regions. I thought she looked most elegant. It was the new fashion among Bombay girls, I gathered, called ethnic chic. We went to the old market where the nine-yard sari ladies still shopped and sat on white cushions, our legs folded beneath us. I bought a deep green border sari, planning to wear it with a red shoe-flower behind my ear. I saw myself sitting demurely in a corner in Merch's room. We then went looking for what was rumored to be the first shop that ever made the original Kolhapuri chappals now worn by all the Bombay girls. We found it finally, an intense hole-in-the-wall run by two doddering brothers. It was in the heart of the old city, and the narrow road was a noisy jumble of cows, bicycles, rickshaws, and vendors selling cheap plastic toys. It was easier to walk, and so we sent the protesting driver home, wandered around instead, and had tea and samosas at Rainbow Lunch Home. I was nearly boisterous, so eager was I to make Ayi laugh. And she did. She did laugh often, but I sensed that it was just a sound, made to keep me happy.

We returned by rickshaw in the evening, laden with packages. In the monsoons, when the courtyard could not be used, the action was usually in the wide, covered back veranda outside the kitchen. The drawing-room lights were turned on only when the men came home from work. The veranda was noisy with aunts and servants and children eating fresh fried fritters from a steel plate. There was a dip in the sound when we walked in. Everyone pretended not to look at Ayi. I knew they were cheering me on. It was as if a bed of nails had opened up to reveal a plump mattress inside. The comfort of a large family I felt that day for the first time.

"Really, Charu, you should go back and finish the term. No sense in giving up like that in the middle," Ayi said that night when we had both gotten into our beds and tucked the mosquito nets around us.

"No, I want to stay," I said.

"No, I tell you, I will be just fine. I will stay here for three weeks, and then, when your holidays come, you come here first, and then we will both go together to Indore." She did not say "to Baba," and again I began to wonder if Baba's secret past had somehow come into focus again. Maybe the looming shadow had pounced.

Ayi was too fragile. I could not ask her now, of all times. But perhaps I could ask Tai.

I looked for a chance to find Tai alone, which was difficult since she was not a contemplative woman. Finally the next evening I came upon her combing her hair with a little bowl of oil beside her. Turned out she wanted to talk to me.

"Come here, Charu," she called, "come, sit down." She pointed beside her. "I want to ask you, has Shalini said anything to you?"

I shook my head. "No, nothing," I said, my heart fluttering like the wings of a trapped parrot. "Why, did—did something new come up?"

Tai appraised me with a shrewd look. "Well, they have to tell you when they want to," she muttered, scowling, as she always did when my little family was mentioned. But then her eyes softened. "She will be stronger, soon, don't worry. You know, Charu, it is a woman's job to protect her family. Everyone has to do it. Soon it will be your turn. Then you'll understand. At a certain age, a woman begins to feel tired of it all. Sometimes you have to put your load down. Your mother is tired. Now you have to help her. We all have to help her."

Tai's hair was done. Oiled, plaited, and wound into a small bun with a net around it. She wrapped up the conversation with a Tai special. Tai was famous for ending all conversations with a broader lecture on life. "I told your ayi. Some things we women just have to ignore. I told her, don't look up. In life, one must always look down at those below you, and be happy."

I had no choice but to be content with that for now.

By Sunday morning Ayi was so much better that Tai herself thought it was wise for me to finish my stint and come back. "It is only three weeks, and we will all look after her," she said.

Tai, of course, chalked this up as a personal triumph. She had come in and solved the family problem, yet again. Her power remained intact. She decided that morning, quite abruptly, which was the way she made most of her decisions, to go to Igatpuri for a week. Surekha, the second sister, lived there, and she had found a prospective girl for Tai's son. Tai was in the midst of choosing a bride for her son and was dashing around looking for the right girl. Her son would then view the selected ones.

"After that, I am going to find you a boy. I have a very good family in mind," she said, and smiled ominously. I was sure it would be a widower from Surat with two young children. He would comb his oily black hair in a Rajesh Khanna puff.

She waddled out of the house in triumph, her breasts preceding her like wind-puffed sails.

From the time I was a baby, the custom had been set. I was taken to touch Dada's feet when I came to Kolhapur, and I went in to touch his feet when I left. So I went into his room to say good-bye. The old man teared up again a bit, but he smiled. "Shabash, Charu, you will be a strong girl," he said. "I am glad, because you will need it." He patted my back. I took it for what it was: It was the truth. He looked into my face again. I knew now he always would.

I left in the afternoon, in the white Ambassador with Sayed driving, the combination always considered safest for long-distance travel. Ayi stood at the gate until my car turned the corner, and I knew that her eyes would be wet. I knew she had put on a brave front; I hoped her front would harden into a shell. But she will be just fine, I assured myself. I was armed with fresh-ground garlic chutney, a bag of good Kolhapur rice, and a knack for making bhakarwadi. Tai, Ayi, and I had rolled them out for a huge Sunday lunch.

"Shalini tai is much better as soon as she saw you," said Sayed while driving back. He had always been the driver trusted with the girls. I think he had even carried me as a child, from the car to my mother as she shopped for saris with her sisters, and I felt he was proud of me. I realized this was the first time in Kolhapur when I had not felt that the blot covered my entire face.

As we turned the corner on the ghat up from Vai, the fog became thick, and soon we could see almost nothing. The rain became heavier as we climbed up the ghat, and Sayed slowed the car to a crawl. It was a like a punch to the head, diving back into the Panchgani rain.

ELEVEN

Transport

I WALKED IN just as the school was sitting down for dinner. The tin-roofed rain walk led straight down through the center of the school, plunging me into the post-grace chatter of the dining room. The lights had gone off. The dining room was lit by four hissing gas lanterns hung on hooks from the ceiling. I took a candle from the dispensary, called a cheery "hello" to Sister Richards, and put down my bags, meaning to change and go for dinner. But I could not. I could not even stay in my room for more than a minute. I washed my face, smoothed my hair, and walked out into the wet night. I felt an urgent need to see her. I feared that something terrible had happened to her.

I decided to go to Merch. Maybe she would be there. I stood outside, the rain dripping down my nose, and looked in to see Samar and his wife laughing on the carpet, but not her. I could not go in. I went on to Sunbeam. Let her be there, I prayed to my emergency god. Let her be there, and I will hug her, hold her, feel her heart beat against mine, and leave.

She was wearing a loose white khadi shirt, her sleeves rolled up to the elbow. She was sitting on a mattress, smoking a joint. Her knees were folded up to her chin, her lips pouting. She did not see me at the back window. I walked through the dank, dark kitchen and burst into her room. I do not know when she jumped up. But, lithe as a cat, she was at the door. We hugged and hugged and hugged again, and then were on the bed. And it was I who made love to her. After all those kisses, after all those stolen kisses, all those times in the backseat of a wet car, or wet outside my bedroom door, or in the wind on Merch's balcony, after all those times when I had pulled away in fear or guilt, we traveled a new world together that night, this I know. Our lovemaking was so smooth and sweet, it was a night dipped in honey.

Before dawn, while she was still sleeping, snoring softly, with her nose in the pillow, I sneaked out and walked back to my room, followed by barking dogs. The rain had turned light, but it still dripped around my raincoat hood like a curtain. The town was asleep. I was afraid for my life, but I held her body like a warm shield under my raincoat. As I was going down Oak Lane, I heard a swish, and a long minute later, a bicycle went careening down the slippery slope, the milkman whistling above his jangling cans.

From then on, we could not stay apart. We started meeting in the afternoons, on the days I did not have class. I would walk out from the back, straight after lunch. I felt invisible in the pouring rain. She had the keys to Merch's rooms and would be waiting for me, listening to music.

Merch, she always said, was playing bridge with Mr. Blind Irani. I did not once ask her if Merch knew about us. I did not want to know. I felt I loved Merch too, in a fashion. There was a romance between us, but it was like lace.

It was a flirtation of smiles and small confidences. I thought of myself as a listener, but I found that with him, I talked. Our friendship was mellow and light, like the cigarette smoke that curled between us beside the table lamp.

If Merch was air, Prince was fire.

On a voluptuous afternoon, she slid my hair around my body. "Charulata unbound," she said.

She did not talk about her past. When she brooded, I did not enter. I could see the shift in her brittle eyes.

I was shuttling between green eyes. But they are so very different, the green eyes of the two people I love most, I thought. Ayi's eyes were transparent. They were like two little conductors. They passed on her love, her laughter, her sadness. Everyone—government clerks, vegetable vendors, neighbors and schoolteachers—everyone was always enchanted by Ayi. My mother was the lovely lady with the light eyes.

Pin's eyes were flecked with yellow. They were like marbles, glassy with hidden secrets. "What does it feel like," she whispered once, as we lay in bed, "to be loved without conditions?"

"Nobody is loved without conditions," I said, automatically.

"I bet you are," she quipped, licking my shoulder.

"Well, I guess I am," I conceded at first, and then thought about it. "I guess I am the center of their universe. I mean my parents'. But it is conditional. As long as I go along with their values. I suppose as long as I am a good girl."

"You are?" she mocked.

I don't know if she ever guessed the sudden turmoil that could sometimes overtake me. I put our secret world in a separate compartment and tried to pretend it did not exist.

"And if you were not a good girl, would they love you?" she asked. She always played with my hair.

I broke into a sweat. If Ayi Baba saw me now, could they love me?

"Parents must love their children. Even if they cast them out, deep down, they love them. It's the nature of life," I said, hoping it was true.

"Nope," said Pin. "Not true. I don't think *they* did. In any way whatsoever." She did not refer to them as parents.

It was a part of the romance of her, the brooding and the mystery. "I'm certifiably unlovable. You should know that," she added, flippantly.

"I love you," I could have said, but did not have that kind of confidence. "Why, were you terribly naughty?" I asked instead.

"I was flawed goods to them. From the beginning, I think," she said, shrugging her shoulders to show she did not care. "They just loved the Lord. I was always different from them. I remember thinking they were idiots when I was about seven." And then she changed the subject.

I did not understand. If her parents died when she was an adult, she was not an orphan in the traditional sense. So why was she tied to Nelson? I brought it up once, on a late night cigarette run with Merch, when we had left Pin behind with a gray cloud perched upon her head, angry about some slight from Nelly.

"Why does she have to hate Nelly so much? Nobody is *forcing* her to stay here," I said, though of course I did not want her to go, I just wanted to dig deeper. "Why does she have to take everything Nelly does as a personal insult?"

Merch did not answer at once. He watched his gum boots squelching in the mud. "She's going through a tough time. She feels alone in the world. She feels they all betrayed her."

"And did they?" I prompted, after a pause in which he added nothing.

"It's her story, really," said Merch gently. "She'll tell you when she is ready." I imagined a small reproof in this and decided to ask no more. But I always felt safe with Merch after that, knowing how he guarded his confidences.

"At least if they had died when she was a child, she could have imagined how they would have loved her," he said.

"So you think it's true that they did not love her?" It popped right out, though I had promised myself a minute ago to delve no more.

"It is true," he said, handing me the umbrella to hold while he took out two cigarettes. "It's her truth." The rain splashed around our ankles, and our heads almost touched as we lit our cigarettes with a single match.

The bidi stall was just a five-minute walk from Merch's. At around eleven, just before the bidiwala closed for the night, Merch would usually offer to go and replenish the cigarette stock. I would stand up and walk out with him. We took Merch's large black umbrella and walked in step, our faces wet with windblown drizzle.

I had begun smoking cigarettes. I liked Wills, though

Merch and Prince smoked Charminars. I started just because the smoke, the lighting, inhaling, and languid curling, was so much a part of those nights. But I had not smoked a joint yet. I would always smile and shake my head when it was passed around. I helped Merch make the joints, though, mostly because it gave me something to do. I would empty the cigarettes, Merch would burn and soften a part of some large ball of hash of which he seemed to have a steady supply, and I would mix it into the tobacco. He would refill the cigarettes with the mixture. We always made three joints at a time.

Sometimes, in the days of the long rains, when we did not feel like slicing through to the bidi stand, we would assure each other that we had quite enough cigarettes of all brands and would just end the party when they were over. Then, deep into the night, we would set off in the Fiat, searching for cigarettes and strong sweet chai. They were always wonderful nights.

I can cut my time in Panchgani into two with a warm knife. The second half began after Kolhapur. I was in hell one minute, and in heaven the next. When I was not with her, I felt I should not see her again. It was her fault. She was turning me into a depraved person. No wonder her parents hated her. I must stop making love to her, or I would turn into her. I could not even bring myself to say the word in the recesses of my mind. A lesbian, branded for my whole entire life as a fallen woman. But then I ran to her, and wanted nothing else, except her.

My blot began to change. I slept so little, and went through the days in a haze. The long hours I spent composing my face and attending and containing my blot were no more. One morning, I noticed it had turned darker. Then, the edges started wavering and spreading. It began to change from day to day. I studied it every morning with detachment. Once a tight pink coin, it turned into a dark brown amoeba whose edges seeped into my face.

I wondered if Ayi would notice the changed blot when I saw her in two weeks. I wrote her short bursts of notes, dashing off two-liners on postcards before I went for dinner. "*Counting the days to seeing you*," and "*Remembered you today when I made aloo puri at Sunbeam.*" She wrote once, a letter that gave no indication of her state of mind and ended with "*You must be busy with end of term work. Do not worry about me. The two Bhabhis look after me so well, always making my favorite dishes.*" I chose to find the letter reassuring.

I was tired and dazed during the day, and sometimes short-tempered with the girls, but discovered to my delight that they were better for it. They were less inclined to be cheeky. I began to go into the class with almost no preparation. I went with the flow. In standard ten, we read *Macbeth* and dissected it backward and forward and sideways—guilt and war and A-line dresses, and Indira Gandhi's non-effect on changing the role of women in India. I beamed specifically to Nandita, who seemed to process every word.

I often came across Nandita with two other girls, Ramona and Akhila, after class. Ramona was a gangly, high-strung girl who was prone to giggling fits. Akhila was a cheeky chimp of a girl who always drew a smile after her name. In their free time, the three of them often sat on the covered steps leading down to the hospital. They were always engrossed in secrets, and stopped abruptly as I passed them on my way to my room.

"Good evening, Miss Apte," they chorused, waiting until I turned the corner before resuming.

Miss Nelson smiled at me one day in the staff dining room, and said, loud enough for all to hear, "Charulata, you are doing very well with the tens. I heard you as I passed by yesterday." Praise from her was enough to puff you out for a day or two.

But my spot in the sun was getting increasingly precarious.

Soon it became difficult to restrain Pin in school. She would run up to me and pull my plait from behind. She tried to kiss me in the staff room one morning when we found ourselves alone.

"Can't you please, please behave in school?" I begged. The last place I would choose for a kiss would be the staff room in the morning.

"Now you want to put me back in the box, Miss Charu?" she would say darkly at times, and "OK, promise, ayi chi shappat," another.

But she would not stop. I lived between the dread of being caught and the pure excitement of running into her in a hallway. The rain was liberating. We walked away from the covered corridors and broke out into the rain as soon as we spotted each other. The hockey pitch and lower gardens were always deserted. The rain became our very own portable curtain.

Miss Henderson accosted me near the long steps one afternoon. "Where are you these days, dear? Come and have tea with me," she said, adjusting her ringlets. "You never come now." Her smile seemed a bit cold.

"Everything fine with your family, dear?" she asked as I bit into the biscuit. "Too bad I missed Padmaja. She, now, has the stamp of breeding. I told the girls, I always said, all the girls from that family have it." And then, after a stitch, she said, "Even you, my dear, I know that stamp of breeding when I see it."

Then, looking intensely down at her table runner, she said, her voice soft and firm, "I am sure you feel far from home here, but you must be careful about the company you keep. People talk too much here." I did not ask her what she meant. I pretended I had not heard and talked nervously about Padmaja's daughter for a short while before standing up abruptly and saying good-bye.

I wanted to sneak into my room and lie down and think for some time, and was tiptoeing down the hospital steps, quaking, when Sister Richards called, "Come and have a brandy, child, to dry the bones. This wretched rain. Pah. All my life."

Sister would often hear me bustling in my room in the evenings before dinner, and call out to me. "Come and join, my girl," she would say. I did go in sometimes and listen to her rambling. I always refused the drink.

"In the war, of course, we all drank," she would say every single time. "And then, got so used to it, can't sleep without it, you know. Mind you, I never drink more than two."

The dinner bell rang at seven. I always left her drinking her "second" drink as she waited for the ayah to bring her dinner.

Today, still turning hot and cold from Hendy's meeting, I accepted a brandy from Sister. "You were as timid as a rabbit when you first came. Used to scoot out backwards when I asked you for a drink," said Sister, smacking her lips after the first long sip.

"That's what I said to that Raswani woman. I told her,

'They're youngsters, why not be friends?' I like Moira. She stayed here when she was sick. She would come down and have a drink with me. She's been to England a few times, you know," she added, approvingly.

I began to feel faint with fear. I knew for a fact that Sister Richards and the Hindi teacher were enemies. I had seen the way they threw dagger looks at each other. If they were holding a conversation about me, everyone in school must know, must know something, but what did they know? My thoughts were scurrying and screeching like rats in a metal maze.

Common Knowledge. I felt dizzy with it. The Hindi teacher hated the world in general, but she hated Sister Richards more, and she hated Pin the most. Pin baited her like a matador, red cape just outside her reach. "See the smoke coming out of her nose," she sniggered as Raswani snorted and pawed the earth. "Can you imagine, the other day she called me 'a burden to mother earth'?"

"These women here can drive one to madness," said Sister, after a refill. "That Raswani woman, you know, she used to be in your room when I first came to Timmins. She's cuckoo. Just plain crazy. Pah." She spoke with venom, the "pah" short and sharp, as if she were spitting. "No life. Nobody. Stays here through the short holidays. Rents a room somewhere in the December holidays. Just imagine, wanted to come with me to Deolali. You know, my brother Cedrick and his wife, I have a room there, anytime, waiting for me." Sister usually talked in shorthand after her first drink. "Everyone hates her. Everyone. Girls, teachers, servants." The whole school lived in terror of Miss Raswani.

"Except for Miss Nelson," I pointed out.

"Pah. That Nelson of yours wouldn't admit it if she had a viper in her bosom," said Sister with a dismissive flick of white curls. "That Raswani is plain crazy. I should know. We had to treat so many people driven crazy by the war. She's twisted. Should be locked up. I could tell you a thing or two about her."

I was still too roiled about my own good name to be too interested in the Hindi teacher's madness. But Sister continued.

"You know, I saw her peeping into my bathroom one day, those mad eyes of hers. I went to Nelson straight and told her. That Nelson, so saintly, just smiled and said, 'Maybe it was dark, Sister.'" Sister pursed her mouth and mimicked. "But next day, I went to her again. I said, either I go, or she goes. Cannot live with that wretched woman. Always muttering and praying in her room. Now she's next to Nelson. Bet you she's spying on her."

The brandy crept into my veins, and I began to feel less fluttery. Sister would not be so casual about it all, talking to me like this, if Raswani had seen Pin and me kissing behind the gulmohor tree at the outer edge of lower garden, as we had done, just once or twice.

Raswani must have seen us walking in the rain and laughing. We did that all the time. But it was innocent. In fact, I was the picture of innocence. I knew that. Even if she had seen a hint of something, no one would believe it. That quiet little Maharashtrian girl with a blot on her face, who could think she was carrying on with anyone at all, let alone a woman—and let absolutely alone the dangerous Miss Prince? That was it. They all thought we were a bit too friendly. Maybe they even thought the Prince was trying to seduce me. My secret was safe. If they had known, if Hendy or Sister or Raswani knew, all hell would have broken loose. Surely.

Tai's voice came floating back from a still afternoon in Kolhapur: "Chastity. Let chastity be your sword." I was sitting on the floor while Tai was advising Padmaja's older sister Joytsna, who had been caught kissing her fiancé in the car at night. I must have been around fifteen. "A woman has her own power," said Tai. She was sitting on the bed, legs apart, like a pasha.

"Whatever *they* may want to do," she said, her face screwed in disgust. "We have to take a firm"—she pronounced it "farm"—"hand. Chastity," she said to the squirming Joytsna, "chastity should be your sword"—she pronounced it "swared."

And innocence shall be mine, I thought. Chastity has gone, but I still need a weapon. Innocence will be my swared in this battle. I will smile and dimple, as I always do.

I skipped dinner and went to Merch.

"Ah, Charu on a weekday," said Merch with a giggle of pleasure. Soon, Samar came by, we picked Pin up from Sunbeam, and drove up the back road to table-land. Before I knew it, we were at Shankar's fabled den in search of some Afghani hash. It appeared that Shankar had passed Samar in the bazaar that morning and indicated that he had some good stuff from a foreign hippie.

Shankar, the school handyman, lived a double life. By day he bustled around the school mending and lifting. At night, he sold hash and illicit liquor from a cave halfway up the table-land cliff. Strange though it seemed, the missionaries did not seem to know that he ran a thriving illegal business on the side. I knew Shankar quite well in school. He had come and fixed a leak in my bathroom. It was I who broke the ice, by talking to him in Marathi. He said when he saw me he always thought of his daughter, who was in college in Vai.

After that, he showed me her photographs and her letters, which he insisted she write in English, though he could not read them. He carried them around in his pocket and showed them proudly to select teachers. Miss Nelson had promised that his daughter would teach Marathi at the school as soon as she finished college. This was a vaulting leap up the ladder for her, and he could not contain his enthusiasm. "Bhagi will be like you," he often would say to me as he stood on a ladder fixing a light or sloshed through puddles in his knee-high black gum boots. "You must be her friend and help her out." And I would nod my head and assure him that I would, although I did not really plan to be around for so long. But we had met each other with our good school faces. I had never been to his den. And I did not wish to go.

Pin and I had stayed behind in the car as the boys walked up the final steep path to the cave. We stopped kissing and squirming when I heard them splashing back. I pushed Pin away and adjusted my clothes. I never let Pin touch me in front of the gang. Samar directed a dim torch light at the backseat. His bulging eyes, which got very red and glassy when he was stoned, peered down at us. I composed my face. "We're taking Shankar to the bazaar," he said. I saw Shankar's smiling face perched like a moon on his shoulder. I saw his smile freeze, in slow motion, when he saw me there. "Charu!" he said, terse and shrill. And then he looked away. He got into the front seat and did not look at me through the ride, not even when he got out. Shankar was in shock. I had taken on the responsibility of being a daughter, and then he had found me at night among the depraved and debauched. Veils and virginities were being stripped away so fast, I had no time to think or feel.

I'll deal with it tomorrow, I thought, and reached out for the joint as it was passed to Pin. I smoked my first joint that night.

Now that I can sometimes see my life swirling like a bowl of clear soup, I cannot quite recall the intensity of those days when the door first opened. I remember the panic, the fear of falling, and then, the music.

Samar had rigged two large black speakers in the car so we could have the right kind of music. It was Cat Stevens that night, hammering his sad voice into my small soul.

Lisa, Lisa, sad Lisa
Tell me, what's making you sad, Lee?

I heard the pauses for the first time. They were wide and deep and dangerously lovely.

After that, Pin would always produce a rumpled cigarette at choice moments. "Let's have a small one," she would say with a sheepish grin. I soon learned to tighten my throat and inhale properly.

The effect was instant. It was wide, wild, wondrous. I walked in wet and tense, and tight as a button. After the joint, we would roll around, or play and talk and giggle and kiss. We smoked, we kissed, we looked into each other's eyes and sighed. We lay on her satin sheets, her body white and soft as a goose feather. In the dim red glow of her room, we would whisper and laugh, we would start playing with each other and fall asleep warm and wet and entwined. The drumming of the rain became our own private dancer.

TWELVE

The Vortex

IT WAS THE fortieth day of rain. Even Mr. Blind Irani, the oldest Panchgani resident, could not remember such a long stretch of constant rain. The light was dim and gray, the sky always overcast. The rain on the tin roof had become a steady beat in all our heads. It was as if the whole entire school were living inside a giant drum.

That night, the rain had been angrier than usual. There was a high wind. The lights had gone out again, and I was in my room correcting exam papers after dinner, with the lantern turned so high it was smoking. I was bored. I was wondering whether to pass or fail Daksha Trivedi for a rather dim essay on Lady Macbeth when I heard a banging on the bathroom door. No one ever entered my room through that door except me and the servants.

I opened the door to find her, drenched, on my doorstep.

"I just couldn't wait another minute," she said as she stepped into the room, putting her wet hand under my blouse. "Hmm, you're toast," she said, nuzzling.

She dropped her clothes in a damp heap on the floor. "Dry me up," she whispered. "Rub me till I am safe and warm."

My lips were stiff, and my tongue refused to move against hers. I was angry. She knew I needed to keep my two worlds apart. She did it to mock me, to mock my middle-class morality. "*So* unlike the love life of our own dear queen," she retorted once, grinning, when I blocked her roving hands near the music room.

But I could not send her away. I locked the door, dimmed the lantern, and got out a fresh white towel. I sat her down on my only chair, a low-backed one whose corners always poked into my midriff.

I stood behind her and starting rubbing her hair. Her head became a rag doll, swinging limp against the cradle of the towel. Her eyes were closed. Still standing behind her, I started kneading her shoulders with the towel. I strayed down, briefly, to pat dry the valley between her full-moon breasts, then pulled back to the shoulders, smoothing out the knots of tension. I did not touch her wide warm nipples. Time moved in large long seconds. I dried her back and then came to face her. I knelt at her feet. Slowly, slowly, I pried open her small neat toes and rubbed the towel between each one. The towel smelled of sigri smoke. I felt a serpent coiled inside her that night.

She got up abruptly, searched through the pockets of her jeans, found her packet of cigarettes and lighter, and sat on my bed. I remember us both on the bed, naked, smoking a joint.

We sat with our legs cradled around each other, and it seemed we murmured for hours.

She talked of England, a small town by the sea. "I am going to leave this place, Charu," she said. "I really am." She was pensive, and I had never seen her like that. She told me "they" had left her some money and a small house on the coast. She said her time here was over. "I feel it in my bones," she said. The sheets lay loose at our waists. She painted patterns with the tip of my hair on her open palm. "Come with me, Charu. I will buy you fish and chips in a paper cone, and take you swimming in the sea," she said. This was the only time we ever spoke of being together in another place.

"I want to take you to the witch's needle. Let's go now, to the witch's needle," she whispered later as we lay with jumbled legs. "Let's go naked. Just put on our raincoats and run." The witch's needle was a tall black rock on table-land with a hole on its top like the eye of a needle.

"Not in this rain. And it's so windy tonight," I answered. We were so close and warm and cradled.

"But on a night like this the wind whistles through the needle. You'll love it, I swear." She told me she went up there sometimes when she could not sleep, and sat under the needle. "It's so peaceful," she said. "The wind through the eye makes this amazing high-pitched sound. Like a lullaby. One time I stayed there until dawn, and then went back to my room and slept like a baby until noon." She said once when it was raining hard she slipped off the edge near the needle. "I nearly died," she said, smiling as though it were some great personal achievement.

"That's exactly why I don't want to go tonight. Too close to the edge for tonight," I said.

"But you know, I almost let go that night," she said. "It was tempting. Really, it was. I was hugging this rock, it was so windy, I was sure I could let go and fly." She had never opened up to me like that.

"Stoned," I said. "You must have been stoned. Please don't go again like that." I ran my hand through her hair and held her tight, feeling a tenderness welling up inside me. "I'm not going to let you go there ever again."

"But tonight, Charu. Let's go tonight."

"Why tonight? It's pouring cats and dogs, don't you hear it?"

"Because, my darling, tonight I am not Moira Prince."

I searched her face for a trace of a smile, but there was none. She had a nervousness and intensity about her that I had never seen before. I was afraid of it.

"Is there a riddle here that I am supposed to solve? What does it mean, 'Tonight I am not Moira Prince'? Who are you, then?"

"Come with me, and I will show you," she said.

"Where? To table-land?"

"Don't ask. Can't you just trust me and come? Please?"

I did not trust her. She seemed edgier than ever. Did she think she would turn into Pan or something? I was afraid she might be going mad. I searched my mind for something flippant, something to change the subject.

"Just for a night," she said, her voice cracking with intensity. I said nothing, but stroked her back as one soothes a child.

I had a cold that night, a sudden-blobs-of-snot kind of cold.

She leaned over and scooped a blob of snot from the edge of my nose.

"Chi, don't do that," I said, turning my face away.

"Only your own family will tell you when you have snot on your face," she said wistfully. "Only your very own people."

She did not look at me. She stared gravely at the yellow blob on her finger. And then she licked it. I should take that hand and lick the fingers, I should shush my inner Brahmin. But the Brahmin remained firm. I took her hand out of her mouth and wiped it primly on my sheets instead. I bent to kiss her, but in the dancing shadows of the wavering wick her face looked hollow, her mouth a gaping hole. This is how she will look when she's old, I thought, and felt a wave of revulsion sweep over me.

"If I were a man, Charu, would you marry me?"

"I doubt it," I said flippantly, though I knew she wasn't joking.

"Why?" she asked.

"Because I prefer you as a woman," I said. I did not mean any of it. I was suddenly thinking, I want to get out of this. This is not me.

I knew I heard a sound then, and a sharp intake of breath. I thought I heard a whisper.

There were three girls with mumps in the hospital. They chirped around happily all day in pajamas, with slightly grimy cloths tied like rabbit ears above their heads. They must have heard us. I sat up, gathering my sheet nervously around me.

I was embarrassed at her naked body in my bedroom, repulsed by what I had become. I imagined the entire school staring with unblinking eyes into the room; I saw them lined up behind the curtain of water as on the day I had run out into the rain. On that first day of rain I had felt my blot prickle with her hard look. Now I wanted her to be gone. I recoiled from her, this white woman slouching.

She could see my naked feelings on my face. She jumped off the bed.

"I just don't think it's wise for you to walk in on me like this," I said, harsh with fear. "I am sure they heard you knock."

"But fuck all that," she said fiercely, not bothering to lower her voice. "Let's go out together. Come with me."

"It's all right for *you*," I said. She was the bad girl. I was not. I did not want her life, people turning away from me and whispering as I passed.

"Yes, of course, always all right for Pin," she said sullenly, and I felt a bad mood rising. Her mood could change in a minute. "Pulling you down, aren't I?" she said in a tone she had never used with me before. She reminded me of a crouching cat. "Well, you can keep your precious little chastity, Miss Charulata Apte. I will never come *here* again," she spat. She pulled on her clothes with her back to me and left. I did not move, I did not look at her. I lay on the bed staring at the ceiling. She was true to her words, you could say, for she never did come back to that hospital room.

"And thank god you're still a fucking virgin!" she said, flinging the words over her shoulder as she walked out. She banged the bathroom door. I know she did it to spite me. She wanted everyone to know she was in my room at night, I thought.

I lay there like a mummy. Good, I thought, if this is the

end. Let her go, and I will be free of her. Next term, I'll lead a normal life.

I do not know how long I lay staring at the ceiling. I do not know how long I stayed there after the rain stopped. I know only that I heard the back door banging loudly with the wind, and noticed then that the drumming inside my head had ceased.

The rain had stopped. It was eerie, the sudden silence in my head.

The sequence of the night settled in my head. She was wrong to have come to me in my room. But she had never done it before. She had come because she needed me.

Poor Pin, wandering the world alone.

It was as if the room, the night itself, pulled me off the bed.

I threw aside the sheet. My naked body reflected in the mirror, smooth as silk. I would go to her defenseless. I needed to tell her that I loved her. I wanted to run after her. She had to know that I loved her.

I will go naked, as she asked me to, I thought, and reached for my raincoat. The raincoat felt wet and rough, like the slap of a cold slug. I slipped my bare feet into my gum boots and shivered as I ran out into the slush. I did not even stop to take a torch, I did not stop to think where I would find her—I knew she would go to table-land. I imagined us again, with the wind in our hair, and the rain in our mouths. I would open out my raincoat and lie naked in the middle of table-land. "Ferry me across the water, do, boatman, do," I was chanting, singsong, as I walked as fast as I could through the shuttered bazaar. It was what Merch had said to me one night, one of those lines he slips like a smooth stone into a lake. The ones that continue to creep up on me at odd moments of my life and turn into a mantra. I began to run and trot and stumble, slowing to a fast walk when I thought I heard a voice at my back.

I knew she would be by the witch's needle. I imagined her leaning against the tall rock, hunched and smoking. I was running to her, aching to hold her tight, her body that was so secretly plump and warm, wanting her, just wanting her. She has never been loved, I thought that night. And I, I who had been so beloved, all my life, I had not loved her back. But I would do it now.

I came to the needle from the back. I saw her standing too close to the edge, raincoat flying like a cape. She was looking out to the mountains behind the mist with her chest open to the wind. The wind from the valley plastered her hair back against her skull, and her cape became a gusting rubber sail. I could hear it thrashing.

I was afraid that she might jump. I wanted to run and pull her back.

And then I saw a white blob flapping in the wind, on the rocks between us. As my eyes adjusted to the black rocks, I could see the outline of her broad, straight back, I saw the tight curls on the back of her head. My heart jumped into my throat like a frog. Miss Nelson. Miss Nelson! To be near naked, on table-land, on a monsoon night, and then to see your school principal in between you and your lover.

There was nothing to do but watch and wait, on a night like this. I sat down on the flat, wet earth. I could feel the hollow earth, I could feel the dank raincoat rub against my skin.

I do not know if I sat there for ten minutes or for twenty

or for forty. I do know it was a *Macbeth* minute. Suddenly I saw Miss Nelson get up and walk to the Prince. She walked in a trance. She put a hand on her shoulder, from behind. The Prince did not turn around. Nelly caressed her hair for a brief moment. She did it as if she couldn't stop herself, as if it was something she had longed to do. The Prince continued looking, chin jutting, at the mountains beyond the clouds. Nelly let her hand rest on Pin's shoulder briefly, and then she turned around and walked down from table-land, her back ramrod straight, her purse dangling neatly on her crooked arm. It seemed to me that her walk had an almost jaunty air. White pajamas and a dangling white purse, on a principal, in the moonlight. The night, I thought, was getting curiouser and curiouser.

Abruptly, Pin sat down on the very edge of the cliff, her legs pulled to her chest. I would have never let her go so far. I would rush to her, pull her back, and then we would sit, I would massage her knotted shoulders, I would lay my head on her shoulder, and I would take her hand and put it to my naked breast. But my naked breast felt cold and damp, and I found I was shivering.

I walked towards her. Her back was to me. I stood behind the needle. But now that I could run to her as I had dreamt, the urgency of the night drained from me, like blood. I could not go to her.

Because of my blot, I had it in me always to step back, to pause, to watch. But that night I was different, rushing headlong in every direction. It was my weather-vane night. One minute I was looking at one life, and the next I was turned all the way around.

She was not for me. I saw it all, in a moment of clarity. I saw her, so proud and broad-shouldered, so hunched and curled, dragging me in her magnificent, muddy wake. I could not do it. It was a night of magic and mystery, for I saw my ayi now, sitting on the rocks where Nelly had been. And I could not cross her.

For a spun moment I stood there, longing again to be in Pin's arms, to be in her arms so that I could become completely beautiful. No one had ever made me feel so beautiful. Perhaps no one ever would.

I turned and walked back.

I have lived with that turning ever since. Like Lady Macbeth, I have begged the spirits to thicken my blood, to stop up the access and passage to remorse.

But not that night. That night, I felt light and free. I ran down though the mist, all the way down the winding path. As I passed the Woggles' garden, I smelt the fragrance of jasmine.

Jasmine, the memory of my first kiss, of my first love.

BOOK TWO

The Rule Breakers' Club

Nandita

This Place Panchgani
Is so nice and Sunny
Except when it Rains
It gives us Pains

—MR. JOSHUA JOHN
The St. Paul's School Chronicle,
1969

THIRTEEN

On Table-Land

IN STANDARD TEN we formed the Rule Breakers' Club. We knew that once we got to standard eleven we would have to be responsible and take our board exams, and so if we wanted to make school history and break all the rules, it would have to be in standard ten. The Rule Breakers' Club of 1974 consisted of our entire class, except for Neeta and Kareena, best friends, both grave and serious and very Christian. There were thirteen of us, which some considered unlucky.

The first few meetings of the Rule Breakers' Club turned out to be a disaster, because although there were at least a thousand and one rules in Timmins, there was no rule book.

The timid ones wanted to break inane rules such as stripping off their name tapes from all their black ribbons, the bold ones wanted to run away into the valley and live off the land, and the crazy ones wanted to meet the boys behind Sydney

Point at night. Finally, it was decided by us, the wise ones, that it would be right to have a list of breakable rules.

It was decided to term all housekeeping rules and eating-in-the-dining-room rules as too trivial to break, and the "sin" rules involving contact with members of the opposite sex—which could get us thrown out—as too grave. They would have to be middle-ground rules. But the breaking of these rules would have to contain acts of courage and daring.

By the end of standard nine, we had agreed upon the final version of the list of breakable rules.

Rule Number Nine was skinging. Skinging meant leaving the school premises by day or night. This was the gravest of the breakable rules. We Timmins girls were allowed out of school only in a formal formation of twos—a docile crocodile—and always in school uniform. One could get expelled for leaving the school without a teacher. But no serious list aiming at a place in Timmins history could be complete without skinging. It was also the most fun rule to break. There was so much that could be done in the world outside the iron gates of Miss Timmins' School. Hot kheema-pau could be had for two rupees at Kaka's Bakery and Eatery, a movie under the tent near Sandy Banks, a cigarette behind the haunted house. No respectable Rule Breakers' list could be complete without a decent skinge.

Akhila, Ramona, and I, Nandita, decided to skinge together. All three of us had joined the school too young and had been scarred together by evil matrons with large curvy whips. We were not really best friends at that time, but we knew each other like sisters. We were all fifteen that year.

The decision to break the skinge rule together was purely

circumstantial. We were all prefects at Pearsall, the lower middles dorm that year, and we collectively had been entrusted with the key to the back door—to be used to let the girls out in case of fire. It would be easy for us to sneak out together.

We decided to skinge in the monsoon term, under cover of the rain. We had planned our night on many delicious Sunday evenings, sitting after dinner on the steps outside the hospital. We were going to go to the pan shop at the corner, buy a packet of Wills cigarettes, smoke, and come back through the hedge in the upper netball field.

The monsoon had settled in, and it had been raining for a month. Everything was wet. Our clothes came back damp from the wash smelling of sigri smoke. There were squishy black snails in our dorms and fungus on all our shoes. In the evenings we were taken on long walks in the rain. With water sloshing in our gum boots, with rain pouring down in a stream to our noses over the hoods of our rubber raincoats, herded in formations of twos through the drenched streets, we discussed our great escape.

When shall we three meet again?
In thunder, lightning, or in rain?
When the hurlyburly's done,
When the battle's lost and won.

We would chant maniacally, feeling as powerful and diabolical as *Macbeth*'s witches almost every time we parted.

Our chosen day was August 27, just before the end of the term, which was September 9. It was the second day of exams.

The desks were all lined up in the gym, as usual. End-of-term excitement filled the damp halls and dorms with high-pitched laughter.

Our estimated time of departure had been set for 10 p.m. My dorm was closest to the matron's room. At 10, making sure that all sounds from Mrs. Wong's room had stopped, I was to walk to the back, shining my torch briefly as I passed each of the other two dorms. We were to convene with our raincoats on at the back door.

As planned, we walked out the back door and out of the school through the gap in the hedge near the netball field. It was only then that we realized, quite suddenly, that the rain had stopped.

First the rain died to a drizzle. Then the drizzle became a fine mist. The sounds of the night changed. With the drumming rain turned off, it was the gushing water in the open drains, the wind in the silver oaks that became loud and clear. We had counted on the rain as our ally. But now, suddenly freed of it, our high spirits turned into a fountain of hysteria. We burst into streams of stomach-bending giggles at every little detail of every little adventure on the way out, and came staggering into the bazaar in our green and yellow raincoats. The bazaar was dark and deserted. The mist surrounding the dim bulb above the pan and bidi stall cast a yellow pall over the leering face of the paanwala.

"Babalok run away, ha?" he said, but was quite happy to sell us three completely damp and stale Wills cigarettes. We also bought a matchbox. But there was nowhere to smoke. It had been so easy so far, like a knife cutting butter. No one had expected the rain to stop, no one was out, and we felt so safe in the surrounding mist that we decided to walk out of the bazaar a little and "have a nice, relaxed smoke," though only one of us had ever smoked a cigarette before.

Soon we found ourselves, cigarettes unsmoked, walking up the road that led to table-land. The mist began to shine with the light of the moon, and opened and closed around us as we walked up the winding road leading to the plateau. There was a lake on the right where we had skipped stones since we were seven. We saw the full yellow moon reflecting in the lake through the mist. It went to our heads like a drug. We could not sit. Let's walk around the whole table-land, we cried, though we knew its sharp, sudden drops were dangerous in the mist. We won't go to the edge, we promised each other. We'll walk around the middle, around our hockey field and the boys' football field.

The moon disappeared again, but its white glow remained on the clouds that lay on the flat, hollow surface of table-land like a pillowcase. We spread out our raincoats in the middle of the hockey field and lay on our backs, holding hands and watching the sky, feeling the empty darkness beneath us. No falling asleep, girls, we told each other, and finally sat up to smoke our cigarettes. There was a very fine wet spray in the tired air, from all the days of rain. Our matches were damp and would not strike, our cigarettes were wet and would not light, and our hands were wild and shaking from adventure and cold.

Soon, the entire matchbox was finished, but for one match. Let's save this for later, girls, we said, and put our cigarettes away in our pockets and walked on. We decided to leave our raincoats there and collect them later. It was such a pain to lug them around, and we felt so light and free without them. A fine, flirting wind played with our hair and dresses, and we made an elbow chain and went around singing loudly in the empty air. We all knew the same songs from cold countries to which we had never been. We sang songs of love and longing. I remember we sang "Shenandoah" and "If you miss the train I'm on," and were soulfully belting out "Those Were the Days" for perhaps the third time when we saw a figure in the sudden moonlight.

When we saw the great black rocks, we realized we were closer to the steep cliff edge of the plateau than we supposed. Miss Prince was leaning against the large cone-shaped rock everyone called the witch's needle.

She shone a torch at us. "On a night like this," she said, "what made you all come along?" Something in the way she said it, butter-smooth, with a clipped smile, and I knew she would not tell. If we had to have the bad luck to meet a teacher, I was glad it was Prince. With her, you could play and perhaps get away with it. Miss Prince kept smoking her rumpled cigarette, eyeing us quizzically. "Miss, can we please have a light," said Akhila, always the quickest to rush in. Miss Prince silently held her lighter up for Akhila.

"Now scat," she said, "before I am forced to officially see you." And so we thanked her and ran away.

"You know, girls, she was smoking pot," said Ramona, in high-pitched horror, as soon as we were out of range. Ramona knew the most about everything because she had three older brothers. One of them was in college in Bombay. In the May holidays she had even been to the movies and sat in the back row with his friends.

It was close to midnight. We decided it was time to go back. We had brought one bar of Cadbury's chocolate for the outing. We divided it into three, and were eating and walking along when we got the shock of our lives. In all the years that have followed, I have never felt the blood draining from my body as at the moment I saw Nelly sitting on another rock in the distance. We looked at each other in horror and despair. There was nowhere to run, and nowhere to hide. We stood frozen, awaiting the worst. Then we realized there was something very odd. In all the years in Timmins, we had always seen our principal in her belted frocks. But tonight she was wearing long white pants. She was sitting with her head cradled in her hands. She did not turn her head to look at us.

"She's wearing her pajamas," whispered Akhila.

"She doesn't see us," I hissed.

And without another word, with the kinetic understanding born of many scrapes and pranks together, we tiptoed past and walked as fast as we could to the road. We then made a dash for it, running down the dark and winding road to the bazaar. The bazaar was completely shuttered and deserted. We walked at a clip until we got to the gap in the hedge of the netball field and were safely inside our school. I shone my torch on my watch. It was 12:35.

"I think she's finally lost it," I said. "Yes, completely cuckoo." We thought with relish of the stories we could tell the rest of the girls the next morning. We imagined them bringing a van with bars from Poona to take her away. "Did you notice if she had her purse with her? Will they let her take it to Poona? We should have known she was bonkers, the way she always carries that purse and rubs her hands."

We agreed. It had been the strangest night of our lives. First Miss Prince smoking pot, and then Miss Nelson praying in her pajamas, all on table-land in the middle of the monsoons in the middle of the night.

"It's the full moon," said Akhila. "It makes people act crazy."

FOURTEEN

The Dastardly Deed

WE WERE SITTING on the hospital steps the next morning, after prayers. It was the twenty-eighth of August, a Wednesday. The murder of Miss Moira Prince took place either on the twenty-seventh or the twenty-eighth of August, depending on whether it was just before or just after midnight.

For the second time in the collective memory of the school, there were no classes and the girls were left free to wander around in dazed groups and gossip. The first time had been five years ago, when there had been a big fire in the middles dorm, and the St. Paul's boys had been called in to throw buckets of water on the burning building.

Tomorrow there was going to be a special memorial service for Miss Prince in the church. Today was the postmortem to affirm time and cause of death.

That morning at breakfast, there had been no sense of impending doom whatsoever. The three of us were agog with our news.

We had decided it would be dangerous to tell the younger girls that their principal was now mad. Only the standard tens and elevens were to be told. There was no rain, but the light was still gray. We had akoori that day for breakfast, the only egg—the only dish, most insisted—that the school kitchen made well, and I kept making signs to Zarine Zakharia across the table, telling her we were calling an emergency meeting of the tens and elevens after prayers.

As usual, we filed into the prayer hall after breakfast, to hymns on the piano played by Miss McCall. I fully expected Nelly to trot briskly in and say, "Hymn number 420," as if nothing had happened. And then nobody would really believe us, and it would go down as one of those half-believed legends that are passed down during midnight feasts, to die out with the next generation.

But after we sat down, it was not Miss Nelson but Miss Wilson who came to the pulpit. She tried not to look flustered.

"Girls, I have a very, very tragic announcement to make," she said, looking down at the pulpit. "Last night, our Miss Prince fell off the edge of table-land. The fall broke her head. She was found in the early hours of the morning. It appears that her death was instant, and she felt no pain." Miss Wilson's face was red, and her voice was paper-thin.

There was a shocked silence in the room. Miss Wilson said, "Let us kneel," and led us in the Lord's Prayer.

Our Father, who art in heaven,
Hallowed be Thy name;
Thy Kingdom come;
Thy will be done
On earth as it is in heaven.

It is a sepia movie in my head. Blue-checked dresses, blue blazers, a gray morning tired after the long rain, numb voices reciting the prayer.

Then she started up in a wavering voice, "Oh Lord, in Thy wisdom Thou hast seen wise to call Thy child Moira Prince into Thy sheltering arms before her time. We pray that she may find peace in Thee, oh Lord, and to Thy everlasting mercy we commend her soul. Amen."

The whole entire prayer hall gave a collective gasp that could be heard above the scraping of benches as we sat down. It hung in the air like a comic-book balloon. Miss Wilson blew her nose and put her crumpled handkerchief back into the pocket of her orange flowered skirt.

"Miss Nelson is indisposed today. I will be in her office. If any one of you needs to talk, please come and see me. There will be no school today." She did not look at us. She bowed her head and walked out. We filed out in a stumbling mass of imploding energy. I do not know what happened to the teachers, or the other girls, but the three of us found ourselves with legs of jelly on the hospital steps.

Nothing ever happened in the school. We lived on the highs of strawberry ice cream for Sunday dinner, and drew fodder from the daily battles and skirmishes of our closed circle. But could this be true, really true? We were laughing and crying at the same time, lurching from peak to valley and back. Could it really be true that we had been the last to see her? None of us had ever touched death before.

"It was Nelly who pushed her," said Akhila with complete conviction.

The motive, she said, was clear. Pratima Patil's cousin was in Queen Mary School in Bombay, and she had brought the news that Miss Prince was a lesbo. She had been thrown out of Queen Mary because of an affair with Mohini Kapur, an athletic Punjabi girl with short curly hair. At the end of the last term, Mohini had run away from her parents' house in Colaba and was found in Sunbeam with Miss Prince. It had been a horrible scandal, and Miss Nelson, whose pride and joy was her good god-fearing school, was brokenhearted. It seemed quite logical to both Akhila and Ramona that she had done it in a fit of insanity, brought along by the sudden stopping of the rain on a full-moon night.

I just could not believe that Nelly was a murderer. "Maybe she slipped and fell," I suggested. "You know, slippery earth, and she was drugged."

I was a teacher lover. Secretly, of course; I would have scorn heaped upon my head if I admitted it. I was more at ease with some of the teachers than with the girls. I found most of the girls, and even half the teachers, to be too naïve and immature.

I remember this clearly, the first time I realized that not only the girls but many of the teachers were more naïve than I. I was seven. I had been in boarding school for maybe two months, and was still in a state of shock and lockdown. Miss Barnabas was the matron of Little House. I cannot imagine how an Indian woman got such an outlandish name, and cannot now ascertain her age or her place of origin, because she was thrown out when Miss Manson walked in one morning and caught her whipping some poor child's ankles. I remember her small bony face and intense eyes, and have an impression of her wearing blue-bordered white saris and a long black plait. She used to walk around the dorms with a hooked whip. I escaped deep emotional scarring by being a part of the small band of favorites. She used to gather us around her in the veranda in the evenings and tell us her thoughts on life. She looked down on most castes and communities. "Now, look at the Parsis," she said one day. "God gave them such a good color. But what have they done? They have wasted it." For a few days, I thought I had learned one new mystery of life; god must assign colors to every community. I was wondering why he gave Parsis a good color, and what a good color might be, and what color we Bengalis had. Finally, I plucked up the courage to ask.

"What color did god give the Parsis, Miss?"

"White, my girl, he made them white. So fair the Parsis are, don't you see around you? Look at that Zarine, how fair she is." That was when it struck me that I was possibly more intelligent than some of the teachers.

But Nelly was a superior being. I looked up to Nelly, I respected her. "Can you imagine Nelly actually physically pushing Pin? Her purse would have got in the way, that's for sure," I told them dismissively. It sounded ridiculous to me.

"Stop being so bloody wishy-washy all the time, Nandita," said Ramona, "You know there is something fishy. Why did Willy say anyone who needs to talk, come to me?"

"And why has Nelly not come for prayers? Pray tell me that, Miss Nandita the know-it-all," said Ramona. "And why was Nelly there, crouching on the rocks? Come on, you can't tell me that is normal. You think she was sitting there and watching, and the Prince suddenly walked from the needle to the edge and slipped away? And then Nelly went quietly back down?"

"OK, I admit it was strange. Maybe there was a scuffle," I said. "Or maybe it happened after she left."

Nelly had always been good to me. I knew she had a soft spot for me. She had put her arm around me and said "Nandita, if that is what you say, then I believe you" that day I had been blamed for putting a strange lock on the science lab and getting our test canceled. I was close to tears, not because I cared about the punishment, but because I had been wrongly accused, and because I was humiliated that Miss Mathews would not believe me when I said I had not done it. Miss Nelson knew the good part of me, and I felt strong and calm with her, more so than with my mother, who was as capricious as a queen. I just could not imagine Nelly, always so straight and true, as a murderer. Akhila and Ramona had no such qualms. This was high drama, after all.

"Fine, so there was no premeditation," conceded Akhila. "Whichever way you look at it, Nelly still killed her. You'll see."

"I think there was premeditation. She followed her up, didn't she?" interrupted Ramona. Ramona was our wild card. You could never tell what she would say or do next.

We knew we had more knowledge than everyone else. But we did not know whom to tell. How could we admit that we were up on table-land that night without being instantly expelled? This we could not risk. We all swore to take our secret to the grave, the pyre, and the well of vultures as per the death rituals of our various religions. We realized that we were the key to the case. Only we could have seen Nelly there, so mad. We felt cold and breathless. We were a whisper away from death.

We now remembered that we had left our raincoats on table-land. And as per Timmins regulations, each raincoat had full names in black ink written on the inside, just below the hood. In the monsoon term we had to take raincoats and wear gum boots every time we left the school, which was always in uniforms, and always in a line of twos.

We would not last long. We would be caught on the way to church tomorrow evening.

"Let's just get new raincoats," we thought for one mad moment, and ran to find Shankar, to ask him please to take money from Ramona's brother in St. Paul's and buy us three raincoats from the bazaar.

Shankar was usually to be found in the tool room behind the pantry. But when we got there, we found his wife, crying. She was an elegant, giraffe-like woman who only wore pink and red nine-yard saris, always with a green blouse. Her big moon tika was smudged, and she was weeping with drama. Devibai, our Pearsall ayah, who was witness and comfort, informed us that Shankar been arrested by Inspector Wagle. He was suspected of murdering Miss Prince.

That was the second shock. Even the police knew it was a murder. We became quite unhinged, and considering going to Miss Henderson as a compact, sobbing group, baring all. "She'll take us to the Woggle, and he will believe us," we told each other.

But as soon as we began to pull ourselves together, it occurred to us that they might think we killed her. Who would you rather believe, we reasoned with growing panic, a calm and saintly principal who has been in Panchgani without a blemish forever, or three hysterical fifteen-year-olds?

I cannot say what we would have done next had we not heard the new buzz in the lower dorm.

Shobha Rajbans knew something. She had gone in to see Willy in Nelson's office after prayers. Willy had shut the office door. Such a thing had never happened. But she would not tell anyone about it. She had "promised Willy to remain quiet about it, until things pass over," she said with an important air to the cluster of girls around her.

We knew we had to talk to her. "It is a matter of life and death for us," we told each other solemnly, having convinced ourselves by now that we would soon be led out of school in handcuffs.

"Look, we know more than anyone else could know about this," we told her after we had pulled her out of her dorm. Shobha was one of the types you could not pull rank on. She was not afraid of anything. We had to convince her that we had a bigger secret. We took her down to the hockey pitch. The stone benches were still wet and the ground was slushy as we stood around her in a huddle. We swore each other to secrecy, and told our story first. She listened to our tale with growing excitement, and then she told us hers.

She said she was reading *Lolita* with a torch under her bed, after lights out.

"You know, my bed is so close to Nelly's bathroom, I'm tuned to listening for her movements even in my sleep," she began, drawing it out. She was as cool as a cucumber.

I knew that bed in Upper Willoughby. I had it in standard nine. You could hear Nelly's movements and bathroom noises booming through the pipes. Sometimes, we all put our ears against the wall, waiting to hear her fart.

We hardly ever heard voices. She had tea with the missionaries, "special talks," and prayer meetings in her private drawing room, which faced the lower garden and was not close enough for the voices to reach us.

"But last night, after lights out," said Shobha, "I heard murmurs, so of course I put my ear against that exact spot in the wall, and one voice became louder. It was Prince. I know it was. I only heard a few words, but what I heard is etched like the Ten Commandments in my mind. Word for word."

"She said, 'Couldn't you tell me? Just one sign, even? Do you know what it would have meant to me?' She was sobbing, those shuddering kinds of sobs people make when someone dies or something. The wind came up and the rain was spluttering and splattering on the roof, and all I could hear for some time were hisses and murmurs. But I am sure it was Nelly talking and pleading. Then, suddenly, above the rain, clear and sharp, Prince screeched, 'You bloody hypocrite. You bloody bitch. Keeping me here like your pet monkey. So saintly.' I thought the whole of Lower Willoughby would have heard."

And then, Shobha heard Nelly say, "Let us pray. Our Lord will show you His mercy, my child, as He did to me."

Ramona was crying. Shobha, who had not been in the belly of the beast, was very excited. "Let's not tell anyone anything anymore," she said. "Let's solve the whole thing ourselves, then you will be free. And we have so many clues. We'll get poor Shankar out of jail."

We began to feel better. Yes, we saw ourselves as heroines, on the front page of the *Poona Herald*. But first we'd have to solve the problem of the raincoats.

"*That is a step we must overleap, for in our way it lies,*" we chanted, and the reassuring rhythm of *Macbeth* calmed us down.

No one in school ever had an extra raincoat. The school list decreed only one raincoat and one pair of gum boots. We could conceivably rob three raincoats from the teachers, but that seemed far too dangerous. It was Shobha, finally, who had the brilliant idea.

"So let's steal lots of raincoats instead," said Shobha.

If only three of us did not have our raincoats, it would be very suspicious. But what if lots of random girls did not have their raincoats? It would be chalked up as another mystery of that mysterious time.

"Or they might think it is a petty thief," said Akhila.

We had to act right away. The girls were dispersed, talking in tense whispers, and the teachers were in each other's rooms, muttering and crying. Raincoats were hung on a row of pegs outside each dorm. We went to the nearest dorms, and grabbed three or four raincoats, each of the same color, folded them over our arms to look like one, and walked as casually as we could down to the hockey pitch, at the very bottom of the school. There, past the school bakery, was a footpath to the lowest tier of Panchgani.

The road was flanked by three newer, less established boarding schools: Bata, Green Lawns, and Oaks. In all our years in Panchgani, none of us had ever been down that road. We had no truck with those schools. We looked down on them. We decided against entering any of them to leave the raincoats, and saw, after Green Lawns, a small steep footpath used by the villagers in the valley. We dumped the raincoats in a heap behind some trees. "I hope the village children use them," said Akhila. And we ran back and got into the school with enough time to saunter into line when the lunch bell rang.

After lunch, the four of us were back on the hospital steps, when Smita Sheth, daughter of the owners of Panchgani Stores, came looking for us. She lived with her parents, and was one of the few girls who attended the school as a "day scholar." She was greatly valued because she was our link to the outside. She had brought a note from Shobha's boyfriend. Shobha put the letter in her pocket with a proud look, and said she would catch up with us later. But ten minutes later she came panting up to us, so excited she could hardly talk.

"The plot thickens," she announced. Dushant, her boyfriend, had also been there that night, and had seen something very different.

When the rain stopped, he wrote, he and two of his friends had skinged out of school and walked to Shankar's den of vice, hoping to buy some cheap rum.

No Timmins girl in living memory had ever gone to Shankar's den of vice. That was way beyond the outer edge of the Timmins code. The cave from which Shankar sold his wares, a hollow carved of volcanic rock below the steep edge of tableland, was called Devil's Kitchen. It was said to be haunted by the ghosts of the marriage party crushed by the boulder that had been dislodged from there by an eruption of the volcano many, many years ago. The boulder now rested precariously halfway down the hill.

When Dushant and his friends got there, they saw the body at Shankar's feet. Shankar was bent over her. "*We did not stop to look. Shankar told us to leave at once,*" Dushant had written. "*But I wanted to tell you that, on the way up, we saw that strange new teacher, the one with the big red birthmark. She was running down the road from table-land, looking wild, almost mad. Could she have done it?"*

Miss Apte. Why was she there on table-land in the middle of the night? "Curiouser and curiouser," said Ramona, rubbing her hands.

"Let's get serious, girls," we told each other. Ramona's cheeks were red with excitement. With the full weight of all our detective knowledge from Agatha Christie, whom we were allowed to read, and from James Hadley Chase, whom we were not allowed to read but we got from Ramona's brother, we made a chart of the scene of the crime. We became the Find-Outers from Enid Blyton's books, our first detective novels. We knew we must make a list.

All the People on or Around Table-Land That Night, and Who Saw Them

Ramona, Akhila, and Nandita—known to be seen by: Miss Prince
Miss Prince—known to be seen by: the girls, the boys, Shankar, Nelly. Maybe by Apt.
Miss Nelson—known to be seen by: the girls
Miss Apte—known to be seen by: the boys
Shankar—known to be seen by: the boys
Dushant and two friends—known to be seen by: Shankar

We were very pleased with our chart. It suggested that more of these people could actually have seen each other. After some time, we changed the Miss Prince line to read:

Miss Prince—known to be seen by the girls (alive), the boys (dead), Shankar (perhaps dead), Miss Apte (dead or alive?), Miss Nelson (alive).

We should not rule out anyone, said Shobha. But ourselves, we agreed. So we revised it accordingly: "Shankar (dead/alive?), the boys (dead/alive?), and Nelson (dead/alive?)." Any one of them could have seen her alive and been the cause of her death.

We tied together a little booklet from pages torn out of Shobha's Hindi rough book, and wrote "Murder on a Monsoon Night" on the first page as a working title.

On the second page, we wrote "The Theory." The plan was to discount nothing, take nothing for granted, but have a theory so we could have a plan.

My theory was that after the fight overheard by Shobha, Nelly followed Miss Prince up to table-land. She sat on the rocks and she prayed for strength. That is when we saw her. She had not seen us because her eyes had been closed in prayer. After we left, she went up to Miss Prince and tried to plead with her, tell her to change her ways. "She said, 'Let the Lord into your heart, my poor lost child,'" mimicked Akhila. Miss Prince, as we all knew, was completely unpredictable. So maybe Nelly tried to put an arm around her and was pushed away, and maybe, in the scuffle, Miss Prince slipped and fell over the edge.

Akhila and Ramona felt that Nelly had pushed her. They surmised that after the fight, something in Nelly had snapped. She had followed Miss Prince to table-land, said her prayer in the Garden of Gethsemane, and then pushed Miss Prince over the edge, believing that she was doing the Lord's work.

Shobha believed it was Apt. She could not say why. "It is just my intuition, and don't forget, girls, intuition must play a large role in detection technique," she said. "She's a deep one, a chhupa rustam. Looks so good and bland, but she's not. And what was she doing on table-land?"

In fact, said Shobha, Radha just told the dorm yesterday that she had seen Apt with Prince. They were running down the slippery way to the hockey pitch in the rain, the Prince and Apt, sliding and giggling. That sealed it for Shobha. "There was something between them," she said, her eyes round and large.

By no stretch of imagination could I imagine Miss Apte shoving Prince off a cliff. Nor could I imagine her having an affair with Prince. Young girls had crushes on prefects, prefects had crushes on teachers. Friendships between girls became intense and all-consuming and sometimes as obsessive as love affairs, though actual lesbian affairs were not known to happen in our school. But this was all boarding school chatter. Miss Apte did not grow up like us.

The first day she walked into our class, thin and tentative and as nervous as a fawn, I thought, She's going to be as bad as Jacinta and that lot. And when she said "Hello, I am Charulata Apte from Indore" in that terrible vernacular accent, I thought, What does she know about literature?

Served me right for being such a Bombay snob.

She turned out to be the best teacher I ever had. I forgot about her accent and her scarred face. I loved her classes. She helped me think about women's lib and hippies and Bob Dylan and all the things happening in the wide world outside our gates, and *Macbeth* as well.

"I don't think she's the type to have an affair with a woman at all," I said. "She wears Indian outfits, and she's from a small town. Too conventional." Lesbians should be brash and bold, I would think. Like Prince.

"But Radha saw them together."

"So, they slid down the slope in the rain. So what?" I said.

"Must have been Miss Prince trying to seduce her. In fact, I was always afraid walking down the covered steps alone with Miss Prince. God knows what she might have done," piped Akhila.

"Idiot," said Shobha contemptuously. "Like she had nothing better to do but pine to hold *your* hand."

Akhila blushed and bit her lip. But I began to think there might be some truth in there. Prince might have set her sights on the innocent Charulata Apte.

All of us agreed that Shankar was the least likely of the suspects, mainly because the Prince and Shankar were from different worlds.

"He could have been up there to sell her pot, you never know," said Ramona. "We should not rule anything out." We knew that was the first rule of detection. Suspect everyone. That would be our motto. Shankar could have sold her drugs up on table-land near the witches' needle and then gotten into some drugged argument and pushed her down. His den was directly below that edge of the plateau, and although there was no footpath down the steep cliff edge, he could have walked down the main road and come around to his den to see if she was dead. The boys could have come across him then as he was bending over the dead body. It was hard to imagine, though, Shankar in a scuffle with a white woman. Quite preposterous, we agreed.

The afternoon seemed to stretch forever as we sat on the hospital steps. Rainwater stopped running down the gutters, and a weak sun popped occasionally out of the cloud cover.

We had two main suspects: Nelly and Apt. We decided to keep a close watch on both of them. The time is now, we agreed. Akhila had it on the authority of some forgotten book that criminals always revisit the scene of their crimes within forty-eight hours "to check if they left any clues."

It was decided that we would split up into two groups of two, each group taking charge of one suspect. Akhila and Shobha took Nelly, and Ramona and I got the Apt.

When the bell rang to summon us to line up for church the next day, there was, as expected, a commotion in the dorm verandas. We had been told to wear our red-checked dresses, navy-blue blazers, and berets, which we always wore to church in the monsoon term. With Nelly in her room all day, and Willy and Manson closeted with Inspector Woggle, the lines of authority were quite limp. Miss Henderson, confronted with a mass of fifteen girls without raincoats on the way to Miss Prince's memorial service, decided that those girls would just have to stay behind. Sister Richards offered to watch us. "Girls, get your needlework or reading, and sit in or around the dining room," Hendy said as she left.

Shobha, who did have her raincoat, was about to pretend that she did not when we saw Nelly step out of her room and walk slowly up the stairs without looking to the left or the right. She wore a black dress made of shiny silk, white gloves that came up to her elbows, and a black wide-brimmed hat with a net that covered the eyes. We had never come across anyone dressed like that except in Hitchcock movies seen during holidays in Bombay.

Shobha gave us the thumbs-up, Akhila quickly borrowed a raincoat from Rita Bhatia, who did have her raincoat but preferred not to go, and the two of them left for church while Ramona and I watched for Miss Apte, but she did not leave her room that evening. We sat around gossiping in hushed voices, the stolen raincoats now another topic jumping among the scattered girls in their red-checked dresses. The school had the ruleless feeling of the last day of term, when we would be packing our sheets and blankets into our holdalls. Sister Richards launched into a long and gory story of some general who had gone home on leave to find his wife with a lover, pulled out a pistol, shot the two in the bed, and then gone on to shoot himself while his children watched. I supposed it was meant to keep us from speculating about the death in Panchgani. "Or," said Ramona darkly, "maybe she knows something. She may be hinting that it was an act of passion."

Shobha and Akhila reported that Pastor Reese's sermon at the service was loud and emotional, concentrating mostly on the saintly lives of Moira Prince's parents. The Lord was charged to have mercy on her soul and her parents' souls in their heavenly abode. There were sniffles from the back, where family friends from Nasik and Sunbeam teachers with swollen eyes were seated. Miss Mathews had a crying fit. But Nelson sat dark and erect in a corner at the back and the girls could hardly see her, though they craned their necks. After the service, the girls were walked back to school by Miss Raju, a fat history teacher with calloused feet, while the rest of the teachers stayed for the burial in the church cemetery.

No one had died in the school for nearly sixty years. The last Timmins teacher to be buried in the cemetery behind the red church building had been Miss Pearsall in 1917. The cemetery recorded the British dead from the dawn of Panchgani, and we knew every headstone.

The church and the pastor were shared with St. Paul's School, which belonged to the same Scottish Presbyterian mission as Timmins. But the boys' school did not harbor any spinster missionaries, and the Lord's hand rested more lightly on their daily schedule. The boys who came to church were usually the ones interested in looking at the girls.

After the sermon and prayers that day, Pastor Reese announced that a gold plaque dedicated to Moira Prince and her parents, Joseph and Martha Prince, would be hung on the wall of the church. It would be placed next to the one for Mary, Minnie, and Emma, daughters of a prior pastor, who, according to the ornate gold plaque, perished during a storm in Vai.

"The plaque has been donated by Miss Nelson," said Pastor Reese solemnly.

That evening, Willy, Nelly, and Manson, the Holy Trinity, gathered for dinner in Miss Nelson's private drawing room. The Apt did not leave her room, and we saw the ayah take her dinner to her on a tray. We Apt-watchers agreed to sneak out after lights out and watch her room.

"*What ho, Malvolio,*" muttered Ramona when, soon after lights out, Apt's back door squeaked open and she slunk out and started walking at a determined pace down Oak Lane. I was plump and thought I was wise because I lived mostly in my books. Ramona was nervy and wired. She hated Shakespeare, but I had to admit that it was she who came out with the most unexpected and quotable of quotes.

We followed at a distance, holding hands for courage. We wore randomly borrowed raincoats and looked quite anonymous, we thought, like women walking in a Panchgani monsoon. We had spent months planning our last escape, but here we were just walking out like this, so easy. It was, of course, a time of more chaos in school than we could have imagined in our wildest dreams.

We poked each other breathless with excitement when she went to Dr. Desai's dispensary and climbed up the stairs.

She emerged after about ten minutes, accompanied by Merch. We knew Merch, he taught us geography one summer in a listless, funny sort of way. We were doing North America that year, and I remember he said Pawtucket could have gotten its name because it tucked the paw of Connecticut, and I never did figure that one out.

We trailed them at a distance. There was a light mist in the air that night, and they seemed not to even be aware of us. Merch was wearing gum boots and a dark red pullover. He had no raincoat. We did not dare to talk. We walked quietly, heads bowed. Before they even turned up the fork from the municipal park to which no one ever went, we knew they could be headed to only one place: table-land.

Once up on table-land, we had to be very careful. If they turned, there would be nowhere to hide on its flat echoing surface. There were some bushes near the lake, which was to the right of the road as you reached the top. We hid behind them. Merch put his arm around her shoulders as they walked towards the rocks where the Prince had been the night she died. We could see them faintly in the distance, defined by the intermittent glow of a cigarette.

Were they friends, were they lovers? We knew that Merch and Prince were often together. They were so easy with each other, always laughing and smoking in the bazaar. Many in Panchgani said they were having an affair. But we knew the Prince preferred girls.

But what of Apt and Merch? How were they connected? He had put his arm around her. "It is a love triangle," said Ramona, in triumph. She just could not wait to tell the others.

"But on second thought, why should they both be in love with Apt? She's ugly," said Ramona.

The Apt was my pet teacher. I felt obliged to stick up for her. "What about when she laughs?" I said, remembering how her brown eyes sparkled. It struck me for the first time how hard it must be for her to keep those eyes sparkling. I was not pretty, I knew that, and I knew how hard that was, but it must be so much harder to grow up with a big red mark on your face. How many people, I wondered, would bypass the mark and see her? It had taken *me* pretty long.

We were crouching, sitting, and creeping around the rocks behind the bushes for almost an hour, cold and restless, when we heard echoing footsteps. Under the clouded moon we saw the Apt, alone, walking down, a black shawl draped around her head.

Should we follow? Should we wait? We'd have to wait, we whispered, otherwise Merch might see us as he walked down. We could see the glow of his cigarette near the rock. Soon, he came towards the path. But instead of walking down, he turned and came to the pond. He walked to the bushes and looked down at us, huddled behind the hedge.

"How very nice," he said, and his eyes glowed white. "Ramona and Nandita. Just the girls I wanted to see."

Merch had always looked like a harmless sort of bloke. We bullied him when he taught us. But tonight he loomed large and sinister over us.

"I have something of yours in my room," he said. "Follow me and I will return it." His voice was a whisper, but we heard every word. We stood up, squirming, and followed him, heads bowed, down through the bazaar. He did not turn back to look at us.

I wished for Shobha the sure, or for Akhila of the impertinent questions. But here we were, the timid ones, Ramona and I, alone on a night soaked with already-shed rain, dripping, not asking a thing. Like docile little cows, we waited downstairs outside Dr. Desai's, holding hands, too numb to talk.

When he came down carrying our raincoats, I was relieved. I do not know what I expected.

He opened each one and read the names written below the hood.

Nandita Bhansali
Akhila Bahadur
Ramona Dastoor

He paused after each name, as though he were Miss Nelson reading order marks. I think we even hung our heads as we did in the prayer hall. He handed the three raincoats to us, and said in a low and sinister sort of voice, "Now I want to hear nothing, you understand, nothing about anything, from any of you. I trust you will convey this to Akhila also." He paused, looked at each of us in turn, and then said, "I say this out of concern for your personal safety." He did not mention how he had happened to find our raincoats at the scene of the crime, and we did not have the courage to ask him.

There was another significant pause, after which he looked at me. "Nandita, you are the reasonable one. I hope you can impress this fact upon your classmates." He was very stern. "Leave the detection to the adults, otherwise there will be trouble." He was sneering at us. "I can personally assure you of this," he said.

We were both shaking with fear. We realized that we were not just the watchers. We were also the watched.

"He did it," breathed Ramona. "I could see it in his eyes." She started sobbing as soon as we were out of earshot. "I don't want to die," she kept repeating, between sobs.

Ramona was high-strung. She had always been like that. She got very excited and could be a lot of fun. But she could fall apart quite suddenly. "Let's talk it over, the four of us. It all makes no sense," I said, linking my arm through hers. I just wanted to get her back into bed, safely.

FIFTEEN

Panty Day

THE NEXT MORNING I awoke with dread in my soul and went to call Akhila and Ramona so we could have a few minutes to talk before the rising bell. Ramona was the prefect of the second dorm. The prefect beds in Pearsall were front center, with two rows of narrow metal cots lined up against the wall on either side, fourteen girls to each dorm.

Ramona's swollen eyes popped open before I reached her bed. I could see she had not slept. I motioned her to our meeting place in the corner of the bathroom. Akhila sprang awake before I got to her bed, her black eyes crackling with excitement. She dashed out with me in the flowered blue pajamas that were too tight for her, her springy black hair tied in two tight pigtails that bounced around her shoulders.

"Merch is going to kill us," announced Ramona as soon as we met.

"Merch? Merch? You're mad or what? He could not even kill

that bat in the classroom. He went and called Shankar," said Akhila scornfully.

"No. Really, really, really. He looked so scary last night. And he told us to stay out of it. Otherwise, he said, he would personally take care of it. And that can mean only one thing," Ramona said. She was going to burst into one of her crying fits, I could see it coming.

Akhila looked to me. Yes, I said, he did go back to the place of the crime, and yes, he did return our raincoats with a sinister warning. The rising bell interrupted us for the ten thousand and tenth time, and we went back to the playing fields of Eton, herding our charges through brushed hair, made beds, and polished shoes before breakfast.

Just before the breakfast bell, Dina Bhutta came to tell me that Ramona was still in bed, her blanket over her head. She must have crept back into bed after our meeting.

"Ramona," I said, sitting on the edge of the bed. "We are all together in this. Don't have to take it so badly, you know."

She poked her head out and eyed me balefully. *"The Thane of Fife,"* she said, *"had a wife. Where is she now?"*

I wished she would at least smile a little when she said it. But she just pulled the blanket back over her head.

Below the veneer of merriment and camaraderie, there was a layer of sadness in the school. An orphaned feeling in the pit of all our stomachs. We had been snatched from the bosom of our families and left on this hilltop with no one to sing us to sleep or hear our frightened dreams. We were all there for a reason, especially those of us who had been left on the hilltop before we were even ten. My two sisters and I were in boarding because our mother was not capable of looking after us. Our father had told us that. At least this way he knew we were looked after when he traveled, he said, since our mother played cards all day with polished nails. Ramona had been a bed wetter. I remember her being hit by Miss Barnabas on the head and pushed to the bathroom, looking down and holding back tears. "Dirty child, did it again. Ayah, just see what this child has done." We felt for her but we never spoke about it. Many years later she told me that she would awake at dawn in a panic, knowing she had wet her bed again. She would fan her legs furiously under the blanket for a whole hour. "I thought if I fanned it enough, it would dry up and they would not notice it. I even became a Christian for a short while in standard three. I went and told Mrs. Prince—can you imagine, our Prince's mother, remember she used to hold all those intense prayer meetings?—that I wanted to let Jesus into my heart. She knelt with me in Nelly's drawing room, and then she gave me a little picture of Jesus. I remember it so clearly: Jesus had long blond hair and was wearing a blue scarf over his robe. He was holding a lantern that cast this warm glow, and he was knocking on the wooden door of this cozy little cottage. 'He has been waiting all this time for you to let him in,' she said. I would stare at it in bed before lights out and pray for him to help me. I felt very strongly about it for some time. I was always talking in my mind to Jesus. I felt I was in this English cottage, sitting on a sofa with this Jesus from my picture. I don't remember when I stopped being a Christian, but I know I stopped wetting my bed in standard five."

I sent Dina to call in the matron. Mrs. Wong was a slim

and elegant Chinese lady who wore lacy undershirts and slept with curlers in her hair. She regaled us with stories of her aristocratic past in China. All stories ended in the drama of the escape from the Communists, and how the family servants tied her to a donkey and crossed the snowy mountains into India. "Then we run, we hide, we tie cloths on our feet." She would mimic every action with the face of an anxious young girl peering over a mountain ledge. The story sessions happened only when she was in a good mood. Mostly, she was in a bad mood and stayed in her room.

Mrs. Wong felt Ramona's forehead and wrist, asked her to stick out her tongue and show her stomach. "No fevel. No spots," she said, "but stay in bed for morning. We see at lunch time."

So it was the three of us under the banyan tree after prayers. It was a cloudy day with no wind and birdcalls hanging loud in the sullen air.

"I think we should stop," I said. "Let the Woggle figure it out. Why should I care about who killed Prince?" Akhila and Shobha remained unshaken by the tale of the new monster Merch. They urged me to lighten up. Akhila was a wiry little bouncer with ink stains on her uniform. She was one of the naughty girls, confident and cheeky. She was a beloved only child. Her father ran a sugar estate with no suitable schools around. Her mother sent her parcels with home-fried papdis and puris every week, and knitted bright new sweaters for her every year.

As we filed into the gym where we were to spend the morning studying for the afternoon exams, we saw that the good Inspector Woggle had set up a desk in the staff room and was interviewing a very grave Miss Jacobs.

Miss Mathews was the duty teacher. Her sari was in complete disarray, and her eyes were swollen and teary. Within minutes I got a note from Shobha, sitting eight desks down. "She's falling apart. She must know something. Let's pump her."

Miss Jacinta Mathews was the most pumpable of all the teachers. We called her L.S., because she was spacey and someone once said that she was a real Lucy in the Sky with Diamonds. First we started calling her Lucy in the Sky, which was too long, so one day it became L.S.

My resolve to remain aloof from the murder investigation faded, and I followed the two of them to the duty desk on the stage at the front of the gym. "Dark things, girls. Dark things under our very noses," said Miss Mathews, shaking her finger at us, her rosebud lips aquiver.

"But Miss, you must know who killed her," said Shobha. "You lived in the same house. And she liked you. Come on, Miss, we saw you laughing with her on sports duty just last week." I had always been a little repelled at the blatant way that Shobha sidled up to teachers and flattered them when she wanted something. But I had to admit it worked.

"Did the inspector already talk to you?" I asked.

"I am not going to tell any strange man what I heard," said L.S., tossing her head defiantly. "But I did tell him what I saw."

"Miss, you know who pushed her! Your photo could get into the *Poona Herald*!"

We rolled her around like a ball of puri dough.

"I told the inspector I saw a letter on the tray for her the very evening of her death. From England," said L.S., arching her eyebrows with an important air.

"Oooh Miss. So you know what was in the letter. You know why she died. Must be some dark secret."

"Akhila Bahadur, try not to be stupider than the good Lord made you. How can I read someone else's letter?" But then she dropped her voice to a whisper, looking around to make sure no one else was listening. "She came home after dinner, she read it, and then she ran out into the rain."

"For the last time," said Akhila in a sinister undertone.

"But she was your friend, Miss Mathews, did she tell you anything? She hid that girl from Queen Mary in her bedroom for two whole days, remember? Why do you think she did that, Miss?" asked Shobha, playing with Miss Mathews' hair. I saw where she was leading.

"I'll have you know she was not my friend," said L.S., her eyes flashing. She had a small heart-shaped face and very long eyelashes, which she loved to bat.

"Miss Prince was really Charu's friend, no?"

Miss Mathews' eyes started shining, a tear spilling out. "Muttering and moaning in the room, all night long," she mumbled.

And then, like a child who has said too much, she suddenly raised her voice. "Now go back to your desks, you silly girls, before I give you all an order mark," she shouted so that the whole gym could hear.

The Apt, we had to talk to Apt. But lo and behold, as we were sidling out of the gym, we saw the Apt being led out by a fat lady in a nasty nylon sari. She was weeping. A driver in a white uniform carried her suitcase.

The Apt was always neat and well kempt, her hair sleek and braided. Recently she had started wearing cotton saris with borders, and tying her hair in a low knot at the nape. It often came lose, and she would shake it out and then coil it again. She had begun to look quite pert. But today, as they gently folded her into the white Ambassador, her hair was dry and knotted as if it had not been combed for days, and her face was like a cracked egg with the yolk streaming out.

"She's having a breakdown," I said. "They called in her family." My first thought was, Oh, no, I'm going to miss her class. I looked forward to her classes, her questions, her homework, her tests. I wrote better for her. I could see her reading my essays, pencil in mouth, smiling. She gave me very high marks. She once even gave me a nine out of ten, and often read my answers aloud to the class.

"She just likes you," said Anjani, who worked harder than me. "I bet if I wrote your name on the paper I would get nine out of ten too." I did not bother to contradict her. "You are just smarter than most people," my father often told me. "Remember that."

Ramona was back in the dining room for lunch. She gave the thumbs-up—the secret panty sign—as she filed in. I felt betrayed. I had worn my bloomers as usual.

"This morning you were so scared—couldn't even get up," I said reproachfully. "What made you wear a panty today of all days?"

"Well, if I'm going to die, might as well die with a panty," she said. Turned out that even Akhila had worn a panty that day. "I knew no one would be watching, so why not?" she said with a shrug.

It was Rule Number Three on our List of Breakable Rules. It was also known as the Elastic Band Rule. Akhila had suggested it, and it had turned out to be the most delicious of all the rules that we broke.

Wardrobe rules were very strict at Timmins' School for Girls. Each girl's trunk must contain eight blue-checked knickers, two red-checked knickers, two navy-blue sports knickers, and eight play knickers. The whole army of knickers had to be bloomers, held up with elastic at each leg, not more than six inches above the knee. At home, through every holiday, the tailor sat in our balcony for weeks, patiently threading elastic into the one hundred twenty knicker legs of us three sisters. Everyone turned up with tight elastic legs. But the elastic started loosening up as the term progressed. By midterm, we became a straggly lot, each with one or two knicker legs hanging limp below our hems.

Miss Manson came back from furlough firm and resolved. She could have told us to throw the bloomers in the fire then, but that would be the beginning of the end of colonialism. No, Miss Manson took it upon herself to see to the uplift of our brown masses. She set up an inspection regimen.

Every morning when we lined up for prayers, each class would have to knicker snap as Miss Manson walked by. Suddenly, she would stop and turn, impaling some unfortunate girl with her watery blue stare. "Alpa Mohite, let me hear your elastic," she would say in her thin stern voice, and the poor girl would have to produce a respectable slap before the silent school. Those found wanting were pulled out and taken for private screening in the staff room. There they would have to line up and lift their dresses. Girls with badly failing elastic got two detentions.

By midterm, Miss Manson began to think that the Lord needed more of her. We would find her waiting when we turned corners, or she would quietly creep up on us from behind. "Let's hear your elastic, now," she would say, softly. She was always on the lookout for fallen girls, we could feel her X-ray eyes boring into us as we walked by her, we knew she was trying to look up our dresses when we jumped. We began to call her the bloodhound.

Breaking of the Elastic Band Rule required fairly elaborate strategies that had taken many nights of excited discussion and practice. Our ammunition was lots of little bands of elastic. These were to be kept in both pockets of the uniform, to be curled around the index finger and snapped upon demand. We practiced this often. Of course for sports and P.E. we had to stay with the navy-blue bloomers under our divided skirts.

And remember, girls, no climbing trees, no standing up on the big swings, and no running down the steps on panty days, we said. We hid lacy little panties in our lockers and would wear them when the spirit moved us. We could not send them to the dhobi, and so we washed them and hung the wet panties behind our towels. This rule must be kept secret, we all agreed. The Rule Breakers were sworn to secrecy on this, because we knew it would be tempting. We knew that if the news spread, and all the seniors started wearing panties, we were sure to be discovered. We were not to misuse the rule, lest it give us all away. Perhaps only once or twice a month, we assured each other.

But we began to feel so lithe and graceful and free, so full of tingles, so like real college girls that of course we began to wear panties more often. We had now reached the end of the second term, and it was possible that we would get away with it entirely. Only Tara Guha had been caught, once. But then, Tara was bound to get caught; she was wearing panties every day. Tara had started kissing boys at thirteen.

"And anyway, what are they going to do?" said Tara defiantly when we pleaded with her to slow down. "Throw me out and tell my parents that I was wearing the wrong underwear?"

There was a deep breath of dread in the ranks when we saw that it was the bloodhound herself on lunch duty. But she did not ask for a single elastic snap as we filed into the dining room. She announced after grace that Miss Apte had been called home because her mother was seriously ill. "She is in a coma," she added, but was too distracted to offer to pray for her quick recovery.

My knickers felt like a straitjacket. I was itching all over and could not sit still through lunch. Rumors and theories and wild stories swirled around the tables like red rainwater through open dikes. The shock of the crushed skull was now overlaid with the thrill of being amidst dastardly deeds.

Shobha was indignant that her prime suspect had slipped away. "It's a ruse," she pronounced. "Apt found a way to get out of the school. Probably sent herself a telegram. Mother sick. So original. Every year my servant gets the same telegram. But we'll get her. We are practically finding facts by the minute."

We added the facts to our book.

The Apt and Prince were lovers.

Merch knows we were on table-land that night.

Prince read a letter and then dashed out to fight with Nelly.

The first line bothered me, but the girls overruled my objections. "Miss Mathews said they were muttering and moaning all night in the room, and that can mean only one thing, Nandita," said Shobha, and the others nodded in agreement.

We agreed that in a day or two we would be able to march into Woggle's office in triumph and lay bare the entire plot. His stomach would tremble.

But Ramona was not to be tempted by fame and glory. "There is always a second murder," she said darkly. She said she would not take part in any interviews. But of course she would remain with us, she said, as a behind-the-scenes kind of detective. We decided that Sister Richards should be our next interviewee. She was sure to have seen something if Prince and Apt were lovers, since her room was next to Apt's. We convinced Ramona she needed to go to hospital. Akhila and I supported her down the steps.

Sister hated to admit anyone to hospital. Too much bother, she said. If you did not have fever, spots, or a mortal wound, you were subjected to one of the following three: red swab for wounds, purple swabs for sore throats, and bitter medicine for everything else. If you were deemed sick enough the next day, you were to come to the hospital during morning break and meet Dr. Desai. Dr. Desai was a decrepit man who still wore a bowler hat and was hard of hearing.

"Speak up, girl," Sister would say as we described symptoms. "And don't breathe on the poor doctor! Look the other way, child."

"Get yourself admitted," we urged Ramona. "Try and faint. You look so pale anyway. Then you can snoop around Apt's room and gossip with Richards."

"Sister Richards," we called, "Ramona is very dizzy. She

nearly fainted. Mrs. Wong thinks she is very sick. She was in bed all morning."

But Ramona did not look as sick as she could have. We eyed her balefully. Akhila pinched her upper arm.

"Ow!" she said.

"Anything hurt, child?" asked Sister.

Akhila pinched the same spot. "Nothing, sister, a mosquito just bit me," said Ramona calmly.

Sister went to the dispensary to get the bitter bottle. "At least I'm taking the medicine," hissed Ramona. "Why don't you try and find out about Apt?" She had turned suddenly tall and gangly last year, but her chest was still as flat as an ironing board.

"We saw Miss Apte being carried out. Is she sick, Sister?" asked Akhila.

"Poor girl," said Sister. "First her friend and then the mother. Was crying in her room all day yesterday. I said to her, 'You know Inspector Wagle. Go tell him to release Shankar.' Ridiculous. Whole town is talking. They say it is some private vendetta."

"But how does she know Inspector Wagle so well?"

"Same caste. You know. Miss Apte used to shop in the bazaar with his wife. They all stick together, those Maharashtrians. That girl was always talking to them all in Marathi. Even Shankar," said Sister, putting the thermometer back into the bottle of dirty white liquid.

"Didn't know what she was getting herself into, that girl," she muttered, almost to herself, as she went back to her radio.

There was no need to support Ramona back up the stairs, and we were walking back through the hospital veranda, digesting Sister's vendetta story, when we saw three sets of eyes dancing just above the window ledge. There were three juniors with mumps in the hospital, and they had something to tell us. They met us at the back door, breathless with excitement.

The girls said they had heard whispers and movement coming from the Apt's room on the night of the murder. One of them, Dilnaz, had even heard a knock. They were sure there had been someone in her room that night. And then, after the rain stopped, they had heard the back door banging. They knew the Apt had left, because they had knocked on her door.

"We were going to pretend that Sita needed something if she answered," they said. Their bandages were tied in big loose bows above their heads and flapped as they talked. Dilnaz had her baby-blue pajama top buttoned wrong. The three of them looked like the see no evil, hear no evil, speak no evil monkeys on the posters in the dining room. Gandhiji had been fond of these posters, it appears, and had advised that they be put up in all the schools of India.

The girls leaned as far out as they could from their window that night, they said, to where they could see a little bit of the room. "But we never saw anyone," said Dilnaz. They were nudging each other and giggling, and so we knew there was more they wanted to tell us.

"We saw cigarette smoke out of the window," they said, "and Dilnaz, Dilnaz says she heard . . ." and then they started fidgeting and giggling again.

"Yes, Dilnaz," I said, staring kindly into her eyes.

"I heard the word *fuck*," said Dilnaz finally, at which the girls once again burst into giggles.

"Who is that?" shouted Sister, hearing a noise. The girls rushed back to their beds, and we went onward.

By the time we met again, Ramona had it all wrapped up. "It could only be Merch in the room," she said. "He smokes, and he could easily say words like fuck. They are lovers. The girls heard them leave. They went up to table-land, waited till we had left, and killed her for a private vendetta. You heard Sister Richards, even she said private vendetta. QED."

"And that is why he said he would kill us if we tell the Woggle," she added with sullen conviction.

It was easy to be irritated with Ramona, but you could not stay really angry with her. She was just such an innocent, always had been. Everyone in the class understood that. Her excitements were intense and infectious, her anxieties all-consuming.

Right now, she was like a rocket about to burst into some sky or another.

That afternoon, her paranoia became the cause of an indelible event in Timmins history. It cracked the iron back of Miss Raswani, the most hated and feared teacher in school. Miss Raswani taught Hindi in an archaic and rigid manner. Everything went in a two-week cycle. On Monday, she read a chapter aloud standing in front of the teacher's table. Then she made the class read it in turns, a paragraph at a time. For Hindi night study we had to learn the first half of the chapter by heart. On Tuesday Raswani would sit ramrod straight at the desk and eye us sternly. "Punita Parikh, first paragraph," she would bark, and Punita would have to stand up and recite it. Wednesday, it was the second half. Thursday the whole chapter once more. Friday was the test. We had to sit down and write the whole chapter. There was no wavering from the text, no need for explanations. This was how the Vedas must have been taught to Brahmin boys in Benares a thousand years ago, and Miss Raswani saw no need to deviate. I can still recite entire chunks of "Bharat ki Vividh Rituen."

The next week was devoted to corrections. Any departure from the text was crossed through with an angry red pencil. We would have to rewrite it, in pencil, in our Hindi rough books. Sentences with errors had to be rewritten once. Misspellings, three times. As we finished, we would take the book to her to be corrected. We would stand by the desk, quivering, while she spitefully jabbed at the book with her pencil. Even the littlest of mistakes could get the book flung in your face. We had to keep doing corrections in our rough book until they were completely right. Then, the corrected correction had to be copied into the fair book in fountain pen. God help you if you made a mistake in your fair book, where there was no scratching out. Miss Raswani gave the most homework, and the most detentions.

Miss Raswani, who could drive the entire senior school into tense silence as she turned the corner to a classroom; Miss Raswani, during whose class we were afraid to look at each other or put up our hands to go to the bathroom; this very same Miss Raswani left the jeering gym with a quivering lip, as if she were Miss Charulata Apte just arrived from Indore.

It was Ramona who started it.

The gym contained all of the middles and seniors, about a hundred girls whose desks had been pushed out of their classrooms and then lined up in six long rows with a passage through the center to the stage where the teacher sat, so that exams could be fair and firm. I loved exams. I loved writing the answers in the two hours of pin-drop silence, and I loved the marks I got after that. I loved walking up through the crowd to the list to see if I was first or second.

But it was not an exam day. Exams had been postponed. It was a post-murder day. The boundaries were stretched taut, like a ribbon waiting to be cut with a sharp pair of scissors, and it was Ramona who did it, unknowingly.

The gym smelled of sweaty Keds, the everyday brown sports shoes kept in two huge cupboards of cubbyholes just big enough to hold them. The right wall was made up of large lattice shutters that looked out onto the road. I was in the window line, three desks behind Ramona, surreptitiously reading *Atlas Shrugged* hidden inside the textbook *History of British Rule in India*.

"The killer," Ramona suddenly said, loud enough for all the girls around her to hear quite clearly. "The killer is here." She was pointing, either at the road or at the red house across it that belonged to Mr. and Mrs. Nerulakar, who taught in Sanjeevan School, near Sandy Banks.

All I saw was one head bobbing by above the hedge, Mr. George Singh, the sports master from St. Paul's School, a military man who held himself so stiff that there was a story of his head having been cut off in a duel and then glued back on at Devil's Kitchen. He might even have been whistling, since I remember a tune floating by in the leaden air. There was no sign of Merch.

There was a disruption in the ranks. Girls from desks at the other end of the gym began to stand up to see what was going on.

"Who said that?" roared Raswani, her eyes directed towards the girls staring at Ramona, who was staring out at the road.

"Ramona Dastoor, come here at once," she said. Ramona did not seem to hear her; she did not turn her head. A heaving gasp passed through the hall like a huge wave.

She saw me sitting three desks behind her. "Nandita, bring that wretched girl to me," she ordered, banging a ruler on her desk and demanding silence.

I went to take her by the hand. She was ice-cold, and she kept looking at the road, transfixed, though I could see nothing of interest.

"Should I take her down to the hospital?" I asked. But the gym was getting noisy; circles of whispers were swirling around the room.

Raswani banged the desk loudly, and the noise subsided.

"Should I take her to the hospital?" I asked again, though Raswani still did not answer. "Miss, she feels ice-cold, and on top of that she is sweating."

"Come on, Rami, I'll walk you down," I whispered in her ear, taking her shoulder.

But she did not look at me.

"There is going to be another murder," she said in a loud but low-pitched voice, as if possessed, as if she could see it happening in front of her.

I stepped back. Although I had stood beside her naked at the two-ayah bath in Little House—we were lined up and passed like packages from the three-mug washing ayah, to the bad-tempered wiping ayah who stank—I was suddenly afraid of her. I thought she might turn and put her hands around my neck and choke me until my face was blotched and blue.

Pandemonium broke out in the gym.

"Silence," roared Miss Raswani. "I will have complete silence in this room."

The noise actually got louder. Girls began to leave their desks and cluster around their friends. There were gasps and an undercurrent of the inevitable giggles.

"Immediately. I want complete silence right now," she thundered in voice that had been known to wet timid knickers.

No one looked at her. No one paid any attention. Suddenly, as if by silent consensus, the one hundred girls in the gym decided that Raswani's rule of terror had been a skipping-rope, and they jumped right over it to the other side.

I stood transfixed, enthralled more by the way decades of carefully nurtured authority could be squashed like a soft strawberry than by Ramona's hysterical ranting. I realized that Raswani had never had any other strategy but frontal attack. She continued to bang and shout, but a confused and vulnerable frown appeared on her face.

Suddenly the Hindi teacher got up from her desk and started walking through the center of the room with her head bowed. Someone started clapping when she was halfway out, and by the end, the entire gym was clapping in unison. And when she had left without even turning to look at us once, we began to cheer and jump and pat each other on the back in glee, as though we had just won the Third Battle of Panipat or something. "Just imagine," my sister Viny came up to me and said. "We won't have to wake up with the dread of Hindi ever again."

I saw that Ramona had sat down with her head on her desk. She was sobbing. I shook her gently, and she got up and came down the stairs with me and let me put her into her bed without a word.

Since Shobha was not in our class, she did not know Ramona as well as Akhila and I. Not knowing that Ramona had to be babied sometimes, she was getting irritated. That evening, when we gathered after dinner at the hospital steps, Shobha decided to take her to task.

"Listen, nothing is going to happen to you. You yourself say it all the time: This place is a jail. So for once let's be happy about it. Nothing can happen to us while we are inside Timmins," she said firmly to the pale and wan Ramona. We all chimed in.

"Merch can't come in and the Apt has fled."

"And all the dorms are locked at night."

"Does Apt even look like a murderer?"

"Well, neither does Nelly, for that matter."

And who had even seen a murderer among us? No one. It was a crime of passion, we agreed, and in a crime of passion murderers are not murderers in the sinister sense.

"But just look at Apt," I said. "She's so timid. You really think she is going around having an affair with Prince *and* with Merch? A man and a woman? *Come on.* Miss Charulata Apte from Indore."

"And on top of that she is deformed," said Akhila.

"But those are the ones," said Shobha. "They think and think. The sly ones. I have an auntie with a birthmark—I know."

"Ya, but you think there was some kind of tragic love triangle around her?" asked Akhila.

"Well, they must all be so lonely in this godforsaken place, you never know," said Shobha. "I mean, what could they be doing every evening in this bloody rain?"

I thought it was highly unlikely. It was the letter, and the fight with Nelly, I said. That is where the answer lay.

"The letter could be a red herring," said Ramona.

Either way, we knew we must get to the bottom of the letter business. But we could think of no way to get closer to the letter just then.

"She's coming," hissed Tara, walking over to us. The panty girls got their elastic ready.

"Nandita Bhansali, elastic please," said Miss Manson, and I snapped mine as loud as the church bell.

I even let my uniform fly up a little so she could see the blue checks underneath. I felt vindicated. I knew I had saved the day.

"Do you think she looks more like a ferret every day?"

"Doesn't she have anything better to do on a day like this? Nelly hasn't even come out of her room."

"She needs a man, that's what she needs," said Tara.

"Or maybe a woman." And that set us all into giggles.

"Well, at least let's find out how private this private vendetta really is," said Shobha, referring to Sister Richards's comment to us that morning. She went off to find Smita Sheth, whose family ran Panchgani Stores.

"I think Sister meant *personal* vendetta," I called after her.

SIXTEEN

Chinese Whispers

SOON THE PHRASE "private vendetta" was popping out of corridors and dark corners and hovering around bathroom sinks. And every time they said private vendetta I wanted to correct them. It was not a *private* vendetta, it was a *personal* vendetta, I said sometimes, and other times I walked past shaking my head. I was sensitive about the word. I felt I partly owned it, and it bothered me that it was not being used in the right context. We were the Vendetta sisters after all, the three of us, Nandita, Duhita, and Vinita, whom everyone called Viny.

I don't know how it started, but I do know it was soon after my sisters arrived in the school, both of them tender and straggly like young chickens, Viny not even five years old—I remember how she refused a banana at little lunch because she did not know, she told me later, how to open it. The Vendettas, we were called (because all our names ended in *ta*, I think, though it was so long ago I cannot be sure), like some slinky singing sisters, when in fact we were quite short and prosaic. "Like your father, all three of you," my mother would say smiling, for it was established that she was the beauty of the family. Some of us were granted good bones. "You have good bones. They will stand by you when you are older," my mother would say to Duhita and Vinita, though never to me. Apparently I was going to be left beauty-less even when I was older. But I didn't really care, because I was never going to care what she said or did. Because I had my sweet father to myself. My father was an inventor. I would stand beside him on the balcony late at night as he explained his peanut-grading machine or his world bank scheme, which brought the head of Dena Bank to our house for dinner and was very close to making us as rich as princesses. "Observation is the key," he would say, inhaling his cigarette. "You can get to the bottom of anything if you observe and reason."

It was not a *private* vendetta at all that had prompted Inspector Wagle to put Shankar in jail for the alleged murder of Miss Moira Prince, I told Akhila, Ramona, and Shobha as we clustered in the veranda beside the upper netball court. It was not private, because everyone knew it. It was a *personal* vendetta between the two men. But they paid no attention to that.

We were huddled outside our class with Smita Sheth, who knew why the inspector had put Shankar in jail. She also knew why the Woggle believed the Prince had been pushed off the cliff. There were marks of a struggle upon her, her shirt was ripped, her buttons were missing, and there were signs that she had tried to stop her fall. "Her hands were tightly clenched around bunches of grass and dirt, and her nails were torn and bleeding," said Smita.

But what about the footprints? I asked. Aren't there supposed to be signs of a struggle, and aren't they supposed to get shoe sizes and such like?

No, said Smita, the surface of table-land was so bald and rocky that it was impossible to tell.

Smita Sheth had become our daily gazetteer. She was always surrounded by avid groups of girls, and she told the stories with relish. You could tell that her parents' shop had become the center of the village gossip, because she was full of little details and opinions and phrases that you could picture spoken by a pursed-lipped adult. There were no newspapers or magazines in our world. In fact, almost anything written after World War II was considered modern in our school. We had never cared about our dearth of news, but now that we had *become* news, we felt suddenly isolated; we felt we were sewn into a shroud of mist. And so we turned to Smita, whose stories were passed down in an endless chain of Chinese whispers that poured upon the school like rain.

Smita informed us that she edited the stories to suit her audience. "I mean, I can't tell the standard-eight girls the details of the affair. But with you girls, I can talk frankly," she said. She put on her mother's voice and mannerisms as she told this story. Her mother had played an important role, after all, in this event that occurred before we came to Timmins.

When the Wagles arrived in Panchgani, in the late fifties, the good townspeople were pleased to have the affable young inspector, his feisty wife Janaki, and their little twin daughters Pinkie and Yellow amongst them. Smita's parents, the banya couple from Bombay who were making Panchgani history by setting up the largest and most modern shop that would ever be in town, were especially pleased to have another young city couple to help while away the time. "Though of course their ways were different because they were Marathi, and they ate fish," said Smita with a vegetarian shudder.

The inspector lived up to the hopes and expectations of the Sheths. He was often to be seen in his pressed khaki uniform, sipping tea and chatting with Jitubhai in the back office of the store. His wife, though, was considered to be arrogant by some in town, more specifically by Smita's blameless mother, Taruben. Smita's father insisted to this day, every time the conversation came up, that Mrs. Wagle was "quite a beauty, I tell you, in those days," and her mother never failed to counter that she did not like those types of looks, and furthermore, she could see from day one that the lady had roaming eyes. Such a good man she had, but no, Janaki Wagle was not happy.

Gradually, there developed a groundswell of rumors that Shankar was seen riding his bicycle towards table-land almost every afternoon at two. In the summer, sweat pouring down his face and damp patches on his shirt, he was sometimes seen whistling as he turned the corner from the municipal park to Echo Rock Road, where the light bounced off the black rocks and a breeze blew down from table-land even on the hottest afternoons. There were rumors, said Smita, but her mother refused to believe them. "Why would anyone like us have relations like that with a servant?" Smita said in holy terror.

It was Smita's mother, the spiderwoman Taruben, a stick of a figure with hair on her arms so long you might think she brushed it, who came upon Shankar and Janaki in the most compromising of positions.

Most people did not ask her why she had walked all the way from the bazaar up the steep slope to the Wagles' Nest in the middle of the afternoon, but she always made sure to explain, lest they suspect her of being a busybody. Inspector Wagle, she said, had just informed her that his wife would be arranging the women's and children's activities at the Independence Day fair in the bazaar, and she had decided to go up and talk to Mrs. Wagle to see how she could be of help. Of course, everyone was very enthusiastic about August 15 in those days, she would add.

She saw a bike lying lazily by the pink bougainvillea bushes, and a tall steel glass still frosted with drops from the ice that had been in the chas on the veranda table. Through the window she could see the new white fridge standing proudly behind the dining table. Janaki had opened it and shown her all the drawers and shelves two weeks ago, preening because Taruben's own husband did not deem it necessary to have a fridge in the house. He told her she could use the fridge in the shop downstairs. It is more than enough for our needs, you know, no eggs, no meat, only milk and such, Taru had told Janaki in defense of her fridgeless condition, though she could not stop the stab of jealousy in her tiny bosom when she saw the neatly stacked tomatoes in the lovely plastic bottom drawer.

Because of the bicycle outside, Taruben said, she naturally assumed that there was a guest in the house and that she would find them seated in the shaded living room beyond the fridge, and so she walked in. She heard a giggle and murmurs from the closed bedroom door. "Janaki Bhabhi," she began calling, her tentative voice growing louder each time. She happened, she said, to be positioned right outside the bedroom when Janaki burst out adjusting a crumpled sari, and Taruben saw Shankar lying on the bed with a white sheet pulled up to his naked chest. She said he had a tuft of hair on his shoulders, and that during the split second before the red curtain fell back into place, they stared at each other, and she saw him leering at her. He did not even look ashamed, he looked proud, she said. Her whole body recoiled in horror. Even the sheets must reek of his smell, she thought, with the sour acidity of bile rising to her mouth.

She dropped the notebook marked "Independence Day Ideas," and ran back out and all the way down to her shop, and although she knew herself to be the last person to be starting any gossip, she wondered whether she should tell the inspector about his wife, and in her indecision, she discussed her dilemma with Mrs. Dubash, who had come by to buy a new Duckback raincoat, since of course Panchgani Stores had the largest selection. And perhaps the story was even heard by Pandu, the peon whom Taruben had taught to make a most superior masala chai.

It was not clear who informed the inspector that his wife had been unfaithful, with a lower-class man, no less. But the news was flying around the town, and it was inevitable that he caught it. The people of Panchgani waited to see if Inspector Wagle would leave his wife or beat her; they looked for bruises when they saw her walking through the bazaar with laden bags. They watched and waited, but the inspector did nothing. He continued to do his rounds, with his loud jovial voice and his starched khaki uniform that was always a little too tight for him, but everyone could see that his smile was pasted on. Soon after, when Janaki produced a son, Panchgani shook its head. Look, he is so much darker than both of them, they said. But the inspector did nothing to indicate anything was amiss, and young Kushal was often seen wandering around in the police jeep or in the bazaar with one of the older hawaldars.

Shankar became arrogant. He would slow his cycle as he sailed past the police chowki, which was just past the municipal park, outside the bazaar. Soon he set up his illicit den in the cave under table-land. And the inspector was unwilling or unable to shut it down.

"All those years I've known Shankar, and my goodness, I cannot imagine him and the inspector's wife, can you?" said Smita. She had not known the story growing up, she said, though she was used to hearing a sigh after the inspector's name. What can he do, poor man, his wife stabbing him in the back like that? people would ask. His own policemen are taking bribes from his enemy, and yet he is afraid to stop it. "She has just finished him," Taruben would say shaking her head. "*F-I-N-I-S-H-E-D*, that man."

And then, more than a decade later, when Shankar was found leaning over the dead body of a white woman on the rocks outside his cave of ill-repute, it was as if God had given Inspector Wagle a second chance. He arrested Shankar immediately and sent him down to Poona the very next day. He knew how they beat up the lower classes at the Poona jail. They would beat Shankar into submission and get a confession out of him. And the murder of a white woman could keep him in jail for life.

The papers reported that a local man who was a servant in the school in which the white woman taught had been apprehended and was being held prior to trial. "He has been a petty criminal in Panchgani for years," the inspector was quoted as saying. The small article appeared on the second page of the *Satara Daily* the evening after the Prince's death. Failing to find a photograph of either the Prince or Shankar on such short notice, the newspaper had seen fit to run a photograph of the inspector himself, who smirked for all the world like a man who has just killed two birds with one stone. The newspaper mentioned that Mr. Wagle was the son of Ishwardas Wagle, a prominent Poona politician. Smita brought a clipping of the article to school. She did not let it out of her hands. We clustered around her as she read it aloud, and then carefully folded it and put it back in the pocket of her blue blazer.

The town took sides. It was clear from the beginning that no one cared even one bit about the murdered white woman. They hardly knew who she was—though they had seen her often in the bazaar hanging around with the ruffian youths—and they did not care that her death had been tragic or that her life had been cut short by someone in their midst. They cared only to sit for endless hours and discuss whether or not Shankar had killed her, and whether or not the inspector did the right thing in arresting him. In school the ayahs looked sad and resigned as they sat on their haunches deftly making pans and popping them in their mouths. Shankar's lovely wife was often with them, wiping her doe eyes with the edge of her sari pallu.

It was Mr. Blind Irani's letter in the *Poona Herald* that took

Panchgani by surprise and upset the regular balance of the town.

> It is difficult to imagine what were the grounds for arresting Shankar Tamde for the murder of the British teacher Miss Moira Prince from a Panchgani school. Although due to signs of a struggle on the body of the dead girl, it might be fair to assume foul play, it certainly runs against the grain of justice to lock up a poor man because he cannot defend himself. It would be a crime to consider the case closed. Small towns are hotbeds of gossip, and it is indeed shameful to see the state of our law and order system. Have we sunk so low that a man can be locked up on the basis of a private vendetta that was played out more than a decade before this time? This would not have been tolerated by the powers before this Independent era. What use is our democracy when a man cannot defend himself against charges that were likely trumped up?

The people of Panchgani were stunned. Mr. Blind Irani should have been on the side of the inspector. That is where he belonged. Inspector Wagle sometimes filled in to make up the bridge club that met on Tuesday afternoons. Who would have thought that the old man would care so much about a man like Shankar, a servant-class man?

The town divide should have run along the English fault line. Those who read the English papers versus those who either read the Marathi paper or could not read at all. Hotel owners, semi-retired Parsi couples, and ex-tuberculosis patients who had come from Bombay and Poona for a cure and stayed on would be in the English camp, on the side of the inspector. And the villagers, the wiry ghat people who had inhabited the mountains long before Shivaji's day would be behind Shankar, who was one of their own. It was only the English side that mattered, of course, since the others barely had a voice. Mr. Blind Irani's letter thrust the two sides onto a nearly equal footing.

Everyone agreed that it was the hand of Merch. It was Merch who sat with Mr. Blind Irani at the corner table and read him the newspapers and the correspondence of like-minded letter writers. It was Merch who wrote out the letters that he dictated for the *Poona Herald*. It had to be Merch who had pulled Mr. Blind Irani to the other side of the tracks.

Mr. Dubash's rebuttal appeared promptly two days later.

> If the man, Shankar, was falsely accused, let him bring forth the evidence. Let him come out and confess what he was doing at the bottom of the cliff, bending over the body of the dead girl in the middle of a rainy night. The arrested man is known in these environs for his nefarious activities and has been a corrupting influence on the schools. Further, his dealing in narcotics has attracted young men of dubious character to our town. The law-abiding citizens of Panchgani have been at their wits' end. It is time he was brought to justice.

The core of the Panchgani Stores gang, which had the benefit of Taruben's brilliant tea as they sat around on folding metal chairs in the back room, consisted of the owner of El Cid Hotel, a red-faced man named Rohington, the Dubashes of Dalwich House, and of course the Sheths themselves. Inspector Wagle was very busy collecting evidence, but he did drop by on his way home in the evening. Since the Sheths did not partake in spirits, he could not take his evening beer with them, and so he soon went home to his strange household: a wife whose former lover he had just sent towards the gallows, and a son who had his enemy's blood in his veins.

Everyone stared and moved away when the inspector's wife walked into town. No one knew what she thought and no one dared to ask. She had withdrawn from the town after the affair. She had made not a single friend in Panchgani all those years. Instead, she spent her days at home, cultivating fragrant roses and jasmine and pink and white bougainvillea that crept along the arched garden gate of the Nest, so that everyone stopped to gaze at her garden before they turned towards the Muslim cemetery on their way up to table-land. You could see her garden from the left tip of table-land, hanging like an embroidered handkerchief halfway in the sky. As she walked down to the bazaar with a flower in her bun, the women thought of how she must remember those hot afternoons of pleasure, and felt a pang of sorrow for their own wasted lives. Some of the more charitable older women blamed the water. We have seen it before, they said wisely. When young women first come to Panchgani, desire explodes in their loins. But it dies soon and then the water turns bitter in their stomachs.

Mr. Blind Irani found himself aligned with the mochi who owned Vidya Shoes and Slippers for Every Occasion, a small narrow shop across the street from the Irani Café; fat Kaka, the buddha behind the cash counter of Kaka's Bakery and Eatery; and Hafeez, the Muslim contractor who painted the red roofs of Timmins School every two years. And of course, Merch. But Merch was considered to be a fringe person and did not count.

"The first three sentences of Mr. Blind Irani's letter, right up till '*It would be a crime to consider the case closed,*' are from the hand of Merch," I informed the girls. "After that, the old man starts his ranting. You can see the difference."

"Wait, wait," said Akhila, bouncing up and down, her new breasts jiggling happily in her blue-checked dress. "You know, it could have been the inspector. He might have pushed the Prince and then put the blame on Shankar. He finally found a way of getting rid of his enemy. Think how he must have hated him all these years. His house is right there, he must have seen Prince walking up, followed her . . ." She petered out as the many holes in the theory became evident to us all. How on earth could the inspector have known that Shankar would be caught bending over her? And why should he have to murder a white girl to get at his enemy, after fifteen long years?

"We should write it down in our book anyway," said Shobha. "After all, there was a motive."

Stranger things had happened, especially in detective novels. But I could see that the tale was too hollow to hold any truth. "No," I said. "He was handed an opportunity and he took it. Simple as that."

We were sitting on the long green bench outside the senior classrooms, facing the abandoned throwball court that was overrun with electric green grass. Small fine clouds were passing through us as they moved over the mountain. We were chewing on stalks of khatta mittha bhaji, a juicy weed that flourished in the rains under the eaves of the sloping roofs. We were always looking for things to eat. In the summer we sucked the honey from the stems of the shoe-flowers.

"The stakes are higher now," said Shobha. "We have to find actual evidence." We realized that we could not just go in now and tell the inspector what we saw, and what we thought about it. The inspector was not after the truth. He did not want to solve the case. He was planning to put Shankar away for life. So if we wanted him to take us seriously, we would have to present real evidence.

Ramona, Shobha, and I sat in a row, chewing like sober little cows. Akhila paced excitedly up and down in front of us, bobbing and fidgeting. She took out her bottle of Vaseline from her pocket and applied large amounts to her lips to make them glossy. She had two large, pussy pimples at the edge of her nose, and kept trying to squeeze them out.

"Only we can do it," she said, rallying us to battle. I imagined her on a white steed, her breasts bouncing. "Only we can save Shankar."

"It is the hand of Merch. The whole thing. And now we cannot even go to the Woggle and tell him, because he will never release Shankar," said Ramona, shaking her head.

"Ramona, you have it wrong, don't you see?" I said. "It is actually because of Merch's letter that we *can* go to the Woggle. Now he knows he has to listen to us, because we could go to Mr. Blind and he might write another letter. Merch is trying to save Shankar, same as us. That makes him on the same side as us."

"But then why is he stirring things up? What is his motive?" she asked, getting belligerent.

"Are you some sort of specter of doom, or what?" I asked, and she looked chastised.

"No, but I just want you to be cautious. I feel we are getting into deep waters here."

"I think we need to drop her from the investigation," said Shobha as soon as Ramona had left. "She'll get us into trouble."

"So you mean we pretend nothing more is happening?" I asked.

"Or we could make up some stuff to feed her," said Shobha.

Akhila looked at me. I nodded but said nothing. It was a good idea. It should have come from me.

SEVENTEEN

The Scream

AT THE END of the monsoon term, there was a blight of lice in Pearsall, where I was dorm prefect. The first five cases were discovered on a Saturday morning during a routine and cursory nails and hair inspection. Mrs. Wong called in the ayahs. Grumpy ayahs wielding lice combs pulled angrily at our hair. Girls with long and curly hair screamed in pain. Those with lice were flung like dirty socks to the left of the room. Soon the lice-line became longer than the non-lice-line. Mrs. Wong paced up and down the row of liced girls ranting and raving.

"Never seen so much lice. Never in all my years. Even my head is scratching. The floors will be crawling with boochies." She took big steps, her hands behind her back. We did not dare to speak. We tried not to scratch our heads.

The next morning she emerged from her room with a solution. "DDT powder," she announced merrily, her eyes twinkling. "That will put an end to it. Sister says they used it in the war."

Mrs. Wong ordered a sack of DDT. It was two days after the funeral. After dinner, we lined up in our pajamas with towels draped across our shoulders. Each girl was to put DDT on the hair of the girl in front. Pillowcases filled with white powder were passed around. We threw handfuls of it in each other's hair. We began to look like old ladies in Hindi movies and school plays. The air was white. Soon we took the pillowcases filled with powder and started pillow fights. "Snow, it must be like snow," we were shouting in delight, skidding on the DDT powder strewn across the stone floor.

Mrs. Wong popped her head out of her room, her powdered hair tied deftly in a red scarf knotted at the forehead. "Nandita," she called. "Lights out. I want everyone in bed now."

We turned off the lights, but it was not a night for sleep. We all felt strangely elated. "Please, please, can we stay up and tell ghost stories? Please Nandita, tell us a ghost story," the girls said, clustering around me with white powder drizzling from their hair. I relented, even though I was trying to be the perfect prefect.

We spread blankets on the damp floor and sat in a tight circle between two beds, leaning against each other. We lit our torches and laid them face down in the center of the circle.

Farida Naturewalla's father had just sent her an extra-large bottle of Phosfomin syrup that she generously offered to share. No food was allowed in the dorms, but we could keep tonics in our cupboards. It was easy to get parents to send tonics, and tonic parties were one of the pleasures of our lives. Phosfomin was a bright green tonic that smelled like alcohol and tasted like peppermint. Farida measured three large capfuls into each glass.

The first story was always the Pearsall Story. Miss Pearsall had been the only teacher to die in the school. Now of course, there was the Prince. But her bashed head on the rocks was too raw, not yet a midnight-feast ghost story. So I decided to stick to Miss Pearsall's ghost.

Miss Pearsall was a missionary. According to the golden plaque in the prayer room, Miss Pearsall had been the principal from 1910 to 1917. The plaque did not mention how she died. But the midnight-feast version had all the details.

Miss Pearsall was a cripple. She had polio as a child, and she wore a huge polio leg brace. The shoe of the brace had a thick platform, and she often had to use crutches. One rainy night, Miss Pearsall's crutch had slid on the stone steps outside the dining room. She had lost her balance and tumbled all the way down. Her body landed on the sharp stones around the flower beds. The fall had broken her head.

She was buried in the graveyard behind the church, beside Mary, Minnie, and Emma, the three daughters of the unfortunate pastor, surrounded by headstones of women and children of missionaries and civil servants who had wilted and withered. Miss Pearsall was unhappy because she did not die in England. Her body was trapped forever in the dirt of the wretched colony she had come to improve, dreaming always of steak-and-kidney pie by the fire at home. And so her soul could not move on. She haunted our school.

We had put our torches in the center of the circle, their red plastic hoods face down. The scene is trapped in my mind in red plastic light—fluorescent green Phosfomin, white-haired girls in tight pajamas with missing buttons, white poison dust clouds colliding over our heads.

"You know the sounds you hear at night on the stairs? Thud, thud—one light, one heavy? That is Miss Pearsall limping down the stairs," I said, draining my glass. It burnt an arc down my throat to the center of my stomach.

On cue, the stairs creaked, thud, thud, bad foot, good foot, and then as an extra measure a gust of wind blew the window above the stairs open into the dorm. Girls hugged each other and screamed.

"Wait till I come and catch you. Get back into your beds you little monkeys," Mrs. Wong shouted.

"All right, girls, quiet now," I said, loud enough for Mrs. Wong to hear.

"Now, girls, no need to get so afraid," I said. "In fact, Miss Nelson says that that old wooden stairs always creak. Expansion and contraction. Everyone knows that."

"But it does sound like a crutch and then a foot. Shh, listen."

"I think she is a good ghost. She guards our school. Especially our dorm, since we have her name," said Maya Desai.

"And no one has ever heard anything but the steps."

But the wind started rattling the doors and windows, and even I felt a chill creep up my spine. Not from the Pearsall story. From the Prince story.

"And imagine, they both died of broken heads, they were both British, and the best of it is that both their names begin with *P*," said some squeaky voice on my right.

The noise level was rising again. "Into bed every one of you," shouted Miss Wong, and so we dispersed.

Even if you believed in ghosts, Miss Pearsall was quite harmless. She had been with us for many years, and she was but a thud on the stairs. No one had heard a peep out of her. I was fifteen years old, and in spite of eight years of ghoulish stories at midnight feasts, I did not really believe in fate or ghosts. Until that night.

I do not know if I woke up because of the scream, or just before it. In my dreams, I think I awoke in the hushed split second before the scream.

It was deep into the night. It was a low scream, with a growl in it. It could only be described as chilling or bloodcurdling, or both. It was the most frightening scream that I have heard ever before or ever since. Everyone who heard it says so. Little Supriya Chatterjee was found shivering in the rainbow room, and Bindu Mathais and Neela Khanna had locked themselves in the last bathroom. A lot of girls just slept through it, and I felt they were the lucky ones. They would not be haunted by it. Those of us who had woken up could not go back to sleep, and we spent the night clustered two and three to a bed, whispering. The wind came up in sudden gusts, swishing the trees. We were shivery with fright, holding clammy hands under the blankets, waiting with dread for the next scream. The long, single howl that hung in the air, perhaps a banshee scream sounded like that.

We had been left on the hilltop to be broken by demented women with foreign customs, and we had formed together into a lumpy clay pot. Although the scream sank into the dark waters of childhood terror and became a seamless part of the morning dread of our adult lives, it was Ramona who was most affected by it. The scream, and the haunted night that followed, marked the turning point in Ramona's life.

We discovered at breakfast that the scream had also been

heard in Upper Willoughby, Lower Willoughby, and Harley Street.

The Lower Willoughby girls said it was Miss Raswani.

Miss Raswani's room was above Lower Willoughby.

"It was her. Falguni saw her standing at her window just after lights out. She had her white stringy hair down, and—can you imagine?—wore a long flannel nightie," said Pooja Patel.

"What color was it?" asked Akhila. But Pooja said there was not enough light to see the actual garment.

"She always paces and mutters in the night. We are all used to it. But since the death, since the rain has stopped, we hear her talking loudly and sobbing, even. After the episode in the gym yesterday, she must have cracked completely. We heard the scream coming from her room. It sounded like her voice, gruff," she said. "It was like a howl. It was horrible. As though she were howling at the moon. Almost the whole dorm heard it. Zareen started sobbing. She said she wanted to go home. Then even Dhanvini and Meena started crying. We could not wait for it to be morning."

But the girls of Upper Willoughby swore just as surely that the scream had come from Miss Nelson's room. "We heard it come out of her bathroom," said Shobha, proud keeper of the next-to-Nelly bed. "We stayed up all night, the three of us on Lopa's bed, gossiping. We were so scared we could not sleep. We held hands."

It was hard to imagine Nelly screaming. She never raised her voice.

"She is so controlled, but what if she finally let it all out? It might sound like that," said Shobha.

"Specially if you had just killed someone and might be going crazy. I can see her in her white pajamas looking out of her window at table-land, hands to her ears, screaming," said Akhila.

I said that we were all ignoring the obvious. "It was Miss Prince," I said. "That scream did not sound human to me."

If it were Raswani or Nelson, it would have sounded distant. Pearsall was in the junior section of the school, quite far from the Willoughbys and Harley Street, the senior dorms. We had never heard any senior sounds. "I think it was the Prince warning us," said Ramona, backing me up, although I began to doubt my judgment as soon as Ramona voiced hers.

"Of course you heard it in Pearsall, you dimwits. Isn't that why a scream is called piercing? And anyway, Nandita, I thought you did not believe in ghosts," said Shobha.

I did not. "Maybe you are right," I said, although the scream had sounded like it came from just outside our dorm.

I asked Mrs. Wong about it after breakfast. It was a clouded, chilly day, and I had gone back to the dorm to get my blazer. It was dhobi day in Pearsall. Every bed had a towel spread under it, with clothes laid out in decreed piles. Three checked dresses, two play dresses, three checked knickers, two play knickers, one white blouse, one navy-blue sports skirt, one pair of navy-blue bloomers, three pairs of socks, one sheet, one pillowcase. Exactly that. No more and no less were allowed without a divine dispensation. Mrs. Wong was sitting on a stool, pencil and notebook in hand. The dhobhi's wife was squatting on her haunches, sorting the dirty clothes.

I walked past her, hesitating, but then went back, stood near her stool, and cleared my throat.

"Mrs. Wong, did you hear the scream last night?"

"Civet cats," said Mrs. Wong after a moment of silence. "Awful noise they make. Could be baby, or maybe giving birth."

Wild civet cats had overrun our school and maybe even the whole of Panchgani during my early years in school. They made a racket at night, mewing, screeching, spitting, and scampering on the sloping tin roofs. They ate baby monkeys, and they left a stench of urine in the open corridor below the big steps. Their kittens wailed like babies being tortured.

Mrs. Wong went back to her dhobi log, drawing lines with a ruler for the week's table. I knew she was lying about the scream. The scream last night was not a wild cat scream. Civet cats wailed for a long time, and since they traveled in groups, there were always other cat sounds around the scream. And besides, those wild cats had not been seen around our school for years.

"Mrs. Wong heard the scream, but she is pretending it is cats," I informed my co-detectives as the prayer bell rang. We had begun to call ourselves the Famous Four.

"Can I see you for a minute, Nandita?" called Miss Wilson as we lined up for prayers. "Can you please do the Bible reading today? St. Matthew, chapter seven. Go into the staff room and look over it, while I start."

It was too sudden. I had no time to feel nervous. I am going to be the head girl, I thought. I am a leader. I liked to be calm and composed. That was the only way I felt good inside. "Nandita will be the steady one in the family. She will look after her sisters," my father often said. "Not like her mother," he would usually add, especially when my mother was just within earshot.

And so I walked calmly and slowly into the prayer hall, and read in a loud unwavering voice, though I do not recall a single word.

Miss Wilson went up to the pulpit when I was finished.

"Let us bow our heads in prayer," she said.

"Oh Lord, we beseech Thee today to cast Thine light upon us, and give us strength. Thou knowest our weaknesses, and in Thine infinite mercy, Thou knowest also our strengths. We pray that You give each of us in this school, every girl and every member of our staff, the courage and strength to face the trials and tribulations that may lie ahead. And to Thy safekeeping we commend our souls. Amen."

There were sniffs and sobs from around the room. The teachers' seats at the back of the hall were half empty. Neither Miss Raswani nor the Sunbeamers were present, and for yet another day, Miss Nelson had not emerged from her room. The teachers' faces looked ashen in the sullen light. The scream crouched above the prayer hall, snarling, its fangs bared over our frightened faces.

After prayers Miss Wilson cleared her throat and, mustering a firm voice, made the announcement slowly, with weighty pauses in between.

"We have decided to close the school early this term," she said. "Exams are to be postponed until next term. Today, Miss Manson, Miss Henderson, and I are going to try and contact all your parents, by telephone, where possible, or by telegram. Parents will be encouraged to come and pick up their children. Of course, for those of you whose parents are far away or cannot come, and for the girls from abroad who were going to spend the holiday in school, the school will remain open. I, as well as some of the staff, will be present. Standards four through eleven will be expected to take their books home and study for the exams, which will be held in the second week of the winter term.

"In the mornings, you will sit quietly in the exam hall and study the subject you were to have written. After lunch, you may remain in your dorms and pack your suitcases.

"The events of the past few days have been very upsetting and unsettling for us all. I hope that, out of respect for the gravity of recent events, you will comport yourselves with dignity and refrain from undue hilarity."

Miss McCall played the piano as the girls burst out of the room as out of a tight corset, overjoyed at the double bonus of going home and no exams. That is what I remember most about those days, how the whole school swung wildly as on a frayed rope.

By evening Shobha had changed her mind about the scream. "I think," she announced importantly after a dinner consisting of the dreaded poky vegetable swimming in pepper water. "I think you are right. It was the Prince. She is furious. She must want revenge."

"Let's call her spirit, then," said Akhila. "Let's do a planchette tonight."

About once a year the planchette craze would start up in the senior dorms. Our school buildings were old and creaky; some of them were rumored to have been built on the grounds of an old Muslim graveyard that the missionaries had bought cheap under the protection of their God. Spirits surely roamed the halls, and would be willing to look into the future and tell us how our lives would unfold. We would draw a rectangle in chalk on the floor, with alphabets written out on one side, numbers on the other, and place an overturned steel bowl in the center. After lights out, we would call the spirits. Three girls would put their index fingers lightly on the katori, and in the torchlight we would ask for a spirit to tell us when we would get married and how many children we would have. I did it many times, with no verifiable results. Sometimes the katori did not move at all, sometimes at a sluggish pace that led me to suspect one of the girls was moving it. Only once had the katori moved fast, as though of its own will, though the answers had been garbled nonsense.

We decided that Shobha would sneak into our dorm, hide in the bathroom until lights out, and then the three of us would meet there to do the planchette. We decided not to tell Ramona. She was too nervous these days, we agreed.

We were always cautious about our spirits. We always said "friendly spirit passing by, please come to our help," because we had been warned against waking up specific spirits who might get angry and curse us if disturbed. But tonight we were going to be bold and ask for the Prince herself.

We were scared, of course, but mostly elated, because we would be breaking another of our list of breakable rules. Rule Number Seven was to be broken with a midnight feast or dorm event that was spectacular in some way.

So far, the Lower Willoughby girls held the title of the best feast. They had somehow managed to procure a large quantity of milk and sugar, and, in an incredible feat, stolen a primus stove from the pantry and made dudh pak.

Everyone agreed that the Lower Willoughby dudh pak was so far the most spectacular midnight feast of the Rule Breakers' Club.

Calling the spirit of Miss Prince, and having Shobha sneak in from another dorm to attend the event, was to be our way of topping that. And in order to make it a feast, Shobha had mooched a packet of glucose biscuits.

We were to meet in the last bathroom. Shobha and Akhila had drawn up the planchette by the time I got there. "What took you so long?" whispered Akhila with accusing eyes, for it was almost eleven. "Ramona just kept chattering, just would not let me go back to my bed," I said, though it was not entirely true.

I had been in charge of putting Ramona to bed. I had gone to her bed after lights out, as we so often slipped into each others' beds and exchanged dreams and secrets and family stories. I went that night to distract her and soothe her to sleep. We wanted her to be asleep and suspect nothing. Ramona knew one of her brothers would come to take her home, and she seemed calmer now. I got her chatting on about her favorite subject, the pranks they played on her grandmother. I let her ramble on, and was tempted not to go the bathroom at all and later tell Akhila and Shobha I had fallen asleep, because I did not want to face the spirit of that scream. Nothing is really going to happen, I convinced myself finally. We will all just sit around and be scared, and then go to sleep. I felt braver then. I pretended to fall asleep while Ramona was talking, later pretended to awake with a start, and then got up and stumbled to my bed so that she would not suspect the rest of us were meeting that night.

Ten minutes later, I tiptoed out without a torch so that Ramona would not see me walking by her dorm. I had been eleven the first time I was in Pearsall, and I remembered now how long and dark and dangerous the corridor had felt then, and how sinister every creak and sigh. That was how I saw it again on this night. The corridor stretched to be as long as my life, and I arrived in the bathroom with my heart thudding in my chest.

The Pearsall bathroom block was a large echoing chamber with constantly leaking pipes. The sinks were to the right as you entered; the toilets were lined up to one side and the baths on the other. Shobha and Akhila were in the last bath, a small square room with a tap and a drain in the center. The room was dry, but they had spread a towel on the floor and placed two glowing torches at opposite corners. They looked like they were at a moonlit picnic. Akhila's hands were cold and sweaty, as were mine.

We put our fingers on the katori and called to our spirit. We looked at each other, but the katori did not move. "The spirit of Miss Prince," we whispered together. "We want to help you. Do you have a message for us?" The katori did not move, but we looked at each other with round eyes in the dim light, for we felt it was about to. We felt a presence, I know we did. Suddenly, instead of fear, I felt a rush of energy, as if I were upon a stage before a hushed audience about to speak my lines. Akhila and Shobha looked confident too. We were the three witches again, reaching into the nether world amongst the dripping taps. "*Fair is foul and foul is fair,*" I muttered as we waited for her spirit to move.

"The spirit of Miss Prince," we pleaded, "do you have a message for us? Do you want to tell us who killed you, so we can bring him to justice? Miss Prince, we will be your instruments if you will give us just a hint." We were calm and strong now. We knew something would happen that night. But the katori did not move at all, though we sat for nearly an hour. We should have known better. We should have known that the mighty Prince would not stoop to move an overturned steel bowl at our bidding.

We heard footsteps entering the bathroom, and so we put out our torches and held our breaths. And then we heard Ramona, hoarse and terrified and urgent. "Nandita, come quick," she said. "Where are you?"

We rushed out and found Ramona crouched beneath the sinks, her hands up in front of her face, her torch rolling on the floor. She had heard the voice of Miss Prince, she said in a breathless whisper.

"Didn't you hear it?"

"No," we said. "We heard nothing."

"How could it be?" she said, getting even more agitated. She was shivering. Akhila put an arm around her. "How could you not have heard? It was so loud her voice was echoing through the whole bathroom." Her eyes darted nervously around the room. We shook our heads.

"Then it was only to me, or maybe it was in my head, but it was her," she said. "I swear it was the Prince. She was here, in this bathroom, and she spoke to me."

Ramona said she had wanted to go to the bathroom and had come to wake me up to go with her. She found my bed empty. She went to Akhila's bed and found that empty too. She knew we were up to something and was angry at being left out. Instead of proceeding with fear, as I had, she'd run to the bathroom in anger, and before she went up the stairs, near the sinks, she said she heard the voice of Prince say to her, "Leave now. You will leave this place forever tomorrow."

"But what sense does it make?" I asked her.

"How do I know? I didn't make it up. I am just telling you what I heard. Wait a minute. Maybe she was warning me. Telling me to leave the school, or else I will get killed. Or something like that."

"What was she wearing? What did she look like?"

"I didn't actually see her. From the corner of my eyes I saw a white light. But when I turned, I could see nothing.

"Let's run away now. Let's leave this school. We can stay in El Cid Hotel or something tonight, and tomorrow early we'll take a taxi and go to Poona," she said desperately.

"Yes, and how will we pay for the hotel? And don't you think they'll bring us straight back here? They're not going to give a room to four schoolgirls in the middle of the night, Ramona. Use your head," said Shobha, not masking her contempt for poor Ramona.

"Ramona, let's go to bed now. Anyway, one of your brothers will come tomorrow and take you home. Won't that be easier?" I said.

Later, when we were called by Ramona's family to talk to her about it, in the hope that we might make light of those events, we told her it was a prank we played on her, a cruel prank, we said, sitting in her drawing room sipping tea—although of course we had no idea it would turn so cruel, we assured her. We were very sorry, we told her. We said we had wanted to get her back into a good mood, and we also wanted to break Rule Number Seven. We told her we thought we would play a trick on her and make her laugh. She had always been one of the girls who dreamt of being taken out of school. She had even planned to run away once with Bina and Sameena Rauf, but they did not do it in the end. "So Shobha put a sheet over her head," we told her as she sat across from us tying knots in a pink handkerchief. "We thought we'd tell you that you would leave school and you would be happy, and later, we would tell you the truth."

She looked up at us for the first time then. "Later, when later? You mean like now?" she asked with a flash of her old spirit. We could only nod sheepishly, knowing she would not believe us.

Because Prince's prophecy had come true. Ramona had gone home with her brother the next day, and when her family saw the condition she was in, they took her out of school. She never did come back. And she never did regain her balance. She finished school in Poona, but did not go to college or get married or do anything at all. She grew nervous and paranoid, she began to inhabit a world where "they" were always watching her. They stole her ideas right out of her head; they tapped her phones, siphoned petrol from her car, and were waiting to rape her and kill her. She did not leave the compound of her Parsi family's rambling home, and when we went to meet her, we would find her sitting under a tree staring and muttering, looking increasingly dirty and disheveled.

For a few years she teetered on the edge of sanity when she

became a part of some sort of cult. "I feel so calm and happy," she said. "We just wait for the divine light." The divine light, she said, was white. We called it the white-light cult and wondered if it had anything to do with the light she saw on the night of the haunting.

"I went with her once," her brother's wife told me. "And it was, of all things, a bunch of old Sindhi women who meet every afternoon in each other's poky little flats. Just imagine, all these fat women in white saris; they sit on mats on the floor, and they sing bhajans and achieve some sort of ecstasy by seeing celestial lights. I was quite spooked, I tell you. But anyway, if it gives her something to do, I guess it's OK with us." She shrugged complacently as she plied us with Shrewsbury biscuits.

EIGHTEEN

The Haunting

I KNOW WHAT it is like to be haunted. Not that I looked at it that way when it was happening. That night when we went back to bed after the failed planchette, I could not sleep. I was floating above the earth, through a landscape that was not anywhere I knew, but in it I saw suddenly pockets of places that were my own. I saw our home in Bombay, the small two-bedroom flat in a dirty old building in which my father stooped and sweated to live up to my mother's dreams but could not. I saw my parents' snips of conversation flying above them like knives, my sisters and I running from corner to corner but still getting the knives in our stomachs, in our hearts. I would love my family and my friends and hold them close no matter what, I told myself that night. I always remember that vow and am glad I made it.

I saw that night on table-land. I saw us all on a merry-go-round, Nelly, Apt, Merch, Shankar, the boys, the three of us. The Prince stood outside the circle of swinging horses, silhouetted against the jagged rocks. Children with blue balloons the whole bunch of us, we waved to her as we passed the spot where she stood. Behind me on the merry-go-round, I saw a dark figure, I saw wisps of white hair flying as the head moved up and down and nothing more. I saw everything together, but still sharp and separate, and I know now that it was because I was haunted, carried through the world in the wake of the newly dead.

The planchette we had made earlier that night turned into a jigsaw. The pieces were all lying around: the letter, the vendetta, the love affair, the raincoats. I knew the center piece was mine to find; it was there, waiting. "The letter," I said aloud. "The letter is the key." And as soon as I said that, the letter flew up and spread itself out in the center of the square. The Prince had gotten a letter from England, she had rushed to Nelson and screamed, *Couldn't you tell me? Just one sign, even? Do you know what it would have meant to me?* And then Nelson had been so distraught she had followed her up to table-land in her nightdress. Nelson, who was so proper we used to say she must put her pearl necklace on in the bathroom itself. There was some terrible secret between them. The letter flew away and a dark amoeba that was the secret took its place. I poked it and circled it but I could not bring any light into its dense form.

I may have drifted into a light sleep, because I awoke in the dark before dawn when the birds were beginning to call, with a big new thought bursting out of my head. Miss Raswani. Raswani had to have heard the fight. Shobha heard a little, but her bed ran along Nelly's bathroom wall. Raswani had the other side, where the fight must have taken place. But how could we get anything out of her? And what would she say? She never spoke to anyone; she went up and down the halls alone, shaking her head from time to time.

At first I could not wait for it to be light, so I could go and talk to Shobha and Akhila. But then I began to see how it would be with the four of us, giggling and pinching each other, going to Raswani's door. She would shout and roar and send us packing, for who would tell a dark secret like that to a bunch of arrogant schoolgirls? I would have to go to her alone. I was good with the teachers, they trusted me, and so I knew it would have to be me. I would go to her alone, after breakfast, and somehow feel myself into her mind and make her tell me about the fight. I knew my new strength from the night would not leave me.

Shobha had slept in Ramona's bed, and both of them looked tired. Ramona was pale and wan, and could barely muster a smile when she saw me. You look like you have seen a ghost, I wanted to say, but I did not, because I was not sure she could find it funny. But I said it to Akhila, who appeared to be the least affected by the events of the previous night. "Do you think the Prince was really there last night?" she whispered, her eyes large and limpid.

Ramona was angry and suspicious. "What were you doing locked up in the bathroom?" she demanded, looking at me as if I were the great betrayer. "I did not expect this of you, Nandita, of all people. Stabbing me in the back."

"We were calling the ghost of Prince. And anyway, you said you did not want to be involved in scary things anymore," said Akhila.

"Ya, we just thought you would be more scared, Ramona. We

were protecting you," I said, and it was the truth. I wish I had lied. I wish the story we made up later had occurred to me then.

"Well, you should have let me decide, at least, whether I wanted to be there or not. You are not my parents, or something. And it turned out to be worse. Nothing happened to you. Instead, I walked into the bathroom and had to . . . had to . . . It was real, I swear it," she said, putting her finger nervously into her curls. And then she burst into tears.

"Ramona, can't you see we are all scared? Take a deep breath and calm down, why don't you?" snapped Shobha.

We were at our usual spot, the hospital steps. A large white cloud had settled upon the school, and we could only see outlines of people beyond the steps.

"I am going to meet Raswani. I am going to find out what she heard that night," I announced, bursting into Ramona's hysterical rantings. "Right now, alone," I added for effect, and stood up straight and dusted my dress, though I could feel my knees begin to wobble. I had kept the thought firm in my head throughout breakfast and prayers.

They all looked up at me. Even Shobha was stunned. Shobha and I were wary of each other. From when we were all young, from when we had bonded into a class batch, we had maintained an unspoken rule never to trust anyone from outside the class. That is how we remained so strong. But circumstances had forced us into this alliance with Shobha from a class below us, and now she had taken the center spot. I was not used to someone else calling the shots. I had let myself remain in my usual role, the portly class adviser. The voice of reason, the voice of caution.

But now I was going into the lion's den, alone, and the power of it spread through my body like pleasure.

"Hats off, Nandita," said Shobha, grudgingly shaking her head but still trying to maintain the upper hand. "I had always thought of you as too goody-goody. But you have guts, man. In your own way, of course."

"What will you say? You can't just barge in and ask her what she heard. You have to have a plan," advised Akhila. I could see that she was relieved that I did not want her to come with me.

I planned to knock on her door and begin by asking Raswani what I should be studying during the holidays. I had no idea what I would say after that. This morning, it was as if I had been anointed with some special knowledge. I knew that a leader must not always be cautious. A leader must take a risk when the moment demands it. I had to step in and shape events. But I still didn't know how I could do it.

The mist wrapped itself around me as I walked to Raswani's room. The light was brittle and blue. I felt I was back in the world of my waking dream from last night, with no shadows to hold my body down.

Raswani's room was tucked into a far corner of the senior dorm building. You had to walk over the wooden bridge, up the stone steps, past Upper Willoughby, past the wide, curved veranda outside Nelson's drawing room. I paused outside Nelson's door, listening for a cough or a sniff, or a sound of movement. But everything was shuttered and quiet.

Raswani had a private veranda sectioned off outside her room with a large, badly painted green metal partition. The door was ajar, and so I stepped in. Her bedroom was closed. I knocked softly at first and then louder. I could hear her moving. No one had been inside her room in living memory. No one had even peeped into her room. She did not answer for what seemed like forever. She wants me to leave, I thought, and so I will not. I knocked again.

Finally she said, gruffly, "Who is it?"

"It's me, Nandita, Miss. I wanted to ask you something. About the Hindi syllabus," I said, hoping I sounded calm, though I had to keep myself from faltering.

"Come back later," she said. "I am busy now." There was no roar left in her hoarse voice. With the anger sucked out of it, her voice sounded detached, dispirited.

"But Miss, many of us are leaving this afternoon. And everyone in standard ten wants to know what they should study during the holidays. Only a few minutes, Miss," I pleaded. Although I kept a respectful distance from her, I was not as terrified of Miss Raswani as some of the girls. All we did in her class was learn things by rote, and that was easy for me. She was almost civil with me. I never let myself be open to being yelled at by her. But today I feared I had crossed the line.

I stiffened my spine and straightened my shoulders. I expected a roar. But after a moment's silence, she said, "All right," followed by a deep sigh.

I saw the top of her head first. Usually her thick white hair was plastered to her skull in a middle parting and tied in a tight small knot at the back. But today I saw the wispy strips of hair darting in all directions, as I had in my dream. I knew she was the key to the murder.

"Don't forget to look into her room. See if she has any

photos or anything," the girls had bid me. I was poised straight outside the double doors for optimal viewing, but she opened one door a crack and came out, so I saw nothing inside the mystery room.

I had not laid eyes on her since her ignoble defeat in the gym. She was wearing a purple cotton housecoat, tied tightly with a bow just above her waist. The bottom of her sari petticoat peeped out from beneath it, an inch above her ankles. She wore flannel slippers. She looks like a lonely and confused woman, I thought, surprised. I felt I was looking at her for the first time. She must be at least sixty, I realized, though it had never entered my mind to guess her age before. We always looked at her in a slanting way to avoid her angry attention. When she was on night-study duty, no child even coughed.

In the veranda was a wooden table with a single high-backed chair facing the green metal door. I could see her sitting there on summer evenings, murdering our rote writing with her slashing red pencil. She sat down on the chair.

"Let me see your textbook, and I will mark out the important chapters," she said. The fat Hindi text issued by the government of India's Board of Education was packed with mind-curdling random essays such as "Nehru Chacha Ki Topi" ("Uncle Nehru's Cap") and the life and teachings of Buddha and Jesus Christ as if we did not hear enough about him already The book was devoid of meaning. Any stray bits of interest were stamped out by Raswani's brutal teaching.

She leafed through the pages swiftly, trying to muster some concentration. I could see her mind was not on it. Her hands were shaking.

I was standing beside her, so her eyes were level with my green Rowson House belt. My mind was swirling in a panic. After she gave me the important chapters, I would have to leave. What should I do? What would Tara do? Or Shobha? Or the Prince, what would she do? But then, I thought, none of them would even have gotten this far. Only I can make it happen. I have to go solo, I thought. I felt goose pimples crawling up my back. Lights, music, action. I lurched and then slumped down and managed to be sitting in a huddle at her feet, my head resting on my knees. I was shaking like a leaf. The shiver had crawled up my spine and sent my teeth chattering.

She recoiled in horror. "Are you unwell?" she muttered in a hoarse whisper. Another teacher might have touched my shoulder, patted me. But not her. She must not have touched anyone since she was twenty-two.

"I feel giddy, Miss, not so good," I mumbled with my head still down. I needed to summon tears when I looked up at her. Tears did not come easily to me. Even when my mother berated me—she hated me because I was my father's favorite—I never cried.

"How can there be a murder here, in our school?" I said, finally looking up at her with what I deemed to be trusting eyes. I was still shaking, I knew she could see that. I felt the tension of the last few days winding up inside me and then radiating out. I knew how I was going to play it. Like my mother did in her endless games of bridge. I was going to finesse the queen. I was the best actress in the senior school; I always played the lead for Rowson House. I could see myself sitting at her feet on the stage, and the audience gasping in the dark behind me. It is all just a play, I thought, for what do I really care who killed that woman, the Prince?

"I came to tell you something," I mumbled, looking down again. "I do not know who else I can trust but you." There were teachers like Jacinta Mathews who were susceptible to flattery, and we all knew them. But I doubted if anyone had ever flattered Raswani the monster. No one dared to speak to her. We just ran or hid or prayed to be invisible when we saw her. That was what she seemed to want. "Get out of my sight, you wretched child," she would scream, swollen veins popping out of her neck.

But I knew she was past screaming. And if she knew a part of the story, surely she would want to know another secret. And a little flattery could do no harm. That is what Shobha said. When in trouble, apply flattery.

"We saw the Prince on table-land that night, and then we saw Miss Nelson there. It was the three of us, Akhila, Ramona, and I. We have not told anyone yet. We are afraid. We do not know what to do," I said, speaking slowly and tremulously. It was the truth. But Raswani was the last person we would have confided in. My hands were cold and clammy. I expected her to say, "And what were you doing out on table-land in the middle of the night?" She would pick me up by the collar of my blue-checked uniform and march me to prison, I thought, my heart thudding against my chest. I knew my cheeks were flushed.

But not a sound escaped her. She was quiet for too long. I glanced up at her. She was looking out into the distance. "He is testing me," she said finally.

Then she looked down at me. Those mad eyes with the flaring white rim. In a soft voice that seemed to come from deep inside her—a voice we did not know she had—she said, "I will not ask what the three of you were doing out of school at night. I know you could be expelled for that. But it is not your fault. I know you, Nandita. You are a good girl. It is because of the wicked one. But the Lord took matters into his own hands." She looked down at her gnarled hands.

"Tell me everything," she said, "in detail. I do not care to know what you think. I just want to know everything you saw on table-land that night."

In fact, it was her very own words I wanted to say back to her: "Tell me everything, in detail," I wanted to say to her. "I do not care to know what you think. I want to know every word you heard from your room that night."

But I was at her mercy. If I could not be direct, I must be devious.

And so I told her. I told her how we saw the Prince leaning against the witch's needle, and then how we saw Nelson sitting on the rocks with her head in her hands, and how she did not see us, and how we ran. I left out the other players. I left out the Apt, the boys, and our brush with Merch the night after. I did not want to muddy the waters.

"And then we hear that Prince was pushed over the edge from that very spot soon after. What are we to think, Miss?" I asked her in a frightened voice.

She shook her head and stared at the dripping trees. "The Lord works in mysterious ways," she said finally. She sounded confused, not shocked.

Maybe she was there as well, I thought. Hadn't I seen her in my vision? Maybe she had heard Nelson leave and had followed her up, so that Nelson followed Prince and Raswani followed Nelson. Like a chain of fish each eating the other on the geography sea chart.

She knew the secret. I was sure of it now, seeing her pale, scared face. She knows the secret, and it is big and terrible enough to kill. But she will take it to the grave with her unless I make her tell, today.

"We do not know what to do," I said. "Should we go to the police now, or should we wait for Shobha's father?" Everyone knew Shobha's smooth, capable father. "Shobha says we should wait till he comes this afternoon, and then go to the police with him," I said. Even Raswani must have known that it would be all out of the box once we told Shobha's father.

Then she started to speak. She spoke in a low, even voice. In the distance I could hear the shrill voices and laughter of schoolgirls.

"That night," she said, "I heard her taunting Miss Nelson. I prayed to the Lord, I prayed that I might take her sorrow away from her. Why should she suffer so much? Hadn't she suffered enough? Hadn't we all suffered enough? Exposing these young girls to her wicked ways. Flaunting herself." A dash of her old anger crept into her voice again. "Now she is free of her. Now we are all free of her."

Maybe they murdered her together, Raswani and Nelson, I thought, wildly. They murdered her because she was a lesbian, a serpent in their beloved Timmins. Ideas began to twirl around in my head a mile a minute. Raswani could well have been wandering around on table-land that night. It was a haunted night, and perhaps we were all drawn up to table-land by some ghostly force, like the moon pulls the tides to it.

"She was a saint," Raswani continued in a measured voice devoid of any emotion, as though she were not speaking to me but confessing to a judge and jury. "I prayed always to the Lord to let me be worthy of her, to let me be like her. It was she who made me turn to the Lord for mercy when I came to this blessed place. She would pray with me every night after dinner. But sometimes, when I prayed to the Almighty, it was her face in front of me. That was my only sin.

"But she was hiding a bigger sin. Hiding it in front of all our eyes. The child turned into a monster. A depraved, wicked monster. She became a burden to us all, carrying on with her wicked ways for all to see. She was like a boil upon the earth."

Maybe they were having an affair. That's it, I thought. That explained everything. Nelson and Prince were having an affair. That was the terrible secret between them. And Raswani heard about it that night. I wanted to run and tell the girls. My heart was banging up a storm.

I dared not breathe, I dared not gasp, I dared not make her stop.

Finally she stood up—slowly, using the table for support, as if she had aged ten years while she sat in front of me. She adjusted her housecoat, and, still holding my Hindi textbook in her hand, walked into her room and closed the door. I waited outside, growing more nervous by the minute. I wanted to leave, but I could not because she had my book. I heard her opening drawers and rummaging through her drawers.

When I heard her muttering "Into Thy hands I commend

you" or something of that sort, I realized she was praying. I thought she had forgotten about me, and so I raised my voice and said, "Miss Raswani, can I please have my textbook back?"

She came out with the book in her hand and looked at me. Her eyes were dim, like those of very old women. It was the anger that kept her going all these years, I realized. Now that she is sad, the mad Saturn ring around her eyes will melt and she will die, I thought. This was the first time I felt compassion for an adult human being. I was fifteen.

"Show it to that silly child, your friend Akhila," she said, handing me the book. "Tell her to revise her favorite chapter."

She's daft, I thought, because I knew Akhila did not have enough interest in Hindi to possibly have a favorite chapter.

I held the book tight to my chest and ran breathless to the steps. They were still there, the three of them, sitting in a tight formation on the hospital steps. Although it seemed a lifetime had passed, it was hardly half past nine in the morning, and I must have been gone less than half an hour.

"They were having an affair," I announced triumphantly. "Nelson and Prince were having an affair. That was the fight. And that was the reason for the murder."

"You mean the monster actually told you that?" asked Shobha, shocked.

"Well, not exactly. She said that Nelson was hiding a big sin in front of all our eyes. Those were her words. Raswani told me that her only sin was loving Nelson, of seeing her face instead of the Lord's when she prayed. But Nelson, she said, was hiding a bigger sin."

"She actually said all these things to you?" asked Shobha, giving me the quizzical eye.

"Nandita would not make such a thing up," said Ramona, my stout defender, and Akhila nodded her head in agreement.

I could not blame Shobha for doubting me. It would never have happened, even yesterday. Raswani never talked to students. She shouted one-line commands, and we obeyed. Now she was a broken woman, and I was the strong one.

The news was shocking. But it was possible. After all, as Shobha said, they must be so frustrated here, these spinsters, never even seeing a man of their own kind except the pastor, and how they all blushed and flirted with Pastor Reese, though he had a wife and three young children. An affair between Nelson and the Prince was quite plausible, and entirely possible, we all agreed. That was why Nelson kept the Prince in school, in spite of all the scandals. That was the meaning of the accusation Shobha had heard with her ear pressed to Nelson's bathroom wall. *You bloody hypocrite,* Prince had screamed on the night of her death. *You bloody bitch. Keeping me here like your pet monkey. So saintly.* Because the Prince was performing for the principal. Kept there to satisfy the devious principal's unnatural desires. While letting Nelson appear to be the saint, the Prince the sinner. I, who had looked up to Miss Nelson all these years, changed my mind about her that day. I saw how she had wronged the Prince.

"No wonder she rubs her hands all the time like Lady Macbeth," said Ramona.

NINETEEN

MariOrPiriKuri

MISS RASWANI DISAPPEARED the same day. When she did not come to dinner, the Willoughby ayah took her a meal tray, only to find her room clean and empty except for a pile of brown-paper-covered textbooks on the desk. We were told the next morning.

But by then, Nelson had already been taken into custody. Because of us.

That morning, after I left Raswani's room we garnished the liaison between Nelson and Prince, on the hospital steps.

Nelson liked nymphets, said Shobha, and she should know, since she was reading *Lolita* with a torch under the blankets. That is what she kept in her purse, we agreed. Pictures of young girls, perhaps even of us. Maybe she took pictures of us through bathroom chinks. "Does anyone remember hearing a click while changing in Upper Willoughby?" asked Shobha with an excited shudder.

It must have begun while Prince was growing up with those ghastly saintly parents. They came to our school raising a storm of Christian dust, telling us stories with pictures painted on a felt board. They had an irritating pious air about them, and sang soulful duets. We had no idea they had a daughter until she came to teach abruptly in the middle of the winter term two months after their sudden deaths. There had been a memorial service in the church after they died, when we were in standard eight. I remember Miss Nelson sitting in her usual seat—up front, with the church choir—and blowing her red nose during the one minute of silence.

Nelson, who was supposed to have been their trusted family friend, had ravished their daughter. "Come sit on my lap, dear," she must have said, reading to Prince from the Bible in the evenings. And who would suspect an *aunt*?

Our mothers had warned us about the uncles. No arms around shoulders, no sitting on laps, and if they pat you on the back too often, you just come and tell me. But even the most paranoid of mothers had never thought to warn us against an aunt.

Brilliant. Lesbian aunt ravishes young girl who turns into a lesbian herself. Lesbian aunt pretends to be a saint. After murdering her ravishee, she donates a plaque in the church to the poor parents and their wayward daughter. "Twisted, man, truly twisted," said Akhila with glee.

"You have to admit Prince is the most interesting teacher in this place," said Shobha.

"You mean she was," I said, and felt a shiver down my spine. Actually, I had never liked Miss Prince. I found her self-absorbed and erratic. I blamed her for getting poor Apt involved in all this. I felt Prince had deliberately preyed on Apt because she was insecure and innocent. But now I felt sorry for Prince too.

"Remember the time she brought those balloons to the hockey pitch last term, on that hot day, and instead of playing hockey we filled the balloons with water, split into two teams, and had a water fight?" Prince had kept a stack of balloons beside her and thrown them at us randomly.

"She kept throwing balloons at me. I told her it wasn't fair," said Shobha. "And she said, 'Come here, you little rascal,' and pricked one of the balloons and emptied it out down my front."

All our navy-blue divided skirts and white blouses and navy-blue bloomers had to be put out to dry the next day, and the matrons were all in an uproar.

I was not a sports person myself. I kept a book with me and tried as often as possible to sit out and read. Miss Prince left me alone; I thought she did not notice. But on my last report card, she wrote in the comments section for sports, "Nandita finds it beneath her dignity to run."

We realized how brave she had been. She had the courage to flout their God and their ways. She did not hide herself. This is what I am, she said, love me or leave me.

Even her bad moods, now, we felt we understood.

She was never one of the mean ones. We all knew the mean teachers, the mean ayahs, the mean prefects. She was just unpredictable and had outbursts of random cruelty.

We saw how she must have been buffeted. What with those holier-than-thou parents, and then a saintly aunt who starts pawing her. She had sobbed that night, our poor Prince, laying bare her soul to her evil lover, begging her to show some sign that she cared for her. And instead, Nelly had said, *Let us pray. Our Lord will show you His mercy, my child, as He did to me.*

It was from that day on that we began to love the Prince. Even after the story twisted and turned like a scooter rickshaw in a crowded bazaar in Kandivili, we kept on loving her. Even though she was a lesbian.

Or maybe also because she was a lesbian.

"It adds glamour," I said.

"Why glamour? I think it adds intrigue," Shobha said with a naughty smile.

"What happened that day during detention? Wasn't it totally humiliating when she kept you standing for two hours?" I asked Shobha, wondering if she harbored a grudge, knowing I would have.

"First, I kept standing there, and she kept giving me this cold, sharp glare. It was almost as if I was expected to do something. I couldn't figure out what. So when the lunch bell rang, I started walking out. 'Did anyone give you the permission to leave?' she asked, and so I went back to my place and stood again for another hour."

I could see Shobha, tossing her head, slouching to her spot with a look of contempt on her face.

"Did she ever say anything to you about it?" asked Akhila.

"You know, we never even spoke after that. She would not address me by name. But I was always so aware that she was looking at me, and that day at the Scottish Dancing Competition, I swear to you, man, I knew she was looking at me the whole time. Her eyes were boring into me. I was quite flustered."

"You didn't look flustered to me. I was right next to you, and my kilt was so loose and flappy. But you looked great. And you were strutting away," I said.

"Turned you on, did she?" said Akhila.

"Idiot," said Shobha, and blushed.

I realized with a start that all those times on the netball field when they tossed their heads and stomped past each other, when we had thought they hated each other from that Saturday detention, they were actually flirting.

"And then when Nelly came up that day to send you down to the dorm, did you see anything between them?" we asked.

"Nelly walked in grave as a graveyard," said Shobha. "She did not look at Prince, she walked to me, she raised her eyebrows in sorrow, and she said, 'You can go now, Shobha.' Prince did not look up from her book. Her legs were still on the table. She was leaning back on her chair, absorbed, not noticing Nelson. Nelson stood at the door of the classroom and watched me till I turned the corner."

"That's all? You didn't hear anything more?" asked Akhila.

"You think I would walk away from that? Not a chance. I turned the corner and ducked into the art room. I saw Nelson walk to Prince, take the book away from her, and put it in her purse. Then she put Prince's head to her bosom."

"You mean you actually saw them making out? As if. And all this time you did not even let out a peep about it?" we asked, scoffing.

"Not exactly making out, of course," said Shobha condescendingly. "Prince did not bury her head in Nelson's bosom and start kissing or anything. In fact, she shook her head free.

I mean, they could have kissed or something after that. I don't know because I had to leave. Nelson came walking down the corridor, I thought she might have seen me, and so I ran."

"How could you leave the art room without being seen?" I asked her.

"I jumped out of the window at the back. It's quite easy. I did it once before with Raksha, when we went to steal the school bell for April Fool's Day. It was quite easy, really," insisted Shobha.

I did not believe a word of it. She was making it up as she went. Surely she would have told us about it earlier, had it been true. I suddenly saw Shobha's clay feet—I realized that she was a fibber. She would do or say anything just to get the spotlight back on her.

The Prince had said, *You bloody hypocrite*, stalked out into the night, and gone to table-land to get drugs from Shankar. Nelly followed her and pushed her over the edge because she knew that Prince would not keep her secret anymore, and her perfect reputation would be tarnished forevermore.

This was the logical story. It made sense. We had it all wrapped up. By the time the envelope fell out of my Hindi textbook, I had even put aside my quest for the letter from England that had made the Prince rush out into the raining night.

I see it as my fault. I, who had been trained to concentrate on the details that other people missed. I had suppressed the thought of the letter. Luckily, it slipped out of my textbook onto the red stone step at my feet.

I had the Hindi textbook, fresh from the hands of Miss Raswani, still on my lap. I must have been fiddling with it in an absentminded way—for of course Hindi revisions were the furthest thing from my mind—when it opened to the MariOr-PiriKuri chapter and the letter fell out, still in its blue- and red-edged airmail envelope.

We went to the plastic-covered table outside the dining room, and I copied the entire letter word for word into our murder notebook. I still have those pages today. I remember how I wrote that morning in blue ink with the smooth-nibbed Pilot pen that I loved, and the smell of Mallu the bearer's stinky dishcloth on the plastic.

The envelope was addressed to "Miss Moira Prince, Miss Timmins' School, Panchgani, India" from "Jonathan Birkett, 17 Balfour Road, London, England." The postmark was from August 2, 1974. And it was written exactly like this:

Dear Moira,

Forgive me for not being in touch sooner. You must think I had forgotten about the promise I made to you at Christmas. Let me assure you that nothing could be further from the truth. I too am eager to complete the picture of our family history, though of course I know that your quest is more essential.

I meant to go during the Easter Holidays. But Camilla has been rather unwell, and the care of the children fell solely onto me, and that prevented me from going. That should not have prevented me from writing to you, I know, but I confess I felt guilty—I knew, after all, what it meant to you, and how anxious you must be—and so I kept telling myself that I would write after I had accomplished my task. Or at least when I could tell you with confidence when I would actually go to Norfolk.

Now that the school is finally closed for the summer holidays, and Camilla is much better—she sends you her love, and hopes that you will come for the holidays again this year so we can get to meet our newly discovered cousin, and our children can have an aunt, for we are both only children, you and I—I had the opportunity at last to drive up to Little Snoring. I spent three days there, digging into records and talking to people. I must tell you it is a wonderfully picturesque little village a few miles off the coast. I am sending you a photograph of St. Andrew Chapel, which is a wonderful medieval church.

I am surprised that you had never even heard Little Snoring mentioned once in your home, since that is where your parents lived for many years before they went off on their mission to India. But of course, once they decided to keep your adoption secret from you, they must have had to bury that whole part of their lives.

But why do I rant on like this, when you must be so eager for the results of my search.

According to the village records, there were three girls born on November 20, 1946. If you do have the correct date of your birth, then we have struck gold, since there is an unwed mother on the list:

Amanda, born to Charles and Mary Linn

Margaret, born to Innis and Martha Naar

Charlotte, born to Shirley Nelson

As you see, there is no mention of a father for Charlotte.

I did try to do some digging around, you know. I spoke to the pastor of the Presbyterian church, told him about my aunt and uncle who became missionaries, but he was a young man, and was either unwilling to talk or unknowing of the adoption, which is very possible, because these things were done very informally in those days, as you know. He said none of the names were familiar to him. So I am sending you a copy of the birth certificate, in case it might help you in your search.

I discovered that there was an air force base near the village during the war, which might go a long way towards explaining the circumstances of your birth. The war, the handsome boys in uniform, might have driven the village girls to distraction; I hope you do not mind me saying so.

And though I have taken so long to get this far, let me assure you that I am most willing to help you locate Shirley Nelson—although it is possible that she may be married and have a different name.

We are all still in a state of pleasant shock, but so glad that you tracked us through the card. The sisters exchanged cards on a regular basis. Your mother—adoptive mother, I suppose I should say—used to visit us every four years or so, when she came on furlough. She always came alone by train for the day, we had tea together, and then the two sisters used to lock themselves into the room and murmur.

We sent your parents Christmas cards with our family photo every year. They always sent a card too. I waited for the envelopes and stuck the stamps in my book and looked at them often, the maps of India in different colors. Your parents never sent photographs of themselves. My mother said because it must be hard to take photos in those primitive places. But now I can see that you were their secret.

We are all eager to find out where this journey leads you. And once again, please do call upon me if you need my help. I hope that we can continue to be in touch. Camilla and I have begun to harbour fantasies of visiting you in India.

Jon

And so it turned out that Raswani was not so daft as I had supposed when she said her last words to me, the Saturn ring melting around her pupils. In fact, she had been diabolically clever. *Show it to that silly child, your friend Akhila*, she had said. *Tell her to revise her favorite chapter.* And coming to think of it, MariOrPiriKuri *could* be construed as Akhila's favorite chapter.

Throughout the term, Akhila and Ramona had put up their hands in Hindi class and inevitably asked some dumb question designed to make Raswani say the word again.

"MariOrPiriKuri. Yes, I told you before. You will have to revise the chapter again," she would say. She said it in a juicy way, slapping her lips together as though she was waiting to eat her dal chaval. The chapter was a vapid outline of the life and achievements of Marie and Pierre Curie, but their names had been butchered in our phonetic national language, and Raswani would say them as they were written. She must never have heard of the Curies, we gloated. Not a scrap of information must have entered her head since the turn of the century. We kept thinking she would catch on, and correct herself and say Pierre instead of Piri one fine morning, but she did not.

In our personal Timmins history, Marie and Pierre Curie were more famous for opening up the Great Panchgani Scandals than they were for their Nobel Prize–winning discovery of radium. And they are known forever as MariOrPiriKuri.

No birth certificate was found in the envelope, and there was no photo of the village church. We did not know how Raswani had gotten hold of the letter, or why she had now given it to us. We were too shocked to care.

Nelson was the mother of Prince. All this time. A child born in sin under our very noses.

No one knew, not the rest of the Holy Trinity, and certainly not poor Prince. Nelly, our upright principal who was so fair with us all, had kept her secret love child right in front of our faces. And how callous she had been with her own child. Now that I thought about it, they both did have the same strong jawline.

We knew we had solved the case. We shook hands with each other—"Well done, Sherlock," "Elementary, my dear Watson"—and brimming with power and confidence, we decided to walk out of the school in broad daylight and go boldly to Inspector Woggle on our own. There was no time to waste.

As we were leaving the front gate, Ramona suddenly wanted to go to the bathroom.

"Hurry up; I'll go down with you," I said.

"No," she said, "I might take some time. I have my chum. I think you should carry on."

"Don't ditch now, Ramona," we begged. "You saw her on table-land. You were one of the three. And three witnesses are much stronger than two."

"I am sure to meet Merch. I do not want to meet him," Ramona said in a small, despairing voice. "So why don't you all just carry on and tell the Woggle your story and show him the letter. I can be called later, if they need me."

"And what does Merch matter now?" we asked her. "He is nothing. The case is closed. We have proof of the motive, and we have proof that Nelson was at the scene of the crime. What do you think, Ramona? You think he is just lurking around the bazaar waiting for you? Come on, one hardly ever sees him even."

So she came along with us, but we should have known better.

The mist lifted as we walked through the bazaar, and a soft ray of light pierced through the clouds for a moment, lighting up the puddles. The world looked suddenly fresh and clean. We could smell the end of the monsoons. We felt it was an omen, a good omen. When we got to the police chowki, we were told that the inspector was busy. And so we waited on the slatted wooden bench in the veranda.

"What about Apt?" asked Shobha. "What should we say? Dushant saw her running down. She was technically at the scene of the crime."

"But we didn't see her. If Dushant saw her, Dushant should say," I said.

"As if he would lie," said Shobha, flouncing.

"That's not the point, is it? The point is that Dushant himself was breaking rules, so he has to decide what he wants to tell and what he doesn't. We are not the witness, he is."

Shobha opened her mouth and then closed it. She could not argue with that.

My instinct was to keep the Apt out of it. I had no idea what to make of all the love triangles the girls were drawing, but to me, Apt seemed so soft and innocent, I was sure her role was incidental. I wondered where Dushant really saw her. If he saw her near the municipal park, she could have been walking home from the Sydney Point road. There were a whole bunch of houses out there. No point in bringing her into it. This murder had long and twisted roots. Nelson, who I had thought was fair and kind and wise, had an evil side. She did not want to be the mother of Prince, much as my own mother did not want me. From the time I was little, I noticed the revulsion on my mother's face when she looked at me—she wondered where I had come from. As though it were all my fault. My fault for being short and fat and hairy, my fault for breathing. I was suddenly all choked up with tears. I was sure now that Nelson had killed her daughter.

Two hawaldars sat on their haunches smoking bidis, which they crushed as soon as the inspector yelled from behind the closed door. "Send the schoolgirls in," he said in Marathi. We tumbled into his room, the four of us, self-important and bloated with our news, only to find Merch sitting on one of the two chairs facing the inspector's large worn wooden table.

I remember the stab of fear I felt when I first saw the back of his head, with his straggly hair tied in a low ponytail. He said nothing, just looked at us with his customary expression of mild curiosity. But when he lit his cigarette, I saw that his hands were shaking.

We handed the letter to the inspector, still in its envelope. The Woggle held it up and read it, emitting small whistles of sounds as he moved through the words. Then he looked up, and we wondered what he would do.

The inspector had thick oily hair, slicked back. There were two beads of sweat heading down both sides of his plump cheeks. "This is very important evidence," he said, fanning his face with a slightly grimy handkerchief. "Now we have a possible motive. A very good motive. But a motive does not make a murderer. We have no reason to connect your principal to the fall in the middle of a rainy night. The only person present at the scene of the crime was Shankar. And that makes him the main suspect."

I had a feeling Merch was at the inspector's to report seeing our raincoats at the scene of the crime. But he said nothing.

We told him our tale, Akhila, Shobha, and I talking in turn as we were trained to do, still standing in front of his desk as we were used to standing in Nelly's cold office. We told him about the letter, the fight, and our walk on table-land, where we saw Nelson sitting a few feet away from Miss Prince. We put Nelson, with her motive, at the scene of the crime.

And that was how the principal of Miss Timmins' School for Girls came to be walked out of the school in the afternoon, surrounded by policemen.

The inspector walked ahead of her, his two hawaldars behind. The news spread through the school like wildfire. "She is not in handcuffs," shouted Rajvi Tandon, "but she is surrounded." Everyone—girls, teachers, and servants—stood around in gaping groups as she sailed past, looking proudly into the distance. No one said good-bye. In fact, no one said a word to her. Miss Wilson walked by her side, wiping her red nose.

The police jeep was parked under the banyan tree. Before stepping into it, Nelly turned to the crowd that had followed her up. "Miss Wilson will guide you through this. I have entrusted the school to her at this time," she said, and gave Willy a reassuring pat on her back. Willy mustered a strong face, but turned around and walked back into her room as soon as the battered jeep left the school compound.

The disappearance of the Hindi teacher came to our attention the next morning. I do not remember if we were informed of her departure at prayers or even if there were prayers that morning, though of course there must have been.

The rain had started up again, and a sad, slanting drizzle created a hypnotic pattern of crowns on the stone steps. We were all forced to cluster in dorms and damp corridors and soon everybody knew that the Willoughby ayah had found Raswani's room empty.

We wondered where she went, for we knew that she had no home. The most plausible rumor about her life was that she grew up in a Christian orphanage and had lived her entire life in missionary-run enterprises. We imagined her to be a virgin.

She left no note of explanation and no forwarding address. We wondered how she left. How did she carry out all her bags and belongings since the servants declared that none of them had helped her?

So just as one mystery was solved, another came into view. Just as it became clear that Nelson had murdered Prince, we began to imagine that we could prove she had also murdered

Miss Raswani, for that was the sequence of events we had expected from the beginning, and the one that Ramona had predicted. There is always a second murder.

Now you can relax, Ramona, we said. The second murder is done.

Events were falling into the pattern of a classical murder mystery. The first murder is committed to hide some terrible truth. The second, to silence the person who had chanced upon either the terrible truth or the terrible act itself. And Raswani had most definitely happened upon the terrible truth.

If Raswani had disappeared, I could have been the last person in school to see her. She gave the letter to me and fled, fearful for her life. Made sense.

But she could very well have been killed. Nelson did not know the letter was out. She could have killed her for the letter.

"I am told that second murders are easier than the first," said Akhila, as if she personally had tea and toast with first- and second- and third-time murderers.

The entire case lay wide open before us. How did Raswani get hold of the letter? Why did she give it to us? When was she murdered? Could Nelson have killed her? How could Nelson have killed her?

But we had little time to set about solving the case before we were whisked out of the school. We flitted like butterflies from one mystery topic to the next and came up with nothing on that gray morning before Ramona's brother arrived in a creaky taxi from Poona and Shobha's sleek father took her and five girls, including Akhila, in his gleaming Chevrolet Impala.

TWENTY

The Melting Murder

MY FATHER DROVE up two days later with my mother beside him wearing a silk scarf to keep her hair down and a transistor playing Radio Ceylon held at her ear.

I had skulked around the emptying school for the two days, but discovered nothing new. We had prayers every morning, then two hours of sitting silently at our desks and "studying." I read Ayn Rand. We were taken for crocodile walks every evening in three rows: seniors, middles, and juniors. The teachers and matrons were too busy placating the flood of irate parents to think of our moral or intellectual welfare, and certainly too busy to talk to me.

Soon after the arrest of Miss Nelson and the disappearance of the school's oldest teacher, Miss Wilson developed her stiff upper lip. She kept her pleas to the good Lord pretty cut and dried, and whisked around trying to keep the truth at bay. "Until the true events come to light, we will refrain from conjecture and debate," she announced the next morning after we had finished reciting the Lord's prayer. "For the sake of the reputation of our students and our school, we will not discuss the events with the public. No reporters will be allowed in the school, and I have impressed upon your parents, and I do so again with you, to please refrain from loose talk during the holidays. The lawyers, the police, and your teachers will be able to do everything to get to the truth of the matter. We have had a difficult time these last few days, and I want you girls to relax and have a good time at home."

She did not mention that four of the schoolgirls had been instrumental in the arrest of the principal. I was the only one of the detectives still around in those last days when the girls fell out of the school like milk teeth, but Willy did not call me up to her office and talk to me. She knew what I had done, but she showed no anger or emotion. It was during this time that she turned into Wilson the Just.

WE SPENT THAT three-week September holiday after the murder in Bombay, Akhila, Shobha, and I. We spent the days in Shobha's posh flat overlooking the Oval Maidan, eating onion bhajiyas and hot fried potato chips made by her fat cook Deoka, who had been with them since Shobha was four years old. He lives to please me, especially now, said Shobha, tilting her head proudly. We knew that *now* meant after her mother had left her, and asked no more. We were allowed to have as many Cokes with ice in tall glasses as we wanted.

We told our parents we needed to be together every day

of the holidays to study for our exams. And we did sit around and use the tools of our trade. We dissected the events and the words around them like frogs in Miss Mathews' science lab. We used deductive logic, inductive logic, and, as Akhila later pointed out, we used seductive logic. With the juices bursting out of our bodies, our pimples, our periods, coarse curly hairs sprouting on our nipples and chins, we tried to divine the actions and motives of Raswani and Nelly, those two old women who had lived cheek by jowl for so many years.

The murder holiday was like a rest stop in the path of the scandals. It was after the murder of Prince, after the disappearance of the Hindi teacher, after the popping of the first scandal. It was while the world still thought that it was a fact that Nelson had murdered her blood child that we sat around hugging pillows to our breasts, and spinning and whirling and stretching the story as we sucked ice cubes from the frosted glasses of coke.

We wrapped up the story of Prince's murder and moved on to Raswani after the newpaper reports of September, 12, 1974.

ACCUSED PRINCIPAL DOES NOT DENY MURDER CHARGE

The principal of Miss Timmins' School, Panchgani, has not denied the charges leveled against her. Accused of murdering her biological daughter Miss Moira Prince, Miss Shirley Nelson, who is currently being detained in a room in a mofussil hospital, has refused to make a statement either denying or admitting to the crime. Her only words before the Satara sessions magistrate prior to being taken into judicial custody were, "His will be done, on earth as it is in heaven." She has not spoken since. She has refused to retain counsel. Reporters were informed that the State of Maharashtra would designate a lawyer if no one came forward to take up her case.

The report went on to say that a local man, Shankar Tamde, who had been held for questioning, had been released.

The *Indian Express* quoted Nelson as saying, "I am in a great strait: let me fall now into the hand of the Lord; for very great are his mercies: but let me not fall into the hand of man."

The story had now become front-page news. The entire country seemed to be following the dark tale of the two British women who had played out their twisted history atop this remote rain-washed mountain. The Naxalites set fire to an abandoned church in Gauhati, in the state of Assam, protesting missionary presence in India.

It was all so surreal, for we felt inside it and still so far removed.

Shobha's bedroom had a balcony that was level with the top of the palm trees that circled the Oval. The monsoon winds came in from the sea at high tide, and buffeted them around so that when we were lounging on her bed, we could see the bent trees swishing their branches like tails. In the evenings we could see children taking pony rides at the bandstand.

We imagined the sequence of events. On the night of the murder, while Shobha, reading *Lolita* with a torch under her blanket, heard the scream torn from the soul of the poor Prince, Raswani watched from the other side, and with her mad white eye glued to the chink where the wall met the wood of the door between the rooms, she saw the Prince fling the letter at

Nelson, and saw that Nelson did not pick it up to read it, for of course she knew the fact that it contained, had lived in fear of it all these years.

Raswani saw the Prince stalk out, and soon after, she saw Nelson snatch her purse and walk out into the night. She could see the airmail envelope on the table, nearly within her grasp. She knew the bolt on the door between the rooms was loose. You could jiggle the door and drop the latch. And so, while we were running down from table-land and Nelly was saying her last prayer before pushing her daughter off the edge of the cliff, the Hindi teacher went into the room she had watched secretly for so many years, and with shaking hands she snatched the letter and ran back into her room.

She *could* have read it right there in the room. She could have stood over the desk, read the letter, and left it there so that Nelson would never know she had seen it. Then it would have been a different story. But maybe she was nervous, standing in this inner chamber; maybe she did not have her glasses; maybe she expected Nelly to burst into the room any minute. And so she took the letter and retreated to the safety of her room. And did not put it back.

How shocked she must have been when she read the letter—perhaps she had lain rigid in her bed, tossing it around in her boxed brain. And as more time passed, it grew harder for her to get up and go back into the room to return it.

When Wilson announced the death of Prince, the horrible truth must have been clear to Miss Raswani. Perhaps she had even seen Nelly come back to her room later with signs of the deathly deed fresh upon her. Perhaps her clothes were tattered, since it was a known fact that there had been a struggle before the Prince's body went hurtling over the cliff. Raswani could have heard her washing her white pajamas in the sink at night.

But she did not tell the inspector. She did not tell anyone at all, not even Willy, because she was going to protect her beloved Nelson, whose face she saw instead of the Lord's when she prayed at night. *Why should she suffer so much? Hadn't she suffered enough? Hadn't we all suffered enough?* Raswani was really the most simpleminded of the Timmins teachers—nobody with an ounce of intelligence could teach like her—and so we gave her a simple construct. We figured that she saw them as the sinner and the saint. Nelson, who had hidden her love child and then committed murder, was the saint, and the brave-hearted Prince was the sinner because she made love to women and did not hide it.

"The twistedness of this logic is truly horrendous," said Shobha in her imitation Indian Jamsetjee Ram accent, nodding her head from side to side.

"Nelson must be her only real contact with humanity. I bet you no one else has even liked her," I said.

But if that was her motive, we asked each other, biting into salted buttas on the windy ledge of Marine Drive and watching the sea thrash out the last of the current of that long, wild monsoon, if she wanted to keep that secret locked in her soul, why did she give the letter to me, the letter that implicated her beloved Nelson? Why did she give me the secret letter after hiding it for a whole week?

He is testing me. That was the first thing she said when I informed her that the three of us had seen Nelson that night on table-land. I saw now that she must have taken my words as a sign from her God. I was her messenger from God, sent to tell her not to hide the truth. We had seen Nelson on table-land. I had told Raswani that day in her veranda that we would have to tell Shobha's father. Raswani must have known that the questions would begin and the story would soon unravel.

Into Thy hands I commend Thee, she had said, like the good Christian that she was, as she slipped the letter into the book with only a glancing hint. Leave it to the Lord, she must have thought. If He wants the truth to be known, He will reveal it to them. And she had gotten it out of her hands, for she had felt so tainted and so guilty with the letter in her room—after all, she had been a thief in the night, breaking into someone else's room and stealing. She had kept reading and rereading the letter and shoving it to the bottom of different drawers, so when she had finally decided to put it into the Hindi text, she could not find it at first.

She knew the story would unravel, and she wanted no part of it. That is what I believed then.

We agreed that Miss Raswani, who had been such an integral part of our edifice of fear, *could* have ordered a taxi, called the driver down for her bags, sneaked out from the gap behind the hockey pitch at dawn, and disappeared forever, as in a respectable Agatha Christie novel. Or she could have been killed.

We were aware that there were still mysteries at hand.

We wrote in our murder notebook. It was our last entry. I must have been responsible for that "ergo."

Proposed Order of Events on Table-Land on the Night of August 27, 1974

10:45. Girls reach table-land. They do not go near the needle, but wander around.

11:30. They see Nelson and Prince near the needle.

12:35. The girls are back in school.

Somewhere between 12 and 1, the boys see Apt running down.

Ergo: She probably went up before 12.

Somewhere between 12 and 1, the boys find Shankar bending over the dead body.

Whichever way you came down from table-land—unless via the cliff, like the Prince—you had to pass the municipal park.

Apt could have gone up after Nelson left. Between the Apt and Nelson, I would say Nelson was the murderer. She had the motive. Shobha presumed that Apt was the last person down. And she and Merch together had pushed the Prince off the cliff because of some tensions in their supposed love affair.

"I spoke to Dushant today," Shobha announced on the last day of our holidays. Her boyfriend had been in some backwater family factory town during his break and was just back in Bombay. "Dushant told me that the boys have decided to report Miss Apte to the authorities," said Shobha, looking archly at me.

I wanted to warn Miss Apte. I wished there were some way to tell her that a trap was about to be sprung, but I had no idea where she was.

BOOK THREE

The Blot

Charu

TWENTY-ONE

Mr. Much

SOMETIMES I LOOK at the women with their hands folded on their laps and wonder. I see them on Sunday evenings, sitting by the sea with their husbands, their children building castles in the sand. Packing school lunches in the morning, puja after bath, mother-in-law frowning, and sex without a sound. Yes, I could have done it, and my shell could have been my pillow.

I was in Kolhapur, and my mother was in hospital. I spent the days in her hospital room in an anesthetic state of mind, wondering idly about my life, as though it were happening to someone else. I ate heavily from tiffins full of delicious freshly cooked food sent to tempt Ayi, and then I slept for two hours in the extra bed.

At night, in the visiting daughters' room with random aunts lined up beside me, I could not sleep. A knife-thrust of desire would carve a big round hole in my stomach, so that I would have to turn over and stuff pillows under it. I wanted to make love to Pin again. Just once more. I wanted to kiss her for a long, long time. She would pull out, smile into my eyes, give my blot a nibble, and go back into my mouth again. I could feel her teeth on my face. I wanted to bite her and scratch her and twine my legs around her. I wanted to leave small marks on her white velvet body. Just once, just one candlelit night more I wanted. I wanted to love her with abandon. I would drift into a shallow sleep and wake up under the mosquito net with hot blood jumping in my veins so I could not lie down. I would creep out of the room and roam around the courtyard, studying the slate tiles in the moonlight.

Walking into the house from hospital one evening, I found Gopika, a middle aunt just arrived from Jalgaon, slurping tea with my grandmother in the kitchen. Gopika always maintained that everything was better in Jalgaon. Her sons were taller, her daughters were fairer, the milk was better in Jalgaon. Everyone called her Jalgaon Masi.

"They tell me Shalini is much better now," said Jalgaon Masi, "but of course I haven't spoken to Tai yet."

"Yes," I said, "Ayi is better. She is in a stable condition." Ayi was now out of intensive care, off all the machines, and out of danger. She was officially out of her coma, but was still very vague and distant. She was ensconced in a large private room on the top floor of the hospital, attended by a day nurse and a night nurse. But she wasn't connecting the dots yet. She wouldn't speak for days, and then, suddenly, would let out a torrent of dark jumbled fragments mainly about her childhood. We were not sure if she recognized us.

Dr. Tendulkar told us gravely that her brain could have been damaged, since it had been deprived of oxygen.

"But we will watch her for a while," he said. And so we watched her. We took turns, Tai, Baba, and I. Baba slept the night with her, Tai did the evenings, and I sat with her through the day. I sat by the bed and held her hand, I combed her thinning hair, and tried to feed her tomato soup and toast, though she would have none of it. I looked into her eyes, and I was sure she was resting. One fine morning, when I came in, she would say, "Charu beta, get me my knitting, it is on the shelf. No, not there, over there."

The official story was that she slipped into a coma as a result of a reaction to some new medicine for her thyroid problem. The suicide attempt was sealed into a tight family circle; even the younger generation was not to know. We called it the Episode. It had been a week, but we still did not let visitors into her room, for fear of what she might say.

The house went into emergency footing. One car was a hospital ferry. Streams of family members came and went, carrying meals and snacks and fruit and twice-boiled water, thermos flasks of tea, clean towels and sheets and freshly ironed saris and kaftans. The benches outside the hospital room were always filled with gossiping relatives. Dada came every afternoon at 3:30, dressed in his spotless white pants and shirt, on his way back home from his air-conditioned office at Chitnis Transport. The old man would sit outside her room on a straight-backed chair and glare into the distance for exactly ten minutes. And then he would get up and leave. The brothers came in the evening. The sisters began to gather.

"And oh, yes, Charu, there are some people here to see you. From Panchgani," Jalgaon Masi said, blowing into a perfectly poised saucer as I walked out of the kitchen.

I had heard nothing since the day I left Panchgani. During the day I ached for Ayi, and at night I wept for Pin. I was thankful for the rhythm of the hospital. I decided never to go back to school.

"Who?" I asked, my voice high, my heart throbbing in my temples.

"I don't know. They are sitting in the drawing room," she said, pointing with her chin, and I thought she wrinkled her nose in disapproval.

I went in to find Merch, Samar, and Shabir sitting stiffly on the triangle of plastic sofas. They looked very uncomfortable and very stoned. They had been sitting there for at least an hour, they said, and had consumed several cups of tea.

Tai poked her head into the room just then. She was on her way to the hospital. The driver was waiting on the doorstep with the hospital tiffin. She beckoned me out of the room.

"Who is that black boy?" she demanded, her face screwed in disgust. She pronounced it as "buoy." She did not bother to lower her voice. She wore a purple nylon sari with swirling yellow patterns.

I looked at the three of them with Kolhapur eyes. In Panchgani, they were unconventional. But here, in my strict middle-class household where the women all wore saris and covered their heads in front of their father-in-law, they looked absolutely scandalous.

The black buoy was surely Shabir, who was the most outrageous of them all. He was very thin, very dark, and very tall, and dressed in deep-orange pajamas and a hand-dyed vest with a front pocket like the ones the servants wore. His curly hair was loose and strewn untidily across his face. He was nodding his head and smiling at his own private joke. He was smoking a bidi.

"He is a sadhu, Tai," I babbled hastily, trying to walk her towards the door. "See, he is wearing orange clothes. He is a Rajneesh sadhu. You know Ishwar kaka from across the street? Even he is a Rajneesh sadhu." In truth, we had all been a bit shocked when our conventional neighbor with three grown daughters had one day turned up in orange robes and declared that he had become a devotee of Rajneesh, the controversial guru who condoned free love and was rumored to have sex orgies at his ashram in Poona. I imagined that clubbing Shabir together with a fat and balding neighbor might give him a measure of respectability. But Tai was not impressed. Her scowl remained intact.

Samar was sporting a stained white kurta with jeans and thick village slippers. He had a small gold ring in his right ear. Merch was being manful. He was wearing a checked shirt, and had a pen clipped to his pocket. In spite of his glassy eyes, he was the most respectable and introducible of them all, and so I pointed to him. "This is Merch, Tai. He has come to give me some Panchgani news," I said.

Merch stood up straight and took one brave step towards us.

"Oh, yes, Mr. Much," said Tai, looking him up and down sternly.

"So what do you do in Panchgani, Mr. Much?" she asked, her pitted face set in a thunderous scowl. Any young man who dared visit a Chitnis girl must be prepared to produce his credentials. And since no young men of this kind had ever visited a Chitnis girl, Tai was stacking the ramparts with hot oil.

"Photography," said Merch faintly, scratching his head.

"A photographer?" she looked at me, taken aback. Her youngest brother, my uncle Anil, was a professional photographer. She was very proud of him.

But she soon took it in her stride. "Ah, immature," she said dismissively. "He must be an immature."

She waddled out, wiping her face with the polka-dotted napkin. I had no idea what she meant. Merch kept a very straight face. I watched my two worlds collide, not in fire and brimstone, as I had feared, but in comic relief.

"Welcome to Kolhapur, Mr. Immature Much," I said, smiling, happy to see them.

We left the house immediately. I called to Ramu the servant not to keep dinner for me. Shabir had dropped acid, and he could feel it coming on. He needed a safe space. "Give me a good small-town spot," he said. "I've been doing acid so long in the green meadows and rain. I'm looking forward to this." We went to an idli house in the bazaar, but before our order came, Shabir announced that the lights were making him nervous. "Too intense, man," he said. "And that yellow rice that villager was eating, it exploded in my face like a volcano. I think I could even be hallucinating."

We drove around the outskirts of the town and finally found a street with only three little bungalows bunched together on one side. One flickering streetlight stood guard in the middle of them. I sat in the backseat with Merch. Samar parked the car and lit a joint. I took three deep drags and passed the joint to Merch. My arm stretched across a lifetime before it reached him. We had always been three in the backseat, and today, I could not even see her face clearly in my mind. But I knew that her thigh would have been pressed against mine so that my breath came short and fast.

No one said anything. Samar turned the Rolling Stones louder. Shabir got out of the car and walked around the empty street. "I'm seeing the light now," he said sagely as he passed the car, his long, lean face lit in a beatific smile.

"Your pupils are dilated," said Merch.

LSD was something you read about, or heard the Beatles sing about. I did not think it was something that anyone I knew had actually experienced. Maybe they had all done it. Maybe they had even done it on a night when I was with them and not told me. I had imagined that a person on acid would look somewhat like a street drunk, staggering and stuttering. But Shabir was quite calm and coherent. It was as if he were watching a good movie.

Suddenly he climbed back into the car, convulsed with laughter. His springy black hair bounced around his head as he went up and down, slapping his thighs. We could not get a word out of him for some time.

"Amateur," he uttered as he gasped for his last breath. "She meant amateur. You could see her brain turning. That black bouy Much could not possibly be a professional photographer."

"But black buoy was not Much. It was *you*," I said. Shabir laughed harder.

"Too Much," said Samar, snorting. "Too Much. Mr. I. Much. Nice name."

"He could be a minor poet," I said.

It came to mind because he had said it to me once. In his room, I had found a book titled *Minor Romantic Poets of the Nineteenth Century*. The rain was splashing merrily on the roof, the light in his room was sweet and yellow. Shabir and his girlfriend, Raisa, were on the bed, kissing. Samar, his wife, and the Prince were playing Scrabble. The Prince was stooped and restless. She had a bad mood sign on her head, and so no one spoke to her. Samar seemed to be winning, but everyone was waiting for Pin to do a triple word using *J* or *X*. And then she would probably produce a small, shy smile. Merch was rolling a joint, changing the music, and making tea. I picked the book off the shelf and was leafing through it. I knew Merch loved poetry; he said it was the purest of the fictions. Distilled. But still, who would actually buy and read a book that held only minor poets? I was thinking, astonished, when I heard him behind me.

"Minor poets are special. I would be quite content to be a minor poet," he said, his brown eyes shining with pleasure in the dim light.

To be included in scholarly and obscure anthologies, I thought, and found that I had said it out loud in the car. I was used to keeping my thoughts to myself.

We decided to call him Much forever after. Much and the Black Buoy. We began to laugh. And every time there was a lull, one of us would start again. We laughed feverishly, bent over, holding our stomachs, lurching in and out of the car, which stood with doors all wide open like wings, just outside the circle of lamplight. A light went on in a bedroom of one of the bungalows. A curtain was held back for a minute and then dropped again.

Friends could die, family could fall apart, but we could sit in the night on a dead-end road and fill out with laughter. Perhaps I could live through anything, I thought then.

We stopped laughing as suddenly as we had started. And the gravity and gloom that we had held above the laughter settled upon our heads. Samar stepped out of the car. The air closed in around him and became a solid mass of sadness. Merch and I turned and faced each other. The Stones should have been playing "Ruby Tuesday," but they were not. Merch had leaned over to the front seat and turned the volume down. It was too dark to see his face, but the whites of his eyes gleamed. He lit a cigarette and passed it to me. Then he lit one for himself and took a deep drag. His movements were slow and deliberate.

"Do you want to know?" he asked, his voice hoarse, intimate.

No, I did not want to know. I had an affair with a woman, and now she was dead. She was an intense woman, perhaps she was a mad woman. Perhaps I had loved her. But now she was dead. She fell off a cliff on a rainy night. She must have jumped just after I left. But I could not have her back, not for all the perfumes of Arabia. I could still have my mother back, though, if I hoped and dreamt and prayed and cared.

"Yes, I want to know," I said.

All that time with Pin, I had been desperate to get her deep dark secrets out of Merch and jealous that she did not see fit to confide in me. But now, I was afraid.

"Miss Nelson was arrested for Pin's murder," said Merch, slowly, pausing before every word, like a man jumping stones across a gushing stream. "They went to the school and arrested her today, I wanted to tell you before you read it in the papers."

I always remember what I said in the face of this earthshaking news.

"But how did you find me?" I asked, because that was what I had been thinking all evening and waiting to ask.

Maybe he was relieved to talk trivia, or maybe he sensed that I needed to nibble around it. He launched into a lengthy story.

"I knew you were in Kolhapur, so we went to the Chitnis Transport office in the old city first and told the gatekeeper that we were looking for Miss Charulata Apte. A khaki peon came to the car and said Senior Sir wants to see you. The others waited in the car, and I went up these narrow stairs to this small air-conditioned office. This regal sort of Dalmatian was slouching beside the desk, but sat up straight as soon as I walked in.

"Your grandfather ordered tea for me. He looked me up and down while I drank, then he said, so you want to see Charu? I was kind of hypnotized. I just nodded. He told the peon to get into the car and take us to the house. The Dalmatian got up and trotted behind us all the way to the car, wagged his tail twice, and went back. As if the old man had sent his deputy to say good-bye."

Merch was talking, and I had broken up into a hot and seething mass.

"But why Miss Nelson? Did someone see her on table-land?" I asked in a squeaky voice verging on hysteria.

Merch looked at me thoughtfully. He seemed to be about to say something. But he lit a cigarette, instead, and practiced smoke rings. I realized I had not made the most appropriate of responses so far.

I lit a cigarette too. Someone had seen Nelson and Pin on table-land. Whoever saw her could very well have seen me. But it seemed as if they had not. I could have told Merch then of how my role was threaded through that night. But I was used to being a secretive soul. I rubbed my blot instead.

"She told me she considered jumping from that very spot," I said.

"But Woggle insisted it was murder. Too many signs of struggle, clothes torn, and all that stuff."

"It's all so bizarre. Arrested Nelson. Didn't she deny it or something?" I asked, aghast. "She must at least have denied the murder charge. She'll get a lawyer, she'll deny it. Why should she push a girl off a cliff?" I knew she could not have done it. I had seen her walk down with her purse dangling jauntily in the crook of her arm.

"But wait," said Merch. "It gets better—or worse. I suppose one should say worse. The girls found this letter that proves that Nelson was her biological mother."

This time my response was appropriate to the enormity of the news. I clapped my hand to my mouth in disbelief, I ran my hand through my hair, I broke into a sweat, I let out a high-pitched sound. Who would have imagined that her hated Nelson was the one who gave birth to her?

"And what about the parents who died in the bus accident?" I stuttered, still unbelieving.

"It seems the Princes had adopted her and did not tell her. They never told her she was adopted. That's why she hated them all so much. The whole time she was growing up they did not tell her anything. She found out she was adopted just this year, and that too in a roundabout way. She felt they betrayed her. All three of them. Made her live this lie. 'If I was adopted, so what? Why not tell me?' she said, and of course she was right. She was bitter about it. She said she felt somehow dirty, like a hidden wart or something."

"You mean she knew that Nelson was her mother and you knew that too?" I asked, astonished.

"No, no. Pin did not know that Nelson was her mother. Not then. A few months ago she had told me she was adopted. She found out after her parents died," said Merch. The Princes had made Nelson the executor of their wills, and it was Nelson who was responsible for sorting through their papers so Pin knew nothing except what she got as her inheritance. Apparently they had left her a cottage in England and some money, and she was always dreaming of going there.

"Then some old greeting card that was sent long ago and lost in a circuitous sea route or something came for the Princes to Nasik, and was finally redirected to Pin. It was from her mother's sister's family in London. Pin told me she had been completely stunned to see a photograph of this young man and woman and their blond child fall out of the card. There was a chatty letter from a man called Jonathan Birkett addressing her mother as Aunt Martha, saying he hoped they would keep in touch, though his mother had died. Pin figured this must be her mother's sister's family. She had heard childhood stories of her mother growing up—in Dartmouth or some town with a D, she said, I can't remember—with her younger sister, but that was all. No adult stories of this sister or her family were ever told. Pin said it blew her away. She told me that when she first got in touch with the family after receiving the card, they thought her story was a hoax. They insisted the Princes had never had a child. So she went to London last winter. Her cousin, this Jonathan, told her none of the relatives had heard of her. Can you imagine, they had kept her a secret from their own families? She told me she spent sleepless nights wondering why they had done this."

"And so, how did it unravel?"

"Pin and her British cousin finally pieced it together and realized the Princes must have adopted her as a baby while they were living in Little Snoring during or just after the war. Jonathan was not even sure they were missionaries at that time. But he was five or six, he said, when his mother's sister and her husband left suddenly for India. Since his mother was dead, there was no way to verify anything.

"Poor Pin," I said. "In a strange country, all alone. She must have felt terrible."

"She said she was glad. The usual Pin hard-shell talk, I suppose, but she said when she found out she was not their biological child she was actually relieved. She said she had always felt she had no connection to them."

"But do you think she even suspected that Nelson was her mother? If she felt so different from the Princes, do you think she felt some connection to Nelson? Her anger makes so much sense then," I said. Is that what she was thinking, I wondered, as she played with my hair and seemed so lost in thought, and would rise abruptly and say, let's go.

Merch shook his head, said nothing.

"But who saw the two of them on table-land in the middle of the night?" I asked.

"The schoolgirls, you know, Nandita and some others." I had not seen the schoolgirls, so I supposed they had not seen me.

I am glad I was so stoned that night. It sort of cushioned the news.

But why had Nelson been arrested? Had she confessed? Why should she confess? How could she have done it? It was hard for me to keep all these parallel and intersecting events in place. I began to feel breathless and dizzy. "Did Nelson confess to the killings?"

"Well, I mean, what's there to confess? All the pieces fit together. She was seen every step of the way: Pin got a letter from her cousin revealing that Nelson was her mother. She rushed out into the night, she went to Nelson's room, one of the girls heard the two of them fighting from her dorm. She heard Pin sobbing and storming out. Nelson followed her to table-land, where other girls saw her sitting on the rocks behind Pin. They did not know if Pin even realized that Nelson was there. Pin was found dead with signs of a struggle."

There are some steps that are still dark, Mr. Much, I wanted to say, but kept quiet.

"So you mean she found out on the day of her death that Nelson was her mother?" I asked. Hold me safe and tight, she had said, but I had not. Her world had turned more cruel that very night, and she had come to me. I had sent her to her mother empty and wounded.

I thought of her face when she walked into my room and put her hand inside my blouse on that last night. She must have just found out. Must have walked straight to me. I had betrayed Pin twice that night. In my room, and again on table-land. A third time the same night, and I could well be St. Peter of the Bible, I thought bitterly.

I was sweating. Soon I was out of the car, head over the side of the road, vomiting. I threw up everything I had ever eaten, and then some more, and was retching and hiccoughing and sobbing for long afterwards.

It was Shabir who efficiently pulled off my vomit-stained dupatta and held my hair back from my face while I bent over puking my heart out into the ditch. He stood over me, pointing in awe at things I had eaten.

"Psychedelic. This tomato haldi combination, you should see it," he called over to Samar. Samar declined. This was more intimate than I wanted it to be and I was embarrassed at first. But he was so kind and casual and matter-of-fact that I began to feel quite calm, and allowed him to comfort me.

"Your vomit has a Brahmin smell," said Shabir.

When at last I could hold my head up, he went to the car and came back with a thin checked napkin and a bottle of water. After I was done washing and wiping, he fished around in his front pocket and produced a packet of supari to suck on.

"Too much," he said. "Much too much. Want some acid? I have this great stuff. It's very mild."

If it would help, if it could take the world off my shoulders, I would do it. I looked at Merch. He shook his head. "Sit and have a joint," he said.

"But acid is the king of drugs," said Shabir, indignantly.

"Just let her chill," said Samar.

The ground was shifting under us. Now it was two of us in the backseat, and everyone was talking to me. I was no longer peeping at them from behind the Prince, and the man by my side was Mr. Immature Much.

We sat in the car, listening mostly to Shabir hold forth about the benefits of hallucinogenic drugs. In Kolhapur, the monsoons were less intense, and we were in a patch of cool, cloudy days. Shabir seemed somewhat petulant that Merch had prevented me from having acid.

How did she feel, falling so fast, hurtling towards the sharp rocks that broke her skull?

And then I saw her. I saw her eyes as she flew down the cliff. Her face was upside down right in front of me, her hair hanging around her face. I felt the dark rocks around, and the wind rushing past. Her face was transformed with glee, her arms outstretched to embrace the rocks, her raincoat like a cape that Superman might wear. She was happy then, and I knew this was true. She had been dreaming of this, perhaps since the days she had swooped and swirled on her skates in the evening light, playing with the thought of falling.

Merch reached out and held my hand. He held it shyly, tentatively. His hand was trembling.

They deposited me on my doorstep deep in the night and sped off to Panchgani, where they said it had started to rain again. "It will be great to drive in over the mountain at dawn," said Samar.

"Much love," Shabir shouted as the car screeched down the road.

I stumbled into my bed in the corner of the last room. Everything will be clearer tomorrow morning, I thought, as I tucked in the mosquito net around me. Jalgaon Masi was snoring softly in the bed next to mine.

TWENTY-TWO

Outcaste Bhabhi

THE WONDROUS VISION of the night before had vanished when I awoke the next morning with a head like lead. The light was loud, the bed beside me was made, the counterpane down, the mosquito net bunched and tucked. I knew with dread that it must be at least past ten. No one ever slept past eight in the Kolhapur house.

I crossed the chowk and stole into the bathroom. I heard Bhabhi bangles clanking busily in the kitchen, but I did not look in. I had never been one of the sunny children, the ones who were petted and pinched and scolded. I was a slinker, and so the family left me alone unless they had something to say.

The light bounced angrily off the open courtyard, poking sharp knives into my eyes. I kept my head down. In the bathroom, clothes were soaking in green and orange plastic buckets. The white towels and kitchen cloth bucket were still steaming. In the small, chipped mirror, my face was bloated, my blot livid, my hair dry and disordered. Why I had felt beautiful last night I could not imagine. I could not imagine ever having been beautiful. I could not imagine ever being beautiful again.

"Jalgaon Masi has gone to the hospital this morning, so we did not wake you," called majli Bhabhi as I was sneaking back past the chowk. Although the sisters ruled the house, the two older daughters-in-law, whom everyone including the servants called Bhabhi, ran it. The guests, the servants, intricate car schedules, the beds, the meals, the pickles, the clothes, the matching ribbons and socks in the right rooms. They were united in their disapproval and dislike for the youngest daughter-in-law of the house, the outcaste Bhabhi.

Badi Bhabhi, the eldest, walked into the house trailed by Ramu, who was loaded with bulging bags and baskets of fruits and vegetables. She had a fresh jasmine gajra around her bun.

"You look very white, Charu," she said.

"I threw up last night," I said. "And again just now," I added for good measure.

"Where did you have dinner last night?"

"Ideal Idli House," I muttered, too weak to think of anything but the truth.

"Chi, chi. We'll call the doctor."

"No, I'll feel better if I sleep," I muttered.

I pulled the sheet over my head and slipped into a dope drenched dream. The happy Pin I had seen last night was gone. Her face was dark and narrow now. She was more than midway down the cliff, the sharp jaw of the rocks was close. "Putrid, paltry life," she said, and sighed, a long deep sigh that echoed through the cliffs. She sees it all now. In this vast falling moment, she has a second lifetime. She knows that if she can pop back up and walk back down the row of silver oaks, she will have a glowing life. She starts grabbing at rocks and bushes, bruised and desperate.

I stand at the edge of the cliff, where she had stood before she fell. I look down, down. I see her face, bruised and bleeding, filling up the dark cradle of the hills like a cloud,. "I could be with you, Charu," she calls. "I would be good and lovely." Her voice is sad, bouncing around the hills, and then she starts pleading: "Come down, come, Charu. Chaaaruuuu, Charu." I do not know what I am about to do. I do not know what I *can* do. I think I have the power to pull her back again.

And then the dream twists, and it is not Pin at all but my ayi floating through the great black cliffs. Not my ayi with the graying hair and cotton sari, but a cloud of dark air that I somehow know is her. The mist turns gray and smoky, closing around her. But of course her body can't be falling from the cliff. Her body is still in the hospital bed, my dream voice reminds me sharply. *Be back again*. Please, please, please, Ayi, be back again.

"But I must fold the clothes first," I was muttering aloud as I tossed awake, drooling, to find Veena, the outcaste Bhabhi, standing by my bed.

"I heard you were sick," Veena said as she pulled up a chair and sat beside the bed. She had become decidedly more friendly towards me since the Episode.

It was Veena the outcaste Bhabhi who had found Ayi that fateful morning, unconscious on her bed. Veena was the youngest daughter-in-law of the house. She was married to Anil the cross-eyed photographer, the only brother who was not in the family business. It had been a love marriage. The women, in a body, disapproved of her. She was bold, she was disrespectful, she was not from our caste, she refused to cover her head when she saw Dada, she had a brother in America who was married to a fat white woman, she wore pants when she went out with her husband at night. Even the servants said mean things about her.

The outcaste Bhabhi had no children. She did not crowd around the kitchen like the other women, but kept to her room, doing "God knows what." She came and went as she liked, without telling anyone.

"As though this is a hotel," said badi Bhabhi bitterly.

But she had saved my mother. It was eleven in the morning: the children in school, the men at work. The office lunch was cooked and packed and sent out with the drivers, the women were bathed. Nani was in the prayer room, enfolded in flowers and incense. The house was quiet except for the rhythmic thud of the dhoka as Ramu washed the clothes in the last bathroom.

Jivibai, who lived in a hut outside the compound, took some of the credit. "I told Veena tai to go inside and check," she would say, hovering around to interject her moment of glory every time the story was being freshly told. "Doors are always open at this time, I told her."

Jivibai had been working for the family since Ayi and the aunts were young. Her youngest son, Ratan, had taught me to bicycle, running behind me as I wobbled round and round the house. Jivibai came in the morning to mop and sweep the house. When she found Ayi's door closed that day, she asked Veena to go in and check if Ayi wanted the room cleaned.

Veena found my ayi lying on her back, her breathing shallow and labored. Veena first called to her, and when she did not stir, went up to the bed and touched her, and then tried to shake her awake. She said nothing to Jivibai waiting outside. She did not call majli Bhabhi, who was in the kitchen; she did not call Nani, who was praying. She marched straight to the phone in the front room and called her mother, a lady doctor with a thriving dispensary at Makani Manor, who instructed her assistant to call for an ambulance and then came charging into the house, her stethoscope around her neck.

"You should at least have told us," chided badi Bhabhi later when Veena was being lauded as a heroine.

"She was unconscious. I knew there was not time to waste," she retorted dismissively. She became, if anything, more arrogant. The women now began to talk incessantly about her.

"As though we would have wasted any time," complained badi Bhabhi to each sister in turn. "We could have called Dr. Dhandekar. He is right here, and he is, after all, our family doctor. Why get her mother involved? You know she will gossip."

Everyone tutted and tsked. Except for Tai. "She saved my sister's life," she said firmly to them. "Both she and her mother."

Tai marched into Veena's room and hugged her. "Dada and I are going to meet your mother this evening. To thank her also," she said with tears in her eyes.

I looked wanly up at Veena's long, pale face in front of me. I felt as if there were a steel band around my head. I realized that I had smoked too much dope last night. I did not want to talk or listen to Veena. But then I felt a rush of gratitude. She had saved Ayi's life, that was for sure. Ayi had gotten her hands on a stash of sleeping pills, no one knew from where, and then taken them all that morning. The dose was large enough to kill her. It had been a question of timing. I could imagine how the two bumbling Bhabis would have skittered around and called all the servants, and then perhaps their husbands in the office, and then the incompetent family doctor. They could have wasted hours.

"I am so glad it was you who found her," I said.

"They wanted me to call that old doddering doctor of theirs. He gives saline injections to the servants for everything and then charges them 20 rupees for a shot. They are so backward," she said.

Veena had been married for five years. She had recognized me as a fellow outsider from the beginning and would call me to her room sometimes to talk. "Why do you wear only these chudidars? You should wear pants to college," she would say. "After you get married, you won't get a chance." She had even offered me her pants. In those days, I had been withdrawn from her, afraid that I would be seen as being in her camp if I was observed chatting with her.

"It was the best thing you did, calling your mother," I said. She took that as a sign that she could now unburden herself to me.

She launched into a litany of hurts and backward thoughts and deeds committed against her by my family. Everything started with an emphatic "they."

"*They* think that I am defective because I have no children," she said. "As though I am a toy or something. But wait, I'm going to show them."

Jivibai came in to inform me that khichdi had been made especially for me, and the Bhabhis had asked if I wanted to come to the kitchen to eat.

"Can't you see she is sick? Bring it here on a tray," said Veena, imperiously. I cringed. She was always exceedingly short and rude with servants. Jivibai walked away muttering loudly. "Ordering this and ordering that all the time. And who is going to clean up after? They need to get a special maid just for that memsaab . . ." until her voice faded away.

"Want a cigarette?" she asked with a conspiratorial wink.

I had heard rumors that she often smelled of cigarettes. I eyed her tentatively. Perhaps she had even smoked dope. Should I hint at it?

Good thing I didn't. "Your friends last night, be careful. They looked like druggists," she said, leaning towards the bed. "*They* don't know about these things. But I have been around. I can see the signs."

"I don't think I can smoke now," I said. "I feel too sick. But another time."

"Come anytime. I always have some in my room," she said, and left.

I felt sorry for her. Unless she produced some golden sons quite soon, she would remain on the bottom layer of the food chain forever. This was a part of the Hindu Joint Family law, unwritten but sacrosanct. At its center was the great divide between being a daughter and a daughter-in-law.

Daughters were raised on malai and rosewater, loved and nurtured and trained to be sweet and soft and pliant. They were to be led tenderly to the great crossing before they turned twenty. On the other side, as daughters-in-law, they must eat dirt for the first ten years. They must be prepared for a life of criticism and scrutiny and acts of random cruelty.

It was one of the mysteries of womanly life: how at least 88.8 percent of women forgot the bitter dirt they were fed in a household of strangers and started feeding it once again to the wives of their young sons. Perhaps it's a Darwinian thing, I thought once, when I was stoned. Survival of the fittest. Break those lumps of clay when they first enter the house; only then can they become matriarchs. Keep your son in your hand, and only then will he be good to you when you are an old widow. No matter if his wife will hate you for life, just as you hate your husband's mother. Like an intricate group dance, I saw them all, the women of the house doing Scottish dancing in the chowk. In saris, of course. It was almost impossible to imagine all their immense lumpy bodies in kilts.

A woman could rise to the top in her forties. But only if all the "ifs" fell into place. If she had a good marriage with a strong man, if she had borne a good son, she could be forceful by forty. And if she was clever and political, she could become a matriarch at fifty.

I didn't see how poor Veena could get there. I could not see how I could ever get there. For me, there was even less hope. I could end up like the spinster aunts with polio and the impoverished widows in white saris living frugally on the outer edge of the family, peeling potatoes and minding the red chilies drying on the roof. Either timid or bitter. There was nothing else. No Pin, maybe no Ayi, even. No children, no good man by my side.

I sobbed into my pillow with self-pity for the entire afternoon.

I wobbled to the bathroom at three, while the house was in its afternoon coma. The Bhabhis were resting in their bedrooms behind closed doors, the servants were snoring on their pallets in the corridor behind the kitchen. I had a long bath, and creamed and composed my face to a modicum of acceptability, though my eyelids were like powder puffs from all the weeping. I tied my hair in a tight, high knot. My face felt like an open sore. "Back in the days of the blot," I said to the mirror, my heart lying broken at my feet.

Padmaja, my perfectly superior Timmins cousin, bustled in at four brandishing the *Evening News*. I was playing carom with majli Bhabhi's daughter.

"Charu, Charu, did you know all this?" Padmaja called as soon as she had removed her slippers. Her children scrambled out of the car with their schoolbags. She ordered her daughter to take my place at the carom board and beckoned me into the kitchen. The house was bustling again, the children coming back from school, the Bhabhis having their evening tea.

It was on the front page, bottom left.

FOUL PLAY IN GIRLS' BOARDING SCHOOL

> The body of Miss Moira Prince, a teacher at Miss Timmins' School for Girls in Panchgani, was discovered at the bottom of table-land cliffs on the 28th of August. The principal of the school, Miss Shirley Nelson, is being held for her murder.
>
> Foul play was suspected when the 27-year-old British woman was found under the cliffs with a broken neck. The local police initially arrested Shankar Tamde, a servant from the school who was at the scene of the crime. He was being held without bail.

Events have now taken a more shocking turn, in the light of recently unearthed facts. The young woman died shortly after she received a letter which revealed that the school's longtime principal, Miss Shirley Nelson, 46, a British citizen and a member of the Scottish Presbyterian Mission, was in fact her mother. As an unwed mother, she had given the young girl up for adoption at birth. It appears that no one in the school, not even the deceased, had been aware of this relationship.

Students at the school have recently revealed that on the night of the murder, Moira Prince had gone into the principal's room, from whence loud arguments and shouts were said to ensue. Subsequently, both Prince and Nelson were spotted on the top of the table-land cliffs by a group of three students.

"Once we knew that she had been at the scene of the crime, our suspicions became more pronounced," said Inspector Dhananjay Wagle, head of the Panchgani police. Nelson has now been detained for questioning. Because of her position and nationality, she is being held in Vai Hospital. "It would not seem right to put her in lockup with the common criminal elements," said Inspector Wagle.

"Santosh called me from the office. I picked up the evening paper on the way back from the children's school. Look, my hands are still cold. I am in shock," Padmaja was in a state of barely controlled hysteria. "And anyway, who was this Moira Prince? Did you know her?"

And so I began to dole out the truth. I was stingy at first, clutching at the facts, hoarding my nuggets of information like the Timmins girls hoarded their tuck. I still thought of it as my own private truth.

Majli Bhabhi was making up fruit plates for the children and guests. She placed an expertly sliced apple in a steel plate between us. I bit into a sliver, tart and crisp. I still saw the truth as round and finite, something I could cut into discrete little slices with a sharp knife.

"Yes," I told Padmaja tersely, "I knew her. She lived in Sunbeam. But I did not know she was Nelson's daughter. No one knew. Not even Hendy." And then I made a dramatic exit. I ran out of the kitchen with tears clutching at my throat.

"What's the matter with *her*?" I heard Padmaja's voice floating up from behind me. I wanted to run to my bed. But I ran into the bathroom and pretended to throw up instead.

Last night and this morning I had been thinking only of Pin. Of her longing face when she said, *Only your very own people.* I had picked what pertained most to me in the story—the gap between her running out of Sunbeam with the letter in her pocket and the flinging of the letter at Nelson. The hole in the evening that belonged to me. I thought only of how I had betrayed her while she sat in my room with the letter in the pocket of the jeans lying crumpled near my desk. I had sent her to her death.

Reading the newspaper report with Padmaja that afternoon was when the ghastly, ghastly truth came crashing down upon my head and nearly never left.

Nelson was in for murder, and I alone knew she was innocent. I might have to jump into the fire myself to save her.

TWENTY-THREE

Park Benches

THE NEXT MORNING, I decided to go to Panchgani. I told Baba, who was staying in the spare bed in Ayi's hospital room. We sat on the park bench outside the hospital. The sky was purple. Baba and I were eating bananas that we had taken from the shelf in the metal nightstand in Ayi's hospital room. The bananas had gone too ripe, you could smell them as you entered the room, and so we took them out to the park to eat. We sat on a gray granite bench that had been donated by Babubhai Sanghvi to the memory of his loving wife Parvati.

This is the rule of park benches and drinking fountains at train stations, hospitals, and nursing homes across the country. They must be dedicated *to* the memory of a loving wife and mother, or they must be *in* loving memory of a husband and father. The good wife is loving, the good husband loved. No respectable park bench could dare be dedicated to the memory of a loving husband. What would we say for Ayi? Loving wife, mother, daughter, sister. Everyone wanted her love. The bench would be effusive. But at least it would be respectable. Unlike mine.

I had a copy of the previous day's *Evening News*. Of course, Baba had read it. Everyone had. But I read it out to him again. I told Baba for the first time on the bench that evening that the dead girl had been my friend. I started sobbing as I told him how she was my first real friend, and now she was dead. Baba put his arm around me. He pulled out the big white handkerchief he kept always in his back pocket and dried my eyes. Blow your nose, he said, holding the handkerchief to my nose just like he used to when I was young and had a cold. And so I started crying again. It felt good, to be sobbing my heart out.

We sat silently, staring at distant mountains. Baba plucked a leaf and rolled it around absently. Then he held it to his right eye and squinted into it. Suddenly, I saw him in his uniform looking out at foam-flecked seas. I forgot so often that my father was once a sailor and had a sea bobbing inside him.

"I am sorry," he said, still looking at the mountains through his leaf telescope. "I am sorry I have led you to a life seen through a tunnel."

He passed the leaf to me. "See," he said, "how little you can see of the mountains like this? This is the world I have shown you."

You wait for something all your life, but when you know it is coming, you feel almost nothing. I knew I must be quiet. I knew the story was coming now, unasked.

"Your ayi and I used to wonder when you should be told. We always meant to tell you. But of course it became harder as more time passed. Now is as good a time as any, I suppose. Now there is no purpose in keeping my past hanging over your head. It should have been upon my head alone. That is what I thought at the time, when I bowed out."

His voice was detached, as though he had practiced this many times on sleepless nights.

"I do not excuse myself, you must understand that. But in my defense, I will say this. I had reasoned that I retreated to protect you both."

My mind was as still as a pond, waiting.

"But it was a mistake," he said. "I did not even know, Charu. I did not even know that your ayi was as unhappy as I was. I was afraid of losing her. And you. That was the bottom line."

He talked in a quiet, even voice, every syllable of every word pronounced in full. It was how he always talked. He had taught himself English from reading books, he told us often. "I am an autodidactic," he said proudly. He had learned his accent by listening to the officers talk when he first joined the navy, a boy from a small town along the Konkan coast. His relatives were landowning farmers. We did not meet them very often.

His tone was the same, the way he talked was the same, but the sound inside the words was different. I heard a trickle of feeling bubbling up at the bottom of a drying well. We did not look at each other. We did not talk to each other. He was talking to the mountains, and the mountains were echoing his words back to me.

"You see, I rose so fast up the ladder, I became ADC to the Admiral at a young age. He became like a father to me. When I was married and your ayi and I went to the navy parties, everyone would look at me. They envied me, and why shouldn't they? I was a favorite, and your ayi was the most beautiful woman in the world. We were such a handsome couple in those days. Sometimes I would feel that the entire room held its breath when we walked in.

"You know what I loved first about her? Her eyes, her fair skin, her dimples, everyone admired those. But I loved the way she carried herself. Your grandfather had invited me to dinner in Bombay, and we were having a drink when she walked in. She had perfect aplomb. I knew she would always walk upright. I could not believe my luck."

The image popped out, unbidden, of Ayi stooped over, being led to the bathroom.

"I know it is not a charitable thought, Charu, but I can't help thinking it was her revenge. Now the whole world will say how unhappy she must have been with me. All these years, not a word of recrimination, and then, suicide, just like that. She should have nagged and wept like other disappointed wives. I could have lived with that. But this—this slap in the face."

Baba's voice became uneven, as did his breathing. This was not part of what he had practiced telling me. His chest heaved.

Don't cry, Baba, please, please don't cry, I thought, digging my nails into my palms. That will be the last straw. Mothers cry, lovers can cry, but fathers don't cry, except perhaps during death in the family. That is just how it is, and I don't care what they say in women's lib.

Thankfully, Baba regained control.

"I suppose I am to blame," he said. "I was busy containing my bitterness. I left her to take care of the happiness department. And no family can survive without that." A small yellow butterfly fluttered around us with gay abandon.

Baba, I wanted to say, cut it to the bone. Tell me what horrible crime you committed. I was impatient, dismissive even, as I had been all my life with Baba. But then I felt the stab of my own sins and betrayals, and realized how hard it would be to tell them to my parents.

Finally, Baba took up the thread. "I was on top of the world," he said. "I used to go to the Admiral's flat every so often. It was such a beautiful flat, Charu. I used to think, my family will live in a flat just like this when I am admiral. But there was a lot of jealousy in those days. They poisoned the Admiral's mind. He turned against me and helped to frame me."

"But he loved you," I said, remembering how much our lives had been lived in the glow of the Admiral's lamp. *Even the Admiral thought so*, or *What would the Admiral say*, or *Today the Admiral said*—these were the words of our household. Everytime we went to meet him, I was dressed and admonished, and my mother carried a steel box carefully tied with a snow-white cloth containing her homemade amti, which the great man professed to love.

He always pinched my cheek, smiled at my mother, and said, "Ah, my favorite dish from my favorite navy wife." He was tall and fat and had a mustache. His name was Bajaj. I was instructed to call him uncle, though I never actually spoke to him.

After we went to Indore, the admiralisms died away, but that was no surprise to me, since our whole past life had been cast out. I had no inkling that the Admiral himself had played a role in my father's fall.

"But how could he, Baba, suddenly? I mean, how could he turn against you just like that?"

Baba did not explain. He repeated himself, as though that would make it clear.

"There was a lot of jealousy," he said. "They saw me rise too fast to the front. My contemporaries felt threatened, and so they decided to frame me. There was a large smuggling ring operating within the navy at that time. A lot of top officers were involved. This had just surfaced, and we had a sting operation under way. Only the Admiral and a few of us officers knew about it.

"Captain Puri posed as a whistle-blower. He gave testimony that I was the officer behind the whole ring. They cooked up all sorts of evidence. They had people come in and swear that we sent signals from our flat in Walkeshwar. They stated that I had used my position with the Admiral to jockey this posh flat—everyone called it the posh flat, though no one had even seen it—directly overlooking the water. And at nights, I turned lights on and off as a signal to the smuggling boats. They said we landed the goods on Governor's Beach, which was just below our building. For this, they had hard evidence. The goods were landed on that beach, you see, and so in this way they took truths only they knew and wove in untruths along the way to keep their story strong.

"It was hard to prove, because some of my colleagues came out and said that the allegations were untrue and the charges were trumped up.

"The Admiral stayed above it all. He was a smart man. Then, on Independence Day, he gave this famous address on All India Radio. It was a very patriotic speech, which was the fashion in those days. Full of duty and sacrifice. It was clever, I remember, a sort of echo of Nehru's Tryst with Destiny speech.

He spoke about how proud he was of our navy, how honored he was that the people of India had given him this sacred trust of protecting our beloved country.

"Remember, we are still in 1959. A young country still determined to stay on high moral ground. The legacy of Gandhi and all that sort of thing.

"Anyway, after building up the patriotism with a theatrical cadence, the Admiral dropped his voice to a serious register. 'My heart breaks,' he said, 'to have to say this, but within the very institution that you have placed your lives for safe keeping, within our navy itself, among the men who hold the honor of our nation, the men entrusted with guarding our women and children, there is a ring of evildoers. Their crime is not a crime against a fellow human. It is a crime against the nation, and that is the greatest crime of all.' He made an oath to the people of India that he would find these criminals and purge them. 'Bhayon aur behno,' he said. 'Brothers and sisters, if I cannot purge these traitors from our navy, I will resign my post. I will lay down my arms and resign because I am not worthy of the sacred trust of my nation.' I seem to know it by heart, because snatches of it played all the time during news of my trial. He must have used the word sacred at least ten times.

"He was politically astute, of course. He didn't get to where he was for nothing. He stopped short of calling for a witch hunt. He refused to name any names. 'The matter is still under investigation,' he told the press sternly. 'And I will not obstruct the path of justice. You must remember that we are a democracy.'

"So from being a mid-level naval corruption matter—you

know, smuggling of shampoos and cassette players—it turned into a morally charged national issue. "Everyone was watching. Overnight, my photograph was on the front page. "Is He the Traitor?" That was the headline in the *Blitz*."

I cringed for my poor parents. "But did he really believe that you were doing this? How could he?"

Baba shook his head sadly, but did not look at me.

"Captain Puri and the Admiral went to great lengths," he continued. "They even resorted to planting foreign goods in a Chitnis Transport truck, you know. Said we used my father-in-law's trucks. Dada batted it all down, of course, probably paid off all sorts of people and called in some of his favors. Saw to it that the name Chitnis Transport did not appear again in the papers, though the dispute continued about the planted goods.

"In the end, they did not have enough conclusive evidence. I was found not guilty by the court-martial. But it had all gotten murky and emotionally charged. And then your mother lost the child. We knew you were all we had. We decided to take you away and start again."

I turned and faced him. He was fifty-seven years old, but he looked older, he had a shriveled air. I could not imagine him as an admiral. I recoiled from him. I decided to tell him nothing of my guest appearance—for that was how I now saw it—on the fateful night of Pin's death. Many times in my life I have put myself on that spot on the park bench and wondered why I did not even hint to Baba that I had a hand in there. It was a snap decision, composed in equal parts of cowardice, caution, and concern, I suppose. Or a deceitful nature, inherited no doubt, from the father.

"I need to go to Panchgani for one or two days Baba," I said. "I need to meet friends and teachers after this tragedy."

"It is a difficult time for you, beta," he said. "Go ahead. We will hold the fort down."

TWENTY-FOUR

Foreign Dispatches

KAKA'S WAS NOT a nice place for young lady teachers. It was the cheapest restaurant in Panchgani. The main dining room was noisy with the clanking of plates and pots and waiters shouting orders to the kitchen. Farmers from the valley in white cloth caps, mochis in dhotis, and peons in khaki pants sat sipping chai under the watchful glare of the owner, Kaka. *Ladys and familys up the stairs*, said the sign above the cash counter. The upstairs waiter, a cheeky child with a grimy napkin slung over his shoulder, shouted our order to the downstairs waiter. Merch had barely lit his cigarette when two steaming plates of bright yellow dal fry were smartly slapped down before us.

As always, I forgot about the blot when I was facing him.

"I wish I could just run away," I said to him.

The mist drifted in through the open window and swirled around us. We could not see the street below, only faint blurs of yellow and blue raincoats gliding by.

Merch was swiping the last of his dal neatly with a piece of pau bread. He was a gentlemanly eater, slow and methodical. He finished his bite, and then sat back and drank half his glass of water.

"We *could* go across the Sahara, you know," he said, a shy smile lighting his eyes, "but it would have to be in a pink car. With green stars."

I had come in from Kolhapur that morning. I had planned to go directly to school from the bus stop. But instead I had found myself walking towards Merch's room. The rain was coming down in a steady drizzle. A white cloud of mist hung over the town so that I felt I was wandering alone in the world. I was glad, because I did not want to run into anyone just yet.

Merch's door was bolted from the outside, and so I waited under the tree, staring into space, thinking of nothing. I waited for a drop of rain to trickle down my nose, and caught it with my tongue. Finally, he came walking up the lane, in jeans and the usual rust sweater, a large black umbrella mushrooming above him. I realized that he never wore a raincoat.

"Aha," he said with an excited laugh. "Charu on a weekday."

I followed Merch demurely up the stairs and held his books while he pulled the squeaky bolt from the door. Snakes of memories slid out from every corner, wound themselves around my ankles. How could I enter the room when I could still see her lounging on the bed? I saw "our" counterpane spread out on his bed and felt a red flush of shame spread up to the roots of my hair. I wondered if he had washed it before he had spread it. I wondered if he knew.

The Prince and I had started taking an unused counterpane kept in Merch's bottom drawer and spreading it over the bed before we made love. His room had dusty corners, but his cupboard was neat, everything ironed and piled in the right categories, down to the socks and hankies. I felt guilty, opening his cupboard and going through his things.

"Let's not do this, Pin," I said. "He might not like it."

"Do you think he will like our female discharges across his clean sheets then?" she asked, mocking. She knew I recoiled from brass tacks. "Maybe he would," she said, laughing. "With Merch, you never know. And anyway, can you imagine him ever being angry with you?" I could not.

"He may be the Mystery Man, but once he loves you, you can do anything. He'll always understand," Pin assured me.

"So you think he loves me?" I was surprised. But once she said it, I knew it to be true.

"But aren't you the princess?" she asked. She seemed to think I should know it.

"And you, doesn't he love you too?" I said to her, for I myself was sure of it.

"I suppose you could say he does. But I am such a Scorpio. I bite people I love."

I saw a demon pop out of her head and pause above her curls, but then it passed, and she bared her teeth, lunged at my shoulder, and bit it, holding my naked arms pinned against my breast. "And I eat them all up before dinner," she said, continuing the nibble up the ridge of my shoulder all the way down the collarbone.

And so we always made love on the faded green counterpane smelling of soap. Before we left the room, we would fold it and put it back in the same spot, under the clean sheets and towels.

It was hard for me to step over the threshold, and perhaps he sensed it. "Coming to Kaka's for lunch?" he asked. "They make the best dal fry in Satara District." He left his books on the table, and we floated back down into the mist.

Those first days were so raw we walked on eggshells towards each other.

I had come to Panchgani planning to pull Nelson from the gallows. I planned to tell someone—anyone, perhaps Wilson, maybe even the Woggle—that I had seen Nelson leave tableland while Pin was still alive, but I was unclear about who, what, and how, and not willing to think clearly on the consequences this would have for me.

But I allowed the heavy mantle of responsibility to blow off my shoulders as I sat atop the world with Merch. We decided to go on a bilingual journey. Every word and phrase we said would mean something in two languages at the same time. We laid out our phrases like a road map: far white luggage, we could say, after hey bug. What lovely, we could exclaim after we passed paddy fields. And if by chance there was an accident, we could say "tout le monde" (which means "broken head" in Marathi).

"Prepare the car," I told him gaily as I gathered up my things. "We will depart at dusk."

"First stop, Casablanca," Merch called after me as I climbed down the steep stairs and walked to school alone.

There were three Ambassador cars parked in the school compound. Fathers and mothers and ayahs holding baby brothers were milling around.

I came upon Miss Wilson leading a plump dark man in his forties out of the Principal's office.

"Oh, how nice to see you, Miss Apte," said Miss Wilson. "I do hope your mother is better."

She turned and introduced me to the man. "Mr. Bhansali, meet Miss Apte, a new teacher. She has been teaching English and English literature to Nandita this past term."

Mr. Bhansali held out his hand, and when I tentatively offered mine, he pumped it with purpose. The school was pale and shrunken around his vigorous male presence.

"Nandita has a gift for language," I said, feeling I needed to enter the conversation.

"Thank you. She will be pleased you said that. She thinks very highly of you," he said, and then turned to Miss Wilson.

"And please, do let me know if there is anything more I can do. I have complete confidence in Miss Nelson, and in all of you," he said, his voice smooth and reassuring. "As I told you, I can use my contacts if necessary." His smile was measured, like his daughter's.

"I will stop by the police chowki and speak to the inspector and will bring Nandita back for questioning," he said. "But of course, that may not be necessary." And then he winked at her. Miss Wilson, quite unused to being winked at by grown men, flushed and let out a nervous giggle.

The school was as chaotic as a beehive without a queen. Grave groups of parents were being escorted down the stairs and through the corridors and dorms by white teachers with red faces and brown teachers with white faces. They were fielding anxious queries with terse, tense statements. The girls, unbound, were squealing and jumping between them, tearing around the school in urgent, excited tangents.

I had pictured myself receiving the school news from Miss Henderson with the comfort of tea and Shrewsbury. But when I peeped into her dorm, I saw that she was otherwise engaged. I caught sight of her face as she was placating a father. He wore a white bush-shirt with blue diamonds embroidered down the sides. His black hair was gleaming and as polished as his shoes.

"I put my daughters here because I want them to get good convent education. Speak good English, you know. But we have to live in this society. I cannot have them exposed to scandals," he said, gesticulating with both hands, truculent as a turtle.

"Mr. Shah," said Miss Henderson severely. "We are not a convent here. You should know that, with three daughters here. We are not a Catholic school. This is a Protestant missionary school. We are not nuns, I'll have you know."

Mr. Shah looked confused for a minute or two, but then he got his bluster back.

"These foreigners think they can come here and disrupt our ways," he said contemptuously. He seemed to have forgotten that he himself had placed his daughters with these foreign women to learn their foreign language and culture. To his credit, he had perhaps never thought of the culture.

"We are all very upset about these events, Mr. Shah, and have tried to shield the girls. That is why we requested that you pick them up," said Miss Henderson. Her face was puffy, her eyes swollen and red-rimmed. The corners of her lips were lifted in a strained smile.

"But of course, if you feel you have lost confidence, there are many other schools in Panchgani, you know, even a Hindu school. Perhaps your family would be more comfortable in

Sanjeevan. It is behind Sandy Banks. They have holidays for Diwali and everything," she said in the severe voice she used with girls caught whispering after lights out.

Mr. Shah was furious. "Are you trying to tell me to take my children out of your school?" he bellowed.

Poor Miss Henderson took a step back, and stuttered, "No, no, I only meant—"

Mr. Shah drew himself up. He was the same height as Miss Henderson, perhaps even a bit shorter, but he seemed to tower over her, becoming suddenly a powerful man. I saw the white side retreating across the chessboard in disarray before my very eyes.

"You *may* tell me to take my children out of the school if you want," he said, nodding his head vigorously from side to side. "Yes, you can go ahead. Although they are very good girls, I will take them out. You can tell me that." He paused for breath before the punch line. "But kindly refrain from telling me where I *can* or *should* put them. I would advise you not to do that. I will put them in a Hindu school or a Muslim School or a Christian School—wherever I like. But that will be my business."

I felt it was kinder to leave Hendy then. All these men in the school. Never had there been so many men in the dorms.

I walked all the way down to the hospital and found Sister Richards sitting in her dispensary rolling cotton swabs, listening to Radio Ceylon. Sudden gusts of wind blew a patter of rain on the tin roof. I realized that the hospital was an outpost of the school, as surely as the school was an outpost of the empire. No male voices penetrated the enclave. The only sign of the chaos that reigned abroad was a red flask on the dispensary table.

"I always felt it," Sister sniffed. "Felt there was something fishy about your precious Miss Nelson. Too saintly. I've seen the world. When you go through a war, you know a thing or two." She eyed her flask longingly, but decided against taking a sip.

"No wonder that child acted up," she said, twisting her lips. "With that kind of mother. Keeping her here, not telling her."

"But Sister, Miss Prince didn't even know that Miss Nelson was her mother," I said, trying to reason with her.

"Don't you believe that, child. She could feel the pull of her own blood," said Sister, taking a discreet sip from her flask. "Blood always knows."

Sister must be right. It made sense. No wonder Pin could not leave the school. No wonder she hated Nelson so much. I saw Pin bound in a lasso and dragged through the dust behind Nelson riding an irreproachable white steed. Everything seemed to be coming at me from a distance. I wanted to grab the flask and take a swig of rum and wipe my mouth with the back of my hand.

"Are you staying here now?" called Sister as I walked towards my room.

Yes, I was about to say, for that was what I had planned. But the smell of the room brought back my yesterday self. I smelled little Charu Apte, the bobbing virgin, in a tight chudidar. "No," I shouted out in a voice whose vehemence and loudness surprised me. "No, I am just taking a few things for the holidays," I said, more placatingly. I sat on my bed.

The room looked just the same as it had on the first day. I had done nothing to make it mine. Just makeup on the dressing table, books on the shelves, and a bright counterpane that my ayi had sent in a neatly wrapped parcel, together with a bottle of pickle that had leaked onto a corner of the counterpane. Though I sent it to the dhobi three times, the smell of methi inserted itself into the room forever after, dueling with the disinfectant and dirty socks.

Two hospitals, I thought firmly—even two hospitals is one too many. I got up with a sudden burst of energy, pulled out my black metal trunk from under the bed, and began to throw my things into it.

One might, like Clint Eastwood, prefer to die beside a fast-running river, but the truth is that all the big things happen in a cesspit of bright lights, disinfectant, and pain. You are born, you give birth, you die, all in a hospital. And furthermore, everything happens in threes. Three witches below, three gods above. The Holy Trinity; Brahma, Vishnu, and Shiva. The world is held aloft by the magic number three. It was fitting, then, that the season of my rebirth was a three-hospital monsoon, although I would have preferred if fate had granted me three palaces.

The first was the hospital of desire, this room, where my body first awoke to passion; the second, the hospital from which I had just left the sweet shelter of my mother and walked out into the world alone; and the third, Vai Hospital, where Miss Nelson was being kept in custody. The role of this last one is harder to know. It keeps changing still.

I swept through my room like a maniac. I threw my books, my clothes, my towels, my sheets, my photos, my letters into the trunk. Then I took down the small brown suitcase from above the cupboard and put in a few things I might need in Kolhapur. I shoved the trunk under the bed and locked it, deciding I would come back for it another day; in a week, perhaps.

It was three in the afternoon. It was the right time to go to Willy. Or even Woggle. I should go to the Woggle and tell him what I saw.

I was tired suddenly, exhausted from the travel and turmoil. I had become lethargic and used to afternoon naps. I lay down and fell into an indolent sleep. It was evening when I awoke. I lay in bed in the gathering gloom for a while, considering my options.

It would do me no good to be blamed for a murder I did not commit. Once I said I was there, I would have to explain what I was doing. And if the affair trickled out—which it no doubt would, whispers and rumors and what was she doing up there in the middle of the night with that notorious woman, and yes, we saw the two alone in the hockey pitch, no doubt Ayi would die. She was hovering between life and death as it was. This would probably give her a big push to the other side. The Kolhapur gang would blame Baba's bloodline. I imagined Tai's face screwed up in disgust, saying, "The apple does not fall far from the tree."

But my silence would mean that Nelson would be the culprit. And she was innocent. Only she and I knew this. I should go and meet her in Vai, I thought. I should find out how she plans to defend herself.

I changed into a saffron kurta Pin had given me one day when I walked into her room drenched. It was a man's kurta, cut wide and short. I had washed it and kept it on the chair, meaning to return it. But now, no need, I thought, as I slipped it on and took a look at my flared hips in the mirror. Maybe in her clothes I can be as bold and heedless as she was. On the other hand, that might just have gone and got her dead.

TWENTY-FIVE

The Secret Mother

NO ONE ASKED me anything when I landed up in Merch's room that evening clutching my brown suitcase, though they were all there, Samar and Shabir and a boy with dirty feet who had smoked a joint with George Harrison. No one ever asked me anything. That was the beauty of being with them. I blithely believed that they knew nothing. I believed that they never spoke about me behind my back. I considered myself to be smooth on the outside; I thought I was sliding in and out of things, leaving no aura behind.

I had left the school and rushed to Merch's retreat, thinking on the way that maybe I should ask Merch for advice. He is a wise man, I thought, and so much older, almost thirty.

But Merch was edgy, nervous, pacing around the room, not meeting my eyes. Usually I would look up at him and almost always find his eyes on me.

The rest of them were discussing ways of getting a fresh

supply of drugs, now that Shankar's den of vice was no more.

"Rajneesh Ashram is best," said Shabir, and so they decided to drive to Poona that very night. I was worried about Ayi and had been planning to return to Kolhapur by the morning bus. But this was too good a chance to lose, I thought. I must strike while the iron is hot, I must meet Nelson right away.

"Can you drop me off at Vai," I asked, "since it's on the way?"

"Why Vai?" they asked astonished.

"I'll take the morning bus to Kolhapur from there," I said. Vai was the junction town at the foot of the valley, with a large, thronging bus station. "No, no," they said gallantly. "We'll take you. We'll go to Poona, we'll pick up the dope, and then we'll drive you to Kolhapur." They were most enthusiastic. I knew this meandering trip could take days, or weeks.

"At least let's start with Vai," I said.

It was already late when we were ready to depart. We were all stoned. We stopped for tea as often as we could. After each chai halt, we all smoked a joint. I cannot remember the name of the boy who had smoked a joint with George Harrison, because by the time we reached Vai, everyone had started calling him Hari & Son. They said they would call him Hari for short. Hari, who was trying to distance himself from the Beatles, pulled out a Jethro Tull cassette from his orange backpack, which he had bought, he said, from a foreign hippie in Colaba. I was very much in awe of him and hardly looked at him. I sat at my usual window, now with Merch's thigh pressed close, as we lurched down the winding ghat road in a mystical Tull trance.

Merch sat next to me, but we did not talk at all. That night after her death, we had gone to table-land and sat beside her rock. We wept bitterly, but it seemed to me that we had not spoken at all. I do not remember even looking up at him; I remember only that I felt almost safe, with my head against Merch's bony chest.

And now, today, he would not meet my eyes. But those first days were jagged and bittersweet with death—as Merch later put it—still perched on our left shoulders. I did not even find it strange. I did not speak to anyone at all. Not that it mattered. I liked this about being stoned.

We emerged out of the mist at 2 a.m. to find that it was not raining at all in the valley, and that there was a dim light burning outside the trucker's chai stop on the outer edge of Vai. We parked the car and honked and honked for service, and then at last we got out of the car to find the night-duty boy stretched asleep on the counter itself, his red-checked gamcha spread over his face.

He sat up and squinted up at us with bloodshot eyes.

"Khalas. Khatam. Nai hai," he said petulantly, seeing that we were not his regular brawny truck drivers but effete city kids. "It's over, go away," he said. The boy, who was sprouting his first beard, sank back on the counter as if it were the most comfortable bed in the world. He soon let out a contented snore, the cloth of the gamcha blowing in and out of his open mouth like an accordion. We stood around and watched him. A dim bulb burned above his head.

We smoked another joint while we wondered what to do.

"Let's check up on Gaiky," said Merch. "He might be able to help us score some grass here in Vai." I had heard Gaiky thrown into a few conversations, but had never met him.

We awoke Gaiky by throwing stones at his window until he popped his head out, his teeth gleaming white like tubelights. We tiptoed quickly past his deaf boxer, Raja, who barked halfheartedly just after we were safely in his bedroom. Gaiky's parents, *Dr. and Dr. (Mrs.) Gaikwad* as per the sign outside the garden gate, ran the gleaming Vai Hospital and lived in a large bungalow close to it. Gaiky had a whitewashed corner room overlooking the garden. He was the blackest boy I had ever seen; his skin was shiny, blue-black.

Tai should see him, I thought. Surely the original, or virginal—as the boys had recently been saying in a Tamil accent—black boy. The boys were now spending all their waking hours together, since Raisa was pregnant in Poona and Samar's wife, it seemed, had fled. Gaiky was wearing a cream-colored T-shirt that had "Indiana University" written across it in small chocolate-brown letters. I was told he went to college in Poona.

It was past four o'clock, and I could not smoke anymore. I lay down neatly curled at the corner of a mattress, covered myself with my dupatta—it was a red cotton, I remember—and fell asleep, hearing their chatter from afar. I awoke with a start at nine the next morning to find the five boys asleep, fanned out on Gaiky's large, high four-poster bed like the petals of a decaying poinsettia.

In the spare, echoing bathroom, I tied my hair in a tight knot, poured five mugs of cold water on alternate shoulders—head standing straight up as Ayi had taught me—and felt somewhat better after I had an intense, silent five-minute sob. Ayi said she had bathed with cold water even in the Kolhapur winters because Gandhiji had advised the youth of India to do so.

He must have done so to discourage sloth and sexuality from arising in their loins.

I had slept in Pin's kurta, and now, not wanting to go out to the car to get my bag, I put it back on and smoothed it out with my palms. I had begun to put kohl in my eyes, and a red vermilion tika as large as a coin on my forehead. It was Pin who suggested that I start putting on makeup, though I had not done it while she lived. "Bring out your eyes and make a big tika to balance your blot," she said, though she herself kept only a bottle of Johnson and Johnson baby oil on her dressing table, which she used to slick back her hair, and which we had used one Sunday afternoon to massage each other with long, languorous strokes, making ourselves as slippery as slabs of butter when we made love. And now here I was, drawing a round dot in a strange man's bathroom, wanting to tell Pin that she had been absolutely right. It was a bolder face that I was presenting now. I had always tried to get all eyes off my face, not knowing that the blot would suck up all the energy thrown at me like a black hole if I let it.

It was time to meet her mother. Her secret mother.

I tied my hair, still damp and gleaming, into a tight knot between my ears and was drying out the wondrous dupatta, which I had used as a towel, near the patch of sunlight in the bedroom when Gaiky sat up with a start. He had a small, straggly mustache, and he ran his fingers through it. He fumbled to the door, popped his head out, and shouted for two cups of tea.

He did not have to tell me to retreat when the servant knocked on the door. I popped behind a wall as he cracked his door and took the steel tray, his body blocking the servant's curious eyes. A girl in the room might be better than a bird in a bush, but she was not for the household to see.

We sat down like a civilized couple and I asked him as we sipped the fragrant ginger tea if I could meet Miss Nelson, the principal of my school.

"Yes," he said. "She is on the top floor of the hospital. Sort of like a house arrest. My mother said she is very quiet and polite, and always smiling. Come, I'll take you to the hospital. I am quite sure she is allowed to have visitors." He spoke English with a Marathi accent, his consonants thick and dipped in ghee, like mine. We felt instantly at ease with each other for that. The girls called it the vernacular accent, with easy contempt.

We agreed that there was no need to let the household know I had spent the night there. "Why uselessly create tension?" said Gaiky, and so he left the room alone and went and stood outside his window holding up his arms to help me down, smooth as a princess.

Sudden gusts of wind sent gray clouds scudding across the weak sun and shook the pink and orange bougainvillea that lined the stone path leading from Gaiky's house to the square three-story hospital building. Raja followed us reluctantly, as though it were his duty. I was not afraid; I was not even nervous. I realized I was still stoned from the night before, from the Bombay Black, which was purported to have opium. I was aware of everything. Between each step I took, I saw the gray pebbles that parted to allow stray stalks of grass. A pale watery sunlight shone down on the families of villagers waiting patiently on their haunches in the hospital compound.

"They bring their sick in by bullock cart and then sit around like this for days, waiting for them to get better. Or die, of course," explained Gaiky. He summoned a thin mali in ragged khaki shorts who was watering the flowers lined against the building, whispered to him for a moment, gave him some money, and patted him on the back. "This mali has good grass man. Clean stuff. Somu always gets it for me. I think I should take it up as a side business. I could sell it to the white hippies in Poona, though of course they prefer hash." He left me at the hospital steps and instructed a ward boy in white shorts to take me up to the gora memsaab.

I thought I had an advantage when I went in to meet Miss Nelson. After all, I knew she had not killed her daughter. She did not know I knew.

It seemed so far that no one had seen me up on table-land. It was my own personal hour, my borrowed hour. I would give it back when I was ready.

I had to find out what Miss Nelson would do to defend herself.

Her doors were shut. Even the window that opened onto the corridor was shut tight. I knocked on the door and got no answer at first. I waited a while—the hawaldar assured me that she was in there—and rapped louder on the glass pane. After a moment, I heard the tail end of the flush as she came out of the bathroom. I imagined her to be smoothing her dress, hanging her purse on the back of the chair—to see her is to see her purse—arranging her double layer of pearls, and then sitting erect and composing her face. It will be grave sorrow, I thought.

"Do you realize that she controls the whole school with her three looks?" Pin had said to me one night after a Sunbeam dinner as we walked along the winding lane lined with sleeping houses. It was during the days of the long rain, and we were both huddled under our separate raincoats, walking with arms crossed tightly against our breasts so that the elbows did not touch the soggy raincoat.

"She learnt it from my mother. The Three Looks: the smile that doles out praise, disappointment when expectations are not met, and grave sorrow when dispensing justice. No anger, never anger. And under it all, the mask of serene holiness. Control. I saw my mother teaching the bitch how to compose that face."

She turned so that we faced each other under the streetlight. With large golden drops of rain falling between us, she made the holy face for me, lips in a straight line with the corners slightly pursed to draw in the cheeks, eyebrows raised so the eyes appeared wide open.

I remembered now how she had looked eerily like Nelson to me then—her mother, her mother, no wonder now, and to think of her two mothers at the dinner table eyeing her with serene sorrow. I saw my Pin as a tousled tomboy with bruised elbows, squirming between them. Between her sacred mothers. Growing up between the secret sacred mothers, my poor Pin.

"Come in," she said.

I felt my first pang of panic when I saw that her face was puffed from weeping. I could look at nothing but the red rims of her magnified eyes as I walked towards her. She wiped her swollen nose and tucked the handkerchief in the sleeve of her pink pin-striped dress, which had pearl buttons running down the front and a collar with a red rickrack edge. I sat down across from her. She closed *The Pilgrim's Progress* by John Bunyan.

The hospital room was a standard one with the bed in the center and a metal nightstand. The only sign that it housed a prisoner, not a patient, was the two hawaldars lounging on a bench outside her door. There was a large wooden table by the window of her room with three upright chairs. She sat behind the table like a right-angled triangle, her back to the window.

She seemed too overcome to speak.

I wanted to leave her. I wanted to turn around and run back to Gaiky's safe room. But no, I thought, with my nails digging into my palms: *This is a step on which I must fall down, or else overleap.*

She must be waiting to get clearance from the mission in Scotland to get a lawyer to defend herself. I must find a way to ask her.

"How are you?" I asked, and wondered what on earth I could say next.

But she took the decision out of my hands.

"I was waiting for you," she said, as if she were sitting at her desk in the principal's office.

"Me?"

I felt she had just opened the door to my soul and seen the jars of guilt and packets of fear stacked inside. I felt as fluttery as a schoolgirl summoned to her office for the most heinous of crimes, such as cheating, stealing, or meeting a boy behind the senior dorm. Me? Why would she be waiting for me?

Maybe she had seen me up there after all. Maybe she thinks I killed her daughter after she left.

She seemed not to notice that I was faint with fear. "The Lord has prepared me for a messenger today," she said. She was calm and smiling down at me

OK, so that was better. She wasn't waiting specifically for me. She was waiting for a visitor; it just happened to be me. The earth went back to spinning along its prescribed course.

Behind her I could see terraces of emerald-green paddy fields going up the foothills.

"All of my life," she said in a grave, measured tone, "my morning Bible reading has been a staff that guides me through the day. I usually follow a pattern from my prayer guide. But now"—she smiled very briefly as she alluded to her circumstances—"I go to the Bible and read wherever it falls open. I feel closer to the Lord's wishes."

Today, she said, it fell open on First Chronicles 21:7.

There was a silence in the room. A shaft of sunlight burst through the window and fell upon her like a halo. I saw motes of dust dancing above her head.

I waited for her to read it, but she seemed hesitant, fingering her Bible. Then, wiping her nose firmly, and with a hint of her principal voice, she said, "Would you like to read it for me, Charulata?"

"You need to go to the beginning of the passage. Start from here," she said, turning the book towards me. The pages were thin and beautiful as onion skin. On a shelf to the right of her was a bottle of Marmite, a bottle of Mala's jam, and a tin of Amul cheese.

"How much should I read?" I asked her.

"Till the message is complete," she said, her hands folded in front of her.

I read.

And God was displeased with this thing; therefore he smote Israel.

And David said unto God, I have sinned greatly, because I have done this thing: but now, I beseech thee, do away the iniquity of thy servant; for I have done very foolishly.

And the Lord spake unto Gad, David's seer, saying,

Go and tell David, saying, Thus saith the Lord, I offer thee three things: choose thee one of them, that I may do it unto thee.

So Gad came to David, and said to him, Thus saith the Lord, Choose thee

Either three years' famine; or three months to be destroyed before thy foes, while that the sword of thine enemies overtaketh thee; or else three days the sword of the Lord, even the pestilence, in the land, and the angel of the Lord destroying throughout all the coasts of Israel. Now therefore advise thyself what word I shall bring again to him that sent me.

And David said unto Gad, I am in a great strait: let me fall now into the hand of the Lord; for very great are his mercies: but let me not fall into the hand of man.

So the Lord sent pestilence upon Israel: and there fell of Israel seventy thousand men.

I decided that the passage was complete and stopped reading.

Nelson spoke with an effort. "I struggled within myself all these days. But now I know. I must put myself in the hands of the Lord," she said in a soft and steady voice.

I was quite breathless and shivering. How was it that her God was giving her these specific messages? And if she had not killed Pin, what need was there for the Lord to send her pestilence and kill seventy thousand men?

I must control my wandering mind, I said sternly to myself. She had read this passage to herself this morning. And now she had made me read it. She was in the hands of her Lord. All fair and fine.

So what was the significance of a messenger? Was I Gad? Did have a direct line to her God? If so, I had not noticed.

And furthermore, why had she not been surprised to see me popping into her room? It seemed like I had been in this room forever. I saw her as a big black spider, saying, *Come into my parlor.*

I wanted to reach across her desk and grab a wooden ruler and rap my head smartly. Stop. Stop. Stop. She knows nothing. She's probably had slews of Timmins teachers coming to see her every day.

But I was appointed a messenger.

Maybe it was all for my benefit. She had made this whole thing up for my benefit.

But I heard Merch's mocking voice in my head: "And how could she be expected to know that you were about to drop by to her hospital room in Vai?"

No, all pure accident. I felt as if I were in another dimension Everything was happening so, so slowly. The smoke from the hawaldar's bidi drifted through the window, whole minutes went by between each curl.

I looked at her, hating her for the first time. That rock-solid armor of saintliness.

Maybe she knew I was on table-land that night. Maybe she knew I had seen her leave. And she was telling me she would put herself in the hands of God because I had not come forward to defend her. But there was a flaw in this thinking. If she knew I saw her leave, why not just come out and say so? Why not point the finger at me? I could well be construed to have a motive, once the sordid truth came out.

But the thoughts were slow and spluttering like ketchup coaxed out of a bottle. If she saw me see her leave, then she thinks I went up to Pin after she left. She thinks I killed her daughter.

I began to see the room closing in on me. Behind that mask she hates me. Just as she hated Pin. No, if she hated Pin, then why should she hate me for killing her? She loved Pin, she loved her not, I was pulling out petals from a flower, she loved her not, she loved her. I felt her burning eyes, I thought of her hands itching to squeeze my neck. I felt goose bumps up my spine.

And then, in slow motion, her face cracked open, and from underneath, a soft, slug-like face emerged. It was something in the way she screwed her lips.

To my utter and complete horror, she burst into tears. "Even that night, on table-land, I could not hug her," she said, and covered her face and wept, her whole body racked with sobs.

It was like watching a mountain melt into a lake.

I kept staring at her like a dolt, frozen. I looked at her and began to feel sorry for her. But I could not bring myself to stand up and pat her or anything. Better not to.

How must it have been for this woman, all those years,

seeing her daughter grow, not telling her, not a sign from any of them? And then, whispers in the night, while they thought Pin slept. Surely, I thought, the world was divided into two: those who had simple, strong, growing families, and those whose families twisted and bent further with each generation. We were the twisted lot, Pin and I.

The secret mother must have stayed with them in Nasik during all Timmins holidays, and maybe as she sat in the evenings and watched her daughter skating fiercely in the fading light, she dreamt of how she would tell her. I will wait until she is a woman, she might have thought. I will tell her on her wedding day, she might have mused. But as Pin grew with venom and tore her path of rebellion, Nelson resigned herself to her role. She could not cast her out, for she believed this was her lot, this her punishment for the sin of letting a young man in a tight uniform make love to her. But she could not tell her, either. Her child would remain a thorn in her side. And her deepest, darkest secret.

But the secret was out, and her daughter was dead.

Her sobs stopped as suddenly as they had started, and Nelson nailed her mask back on.

I wanted to leave, but not before I solved the mystery of the messenger. I fidgeted, hemmed, and then I plunged into it.

"But, but Miss Nelson, what message did I bring to you?" I asked, my voice melting like ice cream.

"I have my message," she said. She seemed to be looking over my head at some hallowed light or something. "You have passed it on to me, unknowingly. All these years, I thought it was her; having her was my sin, I thought. But now I know this. You have taught me that my sin was not loving her. And for this, I must suffer."

I glimpsed Pin's prickly evenings. How hard that world must be, with two unhuggable mothers.

Suddenly, I wanted to hug my mother. It was a physical need, as strong as my desire for Pin had been. My warm, soft, huggable ayi. I wanted to get up and leave and wake the boys up and make them take me to Kolhapur right away. It was this urgency in my limbs. I remembered the smell of Ayi when I came home from school; I remembered how her soft green eyes always lit up when she saw me.

I stood up to leave.

Nelson walked with me, still clutching the Bible to her chest with both her hands. She may not have taken the purse with her, although I can't be sure.

At the door, she turned to me and handed me the Bible with both hands.

"This was left to me by—" She floundered and flushed a deep, deep red. She stopped for a moment, adjusted her curls, and then she said carefully, with a patina of calm on her face that even Jivibai could have wiped off with a careless duster, "I would like you to keep this Bible."

"Maybe you can read it sometimes," she said, and paused and locked her eyes into mine, "and think of us."

That's it, I thought. This is the reason she is making all this fuss over me. Not because she knows I was there on table-land, but because she knows I was more to her daughter than a friend. She knows we were lovers. She must have watched her daughter like a hawk. But I felt no shame. We were in a bigger moment, after all, concerned with life and death.

"Charulata, I know that you are wiser than your years. You can see more than other people, because you are different," she said. "My father always told me that in this life, one must watch out for special people. I know that you are one of them. You have suffered. And you can feel the suffering of others. You have an empathy and power beyond your years. You have a gift, and you must use it well."

She hooked her eyes into mine. They were deep and charismatic. "But some things in life we must all learn the hard way. One day, you will understand that."

She gave me the Bible because I had loved her daughter, and she had not.

I nearly told her then. But I saw Ayi emerging from her coma and then falling back, or worse, coughing dramatically as in a Hindi movie and swooning to her death upon hearing that her daughter had been accused of the murder of her lesbian lover. My mother, I informed ghostly Pin firmly, is more important than yours. I knew she agreed with me a hundred percent. "Let her fry," I heard her pert voice whisper in my ear, like a demented ghost of Banquo.

TWENTY-SIX

Far White

I EMERGED FROM Nelson's room with an all-consuming need to touch my mother.

The boys were still sleeping, and I could not bear to wait. I asked Gaiky to call for a taxi to the bus depot. "I'm taking the bus," I said, "I need to go."

"Chal, I'll take you," said Gaiky, and I followed him around in a daze as he spoke to various servants and ward boys and finally got into the driver's seat of an ambulance. At the back were two benches facing each other. A family of villagers leading a stooped old man in a dirt gray dhoti climbed into the back. Gaiky motioned me to the front seat.

"Do you ever put on the light and siren?" I asked.

"Sure," he said, and proudly turned on the weak red light and a siren that sounded like a musical horn. Few people showed any interest in moving out of the way as we drove through the rainy bazaar of bright blue dripping tarps, dropped off the locals at their home above a small shop made up of gunnysacks filled with wheat and dals and rice, and then arrived at the bus depot, where Gaiky left Raja barking in the backseat and obligingly procured me a seat in a minivan of pilgrims with red tikas and laddu-eating children returning to Kohlapur. I realized I was ravenous and accepted a fair number of bright yellow sweets.

I was jangled and jittery from the meeting with Nelson. There was a death between us, her daughter, my lover, and so I understood that the encounter must be intense. But I felt it was more than that. I felt as though I had gone to battle and come out defeated, though I could not say why. I still did not know how she would defend herself.

It was evening, and the temple bells were ringing when I reached Kohlapur.

In Ayi's room, the dark little night nurse sat in a corner chair, reading a romance under a metal lamp.

I could see my ayi was awake because she was facing the wall and rubbing her feet together. It was a tic she had recently developed. I brought it up anxiously to Dr. Tendulkar, but he just shook his head. These days he always shook his head and sometimes even sighed. She had stopped talking completely, and ate only milk and bananas. She sat up on her bed, they put a napkin around her neck and peeled her banana. She would hold the banana firmly in one hand and the glass of warm milk in the other, taking big bites and washing each down with a sip. She turned her face if we put any other food in front of her.

The nurses bathed her and dressed her in bright cotton housecoats and took her to the bathroom at regular intervals, and in the evenings we took her for a walk down the center of the ward. She walked on her own, slowly but evenly. You just had to guide her by the elbow. She brushed her teeth when you handed her a toothbrush with toothpaste on it, she lifted her clothes neatly and sat on the commode when you took her to the bathroom, and she insisted on washing herself. My vivacious and glittering ayi had become a zombie person who was always looking somewhere else. The light had been switched off in her green eyes. Sometimes she showed us that she was listening: She sat up or nodded her head vigorously, though it was never quite at the right time. I felt that she was trying, for our sakes, to take interest, but that she had none.

The family powers had decided that it was pointless to leave Ayi in the hospital. She would be much more comfortable at home. They would keep a hospital ayah to take care of her. The large storeroom at the back of the house was being aired and emptied of grains and spices stored in ancient, immense glass jars. It was a somber, mysterious place with small secret places between the jars. I used to hide in its dark corners and dream big dreams when I was small. The jars were taller than me then. I called it the Ali Baba room. It was my favorite room in the house, but it would be a grim sick room for Ayi.

Baba and I had not been consulted in this. In any case, we were too numb and limp to object. Baba seemed to be receding. He had left for Indore the day I left for Panchgani, saying he would return on the weekend. I knew he was uncomfortable in the Kolhapur house. He was a son-in-law and as per protocol he was treated like a visiting potentate, but the veneer of respect was very thin. In the strict hierarchy of the joint family he was one rung above Dipika the fourth sister's husband, who played cards all day long and had never earned a single rupee in his life. Baba was stiff and withdrawn and very formal with them all. I wondered what he would do when Ayi was shifted to the house. I wondered if he would stop visiting her altogether.

I bent over her and smoothed the straying white hair from her forehead. She did not turn, and I could not see her face in the dim light. The nurse looked up from her romance and beckoned me with urgent gestures.

"I have some news for you." She arched her heavy penciled brows and looked towards Ayi, indicating that it was something she did not want her to know.

She held the room door shut, and we stood outside in the bright white light corridor, where a fat orderly in a dirty dark-green uniform was doling dal onto steel plates. "Last night, your mother sat up in bed and asked for you," she said. "Very quietly. She called me to her, and said, 'Get Charu.' I telephoned your family, even though it was 4 a.m. I have seen enough patients suddenly come back at the . . ." She hastened on when she saw the terror in my face. "Your auntie"—she put her arms out to indicate that it was the fat one—"came, and in the morning they phoned your school, but you were not there. We told your mother you would come today. The day nurse said she is waiting all day."

No wonder I had felt that urgency in Nelly's room. Ayi had been calling me.

"I was asked to tell you to phone your family immediately when you come in," she said. "Everyone will be so relieved."

But I did not phone. I lay down beside Ayi, got under the blanket, and stretched out beside her. She turned, and her face was as calm as the face with which she woke me in the mornings for school. I buried my face in her soft pillow breasts, and sobbed my heart out for at least an hour.

I would like to rewind the night and remember that I lay awake in her arms and she stroked my hair and imparted words of kindness and wisdom that I could use as torches through my life, but the truth is that I fell into an exhausted slumber from which I awoke drooling on the pillow in the dead of night, curled, my back to her, with an urgent need to pee and a bone-dry mouth.

I came out of the bathroom and saw her lying on her back, asleep. I watched her breathe for a while, and then shuffled to the spare bed across from her, not wanting to wake her. This was the first night I felt she was near me again. Her spirit is coming back, I thought.

But I was wrong.

The next day, she stopped getting out of bed. She receded deeper into herself, and did not follow us with her eyes. I could not always be sure that she actually saw me. It was not technically a coma. It was as if she inhabited a twilight world. I phoned Baba to come back from Indore.

I usually went to the house at night, but once or twice I could not bear to leave her, and I slept in her room. I don't remember Baba talking to her. He sat beside her all night, reading, patting her from time to time. I slept intermittently. It felt like a deathwatch.

Baba sat rigid through the day on the bench outside the room, his face set in a tight, grim mask. The family thickened, for by now most of the sisters had arrived, some with children in tow. I had barely spoken to him since the day he told me his sordid tale of withdrawing from the navy after being accused of smuggling, although I did believe he was innocent. I could hardly bear to look at him. I had by now begun to invest the last night with deep portent and felt that Ayi had asked me to forgive my father. But I felt only contempt when I saw him sitting there like a sucked slice of lemon. It was because of him that Ayi wanted to die. I would never let a husband decide my life like that, I thought. But she had no choice. No forgiveness was possible. I could only feel anger toward him now. Ayi would have to understand.

It was a few days later, on a mellow afternoon with the first slanting sunlight of approaching winter, that I heard the second part of my father's tale.

The household had awoken from the afternoon slumber and was preparing for the evening gossip session at the hospital. In the visiting daughters' room, I came upon a clutch of women wrapping their saris. Lumpy hips and fat thighs showing through thin petticoats, drawstrings being tied tight around balloon stomachs, blouses being buttoned over bulging cotton bras with bad elastic. They were standing in a semicircle for a slice of the mirror on the cupboard door, their backs to me.

With sudden tears I remembered how I had sat cross-legged on the bed and watched in awe as my ayi swirled and swooped and in five minutes produced the perfect sari. All my life, I thought, all my life I have watched her. I felt faint with fear of a life without her, and had to sit down and put my head between my knees to bring back some blood to my head.

And then their voices came into focus. They had not noticed me.

"I found a boy for her, poor boy, dark, but good family—we have to think of our girl, after all—but when they heard the name of the father, they did not even phone me back," said Tai with disdain. She was at the pleat stage, pallu standing like a flag atop her stiff breasts. "I can't bear to see that man sitting in her room with that deceitful face of his."

"To this day, I don't understand why Dada never even looked into the family background," said Jyotika, a middle sister who was leveling the circle of her sari to the floor with her bare heels.

"Can't you see it is eating him up? The poor man, he will destroy himself like this," said Jalgaon Masi. Dada had shrunk and withered before our eyes in the days since the Episode.

"And now we are stuck with that girl."

"She's looking terrible. So thin and dark."

"Dada is going to leave some money for her," said Tai. "Can't expect *him* to take responsibility for her."

I hated them. I hated *him* too, but I hated them more for hating him. I thought suddenly of the order of my mother's inner drawer. The silver watch that Baba had gotten from abroad would be on top of the hankies and, beside them, a round blue plastic bowl containing three keys: one to the safe in the cupboard, one to the bank safe, and one extra key to the front door. In fact, our whole ordered lives had radiated out from that drawer. I saw it shatter in slow motion before my eyes and felt a surge of anger.

I strode into the room, stepped into the center of the circle in front of Tai. "I know why you hate us," I said. "All of you." I turned and looked at the women around me in various stages of undress, their eyes boring into me.

"You hate us because she loved us. Your precious Shalini did not love you, she loved us. She was always trying to shield us from your blows. It was all of you. Judging her, judging us, and shaking your heads." It is you who are responsible for her condition, I thought, and then to my horror I burst into tears.

Tai stepped up and engulfed me in her viselike grip. But I pushed her away.

"Even if I needed help, you all would be the last person on earth I would go to," I shouted back, turning suddenly to English and knowing it had come out wrong.

This was not the creeping, crawling Charu that they knew. They were all silent for a moment. The industrious ones took it as an opportunity to get more of the mirror.

The decision was being made as I ranted. It must have been a signal that jumped from one face to the other: She should know now.

And so they circled me and told me about my father. Like the stories they had told us children while peeling potatoes in the evening light, stories of sainted wives and brave warriors and capricious gods, they told me how my father had been disgraced because he had been caught having an affair with the wife of the Admiral.

"We did it out of respect for Shalini. We never told you anything. But it is better that you know. A man like him should have been proud to have won a girl like your mother. But no, not him."

Tai and Jalgaon Masi told the story, the others formed the chorus.

"That too, she was the wife of his superior. That man was like a father to him."

"Having an affair with a woman old enough to be his mother. Chi. How could Shalini even hold her head up after that?"

I remembered her, the wife of the Admiral. She smelled of talcum powder and foreign perfume, and left a red mark on my cheek when she kissed me.

"A dirty filthy scandal. How your mother could sleep near him all these years, I don't know. And you should have seen that woman. Painted face, wearing sleeveless blouses. Brought shame on the whole family."

No wonder Baba left a wide and gaping hole in the story he told me on the park bench. No wonder the Admiral had unleashed public disgrace and humiliation—it was a viper he had nurtured in his bosom.

I saw a new Baba, Baba the bachelor boy. He was ten years older than Ayi, thirty-one when he married her. Before he met Ayi, he must have spent his evenings at the U.S. club, where the navy families gathered. He must have had four whiskies and used his charm upon the women. A ladies' man in a crisp white uniform, single and charming. He must have grown used to this life.

"And not only that—he went out with cheap women. People saw him in hotels with secretary types with skirts and short hair," said Gopika with pursed lips. Tai gave her the look, and she bit her lower lip and shut up.

"And remember all that gossip about the foreign woman? She came forward and said the child was his? Remember that?" piped up badi Bhabhi, who had been pleating quietly behind us all this time.

"Chup," said Tai in her most authoritative voice. "Those were all just rumors. No need now to bring them up."

"Did Ayi know all these years?" I asked.

"Everyone knew, by the end," said majli Bhabhi with a sniff, tying a tail of false hair into a bun at the back of her head.

"But Ayi forgave him," I told them.

"But that was Shalini's mistake. Always forgive and move on. But you can tell that she did not forget. She should have left him right away. I went and told her, before she left for Indore. Dada said this could be her home, and yours."

I saw how we might have been, my ayi and me, staying on the edges of the big house, the daughter, and the daughter of the daughter, of a failed marriage. I would have to be subservient to my cousins, and Ayi would have to peel the potatoes in the evening as the Bhabhis fried bhajiyas.

"I am glad she did not," I burst out. "I am glad I did not have to grow up in this cruel place."

"Let her be," I heard a Bhabhi say as I stormed off. "Naturally, she is upset. Poor girl."

I walked towards the little market at the end of the road, my blood curdling at the thought of this wizened man, my own father, consorting with flabby women and prostitutes while my mother waited at home with me.

My Bombay father was always going somewhere. I remembered the house, dark and full of shadows in the evening, lit only by the kitchen tubelight and the dim light of a table lamp beside the sofa in the bedroom where my mother waited for her husband to come home for dinner, the picture of wifely duty. He often arrived after nine. She would not eat until he did, and so she was always in a bad mood. Or at least that is what I thought then, because Baba would put me on his knee and say, "You must tell your mother. A modern woman does not need to wait for her husband. She should take a half-hour nap in the afternoon and eat dinner with you. That way she can be rested and happy when I come home." He would say this loudly, while my mother sat in a huff on the sofa in the drawing room, where the lights were now bright. Sometimes she refused to eat and would go to bed in tears. Sometimes I could hear Baba shouting from the bedroom. In contrast, the Indore house was always calm, at least on the surface.

There was only one photograph from my parents' wedding, a black-and-white image of them going around the fire. She is leading, looking down, tense, smothered in garlands and jewels. It is Baba behind her who shines, his face beaming like the sun, confident, radiant.

I saw the sailor tall and lean, his white hat on the nightstand as he dallied with the Admiral's wife. Deep, delicious afternoons of desire. Like Pin and me. But instead of Pin, I suddenly saw Merch, of the lean and lanky body.

I understood then. Growing up, I modeled myself after Ayi. I would be like her—once the blot was gone—wise and graceful and as ordered as the inner drawer. But in actual fact, it was Baba and I, we were the ones cut from the same silk cloth. Given to the temptations of the flesh. Wanting more than was put on the plate.

I must have walked for an hour. The outside of the walk is a blur. I remember staring at a display of push-up bras, I remember wandering around the field across the street, where the madwoman who was said to have lost her son in a bullock-cart tragedy ranted. But the inside of the walk has stayed with me to this day. I felt that my mother was with me. She told me all the things she wanted to say to me that night. Courage, she said. Be braver than me. Be stronger than me. Be happier than me. Of course, she did not say be more beautiful than me, since that would never be possible.

I did not wait for the family carpool to gather, but took a rickshaw to the hospital, and found my father alone in the room, napping on the armchair beside her bed.

He looked grave and distant, like a minor manager in a transport company. We walked around the large playing field near the hospital. It was filled with brisk evening walkers and game-playing boys shouting "Out!" The word echoed in my mind until it found its logical place.

"We must get Ayi out of here," I said. "We must take her back to Indore." After all, we knew that people could stay in comas for years, and then suddenly come out and lead perfectly normal lives. The household was abuzz with case histories and stray stories of a similar nature.

"She should be with us, yes," said Baba.

"Let us have no truck with them. No truck with the Chitnis family," I said, and burst into a semi-hysterical giggle. Baba looked at me with concern, and then finally cracked a smile.

We were walking on a narrow road lined by bougainvillea falling over bungalow walls. "I have been thinking the same thing, Charu, but I was not thinking of bringing it up so soon. But you are absolutely right. No more trucks, as you so rightly put it."

I wondered if he guessed that I was in possession of the whole truth, such as it was. Not tragic, not magic, not epic. An affair and an allegation, and he had taken us into hiding.

School was to start in two days. I had not given my resignation, but planned to go up to Panchgani and inform them that due to family duties I could no longer teach. I also planned to tell the Woggle what I had seen on table-land.

We made plans to take Ayi to Indore by ambulance. We would bring a hospital ayah with us to take care of her until we could find someone local. As I said these things, I imagined myself bowed and thin in the morning, getting Ayi ready, cooking breakfast for Baba, and then going to some teaching job, my blob as big as my face.

Baba knew my thoughts.

"Charu, I will take her back," he said to me in Marathi. Then he cleared his throat and went back to English. "You go back to your school. That is your duty now. I am sure your mother would agree."

I looked down at my hands, folded on my lap. As much as I wanted to go back to Panchgani, I was afraid. I could go back to playing chess with Baba. And after a while, marry a thirty-five-year-old Maharashtrian Brahmin whose wife had died in childbirth and left a baby with a hole in her heart.

"It is time for us to let you go," said Baba, in a "this is final" voice. I saw him, Ayi at his side with jasmine in her hair, the two of them gently placing a paper boat into a gushing brown river and then turning around and walking away.

"I will come with you and settle her in, and then go back to the school. I will go tomorrow and tell Miss Wilson," I said.

"No," said Baba firmly, and he was not so often firm. "I can look after her very well. I will take her alone. Of course you will come and stay with us when you can get away from your work. There will always be a home for you with us. But now you should go and make your life." And then he paused and patted my back. "Make a good life, Charu. Make your ayi proud."

And so Ayi Baba left for Indore, and I decided to go back to Panchgani for the winter term.

The next day, the *Times of India* reported that Miss Shirley Nelson had refused counsel in the matter of the murder of her blood child, and had neither denied nor admitted her guilt.

> Because of her failure to deny the act, a guilty plea has been entered on her behalf for the murder of her daughter, Moira Prince, by the Additional Magistrate of Satara. She will be tried in the High Court there. The court will appoint counsel for her if none is retained by the accused party.

"I will put myself into the hands of my God," she was quoted as saying in all four of the newspapers I read.

TWENTY-SEVEN

Winter Term

ON THE FIRST day of winter term, it was October 1, a Tuesday, I remember, a group of Panchgani schoolboys told their master they saw the teacher with the mark coming down from table-land—"Looking, don't know, just weird"—on the night of the murder. The master, Mr. Samuel, spoke of it to his girlfriend, Malti Innis—"The boys said she looked sort of crazy"—who knew it was her bounden duty to tell the acting principal Miss Wilson, who in turn informed Inspector Wagle.

Inspector Wagle interrogated the boys in disbelief. "What were you doing there? Can you describe her in detail? Do you know exactly at what time? Are you sure it was her? Are you sure it was her?"

But the boys were firm. They saw the teacher with the mark on her face running down from table-land. They had just turned the corner from the park. They said it was sometime between twelve and one. Yes, they were breaking the rules, they were doing a wrong thing, but still, they did see her. Why would they make it up? They were as shocked as the inspector himself. Why didn't he just ask her? They shrugged and left, not really caring, in the end.

On the third day of the winter term, I was summoned by Inspector Wagle and questioned about my activities on the night of August 27, 1974. I was called into his office in the two-room police station.

It was the Prince in me that said no.

It was as if Pin had died and left me her eyes. Suddenly, sometimes, I was beginning to glimpse the world through the eyes of my first love.

The Princely eye cut deeper than the wry Charu eye. *Just tell the inspector you were not even on table-land that night. That's what he wants to hear anyway. Just walk away and let her fry for it. She deserves it. Who would treat their own daughter like that? Evil bitch.*

"They are just schoolboys," I said, looking the Woggle full in the eye. "And it was a monsoon night." I knew it was my word against theirs. I had not lied yet. I had only castled first, as Baba always said I should. Shored up my position.

The Woggle looked happy and relieved at my implied challenge of the boys' observations.

"And they had gone to purchase illicit liquor. They might have been inebriated. Will not stand," he said, nodding energetically. His hearty inspector smile—the "it is all under control now" smile—returned to his fat face.

He dropped his voice a little, so I would understand he was making an off-the-record remark. "It is their own white matter," he said. "We should not poke our heads into it."

"Far white," I could not resist replying, tilting my head with a winning smile.

He looked up at me, his plump face puzzled. He was wearing a military-green long-sleeved pullover with his khakis. I could not see how it stretched over his stomach because I was seated across his massive desk in the center of his office. The detention cell was next door.

"When we heard that you were often with that strange boy Merch and his lot, I told Janaki, this will not bode well for Charu. She is too innocent. They are wastrels, or worse."

I concentrated on a blot of red paan spit on a corner of the whitewashed wall behind his desk.

Woggle had begun to connect the dots. He had drawn a line from Merch and the hippies to me. The line would soon lead to the Prince.

And then, like my father, I would spend my whole life hiding from people who knew. All those who knew the truth. The truth that I had been up on table-land on the night of the murder, and the truth that I had lied about it. Then they would look at me and say, she did it, she had an affair with the white woman and then pushed her down the cliff. A sleazy, slinking type of life. I would walk with a bent head, like Baba.

The blot on the wall became the blot on my face, which became the blot on my world. I felt the cold terrazzo tiles as I sat on the floor of the Indore house, reciting my tables.

"Yes," I said, "I was on table-land on the night of August twenty-seventh."

Although I sometimes used to dream of becoming a lawyer, my only contact with the criminal or legal world was from movies. That moment I had an image of a lady lawyer who wore a gown and wig and said, 'Yes, milord." I wondered if I should say I wanted a lawyer. But that would make me guilty.

I decided to charge in with Tai's Sword of Innocence instead.

"I did go up to table-land that night, but I saw no one there. So I came down." Then I remembered that the boys said they had seen me wild and muttering. "I mean, I walked down," I added, for dignity.

"What would you say was the exact duration of your time on table-land?" said the Woggle gruffly, avoiding my eyes.

I found the "would you say" part a bit ominous. Next thing I knew, I could be in the detention room next door. I imagined myself in a Western, calling my father from a telephone horn in the sheriff's office.

Nelson had her God to help her. I must wield my own weapon. I polished my Sword of Innocence. I knew I had a better chance of finding the truth and freeing Nelson than the clueless Woggle.

"Moira Prince came to see me the night of her death," I said. "She said she had come to know something terrible beyond imagination. She did not tell me what it was. She was very disturbed. She said she was planning to go to table-land and jump off the edge. I calmed her down, and then she left. I did not know anything about the letter. After she left, I attempted to sleep. I fell into a shallow sleep, but I dreamt that she was jumping off the cliff. I awoke with a start, hurriedly put on my raincoat and rushed to table-land. I walked around near the edge and saw nothing. So I left. Then I had to rush to Kolhapur because of my mother."

"And at what time would you say you were on table-land? And for how long?"

"I ran up in a hurry and forgot to wear my watch," I said, and this, at least, was absolutely true. I had gone up in nothing but the raincoat. "I was up for I think about half an hour, maybe forty-five minutes. I started near the lake and walked around it, though not to the far side. I did not go right to the edge, since it was slippery and I am afraid of heights. I kept to the borders, looking for her."

"And you saw nothing?"

"I saw nothing," I said firmly.

"Would you estimate that you were on table-land between twelve and twelve-thirty?"

I did not know what time I had turned and walked back. The autopsy estimated Moira Prince's death to have occurred between 12 and 2 a.m. And the girls had reported seeing both Nelson and Prince alive near midnight. The boys saw neither the girls, nor Nelson coming down. The boys saw me. That made sense, since I was the last person to come down. I could have come down by one.

Pin must have jumped as soon as I left.

"So would you say you were on table-land between twelve and twelve-thirty?" said the Woggle again, showing that he was a man who wanted to do his duty, however unpleasant it might be.

"I know it was later, because I fell into a sleep after Miss Prince left my room. I do not know how long I slept. The bazaar was dark when I walked up. It must have been past midnight," I said.

"So you would say that you were up on table-land between twelve and one?" persisted the Woggle.

"Or it might even have been between one and two," I said.

"You will have to make an official statement," he said in a firm but kind voice. "And did you go up to the needle?"

"No," I said, "I did not go right up to the needle."

I had not gone up to the needle. If I had gone to the needle, I would have walked down with Pin, and she would still be her wild self. I wanted to fall to the ground and rend my clothes and tear my hair and shout woe is me.

The Woggle harrumphed in embarrassment. "You should have informed me of your actions earlier," he said.

I could end up in the hospital room in Vai beside Nelson. Day after day, she would sit upright and read *The Pilgrim's Progress*, and I would curl up in my nightie and read Harold Robbins, and soon I would end up in jail for the rest of my life.

"I was delayed due to a family emergency," I said. "Since I did not see anyone up there at all, I thought it could wait a few days. You see, my mother was in a coma, critical condition." My voice did genuinely wobble as I said this.

"So sorry to hear," said Inspector Woggle gravely, but he did not invite me to dinner, or even to tea, he just shook his head—regret or disbelief, I did not know which.

He called Mr. Kirloskar, the typist from the bank next door, to type out my statement and be the witness. "Since you did not see anything of importance, perhaps it will not be necessary for you to be a witness," the Woggle said. "Will depend on the lawyer. However, you need to inform us of your whereabouts if you leave Panchgani to attend to family matters." He spoke without looking directly at me.

"Due to the circumstances—you know we cannot keep that

white woman in a hospital for too long—the proceedings will be speeded up. The first court date has been set for December first," he informed me.

I had two months to get to the truth. Miss Nelson might fancy martyrdom, but I wanted to know the truth. For Pin's sake, and for mine.

AS SOON AS I entered the green iron gates of the school, I was asked to see Miss Wilson. Miss Wilson called me into her office, which was the same as Miss Nelson's office, though it felt suddenly less cold and hushed, but that could have been because the rain had stopped and tourist couples in bright sweaters were buying chappals and channa in the bazaar.

"Don't you think it would be better, Miss Apte, if you did—um—not teach for a while?" said Miss Wilson patting her straggly curls nervously. "I think your heart is not in it at this time." I am fated, I thought with her pointed collar in front of me, I am fated to sit across the table from white women and be told frightening things.

Then I surveyed the scene with a Princely eye and thought, No, she cannot really frighten me. The worst has happened already.

I could not bear to be in the school anymore. Miss Henderson looked past me, rearing her head and sniffing like a nervous filly. I would have been glad to obey Willy, to never come back to the school again. But I could not.

It was an affair and an allegation that had felled my father. It was the same for me, though my affair could be argued to be more illicit than his, and my accusation could be murder instead of shampoo and underwire bras. I was at the crossroads, and my father was pointing the way. He had retreated, so I could not.

"I think I should finish *Macbeth* with the tens, Miss Wilson," I said earnestly, showing a concern for the unformed minds that I most definitely did not possess. "It will not be fair if I do not finish it for them. After all, it is for their I.S.C. exams."

"Oh, please, don't worry about that, Miss Apte. Miss McCall said she would rather like to try her hand at *Macbeth*. A perfect fit, don't you think?"

Was she saying my teaching was of a lesser quality because I was not white?

She saw I was distressed and blushed, and began to explain. "Oh, you taught it most wonderfully from everything I gather. I hear the girls quoting *Macbeth*. You did most certainly capture their imaginations. I only meant, you know, it is after all about Scotland, and Miss McCall is Scottish. Grew up where it takes place, that sort of thing. Nothing personal at all."

On a personal level I would have loved to loll around with the hippies and do drugs all day and all night, instead of just all night, which is what I was doing now. But I knew the mystery was in the school, and so that was where I must stay.

And they had lost a lot of teachers.

"You must be so shorthanded now, with three teachers gone. Are you sure you don't need a stopgap Hindi teacher?" I asked. The disappearance of the Hindi teacher was another mystery, connected, surely, to the first one.

"Oh, don't worry, we are all pitching in," she said with a

forced jollity, as though they were all filling up a hole in the hockey pitch.

"Mrs. Paranjpe has offered to teach Hindi to the seniors." Mrs. Paranjpe was Maharashtrian Christian, a combination I had never come across before, a short and stout woman who chewed paan. She lived somewhere below the bazaar and taught Marathi and, for a brief time, French, until an entire class failed French in the I.S.C., and French was struck off the list of offered languages.

Rumor had it that her husband, who never missed the gymnastics competition and loved to leer at lithe young bodies, had offered to teach sports "in lieu of the demised teacher," he had added smirking. Miss Wilson had refused.

But now, with me gone, there would be a fourth teacher missing, and I could see Miss Wilson waver in her resolve. She considered me thoughtfully and gravely: I might be as innocent as I looked after all.

"I went to Hindi medium school for some years," I added to strengthen my case, and it was true, I had when we first moved to Indore. Baba had started talking to me in English, so I could "keep up with the language." It became a habit, and now we always spoke English with each other, and Marathi with Ayi.

"Well," said Willy after a long pause. "Thank you, yes, it would be quite helpful. You could teach Hindi to the fives, sixes, and sevens. Let me see."

She got up and walked to a large chart on the wall. A complex chart in three colors, dotted with gleaming bronze drawing pins. Teachers cross-referenced with subjects and classes. She began to shift the drawing pins around, then stand back and rub her chin and stare, and then go back and change a few more, like a general moving armies. I wondered if she was old enough to have been a Wren in the war.

"We could switch their classes around so they are back-to-back," she said. "And sometimes we could do two grades together. You could read a story or have a debate. Something like that might be quite interesting for them. I think we could do it by having you come in for a few hours, let us see." She again rearranged the drawing pins. "Yes, we could do Mondays, Wednesdays, and Thursdays. From ten to twelve-thirty. Would that be convenient?"

I got the message. I was to keep my interaction with the school short and simple. No lunch in the dining room. But now that I had a foot in the door, I could squeeze myself in. I would hang around the staff room before and after classes, I could even pump the schoolgirls. And I would not have to stay in that horrible room smelling of disinfectant and dirty socks.

"I will find some rooms outside," I said, feeling a surge of freedom gathering in my breast.

Now that I had been firmly placed coming down from tableland that night, "looking absolutely mad," I was going to be pointed at. And then talked about. And then, if I was not careful, I would be in jail, snap, for the murder of Moira Prince.

I knew what I must do. Walking past the music room, I had once heard Miss McCall, the music teacher—soon to be the teacher of *Macbeth*—say to some struggling piano player, "Bite the note before it bites you." I would have to bite hard.

"Of course, we will adjust your pay accordingly," said Miss Wilson, closing the meeting. "That would only be fair."

TWENTY-EIGHT

Sister Richards

THE FIRST TIME in my life that I got drunk was with Sister Richards. I had at least three large glasses of rum and Campa Cola with her one evening, soon after my return to Timmins.

I had left the school and was an independent part-time teacher living in Aeolia, a windy villa perched on the cusp of the valley, on the way to Sydney Point. I was paying 200 rupees a month for three rooms temporarily vacated by Shabir and Raisa, who had moved to Poona and rented a house in the Rajneesh Ashram so their child could be born there.

Sister was happy to see me when I walked down to the hospital at sunset. She called it her "medicine hour," with a sly wink. She drank usually in her dim room, but today we pulled out two chairs and sat at the edge of the veranda near the dispensary so we could quickly hide the drinks if a hurt child was to suddenly appear. We were facing a patch of red roses and a bush of shoe-flowers in full bloom. There was a chicken-pox girl in the hospital, poor Malini Hathiramani, whose parents "did not even bother to check that she was red and feverish, just put her on the train," Sister grumbled, going to get two glasses. "And now it is bound to spread."

"So now you're wearing saris," she said, pouring herself a generous amount of triple-X rum. "But my, you've grown thin. Yes, very thin. Have a drink. Calm yourself down."

"I'll have the same as you, just a smaller peg, please," I said. I was planning to get information out of her. She just had to be dying for a good gossip.

"Where could Raswani have gone?" I asked. "Poor thing, she has just been sidestepped with all this mother-daughter drama."

Sister nodded her head in vigorous assent. "Yes," she said lustily, "suddenly one day, just gone."

"And even her room clean. That's odd too. She didn't just walk out, she took her things."

"Or someone packed her things to make it look like she took them. If you ask *me*, I smell a rat. Maybe she was knocked off too, you know, just like our poor Moira. She knew too much, living where she did, cheek by jowl with *that* one." She said it like she might say the evil one.

The drink smelt like cough mixture and tasted worse. I saw no point in savoring it. Sister watched me take great gulps with approval.

Then she launched into the story. "You know, I heard them talking once. Mother and daughter, though I did not see the conversation in that light that day. And neither did she, then, poor child."

Sister took a long draught, put her glass down to rest, and did not take another sip until she finished the entire episode. She did once or twice pop a channa or two into her mouth, pausing her tale as she ground it down with her tiny set of false teeth.

"It happened that Moira had a bad patch of dysentery after she came back from England. So she was here"—Sister pointed to the infectious disease room that was on the other side of the dispensary—"for two weeks.

"Moira was very gloomy those days, stayed in her room and then in the evenings dressed up and went out and didn't come back till very late. Slept all day. Nelson came by a couple of evenings to see her, but she wasn't there.

"'How is her stomach condition?' Nelson asked me. 'She does have loose motions,' I said, 'and sometimes still runs a temperature.' 'Then she should not be going out, Sister,' she said, as though I could have any control over *that* one. Anyway, once she found her in. I was in the dispensary, rolling cotton swabs and such. I heard the conversation, didn't know what to make of it then, but now it comes back quite clearly, and I keep thinking, that Nelson of yours is evil, I tell you. Scaring the poor girl like that, why would she do it, unless she had a motive?

"They talked of her trip to England. Moira was telling Nelson about the house that her parents had left her. She was quite excited about it, describing how you could see the sea from the bedroom in the attic. She said she was planning on moving there. Dorset, she said, or maybe Dover. Something with a *D* anyway, some small town on the coast. I didn't ask her about it, because of course I couldn't let them know I had heard that conversation, could I?"

Sister and I were quite cozy now, and getting closer.

"Nelson was quite discouraging, you know, saying what would you do there, and you won't know anyone there, and that sort of thing. Moira said she would teach. 'There'll always be a school there, and at least I look white, though I felt Indian when I was there,' she said, perky as you please. Sounded happy. I thought it would be a good thing. If you ask me, she should have done it. Gone and started a new life. But that Nelsonofyours (she said it as one word, as though it were her surname or something) was not about to let that one out of her clutches, oh, no. 'You can't teach in England,' she said. 'You have not gotten your teachers' training. They are quite strict about that there.' So saintly, pah. Makes my blood boil. But that Moira was not to be stopped. 'I never really wanted to teach—I just said that because I thought it would keep you happy. Actually, I plan to have another career altogether,' she said, as proud as a peacock. 'I'm going to be an actress.'"

I remembered her as Freny in Merch's room, bent over with laughter before she delivered her line.

"You know, she was much happier recently. Since she met you. But when she was ill and staying here, I would kind of know she was in a mood and leave her alone. Mind you, she did come in and have a few drinks with me. She would saunter up and say, 'Isn't it triple-X day, Sister Richards?' And I would say, 'But drinking is not good for your condition, child.' And she would say, 'Oh, but it is, Sister. I promise you, it is very good for my condition.'

"But those days she was much more ready to fly off the handle, and when Nelson said, 'Do you think that is wise? There is no security in that, and you will be all alone,' Moira let her have it. 'For your information, Miss Shirley Nelson the know-it-all, I do have relatives in England. And I met them all. A cousin, his wife, and a nephew. I met them and I slept in their home and I ate meals with them and took the child to the park. Anyway, why should you care? You'll be happy to see me go, I bet. Then your precious school will be clean again.'

" 'Relatives, what relatives? You have no relatives, I know that,' she said, in a sharp voice. That is the only time I have ever heard that voice out of Nelson. She was shaken up, I tell you. Shaken up, voice rough and hard, not her usual saintly voice. And you know what Moira said?

" 'I thought my parents told you every time I sneezed, for God's sake. They didn't show you the Christmas cards? I can't believe it. You didn't know she had a sister, did you? You didn't know that they lived their saintly lives on a pile of dirt, did you? I used to imagine they were some sort of spy couple in hiding, the way they carried on in England not wanting to be seen. Sometimes I thought it was because of me. They were hiding me because I was such a bad girl. All the holy holies would see how rotten their child was. And then they would not seem so good. That's what I thought.'

"And then Moira dropped her voice, and they were talking for a long time. You know, I am getting deaf these days. The other day I didn't hear what's-her-name, Alpana Modi. She was standing outside the dispensary calling for quite some time, 'Sister, I have cramps.' So after all these murmurs, I had to tie a bandage on some scrape, and I lost their thread of conversation. And then when I went back to—you know, got back to rolling my swabs—Nelson said, 'But I am your family. Your dear parents, they were all the family we had, you and I. And now I am your family. I will look after you.' And there was all this sniffling and blowing of noses, so I decided to go into my room so she would not have to pass by me when she left. At that time, I thought they must be crying about the death of her parents. But now I think Prince must have told her she had just found out about her adoption.

"Mind you," said Sister, holding a small round channa ready to pop into her mouth, "she didn't know it was her own mother she was talking to."

"Yes," I agreed. "She found out she was adopted when her parents died. And she found out about these relatives. The letter came much later." I saw the Prince as Mandrake the Magician, a cape of secrets swirling around her. I talked and talked about my life, and Pin listened with a crooked smile on her face as I chatted. I wanted to know about her; I wish I'd had more time with her. My eyes began to burn, and I felt a welling of tears arise in my throat. Stop, I told myself sternly. This was not the time to distract Sister. It was a time to collect all the scraps of information like a bird building a nest.

"Coming to think of it, that could have been the actual night when Nelson decided to knock her off," said Sister, whose eyelids were beginning to droop.

By this time, we were both maniacally chewing channa in a conspiratorial manner. The dinner bell had rung, the lights had been switched on, and moths and other varied insects were hovering above the naked light bulb in the veranda. The ayah came in with two dinner trays, one for the poor pocked girl, and the other for Sister, who ignored it completely.

We took our chairs into the dispensary to avoid the mosquitoes and poured ourselves another drink. "I am ready to take the bet that Nelson did away with Raswani too," said Sister.

"But then where is her body?" I asked. In the early days, I was convinced that Raswani was a centerpiece in this matter. If we knew what happened to her, we would know what happened to Pin.

No one had seen them go out of the school together. Everyone knew that Nelson had not left her room for three days after Pin's murder. If Nelson had entered Raswani's room through their connecting door and hit her with a bludgeon or choked her in her bed, her body should not be too far.

That is why the flower beds were being dug up.

Three sakarams, with one overseer in long pants from Poona, had tramped around the school for days during the holidays and dug up the long-jump pitch and the slope down from the bakery. The school's two malis had been put to work digging up the neglected vegetable patch outside the kitchen, and Mrs. Cummings, the kitchen mistress, was distraught. But no evidence had been unearthed to date, no smells of rotting flesh assailed us as we walked past tall piles of raw red earth around the random ditches. Searches had also been made at the bottom of the cliff, behind Sydney Point, and down the valley from Parsi Point, just in case she had been taken for a walk and pushed off.

"I did her shopping for her when she lived here," said Sister. "She was so stingy, used one tube of toothpaste and two cakes of soap for the whole term. And in her room only a few saris, one umbrella, and one raincoat."

"Any photographs or pictures in her room?"

"She had a framed Jesus picture: 'Suffer the children to come unto me.' Nothing else. Lived like a nun."

Raswani had disappeared into thin air, and though she had been missing for more than a month, not a single relative or friend had appeared to inquire as to her whereabouts. Miss Wilson had inserted a notice nationally in the *Times of India* more than once.

> Miss Usha Raswani, teacher of Hindi at Timmins School, Panchgani, has been missing since September 5, 1974. Any information regarding her current whereabouts, or her past, would be very much appreciated. Please address all letters to Miss M. Wilson, Miss Timmins' School for Girls, Panchgani, Satara District, Maharashtra.

There was no accompanying photograph, because no photograph of her could be found.

Shankar had told me that both Nelson and Raswani were there before him when he came to Timmins as a young mali and roamed the lower gardens with a huge metal watering can. Shankar says it must have been before 1955 because he remembers that Bhagi was born, but then he says his father was still alive then, and he is sure that his father died more than thirty years ago. So the date of his arrival has not been confirmed. It is confirmed that he wore khaki short pants.

Nelson was learning Marathi, Shankar told me, and he would help her and have conversations with her. "She trusts me to run the school," he said proudly. "I look after her. Protect her from all these banyas. They would fleece the school."

Everyone in the bazaar knew that Shankar took his cut, but everyone also knew that the white women would be overcharged anyway, and so in the end, the school came off better because at least he got work out of the contractors.

Maybe Nelson and Raswani came to the school together. It was possible they knew each other from Nasik. But then Pin should have known her too, and I knew that this was not so. Pin had told me of her first encounter with Raswani, in the school staff room, how she had turned her head away and refused to take Pin's proffered hand.

"Where do you think she came from? Does anyone know? No one even seems to have known her first name," I said to Sister. Although Merch and company did drugs on a constant basis, there was rarely any alcohol around, and I found that I was warm and expansive without knowing that I was drunk. "And who would have thought her name was Usha? I have an aunt called Usha. Such a soft, sweet little name."

"Twisted place, this is. Pah," said Sister, screwing her lips. "I keep to myself, as you see. I go up to the dining room for breakfast, then go up for prayers. That's all. After that, this is my kingdom. With these kinds of women, I tell you, the less you talk to them the better. If you ask me, I personally prefer blood and guts to this mess. But I did hear that Raswani was from the north. I think from Allahabad. Don't ask me who told me that, but I think they all know she is from Allahabad."

Sister and I had passed the realm of careful conversations.

"I think Raswani might be the killer," I said. "She's mad anyway, and you know she hated Pin. I mean Miss Prince." I stumbled over her name. It was impossible to refer to her as

Moira, for it was not a name that fitted her at all. "She could have pushed her off the cliff and then run away. Perhaps back to Allahabad."

This was one of my theories. Since I knew that Nelson had not killed her own daughter—I had seen the way she stood behind her, I had seen the way she patted her so lovingly on the shoulder, I had seen the way she walked down the hill, so light and jaunty, as though she had made her peace with her daughter, I felt in my gut it could not be her—I began to think that the murderer could perhaps be the mad Hindi teacher.

Sister poured the refill. I wasn't counting her intake, but for me, it was the third, or just maybe it could be the fourth. She made mine weaker than the last.

"More likely, though, I think she ran away because she was afraid," I said. "Remember, she ran away before the arrest of Nelson. Maybe she was afraid of Nelson, in the next room, after she gave the letter away."

Sister took another long draught and brought her glass down with a decisive thump, her eyes gleaming with excitement, her cheeks flushed, her face haloed with white tendrils that had escaped the pins.

"That is the exact reason that I know she is dead. Killed off. She could never have survived a day on her own. This I can put down in writing," she said triumphantly.

"Why?"

"I am the only one here besides Nelson who is party to the fact that Raswani does not—just, you know, *cannot*—handle money. When I came here in 1966 Miss Raswani was staying in your room. Nelson called me for tea one day and requested that I do her a personal favor. She asked me to please do some personal shopping for Miss Raswani. 'She's a child at heart, she needs our help,' she said to me, giving me that smug smile of hers, trumpeting her saintly self. Miss Raswani used to leave a list in the dispensary on Wednesdays. You know, toothpaste, talcum powder, and the like, and I would buy them when I went to the bazaar and hand over the bills to Nelson."

"What about her underwear? You mean she never had ever bought herself a single thing her whole life?" This was a stunning new revelation.

"I don't know about her whole life. But here, she hardly ever went out of the school. Grown woman like that, unable to buy herself a peanut. What kind of example to the girls?" muttered Sister scornfully. "I tell you, that Nelsonofyours likes to collect these wounded women so she can play the heroine. I stopped being shopping assistant the day she moved out of here. Wonder who does—oops, I should say who did—it for her."

The unfinished mother picking up lost souls to nurture. I could see how she was opening up her wing to take me under, another fallen bird. Sister walked to her room, swaying slightly, came back with the remainder of the packet of Mama's Channa and emptied it into a white saucer.

Suddenly, I nearly choked on my channa.

"Sister, remember the first day you took me to the bazaar? At Panchgani Stores, the day they found Jitubhai with the dirty magazine?"

"Oh, that was the funniest thing to happen in Panchgani this year," said Sister with a chuckle.

"But don't you remember, we came upon Raswani that day, standing at the counter?"

Sister's mouth went slack. "My goodness, it did not even occur to me till now how strange that was," she said. "But I did not see her buy anything"—there was a trace of triumph in her voice—"No money passed hands. Maybe she came to ask a question."

I made my escape just as Sister was launching for the tenth time into the story of Raswani peeping into her room with those mad eyes of hers, and walked back to Aeolia.

Two days later, I walked up to Sunbeam with a deep October sunset around me. "Good-bye, Ruby Tuesday," I was singing as I turned the corner onto the back road I had first walked with Pin. The song played in my head all day, and when I was with the gang at night, I always asked for the Rolling Stones and closed my eyes and thought of Pin.

I walked in as the ladies were sitting in the drawing room waiting for the ayah to lay out the dinner. The table was already set. I was neither invited nor expected. They were flustered to see me, as I knew they would be, since they had been avoiding me in the staff room, just nodding and walking past.

I saw their sheep eyes across the fence and felt my fingers turn into plug points, conductors of the smooth blue charge of electricity that surged through my body. This was what Pin must have felt, the power of being outside the fold.

We sat around surrounded by brown-covered notebooks. Jacinta bravely started some inane conversation about Kalpana Mehta's frog sitting up suddenly amidst a dissection. "While being dissected, he sat up. Literally. One of the biggest frogs I have ever come across."

I interrupted her abruptly. "Did you know Miss Raswani in Allahabad?" I asked, turning to Malti.

"Yes," said Malti. "I did. She used to spend the long holiday with us."

Malti's father, I was told, was a vicar and attached to the same or a similar Protestant mission in Allahabad. When Malti was around ten, Miss Raswani had suddenly turned up with a metal trunk and set herself up in a small room in the bungalow across from the church. She came every year in the first week of December and stayed until February 4, the entire duration of the winter holidays. They used to see her sitting in the veranda and going for a walk in the evenings.

Malti was happy to give me as many details as I wanted. I could see how relieved she was that I had not come to confront her. She was the one who had informed Miss Wilson of the fact that I had been seen running down from table-land, after all.

"In fact, it's because of her," she said, "that Beena and I are in Timmins today. Every time she came, she had dinner at our house the first night and handed my father an envelope." It was a letter from Miss Nelson, thanking them for taking care of Miss Raswani. It always contained a hundred-rupee note in case she needed anything. The envelope was always sealed. Malti remembered her father tearing the flap and taking out the big blue note.

"Just imagine, she carried a letter about herself and did not read it even. Like a kid coming to school or something," added Beena. Raswani was a safe topic, and they were all happy to jump in.

Malti's father had started sending letters back to the principal with Miss Raswani. Soon they had a sort of pen pal–ship going. Her father was in awe of Miss Nelson. He would shake his head and say, "She's a great lady. How she looks after her teachers. And so they decided to send me here to teach, and we convinced Beena's parents to send her too."

"But was Raswani from Allahabad? How did she find that spot? Did anyone know her?" I asked.

"That's what I'm realizing now. We did not know where she came from. Can you imagine, we did not even know her first name? I was surprised as anyone else when I saw it in the papers."

"But all those Christmas dinners and everything, you mean you didn't talk to her?" I asked, incredulous.

"We didn't care, I think. We treated her like a madwoman. My brother and I and the other children from around there, we used to run after her and make faces behind her back. She would pretend she did not see us. Once we went too far. It was my brother. He stuck out a stick from behind a bush when she was passing, and she tripped. She ran into her room crying. I feel sorry for her now, actually. Even on her holidays she had to deal with the brats. Poor woman."

"And later, after you were in Timmins, did you go together to Allahabad?" I asked.

"No," said Malti. "My father died last year, soon after I came here." She paused and sniffed and Beena patted her back. "We had to vacate the parsonage, and my mother moved back to her family home near Darjeeling. So now I go there for holidays."

I never imagined that they shared a past. "Did you talk often, here?" I asked her.

"When she first met me, she said, once or twice, 'Give my regards to your father,' and sometimes I would say, 'My father sends his regards,' and when he died, she gave a sympathy card to send to my mother. But then we stopped, just pretended we never had any past. Actually, I sort of tried to avoid her. She was always glowering at me. I always felt she hated me, because of those pranks."

"Or maybe because she knew she had been treated like a madwoman," said Beena.

"Maybe that's why she was so stern," I said. "Afraid that she would lose control."

"You can say that again. I was always terrified of her," said Jacinta. "She hated me. I always thought it was because Miss Nelson"—she blushed and fluttered her eyelids—"liked me. She was jealous." There was a moment of embarrassed silence for poor naïve Jacinta, although there probably was a grain of truth in what she said: They both saw Miss Nelson as their very own charismatic mother figure and had to compete for her favor.

"When she smiled at Miss Nelson, she looked quite soft," said Susan. "I saw her eyes twinkle, she looked so different."

No one knew anything of the Hindi teacher's pre-Allahabad days. No one knew where she had been born or bred, or how she came to Timmins and became a pet of the British principal. Everyone assumed it had something to do with a mission connection, that she had been an orphan or something and been brought up in mission schools, just like Estelle of Rowson House.

"But the name doesn't jibe," said Beena. "In the orphanage, they would have given her a Christian name." Not Usha, Hindu goddess of dawn.

So it was not like Estelle of Rowson House, we agreed, feeling for a short moment the easy camaraderie of the monsoon feasts. Just then, the dinner came in smelling so much like the school dining room that I felt a sudden wave of nausea. I got up abruptly and left them to their meal.

They were right. Raswani could not have been brought up in an orphanage. Her name would have been changed. To Rose perhaps. Maybe Nelson had spun this web too, converted some solitary wounded teacher and brought her into her fold. Our Lady of Perpetual Succor.

To get to Aeolia you had to walk out of the bazaar, past the municipal garden and the road to table-land, past the electric-green police chowki, and past the house of Adil and Farad, two brothers who kept a regal young cheetah chained in their garage. I had gone to see it with Pin. We had stood still, elbows touching, watching him pace. Today, when I walked past, I saw the cheetah with Pin's proud face, her wild eyes.

Aeolia was the last house on the road out of Panchgani, the road that led down the valley to Vai. It was barely eight o'clock, but the street was dark and quiet. I began to hear rustlings around me. It's only the wind, I told myself firmly, although there really wasn't one. I shone my dim torch determinedly in front of me. The batteries were low, and it cast a barely perceptible circle of light around me.

I had moved to Aeolia three days ago on the back of Shabir's motorbike, balancing my pointy steel trunk on my lap. They planned to come back after the baby, and had left curtains and an orange bedspread, and plates and pots, and a fruit bowl on the square little dining table in the enclosed veranda, and three valley-viewing chairs on the covered porch. It felt quite homey and wonderful, although at night the wind howled and I was buffeted by wild dreams in which Pin would turn up in my childhood and make love to me in my balcony room in Indore while my parents watched.

Tonight, I was jittery. I checked that every door was locked or bolted, and jumped into bed hungry and read a hardcover book with a forgotten library smell—whether from Shabir and Raisa or from Mr. Sopariwalla, the tottering old owner of Aeolia, I could not say—called *How Green Was My Valley*, and I fell into a restless sleep from which I awoke with a start, sure that someone was in my room.

After a forever-lasting stretch of shivers and terrors, I ran up to the light switch near the entrance and put on the naked overhead light. Then I ran around switching on the two lamps and, for good measure, the porch light. I sat at the little dining table and let myself be whisked into a safer world via the green valley in Wales.

TWENTY-NINE

Mozambique

All drug trips listening to the Doors should be the same, whether they are set in Panchgani or in Columbus, Ohio. But each is different, because as time goes by, you will, say, remember the time we found ourselves in the concrete garden at 2:15 and the neon lights suddenly sparkled, remember the time we saw goldfish glinting in a hidden stepwell on Fort Lohagad and you wrote the poem "Shivaji, Your Goldfish Are Showing," remember the time we watched the moonrise over the cliff on table-land on Shabir's orange acid?

Shabir had come upon a delicious supply of orange acid from the ashram. Some days he would arrive in Panchgani on his bike, with Raisa fully pregnant and radiant in crimson robes, an orange bandana in her hair. We would meet at Kaka's or at Lucky's or if you missed them there you could just wait on Merch's steps.

Panchgani is perfect in winter. The days are as crisp as thin butter toast, the shadows are sharp in the mountain mornings and at night when the moonlight bounces off the great black rocks of table-land.

These days, we did not go near the needle. We walked straight through the center of the plateau to the back where the descent was not so sheer and we could see a steep footpath down into another valley. In the north we could see the last of the five plateaus.

One day we left Raisa curled and sleeping on Merch's bed—I was a little less in awe of her ethereal beauty now that she had the bubble in front of her, and had small tentative conversations with her, about housekeeping in Aeolia and her family in Bombay. 'You'll carry on,' she said without a hint of dismay. 'I'll just sleep here.' We dropped acid and went up to table-land. We watched the flaming sunset sink into crimson and then purple but we did not get high.

Not getting it not getting it, let's take more surely more than half an hour has passed, let's smoke a joint it will bring it on no let's just be done with it and take a quarter more each, what the fuck what will happen we said, and then we all felt the lift together when a ring of lights came on in the valley, bling.

We watched a large yellow moon rise over the fifth plateau and then turn hard and white over our heads, so that table-land shone like a bowl of stone. I lay beside Merch, my arm running along his, our thighs an inch apart. He did not move nearer, and neither did I.

It was as if a switch had been flipped.

AC/DC, swings both ways. That was the joke my college friend Gargi and I understood together in the college corridor, turning our palms from front to back with sly smiles. Swings both ways. I could have read it in a magazine, or heard it from a more boisterous group of girls who sat with boys in the canteen. We thought of men in shiny foreign places, Gargi and I. Not of me.

But there was no denying it. Fresh from that pink corridor I had emerged after one season to swing both ways. For now I was flirting with boys and loving it. I was flirting with all the hippie boys, but most of all with Merch. The monsoon was as intense as a dream. And as distant.

If Pin were here, if she walked into the staff room before the tea came in, skillfully pulled me in a corner and brushed her lips and then her snub nose up against mine, and then turned and left, would I sit down and tingle as I had less than two months ago?

If she had been with me on these long nights with our backs propped against the rocks outside Shankar's defunct den, would I be looking only at her, or smiling into the eyes of some stranger, or jumping up suddenly to take out the packet of cigarettes from Merch's top pocket? I can honestly say that I do not know. I can say that feeling sexy was a current that ran through my body, bouncy and tart, and it was she who started it. Man or woman, it did not matter, I thought. Lovemaking is always with the eyes.

Merch had a dry cough. He would cough periodically and then sit up and slowly light a cigarette, always only using one match, even if the wind was high. After he had finished the cigarette, he would make a joint. He was always calm, quiet, and economical. First he stuck a ball of hash or Bombay Black on the end of a matchstick. Next he put it in a safe spot and emptied the tobacco from a cigarette into the palm of his hand. Then, holding the loose tobacco in his cupped palm, he would light the hash, crumble it into the tobacco, and refill the sleeve, all while paying complete attention to what I was saying. It was a night of deep discussions and walks in various groups and subgroups, because there were five of us, Shabir, Samar, Merch, and I, and Vinoo, a wraith of a boy with big curly hair, a hippie hopeful lured to Panchgani by the rash of newspaper reports of illicit dens in the hills.

These boys with wistful faces brought a steady supply of Bombay Black, or sometimes even fragrant pure Afghani hash, and we drank tea and smoked and sat around swapping thoughts as though we were at a caravansary on an alternative trade route.

We walked down from table-land with looped arms, singing "Show me the way to the next whisky bar" all the way through the sleeping bazaar.

It was November, one month into the winter term. I had been snooping and fact finding, but had come up with nothing. I was nervous and distraught and carried the picture of my ayi with her dead eyes like a steel trunk upon my back. I still addressed my weekly letters to both of them, pretending that Ayi could read. I did not call the house, because I could not bear the thought that my ayi would be right there and not talk to me. I phoned Baba in his office once a week asking about her health. "She's much stronger now," he would say, or "She is resting a lot," or "Today she smiled when I read your letter to her." I revealed nothing of my new circumstances.

I spent as much time as possible with Merch and the gang because they were the seawall that kept out the flood. In their delicious company, I would laugh and lounge for hours and forget the tidal waves of pain and fear and guilt.

That orange acid night pops up vast and iridescent, because things began to speed up again after that night.

The next evening, rested and bathed and vulnerable after the acid, I arrived at Merch's room to find them all leaving for Poona. "Come along," they said, but no, I would not go. "You forget that I have a job. Unlike all you wastrels and worse," I said, although I was well aware that it was Thursday and I had nothing to do for three days.

After a cup of tea and a joint, they were getting into the car when Merch changed his mind. "You'll carry on," he said, pushing hair off his eyes. "I don't think I'll come."

In his room, he went first to his record player. That was the day he changed the music. He spent some time intent, holding a cigarette in one hand, gingerly sifting through his neatly stacked records, and then the deep dark voice that still makes my hair rise swirled into the room. I sat at the edge of his high four-poster bed, my legs dangling nervously over the edge.

It is time, he said, for Nina Simone.

He turned from the music and came and knelt at my feet. He took my foot into his hands and gently unhooked the strap of first one sandal and then the other, and then he sat up on the bed beside me and took me into his arms. I felt my forehead against his bony chest and thought again of how neatly my head fit into the hollow of his chest. And then he pulled me down so that we lay across from each other, fully dressed, not touching, just talking. We did not even mention Pin, then. There was so much we had to tell each other about ourselves. My mother drank her own urine, I said. And my father is a disgraced man. My mother, he said, is touched. She does not allow anyone into the house since my father died. I should be staying with her, looking after her, but I cannot bring myself to do it. He went to Bombay, he said, for film festivals and Jazz Yatra, and stayed with her then. His mother, he said, lived in Bombay on Napean Sea Road, in an old Parsi flat filled with dark carved wood, and that is where he had grown up, in a flat by the sea, just like me.

But of course you were not quite born yet, he said. He was twenty-nine years old, he told me, eight long years older than me.

We could have met at Hanging Gardens in the evening, I said. My bai took me there all the time.

We could have met at the Big Shoe at Kamala Nehru Park, he said, claiming to have loved the shoe. He went in the evening with his ayah until he was ten, while other boys played ruffian games between the cars in the building compound. But he was sure he had never seen me. I would have never forgotten it if I saw you, he said.

But I did not have the blot then, I said. I surprised myself when it came out as a statement of fact instead of an opening into a dark wound.

That would be a different matter altogether, he admitted, and I took that as a compliment.

And so I could have been a baby dressed in frilly bonnets and hand-knitted wool socks in summer, gurgling in a pram while the sensitive Parsi boy with stick legs hanging from his khaki shorts wandered around inside the yellow shoe with the little cottage roof.

I like, I love, I know, I hate, we talked through the day, a stream of pleasure flowing on the bed between us. From the window I could see the far silhouette of a village hut and a patch of bright paddy. I heard a dog barking, and a woman's voice calling "oi mahtara!" in the valley. I should leave now, I thought, in this perfect time before the touching.

But the world melted when we began to kiss, because Merch poured his soul out in that kiss. I cannot remember how we first took our clothes off, but I remember rubbing my skin against his, and his body stretched out beside mine, so that I felt his ribs against my breasts.

I am a virgin, I said.

He cupped my chin in his hands, and kissed me long and slow, and then he climbed on top of me, and he put his hard penis between my thighs so that it rubbed against me with every long stroke, but he did not enter. We got ourselves into the rhythm until his arm got crushed under me, and then we laughed awkwardly and kissed again, and then the passion began to mount once more. For the first time, I knew where the hollow lay, wanting to be filled.

Do it now, I said, put it in, thinking he hesitated because he worried I might want to keep my virginity intact. But he smiled and shook his head. There will be time, he said, and we started talking again in each other's arms.

But how is it, I asked him, how is it that I can love a woman and a man. Something must be wrong with me. Something must be wrong with me when I feel this way about a woman. One minute my body is in turmoil at the touch of a woman, and then, so soon after she dies, I can turn to love a man. I am afraid, I said. I think I am some sort of wanton woman.

You are not a wanton woman, he said, kneading my thighs. You are not a wanton woman, you are a *wanting* woman. That day, with his face an inch away from mine, I shook my head, not liking the label at all. But later I saw that he had given me a line to wear for all of my life.

I grew up disfigured. I imagined people muttering and pointing at me, perhaps more than they actually did. I grew up withdrawing and watching, my hair around my face. But I had stacked up dozens of dreams in colored bottles against the glass pane, and when they did crack open I understood that I was a wanting woman.

Strange gift, though, from a man who himself refused to step out of the pages of his books. And movies and music, of course, I can hear his voice in my head, bemused.

You must learn, he told me quite firmly that day sitting cross-legged in front of me, to stop confusing sex with morality. Sex is an animal act like eating and sleeping. It is only we, the human race, who have ritualized it, glorified it, and tabooed it. It really is as simple as that, he said. He got up, and with his half-risen penis preceding him, he went to his bookshelf.

And that is how the books began to pile up around the bed.

His penis looked like him, long and lanky with a slight upward curve. "Up boy," he said when I began to touch him with tentative strokes, and then he suddenly without a warning swung himself on top of me, and we began a greedy dance, long low strokes until our breathing became fast and ragged and I arched up against him clinging while I came, and then he came in spurts upon my thigh and fell limp on top of me. This, he told me, is called thigh-fucking.

It will be a first time for me too, he said, after we had eaten a packet of glucose biscuits and smoked a joint.

You mean you are a virgin too? I asked, surprised. He seemed so sure and practiced.

No, he said, but you will be my first virgin.

Isn't that a trophy kind of thing, to take a virgin? Supposed to be especially sexy? I asked. I had always been certain that I would be a virgin on my wedding night. But now I wanted to know. I wanted to know if it would change the shape of my desire, to have a part of his body inside my own.

I don't know, he said, but I will have to find out. And he got on top of me again. Just relax your thighs, he said, I'm going in. Don't move, just let them flop. It's the outer hip that is the key, he said, his face screwed up in concentration. It was fun, like an experiment that we were doing together. Yes, he said, I feel it. I feel the wall coming down.

I felt a sharp stab of pain, and then a tingling. And then I felt him sliding around inside me, not thrusting anymore. He rolled back down, and we both lay spent, staring at the ceiling. It had not been like making love. I did not come, and neither did he. Later we found two drops of blood on the sheet.

So did that feel just tremendous or something? I asked when he lay beside me, his head propped up.

Not really, he said. I was quite stressed. I thought I would fall down. The pressure, he said smiling ruefully, of being a man. He mopped his brow in mock relief. And you? he asked, raising his eyebrows into a castle top. Are you sorry to be deflowered?

No, I said, just stunned. It took all of five minutes. No one can tell you how it feels, because it is nothing to the body. Only to the mind.

I wish I had been a virgin too, he said. Then we would both be in the same space. We would grow together and learn about love together. Have you read *Ada* by Nabokov?

No, I had not.

But you must, a book of pure genius, he said, adding the fat book with a torn pink cover on top of the pile beside the bed. Later, I wondered why he did it, whether he had some sort of sinister motive.

But that night, we were still beneath the perfect sky. We stood in the balcony and smoked a joint, and when we were freshly high, I wrapped my brown shawl around us both, and we went to Kaka's, and sat at our usual table in the *ladys and familys* section on the second floor.

Even the surly little waiter smiled at us in the dingy single-bulb light, so that we looked at each other knowing there was a glow around us. And then we went back to his room, we fell into each other's arms once more. I took off all my clothes and did not put them on again until I left, two days later.

On the morning of the second day, when the light was gray and pink, he threw on the shirt left on the floor from the night before and popped his head out of the window, the rest of him dangling naked. He called down to the mali to start a sigri for him, and then get him one packet of Wills cigarettes and two packets of Charminar from the bidi stand, sandalwood paste and a packet of camphor from Panchgani Stores, and fragrant roses and jasmine.

I tugged his shirt from behind. No jasmine, I said.

Only roses, he called, but the most fragrant ones from the puja market.

Tell him to get the flowers first, or else the housewives will snap them up for their morning prayers, I said, and so he conveyed that in turn to the mali.

He then went to the kitchen, where I heard him start the tea. While the water boiled he shuffled to his desk and sat down and carefully rolled three joints and laid them out. His curly long hair fell across his face, and there was a gray-green stubble on his chin. We had spent the night curled and close, between waves of desire. But we had not made love all night.

Deep into the night, I had opened my eyes to find his face buried in my hair on his pillow. I wish it were perfumed, I said, like a princess. I told him I had read how Mughal princesses spent all day in the harem adorning themselves. How they scented their seven orifices, and how their maids held their long black hair above hot coals infused with sandalwood and roses so that they walked in a cloud of perfume all day.

Was this your fantasy? he asked.

This was my fantasy, I said, to make love with perfumed hair.

Let's do it then, he said, and went back to sleep inside my hair.

When we were drinking his strong, sweet tea and could see the clouds rising from the morning valley, I heard the mali walk up the stairs, and I sprang up to hide in the bathroom.

It's fine, murmured Merch, holding my hand down. I don't allow servants in the room. I don't allow anyone in the room, except friends. And no one over thirty-five. I clean my room myself—that explains the dust, I said—and the dhobi leaves my clothes downstairs. The locals are afraid of me, he said, raising his eyebrows, bemused. They think I am into satanic practices or something.

We carefully heated and crushed rose petals and added them to the sandalwood paste. Then we had a hot bath, sliding with soap on the bathroom floor. We washed my hair and rolled it into a towel and wrung it out till it was nearly dry. The coals in the sigri beside us glowed red and warm.

On Merch's balcony, with the sound of the wind in the silver oaks, I still see the two of us, spreading my hair over the fragrant smoke. We put our messy rose paste in a steel dish on the coals, and when it began to smoke we knelt naked on either side of it, holding my hair between us like the girls held out Mahrukh Tunty's bras to dry.

We tried various positions. In the end, I knelt facing away from the sigri and leaned backward into it, while Merch knelt beside me, bolstering my arched body against his, holding up my head with one hand and my hair, above the sigri, with another, so close to the fire that I could see the smoke closing in over my head. I kept my hands locked behind his neck to keep from falling into the fire. This is a job for seven maids, I said, and he bent to kiss my blot, and then we both began to cough with the smoke, and we ran into the room, and I jumped onto his bed and spread my legs, and when he was sliding so smooth and fine inside me I did feel, for the first time, the rhythm of the tide inside me. This is meant to be, I thought, dancing under him. The smoky perfume from my hair got into the pillow and sheets and was in our hands and noses and in our heads because we were nearly one that day.

We are the perfect match, he said, and my heart rose and battered against my chest in hope. We are the perfect match, he said. I think we are the bull and the mare. He pulled out a dusty copy of the Kama Sutra—oh, let me dust your bookshelf one day, I said—and we studied the chart of sexual unions with our legs entwined together.

In his damp kitchen, Merch had one little cupboard, which contained a tin of Nescafé, Darjeeling tea, two bottles of jam, eggs and milk and butter, stale pau bread tied in a newspaper, and a few misshapen bottles of spice. I make the best omelets, he said, and expertly cracked the eggs down the center with a fork, and with the aid of two teacups, he separated the white and the yellow. He beat the whites into a froth with a fork—always forty lashes, he told me, firmly.

We sat cross-legged on the worn carpet with the frying pan between us, scooping up the cloud-light omelet with dripping pieces of bread fried in butter, as Nina Simone's blue-black voice sealed the time in that room.

But what do you really eat all day? I asked him, prying at the little mysteries that surrounded him.

I have a dabba service, he said. Mr. Irani's cook makes me dinner in a tiffin three or four nights a week. I pay fifty rupees a month. Good stuff, actually. He makes chops and sali boti and deviled eggs. Sometimes I only eat at night.

Yes, he said, I am true to type. A Parsi bachelor. He did his Parsi accent, but there was only a hint of Cyrus in his voice, there was no Cyrus without Freny, and there could be no Freny without Pin. I saw the ghost of her against the edges of my eyes. How could I not, when this was the very bed on which I had made love with her?

But guilt, I said to Merch out of the blue. How does this Naked Ape world deal with guilt?

Well, a certain degree of guilt is necessary when killing occurs within the tribe, he said. Maybe I turned as white as a sheet, because he stammered for a moment, and then he hastened to add, I mean, for example, of course, in the extreme case. I mean killing in battle is rewarded, but crimes within the tribe have got to be accompanied by guilt and punishment, for the survival of the tribe, he said, rubbing his beard stubble—the stubble that I had cleaned like a cat, with my tongue, that very morning.

You know, he said later when he had begun to use my hair against me as an erotic device, and I knew where his hands and then his mouth were headed, you do know that in our case, guilt is irrelevant. She was already over the edge, he said, and went on to bite my navel, so that I could pretend that I had not heard it.

After sunset, Merch put on his khaki pants, a red pullover, and thick ghati chappals, and went out to the Irani Café to get some hot gutli pau.

I found *Ada* on the pile beside the bed, and I curled in his bed and read random pages from the musty book, desire spreading and twitching in the pit of my stomach again. I saw how Van Veen loved only Ada, for all of his long life. He loves me, I thought, and I jumped up and did a circle in front of his mirror, my breasts bobbing, my hair flying behind me. And then I stopped and kissed my face in the mirror. He loves me, he loves me, he loves me.

It was the pure day. Of the three days I spent in Merch's room, it was the second. The first day was the shy and awkward day, with nervous giggles and anxious looks. On the third day, our paths began to veer away from each other, because it was on the third day that I loved him the most.

"I read parts of *Ada*," I said to him coyly, angling for a declaration of love. I had turned suddenly cunning in his absence.

"I always saw us in it," he said. "From the day you walked into my room, like Venus emerged from a shell. I felt I wanted to know you all your life. I wanted to grow up with you, to watch you get your breasts, your pubic hair. Ada is the perfect love story, isn't it?"

But this, I wanted to say, this is perfect too, as he lay inside me, limp and resting, and then, one of us would move slowly, and then I would feel him harden, and we would move faster and faster and we would look into each other's eyes and see the worlds we would travel together, and when I came the burst of it was deep inside the center of my soul. This was the life I wanted, this room, this man, this love. And it was when he saw this in my eyes, this greedy need of him, that he began to retreat, although I did not understand this until much later.

I want you, Merch, I hugged him and said, hoarse and fierce and weeping with the strength of my feelings. He took my hair, pulled it up above my head till it almost hurt, and then he kissed me hard till my lips were bruised and I had a blue love bite on my neck. I want you, I said. I want you, Merch, I want you beside me forever. He said nothing.

I awoke the next morning to find *The Hunting of the Snark* by Lewis Carroll on the pillow instead of his tousled head. The room was quiet, the curtains drawn. Merch had gone out without waking me. He will be back with a newspaper and eggs, I thought, and dozed off again to awake at eleven with a heavy head. The room was still silent, and I wondered why he should be away for so long. I picked up the book and saw the poem he had written on the first page.

As birds are fitted to the boughs
That blossom on the tree
And whisper when the south wind blows—
So was my love to me,

And still she blossoms in my mind
And whispers softly, though
The clouds are fitted to the wind,
The wind is to the snow.

—LOUIS SIMPSON

I knew before I knew, as the stomach fell out of my body, as the stars fell from the sky. This was how Merch would do it. This was his way of saying he would not go out into the world as my man. I felt as a newborn might feel, thrust raw and red from a womb.

He would not return to the room until I was gone. Coward, I thought, he takes and props me up as a princess, and then he cannot come and say good-bye. He is not a mystery man, I thought with anger. He is just a common coward. Later, when I was more charitable with him, I granted that, at best, he was an aesthete. Perhaps he wanted to hold the moment forever, like a rose preserved in the pages of a book.

I too got my perfect moment, this I must admit, now that I am older.

But that morning, sobbing, I washed my hair with the shikakai soap in the scrupulous, double-layer soap dish in Merch's dim bathroom. I do not know at what point during the bath I decided to cut it all off, because I know I did not think of it when I went in. I wound my long black hair into a tight tail till the water stopped dripping from it, and then I took a new blade from Merch's shaving kit and hacked off the part of my body that I had always loved, with only the small square shaving mirror above his sink for company. It came off in my hands like a live limb. I wound it into a bun on Merch's pillow, in the place of the book he had left for me there. I buried my face into my shorn hair, as I had done on so many childhood nights. On his pillow, smelling of sandalwood and roses, it became a foreign body, and so I was able to leave it there, sitting like a nest. All he wanted from me, I thought bitterly, was a perfect memory, so let him keep it. Let him miss me now, I thought spitefully as I slammed the door behind me, swearing that I would not need to see him again.

But I could not stay away from the gathering of the gang in the evenings, because that was the lodestar of all our lives. We dream-walked through the days and we came together pulled by magnets and sat stoned and laughing in Merch's room, or wandered around on valiant whims. Merch and I were sheepish with each other for a while, and then one day when the home team, as we called ourselves in those days, parted at dawn, I stayed behind in his room and we began to sleep with each other again and I put my intensity on a shelf and loved him as he wanted to be loved, although it wasn't always easy.

Maybe he still has my hair curled in his cupboard wrapped in a soft white cloth. My beautiful black sleek hair that was my pride; it will be as dry and dusty as our love. I miss my hair now, I miss it swinging merrily around me, I miss it gleaming on my back like an exclamation mark.

But at that time, I did not. I felt light and confident, with wisps and curls around my face. In 1974, I passed through death and dementia and deep and drastic loves, and began to feel that I was destined for a charmed life. I felt that I had cut my hair and stepped from the shadows into the light. Even though the sharp crackle of danger was around me, I walked jauntily along the precipice. I felt I was acting in a story that was sure to turn out right. I was twenty-one.

THIRTY

The Princely Eye

AFTER A MONTH of lying fallow, the case was moving again, and the girls were in a stratospheric state of excitement.

The Scottish Presbyterian Mission in Scotland or wherever such kind of headquarters would be had decided to pay for a lawyer to defend Miss Nelson. Miss Wilson had worn a long navy-blue flowered skirt and closed shoes and a brooch on her white blouse and gone to Poona to meet him.

She had then taken him to Vai to talk to Miss Nelson. But we had heard through Miss Henderson, who told Sister Richards who told Nandita who told me, that Miss Nelson had refused to admit them into her room.

After they had waited for a time, she pushed a note from under her door. She would receive no visitors until the day she appeared in court. She would pray and prepare herself so that she could be an instrument of the Lord.

> Thank the mission for coming to my help. The lawyer can have a free hand in conducting enquiries, and he can send me any paperwork he desires. I will meet him on the day of the court hearing. I have put myself in the hands of the Lord.

"If she is innocent, then she should take the Gandhiji route. Fast and pray. Drink only lime water for forty days." Shobha was holding forth in the detention room on Saturday morning. "I feel so bad for her. Let's send her an anonymous note, telling her to fast. That will get everyone to take notice."

"Nelly knows everyone's writing. There can be no anonymity in this school."

"We'll cut it out of newspapers or books, like they do in the movies. *Fast unto Death for Death of Daughter.*" Shobha raised her voice as I entered the room.

"You're a mean one, Shobha," said an admiring voice from her gallery.

I was glad not to be teaching the likes of Shobha anymore. I enjoyed teaching eleven- and twelve-year-olds. Especially Hindi. I felt I was pouring a warm bath as I read them short stories. They entered Hindi class in a defensive crouch, their senses jammed by Raswani's brutal teaching. When I read "Shatranj ke Khiladi" from *Premchand ki sarvasesht kahania*, the entire class, including the South Indian girls who had probably not understood a word, sat in pin-drop silence for a full minute after I finished it.

But there was still an occasional detention duty, since they were so short on staff.

I don't remember why Shobha had detention that day, but she was clearly intent on goading me. First she passed notes, then she threw notes across the room, then she started whispering, and then talking loudly, until I had no choice but to respond.

"Shobha, stand up now and get out of the room. And do not bother to come back."

Shobha stomped out. But she stopped just outside. She turned around and faced the class with a smirk on her face. The class began to giggle.

"I said I want you out of the class." My voice was quiet now, and controlled. Commanding, I hoped.

"But Miss, how can I leave a detention room? If you throw me out, I won't have done my detention. And anyway, Miss, I am out of the class. See, here is the class line, and I am on the other side."

What to do now? I stared at her malevolently for a few minutes, my hands itching to slap her.

Shobha construed my silence as victory and decided to play to the gallery. "This line will be my boundary from now on. I will not come into the class. I will stand outside here and imbibe your wisdom." Her eyes were insolent. "I will be like Sita, Miss. This will be my god-given boundary line." The class was roaring.

I was wearing one of my tight chudidar sets stitched by Rathode of Rathode & Sons in Indore, and I felt ugly and ungainly, which made me see a deeper shade of red. My blot was blistering, scarlet.

I walked up to her, went really up close to her, so she could smell my breakfast-eggs breath, and stood with my legs apart, hands on hips. She was about an inch taller than me, with mango breasts and almond eyes.

"You will go right now to the library. You will get two order marks. One for disrupting the class and the second for talking back to a teacher. And now you will go to the library and spend the rest of the detention there, reading chapter six of *A Tale of Two Cities*."

Shobha's smirk took on a pasted quality as the muscles in her face became tight. She stood there, not wanting to show a weakness in front of the class.

"If you do not turn around and leave now, you will get a third order mark for disobedience." I liked my newfound voice. It was smooth and icy.

"You can't give me three order marks for the same thing. It's not allowed." But her voice had a waver, had a question at the end.

"You just watch me," I said, standing almost right on top of her.

She turned to leave. But before she walked off, with her back to me, she muttered just under her breath. "You did it. We know."

"What did you just say?" I asked, putting my hand on her shoulder and turning her around roughly to face me.

"Nothing, Miss, nothing at all."

"Look at me," I said, I lifted her chin and held it in place. "You better watch what you say, you stupid little schoolgirl. Or you will regret it later."

There was complete silence in the detention room for the rest of the class, and I relished every minute of it.

"I'M SORRY ABOUT your mother, Miss," Nandita said one day, falling into step beside me as I walked up the winding way around the school building to the staff room. It was called the winter way, because it was used only in the winter. In summer and monsoon everyone used the long covered steps that ran through the center of the school.

Nandita looked at me gravely. She wore thick glasses with square plastic frames. She walked in silence for a few steps, pushing her thick fringe away from her face. Then, suddenly, in a rush, she said, "Miss, you're . . . You know, you're different this term. Everyone says so."

"Well, Nandita, a lot has happened in the last two months," I said. My world had changed. I felt I was a woman on a windy plain in some ancient epic.

"But it feels like—I don't know how to say it, but it feels . . . oh, I don't know, Miss. You seem like a different person."

Nandita had the ability to chat with teachers as one adult to another. I knew she must be referring to my most recent episode with Shobha. Nandita was right. The detention-room drama had the dregs of Prince. Raging Anger was Prince, not me. Charu was silent, stoic, and suffering.

But no point in getting into that. I was pursuing my search for the Hindi teacher.

"Nandita," I said. "It was you who got the letter from Miss Raswani, right?"

"Yes, Miss, it was me," she said

"What made her give it to you just like that?"

"I felt she knew something, and so I went and spoke to her," she said with quiet pride.

"Nandita, well done. No one else could have done it," I said. I meant it. Raswani must have let her guard down, with Nandita so reasonable, so quiet.

"And the next day, she was gone, correct?"

"In fact she disappeared the same day. I was the last person to see her, I think."

"Did she appear to be frightened?"

"She seemed defeated. I don't know if you know about the incident of the day before. She could not control the girls in the gym. She walked out while the girls clapped and jeered. We were always terrified of her. But that day, she walked out with her head down. I saw her face. It was the same look she had on the day she gave me the letter. Like she had lost her roar."

"You girls," I said. "Where do you think she is now?"

"Now that we know the terrible truth about Nelson, mostly everyone thinks she might have killed Raswani. Because of the letter. It is logical to assume that Nelson thought her secret was safe as long as no one knew about the letter, and so she killed Raswani. She didn't know that Raswani had passed on the letter to us."

"No fingerprints, no signs of struggle in the room, and no body," I reminded her.

"I don't know, Miss," said Nandita. "Who knows how efficient these Poona police are? No better than Woggle and his gang, I bet."

Nandita would have been more guarded if she had been with Shobha or Akhila, who were quite wary of me. As it was, she seemed eager to share her knowledge.

"You could be right," I said. "You think her body could be lying hidden under a rock?"

"Or a cave, maybe," said Nandita. "It's hard for us to get out of this place, but I wish I could."

"Well, you obviously managed to get out before," I said in a supercilious tone, asserting my teacher self.

"Yes, Miss, but you know what I mean; I can't just roam around like you," said Nandita, quite unfazed.

She seemed almost as eager as me to solve this mystery. We should team up, I thought.

"Actually, I agree with you," I said. "I have been snooping around. I even went into the Devil's Kitchen two days ago. I saw nothing. No torn clothing, no bones, no smell of rotting flesh."

With Shankar no longer running his den of vice, Devil's Kitchen had an abandoned air when I went there two days ago, on a sunny afternoon. It was windy, but the rock hollow was quiet and dry. The cave must have some aperture somewhere, because it had a diffused glow. There were five metal folding chairs and an upturned box with a couple of half-burned candles, and an outsize overflowing metal ashtray engraved with the words "Tekchand and Sons Water Filters." You entered a wide mouth and then turned to the right, where you were sheltered from the elements and from prying eyes. In one corner was the bar, a plank of wood raised on boxes, with a lantern at either end.

Devil's Kitchen, witch's needle, at first I thought that these were internal Timmins names made up by imaginative girls at midnight feasts. But then I saw a guidebook on Panchgani ("Come visit the Kashmir of Maharashtra, with its sylvan forests, its panoramic mountain views, its salubrious climate") that touted these as places for tourists to view the surrounding vistas, along with Baby Point, Parsi Point, and Sydney Point, the last of which I presume was named after an intrepid British explorer in a solar hat who hacked his way to the hill with the help of a bunch of natives carrying folding desks and foreign newspapers.

"All this Devil's Kitchen, witch's needle. I mean, who came up with these names?"

Nandita smiled and shook her head. "Don't know." She had a very white, even set of teeth. "It's so out of *Macbeth*, isn't it miss?" she said, shyly.

"Have you been to the Devil's Kitchen?" I asked.

"Long ago, when we were in junior school. Before Shankar began to use it, we sometimes went for Saturday walks around the back of table-land to the cave. Once, we went exploring to find the source of the light. Right at the back, there is a hole and you can see a patch of sky from it."

"So then, someone could be on table-land itself, and if they knew how to find the hole, they could slip into the cave?" I asked, astonished.

"The hole is high up, and it seemed very tiny. Like a slit, really. Perhaps a small child on the shoulders of a very tall man could climb though it. And jumping down would be impossible. In fact, after we saw the hole, Tara became obsessed with the cave for some time. She and Ramona had this elaborate prison-break plan where they were going to get a ladder—don't ask me how—and prop it against the hole, and then one day when we went to table-land they would slip through it, run away from school, and live in the cave until the end of term. We were eight or nine then, I think. For some time after that, whenever we went to table-land, we would look for the hole on the surface where the cave should be—but, you know, we have not found it to this day."

"Panchgani is a strange place, no?" I said.

"Don't really know any other, Miss," she said, shrugging her shoulders. "I've been in this school since I was six and a half."

"Is it hard? I mean, I know so many of the girls hate being here."

"I just know that it is the best option for my family, so I don't mind," she replied matter-of-factly.

Sometimes, I thought Nandita was the oldest soul in the whole school.

Since I wasn't teaching the seniors anymore, I did not go past the prayer hall and the big banyan tree, but up the stairs to the middles section, which was perched above the prayer hall.

Akhila came upon us as we turned the corner.

"Good morning, Miss Apte."

"Good morning," I said.

"So, Miss, you found a place to stay?" she said, smirking. There was a nip in the air, and the girls wore navy-blue pullovers over their blue checks. I presumed Miss Manson was still vigilant, and their bloomers were elasticized to the perfect degree, plump thighs forming puffs of flesh on either side of the tight elastic.

I ignored Akhila. I turned to Nandita. "I hear Ramona is not back this term. What is the matter with her?"

"She is disturbed because of all the things we saw, you

know, that night," began Nandita in a measured tone. By the way that she paused significantly before "that night," I knew she was considering her approach. I waited, and we walked a few steps in silence.

But Akhila was not a patient girl, and she blurted it out. "She says she saw Miss Prince's ghost, and it told her she had to leave the school."

Why would I imagine that she had visited only me? She might have visited half of Panchgani, for all I knew.

"Ramona is a nervous girl," said Nandita, embarrassed, giving me a sideways glance, trying to judge my reaction.

"So has she left the school, or is she coming back?"

"We don't know," said Akhila.

"I think she will be back soon," said Nandita stoutly. Nandita tied her green belt too high on her waist, wore her socks long, just below the knees. I saw something of myself in her, an adult facade that I wanted to rip apart. I wanted to tell her to stand on the big swing outside the snuggery and take it so high that it went parallel to the sky, before it was too late. And that is how I often see her in my mind, her dress blowing in the wind, her hair flying, her knees bent to take the swing as high as it could go.

We walked in silence for a while. Ramona was the weak link, I was thinking. She's the one who has seen the most. I should talk to her.

"Did she say she actually physically saw Miss Prince?" I asked.

"No, but . . ."

"And did anyone else, any of you see her?"

Nandita told me of the scream, and of the night when they

called her spirit. I realized that they assumed I knew of this scream. I had not heard even the faintest of rumors.

"Who heard this scream?"

"Everyone heard it," said Akhila. "You can ask anyone."

"Well it's for sure all the girls in Willoughby and Pearsall heard it. So the matrons and teachers around them must have too. The hospital is too far, though. We asked the mumps girls, and they didn't hear it," said Nandita.

"And even you thought it was the ghost of Miss Prince? If only half the school heard and the teachers in Sunbeam didn't hear it, then it was physical, not ethereal, no?" I asked, lifting my eyebrows at Nandita the Sane.

"But Miss, we didn't know about Miss Nelson then, remember? Everyone was confused. The Upper Willoughby girls insist it was Miss Nelson, and the Lower Willoughby girls swear that they heard it like a growl growing out of Miss Raswani's room. So we thought we would consult higher authorities, as it were. Shobha, Akhila, and I decided to do a planchette. I never really thought anything would happen," said Nandita quietly.

All three of us continued to walk, looking down at our feet on the red mud path. "Do you believe that it was really her? I mean, do you think the ghost of Miss Prince really visited Ramona?" she asked.

"Yes, I do," I said softly and saw a lightening in her opaque eyes.

Akhila was fidgeting in the manner of schoolgirls who are about to say something they've been storing up. Usually something you don't want to hear. Finally, as we approached the staff room, she blurted it out.

"Miss, maybe Dr. Desai has some more rooms above his dispensary, you could stay there," she said, stressing "there" and giving me a pleased look as though she had popped a big round sweet into her mouth. I saw Nandita nudge her furiously.

"I have had enough of the smell of disinfectant, thank you," I said, and lifted the pink curtain and walked into the sanctuary of the staff room where no student was ever allowed to set foot. But I heard what they said as they walked past.

"I should have asked, 'Does Merch smell of disinfectant?' That's what I should have done," said Akhila.

"Why didn't you just shut up, you idiot," snapped Nandita. "You spoilt it all."

"But you were supposed to bring up Merch, we agreed." Akhila was saying with a rising tide of disgruntlement. "We were supposed to warn her of the danger. What is the point of rehearsing it"—and then to my disappointment they walked out of my range of hearing and Nandita's soft reply was only a mumble. I turned around with flushed cheeks to see Miss Munim, the art teacher, leering at me with raised eyebrows and a foolish grin. I had no time to think because the bell rang.

Eleven-year-olds still crowded around you and wanted to tell you about their days. They hadn't reached the dueling stage yet, and you could let your guard down.

Divya Moghe of standard six had become something of an acolyte. "We never knew Hindi could be so much fun, Miss," she said. She always offered to carry my books to the staff room, and she always chattered on at full speed, trying to stuff as much into the walk as she could.

The day after my conversation with Nandita and Akhila, Divya was very subdued as she walked beside me carrying sixteen brown-paper-covered Hindi notebooks that I was taking home to correct. "Nandita wants you to meet her in the far throwball court right now. She says it's urgent."

"Did she say why?"

"She does not want anyone else to know." Divya looked at me gravely. I wondered how much of the story she knew. "I think it's to do with the mystery. She says she wanted to tell you yesterday, but Akhila got in the way."

I was on my way to little lunch in the staff room. Little lunch was 10:35 to 10:45. For the girls, it was the only meal left to choice. They could go down to the pantry and get a banana if they wanted. Sometimes there were two glucose biscuits, and on rare occasions, when Miss Cummings felt bountiful, there were two glucose biscuits and a banana, and word would spread quickly and there would be a line outside the pantry. For the teachers, there was a large pot of tea, a tray of Marie biscuits, and a bowl of bananas or small sour oranges.

I loved little lunch. The kitchen in Aeolia was a dark dank outhouse with a Primus stove that took me more than twenty minutes to light. On teaching days I would sit down in the staff room and drink two cups of tea, have a variable number of Marie biscuits, and end with a banana. In winter, they often had small, sweet elaichi bananas, of which I often ate two. Women I had barely exchanged more than two sentences with last term, such as the oily history teacher, the wife of the superintendent of St. Paul's who taught some junior class, and Mrs. Paranjpe, the ex–French teacher who chewed paan, sat down next to me and engaged me in small talk now that I had acquired this aura of mystery.

Meeting Nandita during little lunch would be a considerable sacrifice, but I knew it was for my own good, and so I went and found her leaning against the stone wall that bounded the school

"Miss, I wanted to ask you, do you feel someone has been watching you?" she asked.

I did. After the *How Green Was My Valley* night, my skin crawled after dark. I was afraid to walk to Aeolia at night. The wind howled, the trees swayed, and beneath the sounds I heard the edge of a growl. And when the wind stopped, I heard footsteps and, once, a cough. I could not read because I did not want to leave the light on; I did not want her, him, them, it to watch me. I locked all the doors and windows and lay rigid in the dark, staring up. But I remember one thing: My blot was quiet. Some nights the mali beat his wife and I tried to find her screams reassuring, at least, for sounds of life, but then I began to hear other sounds and screams beneath them. Sometimes I slept at Merch's.

But I enjoyed the quiet, golden afternoons in Aeolia. I came back after school and I could work or read or dream. I took long naps from which I awoke to the evening sounds from the mali's hut. I bathed, dressed—mostly in jeans—gathered my books, and left. I kept some clothes in a drawer in Merch's bathroom.

Shabir had said I was imagining it. "Aeolia is a little spooky," he said. "We used to hear rumblings and rustlings. It's on the windward side. Apparently it's named after Aeolus, Greek god of the wind."

"Or it could be the schoolgirls, spying on you," said Merch.

"They are locked up in that school," I said.

"They did get out that night," he pointed out.

In the safety of the home team I sometimes felt I was imagining the whole thing. But now, I looked at Nandita's face and began to feel she was laughing at me. I had assumed that she was on my side. Now I felt betrayed.

Maybe Merch was right. They were spying on me because they fancied themselves detectives. I imagined the schoolgirls giggling as I changed and talked to myself, as I did so often these days. Or with Merch. Merch. Akhila had insinuated my relationship with Merch. How would she know?

I saw a streak of red before my eyes. "So are you trying to tell me you girls have been spying on me?" I roared, not recognizing the voice that assaulted my ears as my own.

"No, no, Miss, how could we? I know you are innocent," she said, taken aback by my sudden lash of anger.

Shobha was calling to her from the netball field. The Nandita calls became louder as Shobha and Akhila turned the corner near the water tanks.

Nandita gave a resigned sigh. "It's hard to talk with all these chattering girls. But I have so much to tell you," she muttered.

She started to walk away, and then stopped and turned.

"It's all around you, Miss, you must take care."

"What's around me?" I asked urgently, deeply contrite now, verging on the pathetic. "What is all around me?"

Death, I thought, she is saying death is all around me.

Shobha and Akhila were upon us, not at all pleased to see Nandita consorting secretly with me. She turned to them with a placating air, walking towards them with her head tilted, arms outstretched.

"Just look around you, please, Miss. I think you are in danger," she whispered to me before she turned. For that moment, she was the teacher, and I, a thick-headed child.

Akhila and Shobha did not even offer the statutory "Good morning, Miss Apte." They just turned insolently and walked back towards the classrooms.

THAT EVENING, I went for a walk to table-land. I reached the needle in time for sunset.

I sat facing the cliff, as the Prince had done. I sat at the sharp cliff edge, my legs dangling in the void, just as she must have done on the night of her death. Ever since her death, I had wanted to go, but I was afraid to go so far. Today, though, the earth was dry and hard and safe, not slippery as on the monsoon night of her death.

Table-land was empty. I heard no sound except an occasional puff of wind. The distant volcanoes glowed orange, then deep pink as the sun dipped behind them, and then silver in the light of the rising moon as I sat there, calm and Buddhist and untouchable.

I was getting nowhere with the murder mystery, and my affair with Merch was at a dead end. I could see only three roads down from the precipice, each steeper than the next. I could leave Nelson, her Lord, and her lawyer to defend themselves and go home to Ayi until I was needed in court. I could stay on in Panchgani and try to solve my personal mystery:

Was I being followed and watched, was it really the sounds of some sinister scuffling and scrambling I heard in the night at Aeolia, or was I going mad? Or I could go and tell Woggle that my first statement was a lie.

"I did see something on table-land that night, Inspector Wagle," I would have to say.

I have always had a natural tendency to lie. My first lies began with the blot, little subterfuges to protect my own separate world. They blossomed into bigger lies when I loved Pin, necessary deceits but deceits still, because my love was sinful to some, though not to me. I could be nostalgic about them now. They were little lies; there was no loss of life or limb or fortune attached to them. My first lie was of that night on table-land. My first black lie. And I was stuck with it.

Imagine if I went up to Woggle's office—or perhaps I should knock at the Nest on the way down. What if Yellow opened the door with a long plait and a flowered yellow housecoat, and when Woggle came out in his torn T-shirt, I said, "Inspector, I lied. I cannot lie any longer, for I lie awake at nights and need to take shelter in drugs and sex and rock and roll. I cannot lie anymore because my lie might take an innocent person to prison for the rest of her life. I was up on table-land, and I saw Nelson leave while Prince was still alive."

"And why did you lie in the first place?" he would surely ask.

To protect my parents, to protect myself. Because I did not have the courage then. I thought you would think it was me.

He might just believe it. Or he might not.

I could be a bent Baba or a broken Ayi for the rest of my life.

Or I could get lucky.

I was in a trance when I turned to go. "This is good-bye, Pin," I shouted into the void, but the wind snatched my words away.

I had run into Merch in the bazaar on the way up. He had walked around the bend in the road past the municipal park with me. We sat down beside a tree while he discreetly and casually rolled a small joint he called the travel special. We did not ask each other anything, where we were going or what we were doing. "Come by later," he said. "Samar will probably be there." I said I would.

To this day, I cannot say for sure if it was because I was lost in intense stoned thoughts and swung too fast to bring my legs off the edge—but I am not Pin the surfer, I am Charu, squeamish about heights—or if it was because I was given a small sudden shove by ghostly unseen hands. Either way, enthralled by wide vistas and a winter sunset, I tumbled off the cliff.

I took one long deep breath in the abyss. "They say she died near a cave called Devil's Kitchen," I heard Tai say to a circle of mourning women, her face grim. My scream echoed back up to me as in my dream. But by the next breath, I was perched on a ledge, with the emptiness around me. I did not look down.

I shifted my weight on the ledge, dislodging rocks that bounced all the way down to the valley. My slipper came off my foot and hurtled into the abyss. They will find it broken outside Shankar's den, just as they had found her body, I thought.

I knew I could not crouch like a goat in the wind forever. There was no other ledge in sight. No way to clamber up or down the steep rock face. Did Pin hang here suspended between life and death before she fell and broke her head? Did she feel as calm and clear as me?

Above me was a slanting shaft of the black rock face carved jagged with wind and rain. I found I could stand on the ledge and lean against it. I rubbed my face against the sun-warmed rock, and even though I was on a tiny cleft of the volcano, I felt safe. I put my ear to the rock and heard the echo of the wind inside the hollow mountain. I put my mouth to the cleft and sucked its secret air. The ancient air whirled into me, spinning through my body. I felt I could fly.

I realized with a surge of joy that I had stumbled upon the "missing" hole on the roof of Devil's Kitchen. As my eyes opened to the darkness, I could see a tunnel inside the cleft. I hoisted myself up with strength I never knew I had, and got my arms and my head into the gap.

No wonder the schoolgirls had not found the "other side" of the hole in the cave. They had searched the surface of tableland, when in fact it was over the cliff's edge! Surely I was in the hands of my emergency god, because I had fallen on the one ledge that actually had an exit. It is fate, I thought, I will crawl through the tunnel and end up on the folding chairs in Shankar's den.

But it was my hips that came in the way. Typical Indian figure, wide pelvic girdle, good for childbearing but terrible for crawling through narrow tunnels. I found myself wedged with my head and shoulders out at one end, and my legs wriggling into the void.

All the panic crouched in my stomach pounced into my

throat and I screamed, "Bachao, bachao, bachao. Ayi, bachao, save me mother, save me. I was screaming for my mother in the comfort of the mother tongue. My head scraped the roof, dislodging a family of bats who flew around in circles screeching. I had no hope.

And then I saw a pinwheel of light and heard footsteps echoing their way towards me. There was hope!

It was a man, holding a candle. In shadows, he looked like a gorilla. Large, hunched, shambling. He was smoking. He peered up at me in astonishment.

I explained my predicament as best I could to the unseen hulk between the swirling bats. He stood as if glued to the spot below me for what seemed a lifetime, and then he stubbed his cigarette and said, "Thamba," wait. He left and returned with a lantern and a metal chair. He stood up on the chair, reached his giant arms out, and pulled with considerable might, grunting. I wriggled and squirmed and then in the end came flying out like a projectile. I fell on top of him, he fell off the chair, and we were flat on the ground, I on top of him. He smelled of sweat and bidi smoke. I was torn and bleeding and barefoot.

It took me a minute to recognize him. It was Kushal Wagle, the scandal-ridden youngest son of Janaki Wagle, the younger brother of Pinkie and Yellow.

We limped into the den and sat on the metal chairs, facing each other. In the days when I was accepted into the bosom of the Wagle family and sat out in the veranda with the inspector, I saw Kushal rarely. He had a room in the front of the house that he used as his fortress, venturing out only to forage for food or make a phone call. He was sulky and never bothered to look at me, or at anyone else. In those days, of course, I did not know of his paternity issues.

Kushal put the lantern on the table in the center of the den and lit a cigarette. He had thick lips and a chubby, pimply face.

My hair was at half-mast; I knew I must look like a witch. I was shaking. I wanted to ask him for a cigarette, but I knew that would be too shocking.

"Hello, how are Pinkie and Yellow?" I said instead, thinking it was best to go to the common ground to create some comfort in this, the most bizarre of meetings.

"You don't know Pinkie and Yellow, do you?" he said very rudely.

"Well, of course I've heard about them so much from your parents," I said. In the shadowy light, I felt he leered at me.

"Do tell your mother I miss her kokum kadhi," I added. Wanting to remind him how well I knew his mother.

I spoke in Marathi, as I mostly did with his parents. But he answered back proudly in English.

"Oh, yes, yes, you know my parents," he said. He took a large swig from an unmarked bottle containing yellow liquid and then sniggered. "All of them." I realized he had been sitting in the cave alone, drinking country liquor. He was clearly drunk.

In all of the scandal stories swirling around town, they discussed how the inspector felt about rearing the son of his enemy, or how his wife managed to hold her head up in the bazaar. No one had spared a thought for poor Kushal, except to examine the tilt of his head, the shape of his jaw, or the color of his skin, in order to judge who his father was.

The lamp threw an immense, wavering, genie-like shadow on the cave wall.

My throat was parched. "Do you have water?" I asked

He took another swig and passed me the bottle. "Only liquid here tonight," he said, and now there was no doubt about it, he was leering.

I refused, though I admit I was sorely tempted. Never, my mother had dinned into me from the day I could hear, never let yourself be alone in a room with a man. They cannot always control their natures, she usually added, lowering her voice.

The leering man rested his elbows on his knees, hunching forward towards me. "Very soon, I'll have it all going again. I'll have drinks, and even your charas ganja." He spoke the words "charas ganja" in a contemptuous manner. "The old hawaldar, he has promised to get me some of it. You tell those pussy friends of yours—ya, tell those friends to come next week. I will supply all their bad habits." He winked at me.

"Shankar and Son. I should put up a sign outside the cave. That'll show them. That'll show Inspector Wagle. One prick, and he will burst like a balloon." This was Kushal's rite of passage—choosing his father. He was sitting there alone in the dark, scheming of casting his lot with the lowly servant.

I decided it was time to leave. I was shaken up and barefoot, and it was a long way back. First, a clamber down to the dirt road, and then a long and winding walk to Aeolia. I had been hoping to get Kushal to come with me, and perhaps go to the Nest, which was much closer, and get a police car. Or at least a pair of slippers. But Kushal was drunk and mean. I realized I was better off on my own.

I got up to leave. I smoothed my short hair and straightened my clothes.

"Thank you, Kushal," I said. "You saved my life. I am eternally indebted to you. I slipped off the edge of the cliff and fell on a ledge. And miraculously, I found the tunnel. I could have been stuck in that wretched hole forever. That would have been a fate worse than death. It was my good fortune that you were here tonight. I am in your debt."

"Then you should return the favor," he said thickly, and reached out and caught my arm and jerked me onto his lap before I had a chance to react.

"Come on, don't act so proper. I see you talking loose in the bazaar with those boys. I'm sure you service them." I felt a large hard lump rise through the bottom of my thin cotton salwar.

He pulled my hair and held my face just below his. I was glad for my short hair; my tail would have been torture. With the other hand, he was groping my meager breasts. "Ha, you think I don't see you? I saw you going up and down at night from my window. I see you all the time. I see you everywhere. You better be nice to me, or I can get you in hot water. Very, very hot water. You better be nice."

The Sword of Innocence was too tarnished to wield. I would need another weapon.

I relaxed my ramrod-stiff body. I put an arm on his shoulder.

"Fine. Then be a man and do it properly," I said. "No need to pull and tear. Let me teach you. First, light me a cigarette."

He looked confused, not sure he could trust me. But he was a boy of sixteen, and his vanity got the better of him.

He took out two cigarettes from the packet near the ashtray.

I pulled one from his hand and threw it across the cave. "Only one," I ordered. "I'll show you how we can smoke together. I'll exhale into your mouth, and then when we kiss the smoke will swirl between our mouths. We keep blowing it back at each other. You'll see how nice that feels." I grinned at him. I had never done this myself.

He gave a foolish smile and lit my cigarette. He began to breathe hard, his eyes glazed with anticipation. He opened his mouth. His breath was noxious.

I took two deep puffs of the cigarette to steady my nerves, and then I plunged the lighted end onto his tongue, twisting it hard, hoping it would leave a permanent scar. I jumped off his lap and ground my elbow into his still-hard groin, and I ran out of the cave while he was howling in pain.

I scrambled down to the dirt road. I heard him cursing me in Marathi, but thankfully, he did not follow me.

THIRTY-ONE

Merch

AFTER MY TERRIBLE confrontation with fat Kushal, there was only one place to run to. I knocked against his door, praying, and he opened it and took me into his arms.

Merch had quiet eyes and gentle hands. He did not roll me a joint as would be his custom, but produced a dusty bottle of Black Dog whisky and gave it to me and knocked down a large peg himself, neat. My feet were scratched, my clothes were caked with volcanic dust eons old, and I could not stop my hands from shaking or my teeth from chattering.

I had a long, long bath by myself, and when I came out, he asked, "Another whisky or tea and omelet?"

First whisky, then tea and omelet, I said, and when he came to me with the clinking glass, he took my head and held it against his stomach as he passed my chair. I liked the way he could run his hands through my cropped hair. His hands felt warm and big.

As he bustled around in the kitchen, I lit a cigarette and sipped my drink and decided that I had to trust Merch with my story.

Merch is easily the best listener I know. I started with my night on table-land and the descent of Nelson, and went on to the attempted rape. I told him that I had lied.

I do not think he said a word during the whole confession. If he did, I do not recall. I studied his face for signs of shock or dismay, but I instead I saw a gleam of light. "I'm glad you finally decided to trust me," he said, finally, after I had grown silent.

He had known all along. And he did not love me any less.

"Those days everything was so intense, and then, standing in front of Woggle, I thought it would kill my parents. I felt that Pin was right beside me, she was telling me to deny even being there on table-land. I felt so confident, somehow. I felt I could dig around and find out what happened that night, you know, talk to everyone in school, uncover all those old secrets, and get more than those sakaram detectives ever would. In *Macbeth*, Banquo says, '*I must become a borrower of the night, for a dark hour.*' I kept justifying it to myself later, saying I was merely borrowing that dark hour, and I would return it later."

It sounded lame, even to me. "But at least there is one bright spot," I said. "At least I solved one mystery. It's Kushal watching me in Aeolia at night." I scraped up the last of the omelet grease from the frying pan with a piece of pau bread.

"You stay here with me, until all this passes," he said. I was hurt, but tried not to be, because he did not say, "You stay here with me forever."

"But it's causing such a scandal," I said. "Why don't you stay with me there, in Aeolia?"

"And why will that be less scandalous?"

"Well it's far away. We can be more furtive. This place is in the middle of everything. Even the girls were sniggering about it."

He was silent for a minute. "What would you rather do?" he asked.

"I am not safe here. I think I should leave Panchgani. The inspector told me I would be needed for questioning. I am to inform him if I need to leave Panchgani." I said it not because I wanted to go. I knew I could not leave now. I had swallowed Panchgani and could not leave until I digested it. Or maybe it was the other way around. Panchgani had swallowed me, and I could not leave until it was finished with me.

I said it, waiting for him to say, "Don't go, I'll miss you." But he said nothing.

I felt resentment against Merch creep upon me again. His holding back. Why can't he say he will marry me? Then we would live here without the swirling rumors, and he would keep me safe.

But the image crumpled before it was fully formed. I could not imagine the two of us bustling around with children and shining brass pots.

"Why not tell him about Kushal?" he asked. I shook my head then.

But later that night I awoke in a cold sweat. I sat up in bed knowing that I was not safe in Panchgani unless I told the inspector that I was in danger from his son, who was not really his son. And I would never be safe within myself until I confessed to what I really saw on table-land on the night of Pin's death.

Merch opened his eyes. He took my hand and kissed it and held it against his chest, playing with my fingers.

"I don't know if I should be saying this," he said in a hoarse just-awoken voice, "but I love you."

"You should say it if it's true," I said. He felt so safe and clean and good I could not believe it was still the night of the leering caveman.

He stroked my hand as one might a puppy. "But you, you are a restless one."

"And you are not? I think we would be good together. We would be, Merch."

"Let's take it as it comes." He pulled me down and kept my head in the hollow of his shoulder.

I rolled over to the other side of the bed.

"I am not one for commitment," he said, knowing he had hurt me. "But you know I am yours."

As long as it's fiction, I thought.

The next morning, I asked Merch to come with me to Inspector Wagle for moral support. But just as we were about to enter the chowki I changed my mind. I decided I was better off going in alone.

"I need to change my statement," I told the inspector. He looked at me uncomprehending at first. My voice was shaking. "I need to change my statement about my activities on the night of the murder."

He looked very tired. There were large dark pouches under his eyes. "Now what is it, Charu?" he asked.

I confessed. "I did go up to table-land that night for the same reasons as I earlier stated. Moira Prince had come to my room and told me she was thinking of jumping off the cliff. She did not tell me about the letter and the fateful message it contained. I thought I calmed her down. But later that night I awoke with a start from a bad dream and felt that she might still have gone up.

"But when I went up to table-land, I did see something. I saw Moira Prince standing against the needle. Before I could go up to her, I saw Miss Shirley Nelson approach her. Miss Nelson patted her on the back. Moira Prince did not turn. Miss Nelson left and walked down from table-land. I turned and walked back soon after her."

I became bold and strong as soon as I began the first line. It was the most liberating moment of my life.

"She was alive when you left?" he asked. "Did you talk to her?"

"No, I did not go up to her."

Mr. Woggle was eyeing me with displeasure and disbelief. *You mean you went all the way up to table-land in the middle of a monsoon night because you were worried about her, and then you turned and left without talking to her? And how did you suppose she would not jump after you left, since, by your own admission, you were concerned about her safety?* I think this is what he must have been itching to ask—I would have been, if I were him—but I was so clear and confident that he decided to say nothing.

"You will be testifying under oath in court soon," he said. "Nelson is accused of the murder, so you cannot be accused at the same time. But you will be cross-examined by big-city lawyers. Do not take this lightly. You young people do not understand what you meddle and say."

"I did not kill her. If I had, why would I come forward at this stage? To be put under suspicion? I am doing it because I cannot leave Nelson falsely accused."

"It is not as simple as that," said the inspector. "Why did you lie in the first statement?" I noticed he avoided saying my name.

"My mother was in critical condition," I said. "I thought the shock of it would kill her."

"If, as you say, you did not even go up to her, what is the shock?" We were both silent for a moment. A young Brahmin girl from Indore, or even from Panchangi, for that matter, does not reveal her sex life to an inspector. I could not say I went up to table-land to find Prince due to a lover's quarrel. Decorum must be maintained at all costs, even though we were talking of murder.

"And your mother, she is better now?" he asked.

"No," I said, "she is still in a coma."

"Nelson will be tried in court, and if she is found not guilty due to your testimony, it may be your turn next. Have you talked to your family about this?" he asked.

"Yes, I have," I lied, but it was a white lie, with no guilt attached. I had still to figure out how I would tell Ayi and Baba, and what it might do to them in their fragile state.

"Now, you are telling me that the principal didn't kill her and you did not kill her." He looked defeated, I thought, more than anything else. "Who killed her, then?"

"I do not know," I said.

"Well, you can tell that to the court. For now we will record your new statement and pass it on to the relevant authorities." He was silent for a while, seemed to have trouble breathing. Our beer and peanut evenings seemed from another life. "You could face charges for perjury. Or for obstructing justice, if the matter gets really out of hand."

So that was done. Without further ado, I launched into the second subject.

I have a complaint, I said, against Kushal Wagle.

The inspector stiffened and looked at me with distaste. Distaste for me or Kushal or perhaps for us both.

"You are trying to tell me that he assaulted you in Devil's Kitchen at 8 p.m. last night?" he said when my story was complete.

"Yes."

The inspector looked me up and down. I could not blame him, exactly. I had already lied to him before.

"And what do you want me to do about it?" he finally asked.

"I want to register an official complaint," I said. "He should be locked up. He is a danger and a threat."

Even to my own ears, I was beginning to sound hysterical and high-pitched. The inspector must think I am mad. Cracking under duress. He might think I was one of those strange repressed women—often thin and ugly like me—who began by getting tremors and temple trances, and progressed to making up stories with connotations of lewd attacks. He might even think I made up the entire table-land episode.

Inspector Wagle frowned, folds of plump flesh puckering. He called in his hawaldar. The hawaldar stood at attention beside the desk. You could hear the inspector's mind working.

Finally, he said, "Tell Manu to take the car and fetch Kushal here. Not the jeep, the closed car, the Ambassador."

We waited in silence. The inspector pretending to be reading some official reports, I staring at the wall.

Kushal shambled into the office. He gave me a defiant smile.

"So what happened last night?" the inspector asked him in Marathi, his voice curt, his lip curled in disgust.

"Didn't she tell you?" he answered, insisting again on English. "I saved her life. I don't know what she was doing down there, but I saved her life. Heard her scream and pulled her out of the hole above the cave. Maybe she is here to give me my reward."

"But you tried to—tried to threaten me," I almost screamed in anger and frustration.

"Did you or did you not lay a hand on her?" asked the inspector. He stood up, came around his desk, and even though he was at least two inches shorter than the boy, the inspector raised his hand and gave him a hard slap on his cheek. Kushal cowered, and in that moment I saw the helpless eyes of a lost, abused child.

The inspector turned to me. "I cannot control this boy anymore. Go ahead, register your complaint."

"No," I said, feeling sorry for him. "I do not want to record a statement. But I want some kind of assurance that he will not harass me in the future. I think he follows me and spies on me."

"We will see to it," said the Woggle.

"What does that mean?" I asked the inspector.

"Curfew," said the inspector without looking at Kushal. "If he cannot be trusted, then he will be locked into his room at night. I cannot have a member of my own family causing disturbances in town."

"Well, then, I guess I will be safe," I said, and turned to leave.

Kushal showed no gratitude for my soft heart. "Ha!" he said.

"She knows I can get her sent to jail. Instead of punishing me, ask her. Ask her what she does at night when she goes up to table-land with all those boys."

Then he turned, pointed to me, and said, "She's a whore." He used the Marathi word, which sounded even worse. "She's a randi and a murderer."

"Shut up, you bloody idiot!" shouted the inspector. "You dumb son of a bitch, you know-nothing. Why did I keep you and your slut of a mother in my home? Taking advantage of my good nature. And now this. Take him out of my sight." He directed his order to the hovering hawaldar.

I remembered the night of my first dinner with the Woggles, when I had returned to find Janaki wailing. So this must be a regular fixture of family night at the Woggles. The Woggle's torture chamber. Slow drip.

But Kushal stood his ground. "I saw her," he said, pointing his fat index finger at me. "That night from my room. I saw her running down. And it was after the scream."

"What is this babble?" asked the inspector with a snort.

"That night, I heard shouting and screaming, 'Help, help, help!' It was a terrible scream, and I heard it. It was at least ten minutes after that that I saw Charu running down."

"And all this time you said nothing? Don't tamper in this matter." The inspector went to Kushal, grabbed his shoulder, and shook him up. He raised his hand again, but the hawaldar discreetly separated them.

"You can hit me. Coward. Hit me," said Kushal. "But I will record this statement. If you don't take it, I will go down to Satara Court."

"He's lying," I shouted. "There was no scream."

The inspector turned to me. "And how would you know that?"

"If Kushal heard the scream, and I was on or near table-land, I would have heard it. And for that matter, no one else did. Not the girls, the boys, or even Shankar. He was in the cave; he would have heard the scream. He would have said so in his defense when he was arrested."

"You can't stop me," said Kushal. "I heard a scream, and I saw this whore"—he pointed in anger—"I saw her running down after the scream."

All those years of being a good girl were wasted now and gone. I had been accused of being a whore and a murderess. I should have felt distraught, destroyed. But I felt as light as a feather.

THIRTY-TWO

Silver Oak Wind

MY WORLD WAS turning cartwheels. It was straight when I was high and upside down when I was not, and so it was always in the school that the world was most warped, because I never went stoned to school.

But perhaps I could, I was thinking as I walked into school the next morning in my one and only pair of blue jeans and Pin's short saffron kurta. Pin must have come stoned to school. I'm sure I could do it too. No one would ever know. Few people really looked beyond the blot, after all.

The walk from Aeolia was windy, and I was running my hands through my hair. I cast a different shadow in my wild blowing short hair, I was thinking in a pleased manner when I ran into Miss Wilson outside the staff room. There was a strange man in a frayed black suit sitting on the bench outside the staff room. Miss Wilson raised her eyebrows and blushed brick red. "Er, Miss Apte, can I see you in my office for a minute?" she said.

In her office, she stood on the carpet of recalcitrant students, so that I was forced to stand beside her. She handed me an envelope from the Satara District Court. I knew what it was already. I had been expecting it ever since I heard that Nelson had a lawyer. It was a summons to appear before the court as a witness for the defense.

I took the thick envelope and turned to go. But Miss Wilson was not finished with me.

"Just a minute, Miss Apte, I've been meaning to bring up a small matter for a few days now, and I suppose now is as good a time as any. You see, the girls are not allowed to wear trousers," she said quite conversationally, now having composed her face and drawn the mantle of leadership about her. "There was an incident when bell-bottom trousers were confiscated from the senior dorm. It was last summer, before you came, of course, just before the school fete."

I had heard of how Miss Manson made the girls kneel in front of her as she measured the distance from the ground to their hems. And then made them stand up so she could measure the width of their hemlines. But I had not heard of the pants episode.

"Actually, I think there is no harm in them being allowed to wear trousers now," said Miss Wilson. "Times have changed, and it would keep their minds from the minidress. I do think it can be done, but now is not the time. What do you think?" she asked, rubbing her pointy chin.

It would throw Miss Manson, the elastic watcher, out of business is what I was thinking, but I nodded sagely and said, "No, not the time. Perhaps next year."

"Then it would be better for their morale, don't you think, if you did not wear trousers? While you are inside the school, that is, of course."

I knew that Pin was the only woman in Timmins who wore pants, but I presumed it was out of choice that no one else did. And truly, it was hard to see Jacinta Mathews or Willy in divided legs.

I spun around to go, although she had said nothing about the meeting being over. "There were trousers worn by a teacher last term," I muttered over my shoulder. "I do not see why I cannot wear them too."

From the corner of my eye I saw her face redden again, and in her eyes a spark of anger, the kind of anger that Pin must have elicited. I did begin to feel that we were good for each other, the Prince and I, a good cop and bad cop rolled into one, better equipped to solve the mystery of her murder, which was a good thing, because I was sure that my life depended on it.

To my relief, the staff room was empty when I entered. In my cubby was the weekly letter from Baba.

My dear Charu,

I trust this letter finds you in the best of health and happiness. We are both fine here.

Your Ayi is gaining her strength. She drinks chicken soup every night. She is more relaxed, now that she is at home, and her eyes are showing signs of comprehension. You should not worry about her. I judge the prognosis to be good.

We are hiring a new maid for your mother, since

the last one was caught stealing some food items by the jamadarni, who still comes to clean.

It is getting cold in the evenings here in Indore. But the days are pleasant. Ayi and I take our walks at 5 p.m. instead of 6. She walks for quite a stretch now.

Take care of yourself, and do not worry about the home front.

Your loving,
Baba

His letters were always terse and pointed. That is how he must have taught himself to write in the navy.

He knew nothing of my new life as the Panchgani bad girl. He thought I still lived in the back room of the school hospital. Now that I judged the water to be around my neck, I thought perhaps I should tell him that I was embedded in the notorious murder trial.

"I will get a lawyer. I will arrange for you to stay for some time with my brother's niece and her husband in Poona," he might say.

But before that, I would have to tell him a very long story, full of sharp turns and spins. I did not have the strength for it, and neither did they. Let Ayi recover, for now at least.

I came upon Merch drinking coffee at the Irani Café on my way back from school. The café was crowded with Irani boys from Green Lawns swallowing in a manly manner, Adam's apples bobbing with gusto. Merch sometimes gave them English lessons. Today he was sitting alone.

I waved my summons at him.

"Are you scared?" he asked after reading the entire thing.

"Yes, and no. Depends."

"Depends on what?"

"Time and place," I said. "I don't think Woggle can control Kushal. I think he was outside my room again." Yesterday, I had returned to Aeolia in the afternoon straight from the chowki and, tired after all my adventures and upheavals, slept straight through until midnight. When I awoke to use the bathroom, I heard the sound of someone peeing in the bushes outside my window.

"But why should Kushal have it in for you?"

I had figured that one out. "It's the standard-issue Indian male syndrome. Mother and sisters on a pedestal on the one hand, and loose women and prostitutes below the boot on the other. And me, a good Marathi girl like his sisters, consorting with all of you wastrels and worse. Too confusing for him."

This case had stirred up Panchgani. Though a small village, it had many disparate groups who lived in their own watertight worlds. But this case had sliced through the town from top to bottom. Everyone was involved: the white teachers, the brown teachers, the schoolgirls, the schoolboys, the shopkeepers, the police, the malis, the marginals. Everyone was in the pot. Everyone had an opinion. Some in batches, like the ayahs of Timmins who thought it was witchcraft, others in groups of two to five. It was hard to tell who all thought it was I, because some stared and others averted their eyes. I did not really care to judge who thought what. Only Merch. Only Merch knew my truth, and I wanted him to believe every word.

I wanted to convince him of my sense of imminent danger.

But on that matter, he seemed strangely detached. Scornful, even.

"Have you considered," said Merch, lighting a cigarette and taking a deep, post-coffee puff, "that it might have been the girls who pushed Pin? Why should the girls be innocent? They were there that night, and one has to wonder."

"It was a mischief thing, you know, breaking bounds," I argued. It was not possible.

"But they could have pushed her over. There were three of them, and only one of Pin. It might be relatively easy," he said looking gravely into the distance.

"But why should they?" I asked Merch. "Motive, one must have a motive at least. You don't just get up and push a person over a cliff for the sake of it. I doubt if they harbored any deep feelings for her."

"Schoolgirls are nasty creatures," said Merch, "little savages. Socialization is still primitive at that age. Like *Lord of the Flies*."

"You think those rustlings outside my window are them?"

"They could all be there tonight, and they could surround you and have their way with you," said Merch, raising one eyebrow in a significant manner.

"Tonight, why tonight?" I asked.

"Didn't Nandita say it would be tonight?" he said with a furrowed brow.

And then I saw the twinkle light up his eyes and a slow sweet smile spread across his face, and I saw that *he* had been having his way with me.

The girls were hysterical and Merch was an actor.

"This Panchgani is mad. The whole town. Why do all these people have nothing better to do than follow each other around?"

"Exactly, my dear Watson," said Merch. "They have no drugs, no gambling, no bad habits. So they have a lot of time to plot and kill and rape. Bad habits—bad habits are the only hope for Panchgani."

"And to top it all there is the missing Hindi teacher."

I resolved to take him back to Aeolia with me that night. We would put off the lights and pretend to sleep and then we would steal out and look around. Stealthily signaling to each other with torches, we would trap young Kushal, or the girls, since Merch seemed to think it was them.

I decided to say nothing of my plans just yet. We went to his room and made love, and then fell asleep.

It was dusk when I awoke, heavy with dope. I lay looking at the sky go from gray to grayer in the frame of the window. It was that emptiness again, that yellow-fog-rubbing-against-the-mind kind of evening. Merch was sleeping, his lean, long body curled away from me, his springy hair tangled over his eyes. He wore soft khadi pajamas and an old black T-shirt that showed his concave stomach, the line of hair going down from his navel. I felt I was playing blind man's bluff alone, groping around without anyone to touch.

Merch awoke and eventually shuffled to the kitchen. I pretended to be asleep. He pulled the chain of the naked bulb above the stove, and I heard the clinking of spoons. We had a somber cup of tea in the gloom, the dim light from the kitchen casting looming shadows of the two of us crouching on the bed. For the first time in my life, I felt a longing for Indore evenings. Bright tubelights and dinner at eight, served with the purposeful clanking of glass bangles.

"I want to go to Aeolia tonight," I said.

"This must be connected to your supposed watcher," he said, passing me a neatly rolled joint. I took two deep puffs, and soon it became crystal clear to me.

"Yes, I have to," I said.

"Correct," he said. "Be it man or beast."

"Correct," I said. "Be it Kushal or the girls."

"Or the Hound of the Baskervilles," he said.

Why did he need to convince me that this was a childish and hysterical pursuit? Was he foolish enough to think there was no danger at all in this world?

I was restless.

"Let's go, let's go," I said when he smoked a cigarette and pondered if he needed another cup of tea. I felt a sense of urgency, when really and rationally there was none. I was pacing up and down the room, Hindi notebooks in hand.

"Steady," he said as he would to a horse. "We'll have dal fry at Kaka's and we'll walk on to Aeolia. The time will be ripe then."

"Ripe, ripe for what?" My voice rose a register. I knew I was sounding nervous, if not outright hysterical, but I could not stop myself, this was how I felt. In the light of reason, Merch was right, of course. There was no way of judging whether earlier was better than later.

I sat myself down on the mattress on the floor, folded my legs under me, and lit a cigarette. Did he really want me to believe that the girls were dangerous?

I could not remain seated. It was as if I were tied to a string offstage. My knees refused to stay folded, they jerked themselves up, and I began to pace again. The room felt like a pressure cooker. I walked onto the balcony, finished my cigarette, and threw it, watched its burning arc swing down the valley, and then went into the room determined to get him out.

Merch was still in his white khadi pajamas. He took me into his arms and nuzzled his head between my breasts. He ran his hand through my hair and nibbled on my ear. I felt a flash of impatience. I saw suddenly how easy it would be to slip and slide into a slothful life and then dissolve into a little brown puddle.

He should be rushing up with me, with shining sword in hand, ready to hold my hand and fend off all evil at short notice.

But no, not Merch.

He did not want to come with me. He would not come with me. Why lead a horse to water when he is not going to drink? Everyone knows that.

"Merch, just stay a goof for me, all right?" I said. It was an impulsive thing, popped out before I had thought it through, but as soon as I had said it, I knew what I was going to do.

"Ayi chi shappat," he said with a bemused smile. "I promise."

I turned and left him, and did not look back to see if his face registered shock, dismay, or surprise at my sudden exit. I had the definite feeling that the night would go better without him. Perhaps, even, my life. I loved him, how could I not love Merch my whole life? I would, I assured myself as I walked to the bidi stand and bought a packet of Wills cigarettes. I would surely love him my whole life. But not tonight. Tonight I hated him for sending me out alone.

"I'LL SOUND NERVOUS *and intense and mysterious. Just give me five minutes, before she can ask questions, and then come and call me and I can pretend I did not want you all to know."*

"And then we'll go up and finish her off, just as we did with all the others," Shobha would cackle, rubbing her gnarled hands. Akhila would hoot with glee, the shadow of her hooked nose and pointed chin thrown large against the wall.

I was walking to Aeolia, my heart thudding against the brown-paper-covered Hindi notebooks clutched to my chest. I had passed the Government Holiday Home, the garage of the chained cheetah, and the last loop to Aeolia, where the streetlights stopped. Murderers were passing before my eyes like jerky early film clips. The schoolgirls, Mr. Blind Irani, Shankar, and even the plate-throwing little Jacinta, mewing because of our illicit love.

My legs began to shake violently, and I sat down in the middle of the road under the last streetlamp. I could turn around and smile my way back into Merch's room. He would never even bring it up.

Good teacher that I was, even when I flounced out of his place, missing the swing of my plait behind me, I had remembered to take the books. I looked at them lying in a neat pile on the road and, on an impulse, took the first one and flung it up in the air and watched it land spread-eagle in the culvert beside the road. The moonlight filtered in through the swishing silver oaks that the British had kindly planted for our benefit.

And then I threw up another book and another, and then I stood up and started flinging them with abandon—some like discuses, slicing through the air, some simply launched as high as they would go. When only one book was left, and I still wanted to rip and hurl, I began to tear the pages and make them into arrows or crumpled balls and fling them around with passion. I could not quite read the name, but the writing seemed to be that of Ranjana Kothari. When I finished, the road was strewn with papers, and brown-paper-covered books lay around me with gay abandon.

When I started the throwing, I fully intended to pick them up and chastely take them home. But now that I had torn and destroyed one, there was no point in saving the rest.

There was no point in going back tomorrow. There might not even be a tomorrow, for I might die tonight. I might as well burn my bridges, I reasoned. I went back to the brown notebooks lying scattered like dead soldiers on a medieval battlefield, lit a match and set one afire, and then another and another and another. The wind picked up, and burning leaves were churning around me like Diwali rockets gone awry.

They would be found tomorrow. By which time I could well be choked or bludgeoned or pushed off a cliff.

The burning had calmed me down. I felt clear and strong. I could not go on trembling with imaginary ghosts.

I could always shout for the family of the drunken mali. The eldest son was a strapping lad, and he would not be drunk. He would handle Kushal or Raswani or the girls or the Hound of the Baskervilles. I considered taking him with me. But I thought of how I would have to knock on the door of their hut and then they would shout, Kaun hai, who's there, and I would lean close and whisper, Charu from next door, but they would not hear, and so they would shout, Who? and then I would have to shout back loudly, Charu, it's me, Charu from next door, and then she would shout Who? and with all that noise my stalker would slide out and stalk another day. No, I must know tonight, once and for all.

I could creep into my room without switching on any lights. There were two knives in the kitchen, both blunt and rusted. I could die of stab wounds or tetanus if the mystery interloper should run out with a sharp object too. I remembered Merch's Swiss Army knife that he forgot in my room the other evening after using it to burn off a chunk from a ball of hash. I would walk with my soft flat Kolhapuri slippers without a sound. I would walk with swinging arms down the paved passage to the kitchen with the pocket knife pointing out. I crept into my room.

I found the knife, and found that my hand was shaking as I pried it open. Merch had bought it from a Rajneesh hippie at Poona Station, and he was very proud of it. It had the full sixteen attachments, including the bone toothpick. I decided to open all the instruments on one side. The knife, the corkscrew, the scissors, and some others, all sharp.

And then I thought, Kushal will be much more wary this time around. He'll probably gag and bind me before I can lift a finger. I would be better off going in with a bullhorn, like the one Miss Manson used on sports day, so I could shout for the mali before I was gagged. If I had thought this through, I would have picked that up off the hook in the staff room.

Pin's whistle—I had Pin's whistle in the suitcase below my bed. I had found it lying neglected in her cubbyhole in the staff room after her death. I remembered her coming back from evening sports, her hair ruffled, patches of sweat on her blouse, and the whistle still around her neck. I had taken it in a sentimental fit when I was alone in the room, kissing it because it had touched her lips. I slid the suitcase from under my bed and dug it out. Pin's whistle would bring me luck.

With a whistle to my mouth and a sharp octopus object in my right hand, I walked past the mali's smoking hut and was turning the corner to the kitchen when I heard hoarse muttering. Was there more than one person outside my room?

I followed the sound to the back of the kitchen building and paused at the corner. It was a dark night, but by now my eyes were open and I could see quite clearly. It was a woman in a sari, crouching. Her gray hair was no longer in a bun, and her sari was torn and rumpled. She was talking to herself. It was the Hindi teacher.

She appeared stooped and tired. She got up when she saw me turn the corner, moved two steps in my direction, and then collapsed against the wall. I could see that she was panting. She got up and tried to run as I walked towards her, but she did not have the strength. I held her hand as I led her to the mali's hut, but it was more for support than restraint. She seemed broken by her time in the wilderness. She was nodding and muttering; she did not look at me and seemed not to know or care who I was or where I was taking her.

The mali's wife made her sit on a blanket in the corner and gave her water in a tall steel glass. Raswani grabbed the glass with both hands, drank the water in three greedy gulps. Then she lay down in a small curled ball like a kitten and fell asleep.

The mali opened up the drawing room of the main house, from which I phoned Inspector Wagle, who said he would gather his hawaldars and arrive shortly.

But it was Merch who landed up first. I heard a knock on the window of my room and then another. In the dark, from the small slit of a window in the mali's hut, I could see nothing. I sent the mali's son to look into the matter, and he came back with Merch in tow.

In the dim light of the single naked bulb, Merch's eyes were bewildered, accusing. I don't even know if he registered the presence of the sleeping Raswani in the corner at first.

"Why did you just run away without telling me?" he asked in the angriest voice I have ever heard from him. "I thought you'd gone for a walk, or to wait at Kaka's. I came here as soon as I could." I could see his breath still came fast. The mali's wife gave him water in the same steel glass.

The Woggle was in a lather when he finally turned up. He had no place to keep Raswani for the night. "Mahtari," he said, snorting in a derisive manner. "This Panchgani lockup was not designed for old women. I will have to keep her in the school with a hawaldar on duty." He muttered morosely, not relishing the task of awakening those virginal white women in the middle of the night.

As it happened, he did not have to. When he got there in the white Ambassador car, with Raswani in the back between two hawaldars, the school was in an uproar of blazing lights and scurrying girls in flannel pajamas. Nandita had just been found halfway down the table-land cliff. She was unconscious and in critical condition and was being rushed off to hospital.

When she came to, Nandita named the murderer. It was Miss Raswani, she said. Miss Raswani had pushed her over the cliff, shouting garbled nonsense from the Bible, just as she had pushed the Prince.

When I had come upon her behind my kitchen wall, she was returning from the struggle, exhausted and frightened by what she had done. The roaring was finished. She had gone out like a lamb.

Her story was on the front page of the *Poona Herald*, and the third page of the *Times of India*. It was on the front page of the *Evening News*:

HINDI TEACHER ARRESTED IN GIRLS' SCHOOL

The recent mystery of the death of the British teacher of Miss Timmins' School for Girls in Panchgani under suspicious circumstances has taken another sinister turn with the attempted murder of a student at the same school, a fifteen-year-old girl.

The girl, who is in critical condition at Poona General Hospital, has stated that she was dragged by the hair and kicked off the cliff of table-land, a plateau in Panchgani, by Miss Usha Raswani, also a teacher in the same school.

Miss Raswani, who had fled the school soon after the murder of Miss Prince, had taken to wandering around the village at night, it is reported. She has been apprehended and has confessed to the murder of Miss Prince. She has been charged on one count of murder and one of attempted murder, and is being held in Yerwada jail to await trial.

The second victim—whose name has been withheld in order to protect her status as a minor—was, according to her police report, lured by the accused up to table-land and then pushed off. It was the same spot at which the British teacher, Miss Moira Prince, fell off the cliff to her death. By good fortune the minor was rescued that night.

"We have to conclude that these are the doings of an insane mind," said the local inspector. "It is as much for her own safety as for the safety of the community that she is being held without bail." Inspector Dhananjay Wagle had previously detained two others for the crime: a local mali and the British principal of the school. The principal, Miss Shirley Nelson, has been freed, her passport has been released, and she has left for her native England this morning.

Miss Nelson had refused to make any comment to the reporters who had mobbed the airport.

And I was free. As free as the wind in the silver oaks.

THIRTY-THREE

The Tuesday Sari

THE WHOLE SCHOOL loved Nandita as they had never loved anyone before. She was a heroine, she had risked her life but solved the murder. Entire classes sent her individual handmade get-well-soon cards. Some third-standard girls sent her pictures of Jesus with inspirational poems. Teachers and matrons set up a sign-up sheet outside the staff dining room to ensure a steady stream of visitors, and her friends were allowed to miss school and go down to Poona to "cheer her up." Her sisters went twice a week and were given special treatment.

Her spine was damaged, and the general opinion was that she would never walk again. Her father had brought in a Dr. Udwadia, whose name no one had heard before but who was now known through the length and breadth of Panchgani as the all-India authority on spinal neurosurgery. If he could not mend her spine, no one could.

Akhila was with me the day I visited her in the hospital. She was carrying a large number of little plastic-covered autograph books. "Now the whole of standard six has sent these books for her to sign. As though she has nothing better to do," she grumbled, dropping one.

Akhila told me most of the story in Kaka's taxi, where we sat facing the Pearsall ayah, who was her chaperone, and a young boy with two kid goats who continued to have a baa-baa contest all the way to Vai, where they thankfully got off.

"That day, Miss Mathews took us behind table-land for a walk, and we were sitting behind, you know, just below the first loop of the path that goes to the top, and we saw these two village girls walking down to the valley, both wearing Miss Raswani's saris. The Monday and Wednesday saris. She's had them since we were in standard seven. The Tuesday sari is that horrible yellow-brown one.

"So of course we charged down and asked them where they had gotten those saris. They claimed the saris were theirs and tried to walk away, but Shobha caught the hand of the smaller one, and said, 'You stole them. We will report you to the police. You are a thief.' The little one was so cheeky. 'That's what you rich people always think. We people always steal. Go, go to the police, I'll show them where we found the saris.'

"We got them to show us instead. Behind a scrubby bush a little way down towards their shortcut path to their village, they showed us a black trunk. The girls had broken the cheap lock with a rock, it hung dented and loose. Inside we found four neatly folded cotton saris. The two silk church saris were at the bottom. 'See, we didn't even take the silk. Just took two saris from the top. We were going to wash them and put them back soon,' they assured us.

"The rest of the trunk had petticoats and dressing gowns and some papers. There was one dirty torn sari wrapped into a bundle and pushed into a corner. It was her Tuesday sari.

"And she had disappeared on a Tuesday. And so, of course, we all got very excited. And then Nandita became all quiet. I knew she was up to something, because she stopped giving her opinions. We were all saying this and that, and she just nodded. At least if she had told us, this would not have happened." Akhila then burst into tears.

We put on our cheery faces as we walked into the room, but Akhila cried as soon as she saw Nandita's broad smiling face popping out of the brace she was wearing. Then we all started crying.

Her body would turn fat on top as she grew older in a wheelchair, I thought, almost choking with pity. I was glad I was not her, though I knew that she was the heroine, and I was not.

Everyone was crying a lot these days; it was a free-flowing kind of time warp. All three of us sobbed for a time, in separate sorrows. In the end, we hugged, she on the bed and I bending over her in an awkward way, wondering if she would ever make love.

But I felt the strength flowing from her body and knew that pity was the last thing she wanted.

And then we settled down on chairs, spent, and talked of unrelated matters and school gossip and *Macbeth* for quite a while, until it was almost time for us to leave. But I wanted to know. And I was not going to leave without asking the question.

I too had gone towards Raswani that day. I had just been luckier than Nandita. Look her in the eye and say what you want to say, I thought. Deformity we both know.

"Nandita, what made you stay behind like that?" I asked. Akhila was shaking her head vigorously at me from behind her friend, pigtails wagging, mouthing "no, no" and waving her hands in case I missed the other cues.

Nandita's voice took on a dry, neutral tone. "I thought at that time that she was not the murderer. I was quite sure it was someone else. I thought she ran away because she was afraid for her own life. When we were examining her trunk, I saw something move behind a bush, and I thought it just might be her, watching us. Raswani had confided in me once; I thought she liked me. I thought if I waited for her alone, she would come to me. I could get her back, and then they could talk to her. She knew everything and was afraid, that is what I thought."

And then she said, as she would have to for the rest of her life, "I could only do it alone, don't you see? Raswani would never come close otherwise."

We were all quiet after that. I wished I had not made her go through the pain again.

Nandita turned her face away from me. She nodded to Akhila and closed her eyes.

"She is tired," said Akhila, smoothing her brow. "We should go."

Outside the room, Akhila was reproving. "Don't you know you are not supposed to ask her about it?" she said to me sternly.

"No one told me anything about that."

"Well, you aren't," she said, huffily. "Now you have gone and upset her."

"But don't you think she thinks about it all the time? Maybe she wants to talk."

"We have been told not to. By those who know better. Her father and the doctor have said that it will hamper her recovery. Miss Wilson called our class to the drawing room. Her father was there, and he spoke to us. Now that Raswani has confessed, he said, there is no need for anyone to ask her any more questions about it. For now, at least."

On the way back, in Kaka's taxi, with the school's chaperone ayah snoring beside us, and a newlywed couple bound for Vai whispering coyly in the front seat, Akhila could not lose out on the glory of telling the rest of the story.

It seems that, on their way down to school, Miss Mathews had broken the girls up into small groups and sent them to collect tadpoles in jars from the little brown puddles, for use in her science lab. And no one noticed that Nandita had slipped away.

They realized they had lost Nandita when they reached school. The girls went up and told Miss Wilson about the trunk and their missing friend. There was no Timmins car, so Miss Wilson and Miss Manson had borrowed bicycles from Shankar and Mallu the bearer and cycled up to table-land, the entire senior school crowding at the gate to watch them sail away into the evening.

Nandita had been finally discovered on an outcrop of rock halfway down the cliff, lying like a broken doll.

Nandita gave her police report. She stated that Miss Raswani had pushed her off the cliff. And then she said no more.

Nandita had not told anyone the details of the incident. She refused to talk about it. Traumatized. That was the new word all the girls were using. Nandita had been traumatized and never talked about what happened on table-land.

"But that's what bothers me the most. Nandita is so cautious. What made her so reckless that day?" I said.

"It's because of you. She was so intent on saving you. She was blind to her own safety," said Akhila with an accusing look, the resentment she had harbored all day bubbling up to the surface. "It's all your fault."

"Come on, Akhila, do you really think I would want Nandita to be hurt because of me?" I asked. Akhila shrugged and turned her face and stared sullenly out of the window as we shuddered up the ghat.

The residents of Panchgani collected funds to buy the demented Hindi teacher soap and fresh milk in jail. Most agreed that these were the actions of a deranged person. A few said it was Raswani giving up her life for her idol, Miss Nelson. Everyone was relieved that the case was closed.

And I. I packed my bags and left for Bombay as I had always dreamt I would. I did not return to Panchgani until twelve years later, in the summer of 1986.

EPILOGUE

Chinese Lunch

Charu

I FIRST CAME across the concept of the "doughnut truth" in *Ada*. When I learned of the schoolgirls' sinister meeting with Merch on table-land, I wondered if Merch had given me Nabokov's novel all those years ago so I would know about the hole he had left inside the truth.

We were at Kamling restaurant, Akhila and I, shielded from the molten heat of May by deep air-conditioning. We were meeting after twelve years.

Akhila had called one morning when I was ready to leave for college, books under arm, bag on shoulder, tiffin packed.

"Miss Apte? Miss Apte, this is Akhila, from Timmins. I used to be Akhila Bahadur in those days. Remember?"

I really wanted to put down the phone and be gone. I knew I would be late for class.

Much to my surprise, I was leading an almost respectable

life at thirty-two. I was teaching in a Bombay college, I was rearing my child and tending my father. Except that I had no husband.

Ayi lived on for ten years after I left Panchgani. She gradually became somewhat more alert, recognizing us all, saying small words, and laughing at everything. She put on a lot of weight and was like a jolly Buddha. I finished my master's degree, married a rather inconsistent and unsuitable co-student, and had a daughter. We visited Ayi and Baba in Indore as often as we could. When we were coming, she would wait at the window holding out a toy she had bought for Uma. Uma would be looking up as soon as we got off at the train station. "Is that the window, is that Nani's window?" she would whine at every corner, until we arrived and she would charge up the stairs and leap into Ayi's arms. Ayi died in her sleep in 1984, soon after my husband and I parted ways, and Baba moved in with me. He was very active in his retirement, having set up a complete regimen for himself, which included picking up Uma from school, buying fresh vegetables and meat every day, and a brisk evening walk of exactly five miles. I thought of us as a happy family. The Panchgani gang had dispersed, though we still met from time to time.

The white light of summer was blasting into the little room. I began to feel the sweat prickling on my upper lip. I had never been that fond of Akhila. "I'm late for class . . ." I began.

And then I remembered her face framed in Mahrukh Tunty's bra.

One cup was fitted to her head, as snug as a swimming cap. The bra was hooked and hung down to her chest like a demented necklace, the second cup pointy and erect over her left ear.

Mahrukh Tunty's huge round breasts have since gotten her on the cover of *Playboy* magazine, and made her famous through the length and breadth of India and beyond. But in those days, her mountain breasts were a legend only in Panchgani.

Mahrukh was very proud of her breasts then, and happy to parade the evidence. She was prefect of the lower dorm in Rowson House, and she regularly had her minions hold the voluminous underwear over the sigri in the veranda. The center never dried in the monsoons.

On an afternoon of deep rain, I came upon girls gathered and roaring as if around a cockfight. In the center of the circle were two heads in the two cups of Mahrukh's brassiere, bouncing on their haunches towards a stretched skipping rope. The bra strap was fastened at their chins, and they had one arm around each other's shoulders in a lunatic version of the three-legged race.

They scattered when they saw me, and somehow only Akhila was left beside the burning coals, the lacy cup still fitted to her head like a cap, her pigtails popping out from underneath.

"Look Miss. Monsoon swimming," she said, her black eyes dancing. I smiled and walked on, waiting to tell Pin so we could both roll with laughter on her bed.

"Of course, I remember you Akhila," I said, warming to her.

"I saw you at Breach Candy the other day, you had a little girl with you. I waved and called, but you did not see me. I think you were trying to catch a taxi outside Premsons. And then, strangely enough, I ran into Divya Moghe, just out of the blue at some function. We began talking, and she told me she is doing her Ph.D. under you. In Kalina, she said. It must be fate, I thought. First I see you, then I hear about you. I got your number from her. I knew I had to meet you."

Akhila and I agreed to meet for lunch at Kamling restaurant a week later.

I smoothed my sari and sat down across from Akhila at the corner table she had chosen. Her hair was tied up in a high ponytail, she wore a printed salwar, and looked plump and matronly as a mother of two has every right to be. There were big single diamonds in her ears and on the third finger of her left hand. Her thickened features appeared to me as flimsy as a cardboard mask, for I could see the impudent grin of a fourteen-year-old beneath it.

"I somehow remember you with shining lips and oiled lashes," I said.

She burst out laughing. She still had naughty eyes. "Vaseline," she said. "I put large globs of Vaseline on my lips and eyelashes that year. I felt glossy, like a model. Punita Parikh told us that Vaseline made eyelashes grow. So we all started doing it. But I was obsessive. I kept a bottle in my desk and would lather it on between periods."

"Did you know that Raswani died?" she added.

"Yes, in jail, a year ago. Or was it six months?" I still got bits of Timmins news from Divya Moghe.

"But do you really believe that Raswani killed Prince?" she said, putting vinegar and onions on her sweet corn soup with the blue glass spoon.

We had all believed it at that time. We had wanted to believe it. Because we all knew Raswani was mad enough to kill, and we knew she needed to live in custody. And we wanted the case solved, all of us, for our own different reasons. Doubts were discussed only behind closed doors.

When could Raswani have climbed up the hill, where could she have waited, and how could she have come down unseen when it was clear that an unseemly number of Panchgani residents were on and around table-land that night?

"Is it a promenade like Marine Drive or something?" said the judge, who had never been to Panchgani, not finding it as bizarre as it really was.

For a time, I was obsessed.

"No," I said to Akhila. "It does not feel right. In fact, if you want to know, I don't think she was up there at all that night."

Akhila was shoveling chop suey into her mouth with boarding school urgency. She nodded vigorously. "I agree with you," she said. "But not Nandita. Nandita is a hundred percent sure that Raswani killed the Prince that night. She has it on the authority of that time when she spoke to Raswani and Raswani gave her the famous letter. She says that Raswani revered Nelson and finally lost her mind and killed Prince to save her. And then tried to killed Nandita, because she thought Nandita had guessed the truth. And you know how Nandita can be. I am even afraid to open my mouth and say anything." She rolled her eyes up towards the red pagoda lights hanging from the ceiling.

I did know how forceful Nandita could be. Nandita who swept through the corridors of power in her fast foreign wheelchair, Nandita the smart lawyer in a handloom sari, Nandita the champion of the crippled, whom she was now agitating to be called handicapped.

I wrote a chapter for her book *Deformed* (Oxford University Press, 1981). It was a very clever anthology of deformity. I was one of the ten women whom she persuaded to write about their personal bodily defects. There was a woman with buckteeth that flared right out of her lips, a woman with a club foot, a woman who was trying to commit suicide and had been rescued and was now scarred, a blind woman who had remained a spinster and sat mostly alone in the back room of her brother's house, and so forth. Each chapter contained a photograph of the deformed as an adult and, when available, as a child. Some of the chapters were "as told to Nandita Bhansali." Nandita's own story brought up the end. She started out with her fall and her crippling, how her worst childhood nightmare became real, and how you find new strengths, but she quickly broadened the discourse to the need to legislate to protect the weaker sections, this being the duty of any modern society that considered itself humane.

If her chapter was the most potent, mine was the funniest. Not that it was rip-roaring or anything, but it did have a dash of humor, and so Nandita wisely placed it first.

In my teens, at functions and gatherings, I sat in a corner and watched other corner and back-row people. The severely deformed were single and had to be attended to by servants. In addition, entire families who did not fit into the center sat on the rows of chairs that lined the back walls of marriage halls, and I, invisible among them, spent my time formulating the relative ladder of deformity. My chapter, called "The

Greater Blemish," was based on my observation that among couples, the woman was always at least one rung lower than the man. A girl with a bad face might be able to marry a man with a clubfoot. A limping girl had to marry a cripple in a wheelchair; a pretty deaf girl, an old man. A rich girl with a cleft lip could be married to a poor boy who needed prospects. Interclass was permitted because of the other disparities—rich girls with deformities were married to poor boys without prospects—but not intercaste. Caste must be maintained at all costs. A Brahmin could never marry a Banya. Not in an arranged marriage!

That was the essay, and sandwiched in between were the social underpinnings of how women were always at least one rung lower in a feudal patriarchal society; the hierarchy just became more pronounced in cases of deformity.

I could have mentioned that I lost my deformity the day I looked firmly into the mirror and decided that I had been dealt a goodly hand after all. What happened was that the blot popped right out of my soul the day I saw Nandita leave the hospital with her mother pushing her wheelchair, a small, straight smile on her face. I knew my deformity could be dreamt away, but hers could not be. A girl in a wheelchair could not pretend to be whole, not for all the perfumes of Arabia.

"I can understand why Nandita needs to believe that it was Raswani," I said across the half-eaten plates of chicken chow fun. "She told me she still has nightmares about Raswani's mad eyes looming over her, flared in unfathomable anger."

"So if it was not Raswani, and you saw Nelson leave, who could it be?"

"I think she jumped," I said.

It was logical to imagine that Prince went up to table-land that night with every intention of jumping to her death from the top of the cliff. She was a passionate and unstable girl, given to mood swings. And that night, she had felt completely alone.

Only your own family will tell you when you have snot on your face, she said to me that night. *Only your very own people.*

And maybe if I had been wise and courageous, I could have seen that she had something on her mind, that she wanted to talk. She might have shown me the letter that was in her pocket. But I was young, and my head was full of silly romance books. Everything revolved around what she did to me. And so I fought with her, and she stormed out. And then she had her fight with Nelson.

She walked up to table-land, her world as sharp and wounding as the blade of a steel sword. She must have been ready to jump when I saw her. I remembered how her raincoat flapped in the wind. Nelson interrupted her plans by going up to make amends. Prince did not turn, and Nelson did not stay.

Did she know I was there behind the rocks? I believe she did. I believe that it was I who sealed her death. I knew that if I had gone up to her as she sat on the edge, she would not have jumped that night.

"But what about the struggle?" said Akhila. "There were signs of a struggle."

"I think some of it was her grabbing at dirt and rocks as she fell. And the rest, imagined. Don't forget Inspector Wagle needed a reason for putting Shankar in jail."

"I don't think so," she said.

"What do you think then?" I shot back, our old hostility raising its head again.

"The strangest thing is how half of Panchgani was up there that night. In the middle of the monsoon, in the middle of the night, so many people just randomly there. It is out of a detective novel. You have to admit that, at least. I was in the school since I was seven, and I had never been on table-land at night—except once, when Miss Wilson took us stargazing—and there we were, breaking out of bounds, on that very night. We hadn't even planned to be on table-land. I said it when we got back to the school and I say it to this day. It was the rain stopping suddenly after so long. And that too on a full-moon night. It drove us all mad that night."

There was nothing to disagree about. It had been a fateful night.

"Miss Nelson," she said, her words tumbling over each other, lest I not let her finish, "Miss Nelson was the most logical suspect. But then, as in any proper murder mystery, it turned out that she was innocent. We hold up many of the minor characters who, according to storybook logic, should have done it. I mean Mr. Blind Irani, it turns out, was walking on table-land that night and, with his tapping cane, could have banged into her and accidentally pushed her over. Or there was even Shankar."

She hesitated, swallowed a large sip from her second Fanta, and said, "Well, what the hell, it's been so long."

I knew she would not let me go without finishing what she had to say.

"We always boil it down to two," she said. "Shobha felt it

was you. And Ramona will insist to this day that it is Merch," she said, cracking ice with her teeth.

"Merch? Why Merch?" I asked, bemused, for how could Merch the Mystery Man hurt anyone?

"A love triangle. A crime of passion." She mumbled, looking into her food.

She rode it to the end. I had to grant her that. I could imagine she brooked no nonsense from her children or her in-laws. I wondered what bizarre turns their thoughts had taken to pin the deed on Merch, a man whose feet barely touched the ground.

"You really don't know Merch," I assured her. "I can tell you he would be the least likely man on earth to kill for passion." I was very patronizing. I ordered another salted lemon soda.

"You forget," I said, "that I was very close to her before she died. I know instinctively that she jumped. She saw no life for herself, she jumped."

"And all those people, you and Merch and Nelson, up there to watch her."

"Look, I can't explain it all in rational terms. You know that. It was as if she pulled us all to her that night. But none of us could help her. Maybe she called us there to say good-bye." I shrugged. "And for your information, Merch was not there."

Akhila shook her head. "I don't know if Merch is still a friend of yours," she said, "but I wonder about him. I mean, you know Ramona has never been the same since the episode with Merch on table-land."

Merch, who was so gentle and elegant in those days, I could not see that at all. Were they still like schoolgirls after all these years? Were they still seeing the world through the Timmins filter?

"And what are you talking about?"

It was as if I had put a live wire to her head. She seemed electrified. She leaned forward, she sat back."I can't believe it. You actually did not know it all these years?" She shook her head. "I never smoke in public, but I can't help it, what the heck." She continued babbling, fumbling through her lumpy round purse for her pack. "They are not going to believe this. They won't believe it. I wish Shobha and Nandita were here. At least one of them. Otherwise, they just won't believe this. Gosh, imagine. All these years you did not know about Merch's role in this whole murder episode."

"The night of the funeral, when you went back up to table-land with Merch, didn't you know that we followed you?" Her hand was shaking as she rested her cigarette on an ashtray. "I mean, I wasn't there, but I know it like I was. It was Nandita and Ramona. They followed you up to table-land. Didn't you know?"

I shook my head. No, I did not know. I was still disbelieving, but something tripped in my gut, perhaps, because I felt hot and flushed and I had to fan myself with a Kamling napkin.

"Then why did you leave first, alone?" asked Akhila. She narrowed her eyes and looked at me through the smoke of both our cigarettes, for all the world like a Miss Marple from the colonies.

I recalled that night on table-land. We could still feel her presence near the needle, Merch and I, hugging and weeping. And then we sat quietly for some time. "He said he had promised to wait for Mr. Irani and walk down with him," I said. "You know the old man used to walk on table-land at any time, day or night, since he could not see anyway, he said it made no difference to him."

"But he threatened to kill them. As soon as you left, Merch walked up to Nandita and Ramona where they were hiding behind the bushes, and he said he would kill them if they tried to snoop into the murder," she said quietly.

Merch? Our Merch threatening to kill two schoolgirls?

"I'm sorry, I can't see it. I know he would never use the word snoop," I said, and I knew it. How could anyone see him, with his lazy walk, parting the bushes, bending over the girls and telling them with a quizzical smile, "Don't *snoop* into the murder or I will kill you?"

Akhila was quite astounded. "What is it with you?" she said, jerking forward with exasperation. "Was it a '70s pot thing or something? And what about the raincoats? How did he happen to have those raincoats if he hadn't been on table-land the night of the murder?"

Raincoats? This was a new story, after all these years. I listened in silence as she told me how Merch walked the two girls back to his room, giving them the raincoats they had left on table-land the night of the murder along with a sinister threat.

"Ramona's mother tells everyone that her daughter has become touched," said Akhila, patting her temple. "Every time we go there and Ramona spends hours talking intense nonsense, her mother says, as we leave, 'It is a curse. Because she looked into the eyes of a killer as a child. A fresh killer still mad from the murder.' But of course the mother is rather hysterical herself."

I felt I had been dragged through that entire monsoon again during the course of this one Chinese lunch. First the schooldays with the girls floating like blue-checked balloons, and then the raw days after she died, when I was like a dead chicken ready for the fire. I withdrew into my shell, as if I were still twenty-one. I could only look at her, dumbly.

She tilted her head and eyed me with a somber look, resting her case. She had been perky, not pretty, as a girl, and now had a blithe kind of confidence. Her chubby cheeks had filled out into a round pleasant face. I could see her ordering endless plates of chicken sandwiches at CCI Club for her plump children.

I sat back, spent and cold as the air-conditioning dried the rivers of sweat on my body. It was not that I believed everything she said. It was that I felt suddenly certain that I had danced like a snake for the eyes of a killer.

I was possessed all of a sudden with the intensity of those days. I took a taxi from Kamling restaurant, past Marine Drive, where the sea glimmered like glass under the white-hot sky and pigeons picked at peas on the promenade, and went directly to Merch's room in his mother's flat on Napean Sea Road. I ran up the servants' spiral stairway at the back of the building, arriving breathless on the fourth floor to find a lock on the door. I waited a while, heart aflutter like Charulata Apte of the old days, though I had not felt a whiff of that in any of the hundred times I had been to his room in Bombay all these years. The room had a separate entrance, a bed in a corner, and a balcony in the same place as his room in Panchgani. Instead of the layered mountains, the balcony faced a champa tree, on which kites got stuck in January and swung idly all through the summer. In the monsoon, the kites fell to the ground defeated, and the champas blossomed, blowing gusts of scented air into his room in the afternoons as if he were a Mughal monarch. It was the servants' room of his mother's large flat.

The alcove leading to his room had a forsaken air, and so I climbed down and went again up the main staircase and rang the front doorbell. His mother answered and stood as she always did, blocking the front door. She was elegant, in an ironed shift and a shock of short white hair. She was, as always, very warm and friendly, and we stood at the door for a full twenty minutes cooing to each other—how is that nice dark young man you brought with you last time, how is your daughter, I'm sorry I always forget her name—but she did not ask me in. "Sorry, the house is being pest-controlled today, and we are busy covering up all the furniture," she said. She always made an excuse not to invite me in.

Turned out Merch had gone to Panchgani a few days ago. "He said he is going to be there for some time, doing his portraits. He did not tell me anything about when he is coming back. If you see him, please tell him he has to be back by next Tuesday. I need him to sign some papers and the ration card has to be renewed, not actually renewed, but last time the ganga took it they said there is something wrong with it." I left before she could think up any more reasons.

IN MY DIGNIFIED householder stage, I did not dash off on foolish hikes and errands. But the restlessness of the old days took hold of loin and limb, and I decided I could not wait for

Merch to come back to Bombay. That Friday, after classes, I left Uma in my father's care and went up the winding ghat road to Panchgani and entered the room above the dispensary for the first time in a dozen years.

Half the kitchen was now a darkroom. Merch's black-and-white portraits of Panchgani people—portraits of fat Kaka in his restaurant, Mr. Irani playing blind bridge in the sun—were hung around without apparent order.

"What kind of idiot were you in those years, Merch?" I asked him, sitting on the bed, legs dangling. "Who were you in those days?" My mind was turning somersaults after the first joint. "Did you think you were that young man in *Crime and Punishment*? Smoking dope all day thinking of devious plans? I can't remember his name. You know, that young man who stayed in a cupboard and killed the old lady."

"Dimitri Dimitrovich," said Merch. "It's safe to call all Russian heroes Dimitri Dimitrovich."

He must have known where I was heading. There was silence for a time as he went into the kitchen to make me some tea.

"You don't know, Charu," he said, coming out of the kitchen with two steaming cups. "I was obsessed with you in those days. Even when you were with Pin. I used to look at you all the time in the room, just wait for you to look up at me. I felt you were like a rosebud, you had a perfume around you. I concentrated on you. I knew I would make love to you. Even when I saw you with Pin. It was funny, I wasn't jealous or anything, you just kept growing more beautiful before my eyes, blossoming. I knew it would happen suddenly one day, like magic. And it did."

We sat there, lost in our own regrets for a while.

I lit a cigarette and through the distance of the smoke I saw him again. Merch has stopped smoking—"Only tobacco," he always explains, "only stopped tobacco"—now that he is past forty. His hair is still straggly and long, but he has a very small bald patch at the back of his head, which he tries to comb over. I remembered him in this very room, bending over this same record player when his body was lithe and shiny. I could not find him sinister.

"But were the girls right, or were they not?" My words came out in a tumble. "I have come all this way. I rushed straight to your house in Bombay and then came all the way here to Panchgani to ask you two burning questions. What were you doing on table-land on the night of her death?

"You were seen on the cliff that night, you know," I said, accusingly. "Why did you never tell me, Merch, in all these years?"

"How am I supposed to tell you I was there when I was not? We went up together. It was the night of the funeral. That was the night I was up on table-land, with you."

"But we went up together, we sobbed and had this heart-wrenching moment. And then you sent me down alone, saying you had to wait for Mr. Irani, right? Now Akhila tells me you went up to Nandita and Ramona, who were hiding behind the bushes, and you took them down to your room and gave them the raincoats they had left on the night of the murder. There was no sign of Mr. Irani. I don't understand at all."

I had always felt our love started that night, when we hugged and sobbed beside the needle. And to think that he lied and plotted that night hurt, even after all these years.

"You did not even tell me that we had been followed!" I said, disgruntled.

He fidgeted around for a while, blowing his nose with a crumpled handkerchief. "You found out about my fifteen minutes," he said with the shy, shiny smile that had wormed its way into my heart all those years ago. "The two girls followed us up that night. I knew they were hiding in the bushes. So after you left, I walked up to them. It was such a strange echoing kind of night. Poor things, they were crouching and shivering behind the bush. It was so out of Enid Blyton, I could not help myself. I stood over them and told them to leave detecting to the adults. I think I said something about consequences. I did a sort of sinister Cyrus." He was sheepish.

"I need some clarity here. Why didn't you just tell me, instead of sending me down alone first like that under a false pretext?"

"Mr. Blind Irani showed me the raincoats the morning after Pin's fall. He had found them on table-land. The girls' names were below the hoods. I knew Nandita, Ramona, and Akhila. I had taught them intermittently. I thought I would hold on to the raincoats for a day or two and see how it went down. Didn't want to get the girls in trouble. And then I saw the same girls following us. I figured they might have seen you up there that night. So I thought I'd give them a scare, keep them off your trail, so to speak. So I did my sinister act."

It hit me with the force of a thunderclap. "You mean you actually thought, Merch, all these years, that I committed the murder?"

He laughed then, for the first time in the story. "Don't be

silly," he said. "Not all these years, just the first few days. Not that I thought you physically pushed her. I thought that you and Pin might have gone up to table-land after the rain stopped. I thought she might have slipped in some skirmish, and you might have panicked. Something like that. It was quite probable, you must admit.

"And you—so fragile those three days in my room. I felt I held a bird in my hand. And then you asked about guilt, you may not remember"—I remember, Merch, I remember everything—"but you turned as white as a sheet and got off the bed when I mentioned murder."

"Wait a minute. Let me get this clear. So you did that purposely, you mentioned murder just to test me out?" I was getting slowly furious.

"Steady," said Merch.

"But I talked about it all the time, and I mention it as a defining moment in my life. I assumed equal knowledge. And now I had to hear about *your* role in the affair from Akhila, of all people, and that too after all these years?"

"I wouldn't call it a role. More of a cameo appearance, don't you think? All I did was tell these two silly girls to stay out of it. And after it all came out, it hardly mattered. I even forgot about it."

"You forgot?" I asked, unbelieving, because no one forgets those moments. Not even with all the dope. Merch, the Mystery Man. Now you see him, now you don't. That's what Pin had said to me on table-land the night she first kissed me.

"Did you know that all these years the girls thought you were the murderer? Because of that night. And they say

Ramona went crazy because of that night," I said, and then I felt I had been too harsh. "Must have been top-rate acting, that's for sure."

"I think Timmins School education nurtures this sort of nonsense," he said.

I decided to visit the nonsense-nurturing school, even though I knew no one there anymore. Sister Richards had retired, the Sunbeamers had dispersed, and Shankar now owned a bicycle shop in the bazaar with Kushal. It was called Shankarson.

In the principal's chair sat a dark, fat woman in a sari who could have been approaching fifty. I introduced myself to her. "Charulata Apte, I used to teach here a long time ago. During Miss Nelson's time," I said, wondering how much she knew.

She gave a start, clapping her hand to her mouth. "But this is the strangest thing," she said. She was a Syrian Christian, pallu tucked around her waist, thick curls escaping her bun and framing her face, so she appeared harried. Papers were strewn in untidy piles on the leather-topped desk.

I remembered this room always hushed and hallowed. But today, sounds drifted in. I could hear the hum of the life of the school, and floating in on the balmy air came a distant cry of "baatli paaaper" from the street. And though the shape and size and the furniture were just the same, and from the window, when you faced the desk, you still saw the stairs leading up to the school bell, it had relaxed and become an ordinary room. The atoms and particles had readjusted themselves; they had forgotten the stern rule of Miss Shirley Nelson.

"Charulata Apte? Now that is the strangest thing," said the

new principal for the third time, beaming with excitement. She had a well-modulated voice and a Malayalam accent. "You just will not believe this. It is the strangest coincidence, but I just got something in the post for you just last week."

I was staring at her, not saying a word.

The principal calmed herself and continued. "Oh, but perhaps you heard there was a letter for you. Yes, yes, silly of me. You must have been told. Looks like a lawyer's letter, very thick. They may have tried to contact you in other ways, of course. But I am glad you are here. I asked in the prayer hall if anyone knew where to find you. No one knew anything, though of course all sorts of rumors began floating around. I even wrote to Sister Richards, she is with her brother in Deolali, but I haven't gotten a reply. Of course, it's only been one week . . ."

I came out of my trance.

"Yes," I said dutifully, "only a week." The letter must have generated great excitement in the school. Surely the scandals still loomed over the school, just as they did over us all.

She nodded her head vigorously. She was an energetic woman. "Only"—she pronounced it *wonly*—"a week, and really today wonly I was going to send a note to the Chitnis family address I found in an old book, to Kolhapur. I see lots of Chitnis names on the sports records in the gym. Must have been smart girls."

She fished out the envelope and handed it to me. She did not sit back down immediately, but stood watching, hands on hips, waiting for my reaction.

It was a substantial cream envelope, official and foreign, sporting a typed address and an important air. From Stephen

J. Bender and Associates, Esq., London, England. I had never heard of them.

I mumbled my good-byes and swung out of the room, feeling the whoosh of air from the plait turning behind me like an absent limb. I heard *seven times seven is forty-nine*—that is how I always remember that piece of the multiplication table, from an upstairs window on a warm afternoon—as I floated off to the far throw-ball court, where I had met Nandita whole for the last time.

I tore open the envelope to find, inside, another envelope nestled within a crisp typed letter.

I was meant to read the wraparound letter first, get the outside story before the inside story, and so with shaking hands and a hammering heart, I did.

Dorothy Bender of Stephen Bender and Associates informed me that Miss Shirley Nelson had passed away on March 13, 1986. She had died in her sleep and been discovered two days later by neighbors who called the police. Among her papers was this letter, sealed and addressed to me. Ms. Bender continued:

> Although all her affairs and papers were well ordered indeed, there were no instructions pertaining to the letter. But since it was in the box marked "Upon My Death," and contained her will, directions for funeral arrangements, and other bequests, we feel that she intended it to reach you. We are sending it care of the school, assuming it to be the most current address she had of you.
>
> Since we have no indication of the date when this was written, we cannot know if it will, indeed, find you.

The envelope, in Miss Nelson's refined, even hand, was addressed to:

Miss Charulata Apte
c/o Miss Timmins' School for Girls
Panchgani
Maharashtra State
India

I saw her on my first day at school. I heard her say the hard *t*. "We'll look after Charulata here," she had told Baba, putting her arm around me with a reassuring pressure to the shoulder. I had felt safe and warm under her wing.

Inside the envelope was one sheet of paper, a foolscap sheet in her looped, slanted handwriting, with a blue ink pen.

Three witches were called,
Three witches came—
The mother, the daughter, and the lover.
Three more witches arrived on the wind,
Drawn by the shining eye.

They came uncalled and left their robes on the mountain.
They stood unbeckoned beside the witch
Who held the needle that stitches earth to sky.

They took a spark from her fire,
Twisting the tale in their hands.

The blind messenger carried the robes back that night
Anointed in blood.

The marked fool would bear false witness.

I folded the page carefully, put it back in the smaller envelope, folded the second letter around it, put it back in the larger envelope, put it all in my purse, and walked out from the gap in the hedge past the paanwala to Merch's room. I was glad to see that he was not there, but had left the key hanging inside the window that you had to push open.

I walked onto the balcony and sat on the mattress that had been dragged out for sunset-viewing, and read the poem again and again without any understanding, as if I were by-hearting a poem as a child.

It was hard to by-heart. It was clumsy. She could have done better than that, I thought at first, but then I realized she must never have been a writer. I saw her sitting in a gray-blue flat in some suburban spot near London night after night.

And then I curled up and drifted into a shallow sleep, thinking, I am the third witch, I am the third witch, I am in a story written by someone else. She was clever, to take me back into *Macbeth*.

I dreamt that as I sat across from her in that hospital room in Vai, the head of a snake popped out of her mouth and said in a saintly slithering Nelson voice, *I did it dear*, as she handed me the black-bound Bible.

It was as if I had known it all along. As if this had been the reality between us on that afternoon in Vai. The smell of the room came back to me intact, the smell of lavender water wafting from the handkerchief she held before her streaming eyes. And underneath, the strong smell of disinfectant masking the smell of decay and death.

I awoke with a square of moonlight on my face, the valley spread below me. Merch's balcony was the same—it still held the two of us, suspended over the smoke of the burning pink petals—but the valley below had changed, like a slide in a viewmaster. The Krishna that had meandered thinly through Merch's valley—it came out of the earth inside a cavern in old Mahabaleshwar—had been dammed and transformed into a glimmering glass lake. The envelope was under my pillow. I switched on the dim balcony light and read the poem again.

Merch was snoring softly on his bed. I folded myself on my balcony mat and lay shivering, staring at the majestic valley, my thoughts dancing in demented circles.

Three witches were called,
Three witches came—
The mother, the daughter, and the lover.

I was the third witch, the lover, that was for sure. Nelson had given me the family Bible that day in the hospital room at Vai; she had known that the Prince and I were lovers.

Three more witches arrived on the wind,
Drawn by the shining eye.

They came uncalled and left their robes on the mountain.
They stood unasked beside the witch
Who held the needle that stitches earth to sky.

They took a spark from her fire,
Twisting the tale in their hands.
The blind messenger carried the robes back that night
Anointed in blood.

The schoolgirls were the additional witches, who left their raincoats on table-land. They were the twisters of the tale. They had gotten hold of the letter and broadcast it to the world.

The blind messenger was Mr. Irani, who had found the raincoats and given them to Merch.

There was no mention of Raswani. She was not any of the three witches, and neither was she an additional witch, because she left no robes on table-land.

I had heard through Divya Moghe that for the past few years the ex-principal of Timmins had become reclusive and lived by herself with many cats. It was rumored that she had gone quite mad, although there was no substantiating evidence to support this theory. There was a trace of madness in her poem, but it rang true. It was an allegory, written and rewritten over the years. Every word had a meaning.

The murderer was the anointer of blood on the robes. But would that mean that the schoolgirls killed her? Or was the anointer indeed the Hindi teacher, who remained nameless? But why mention everyone else except the murderer?

The marked fool would bear false witness.

Maybe Raswani was the marked fool—marked as in marked by fate. But then her role was that of a witness. She was not the perpetuator of the crime.

Or it could be me. I was marked. Obviously I was marked.

If I was the marked fool who would bear witness, then Nelson knew I was there behind the rocks, watching her. She went up and petted Prince and walked down for my benefit.

I did it, she had said to me in my dream. And this is what she was saying to me with this poem.

She had trumped me, and she wanted me to know it, albeit after her death.

I saw the night again. I imagined Nelson as she walked up to table-land in her daughter's shadow. With one step, she loved her, with the other, she hated her. Left foot, she wished she was dead, right foot, she wanted to hug her to her bosom until the day she died.

Her daughter would not turn to her. She did not look back, even though she knew the secret mother walked behind her. With the raincoat flung over her shoulder like a cape, she walked with big steps and stood arrogant beside the needle.

The secret mother waited. I imagined the turmoil within the principal's breast the saintly mother of perpetual succor fighting the secret mother, the sinner mother. She knew only one could live this life. If the sinner were discovered, the saint must die.

Tomorrow, it would be over. Her daughter would tell everyone the truth, and she herself would be forced to flee the school disgraced.

Or she could kill her, tonight.

Surely, that is how it happened that night.

She sat still, letting the thought settle into her head. She would walk up from behind, she would give her a quick shove. They would think she slipped. It was for the good of all. It would bring order back into the world. For what good would it do for her, Shirley Nelson, to live disgraced when she was so good and strong in this garden she tended? Her daughter was just a thorn, asking to be cut.

And then the clouds parted, and the principal saw the schoolgirls under the needle. And then, as she knew they would, she saw them stop in their tracks as they saw their principal. She did not look up, and she heard them turn and run as generations of guilty girls had run when she turned her blind eye.

She felt the life drain out of her, knowing that she could not do it now. She could not commit this act that she could not even name now that the girls had seen them both. She knew that all she wanted was here, in Panchgani. She knew how strong and true it was, the urge to have her daughter dead. She should arise and walk back. But she did not have the strength. She felt as if she were grounded to the rocks by roots that pulled at her from the cave inside the mountain.

And then she knew it was fate when she saw the marked girl behind the jagged rocks that circled the needle. She knew that her witness had come. She arose and walked slowly up to her child and blessed her, and then, with a blind eye to the marked witness, she walked down the hill.

She turned as she came to the bushes by the lake. It is fate, she thought, as she waited. It is in God's hands now who lives and who dies. I am His instrument.

If the Prince and I had walked down the road together, perhaps the principal would have lain dead beside the cave that night. But I played my part, I turned and walked down alone, and Miss Shirley Nelson pushed the child of her loins off the cliff.

She could be a secret mother now forever. No one she knew would ever know how she was connected to the Prince. She felt she walked down the aisle to meet her new clean life.

But the story had begun to leak even as she turned the corner to the municipal park. The letter had left her room. With this turn, the stakes were higher. She was now to be exposed as a secret mother *and* a murderer. And so she stayed in her room all day and all night, waiting to steal the letter back from her neighbor, the Hindi teacher.

But the letter, slippery as an eel, swam away, and the story became the front-page news. And now she wanted to live. Now that the First Sin had burst forth into the sun, it was revealed to her as moth-eaten and musty. Now she wanted to live. Survival trumps self-image.

And so she took me into her hands. She picked me up like a pink plastic doll, she used my love for Pin to wind me up. In the hospital room she played the martyr.

You have taught me that my sin was not loving her. And for this, I must suffer, she had said to me in the hospital room, rubbing her hands in deep sorrow. Playing on my love for Pin, pushing the envelope of her sainthood, showing she was ready to be punished for a crime she did not commit. Hoisting me up on a pedestal for loving her daughter—you are special, she said to me.

She pretended to cry, but she was rubbing her hands in glee. She would say nothing, she would stay above the fray and make the marked fool clear her name for her.

As it turned out, Raswani did it for her instead.

Poor old Raswani, dying in jail, turned completely insane, not even recognizing Miss Henderson, who had visited her—Henderson told Nandita who told Akhila who told me over chicken chow fun. "It was so depressing," Miss Henderson had said. "She was as mad as a hatter when she died." And poor Pin, without a chance to straighten herself out.

All so that Miss Shirley Nelson could take her fat bottom back to England and dream of the mountain school that she had once ordered, a place where brown, bandaged teachers had padded around her like pets.

The Princes must have saved her. We'll take her away, they could have told her father. We'll look after her, and no one will ever know. We will adopt the baby and Shirley. Shirley will live like a clean woman in the world. You need never worry about her. No one is to know. We will never come back here, they might have said. The child must have always been wedged between them, though.

It was the loneliness that could have driven Nelson to do it, made her write the letter to me, the marked fool. If she did not tell, it must have seemed to her that she did not live.

I saw her playing obsessively with confession. I imagined her, night after night, writing confessions instead of praying. Many, many confessions, to many, many people. And then she burnt them. And now only this remained. This cryptic note, gothic as the act itself, a riddle that would always leave a little room for doubt.

I was pacing from bookshelf to balcony in a shaft of moonlight.

If I had comforted Prince when she came to me, if I had walked up to Pin at the needle, or waited until she turned to walk down and walked down with her, she might have lived. A whole different life, it would have been, for us all. Not better, necessarily, just different.

I felt my blot awakening. The blot and I had been at peace these past twelve years. It was mostly quite calm. It broke out and became red and sore and spread into my upper cheek sometimes, and then I rubbed it with Ayurvedic creams and mostly forgot about it. The blot, I thought, had waned. But now it began to prickle and then to creep and crawl and then to grate and it came back to me as if it had never left.

Baba had gotten me flannel mitts in the days of the cow-dung bandage. They itched my palms, I hated them the first night, but I could not take them off without waking Baba. My mittened fingers could not untie the naval knots that I refused to learn from him. And so I had to scratch my palms, and the outside of my bandage, on an anger and appeasement basis. I realized much later in the night that scratching my hands distracted the main itch. And so I began to put the mitts on every night—even after the cow-dung bandage was abandoned—and I curled up in my bed furiously scratching my palms. I managed to mostly eliminate night itches that year. Mostly, but not completely. I always slept with the mitts under my pillow. Until Panchgani. But it was desire that spread through my body then and sucked the juices out of the blot and left it dry and shriveled. Sleeping, but, I knew now, not gone. I found I was rubbing and rubbing and rubbing my blot in Merch's moonlit room.

I shook Merch awake. I switched on the light, thrust the paper at him, and then snatched it away when I realized he would not be able to read it without his glasses. I read the poem aloud, twice, without comment or explanation.

"It's all over now," I said, lighting a cigarette, pacing up and down as he fumbled. "Can you imagine, after all these years? It's all over now. And no one knows but you and me."

Merch rubbed his eyes and reached for his glasses. He blew on each lens, polished both carefully with the edge of his nearly white khadi kurta, and then put them on and looked at me gravely. "What's all over?" he said. "What?"

Glossary

Ayi: Mother.

Ayah: Maid.

Auntiji: The suffix *-ji* is tagged onto the ends of names or titles to denote respect.

Baba: Father.

Babalok: Children.

Badi Bhabhi: Older brother's wife.

Banya: Businessman.

Beta: My child, used as endearment.

Bhabhi: Brother's wife. Also tagged onto names of women to be used as a term of respect.

Bhajiyas: Fritters.

Bhakris: Flat bread.

Bidi: Cheap Indian cigarette; tobacco rolled in a local leaf.

Brahmin: The highest caste in the Hindu caste system.

Carom: Board game played by four people.
Chal: Come on.
Channa: Roasted chick peas, eaten as snacks.
Charas: Grass, pot.
Chas: Buttermilk.
Chi: An exclamation denoting something gross. Like "yuck."
Chowk: Courtyard.
Chudidar: Indian dress consisting of long tunic and tight pants.

Dal: Lentil curry.
Diwali: Hindu New Year.
Dupatta: Long scarf worn over Indian outfits.
Dhobi: Man who washes clothes.
Dhoop: Evening cleansing of home with incense.

Gajra: A string of fragrant flowers, worn in hair.
Ganja: Grass, pot.
Ghat: Mountain range in western India.

Hawaldar: Policeman.
Hindi: Indian national language.

Idli: Puffed rice cake, a south Indian staple.

Jhansi ki Rani: The queen of Jhansi, famous for her valiant role in India's first war of independence against the British in 1858.

Katori: Small steel bowl.

Kerala: State in southern India.

Khadi: Rough, homespun cloth.

Kheema pau: Mince and bread.

Khichdi: Rice and lentil, overcooked until it is soft and mushy.

Kokam kadhi: Sour curry.

Kurta: A long, loose shirt with embroidery in front. Traditional Indian clothing worn by men and women.

Maharashtra: State in western India (Panchgani is in Maharashtra).

Maharashtrian: A person whose mother tongue is Marathi.

Mahtari: Old woman.

Majli: Middle.

Malayalam: Language spoke in Kerala, a state in southern India.

Mali: Gardener.

Marathi: Language spoken in the Indian state of Maharashtra, in western India.

Masala Chai: Spicy tea.

Methi: Particularly pungent smelling spice used in pickles.

Nani: Maternal grandmother.

Pallu: The end of the six yards of sari.

Paan: Betel leaf with condiments, chewed after meals.

Police chowki: Police station.

Paanwala: A person who sells paan; stalls selling cigarettes, sweets, and paan are a fixture of every town and village in India.

Parsi: A small, distinct community in India consisting of worshippers of Zoroaster who migrated from Iran.

Puri: Fluffy fried bread.

Puja: Hindu prayers.

Rajesh Khanna: Film star who was very popular in the 1970s.

Rani: Queen.

Sari: Indian national dress.

Shivaji: A hero who used guerilla warfare in the Western Ghats in the seventeenth century.

Sita: Wife of the god Rama in Hindu scriptures. Was captured by the demon god Ravana because she did not stay within the bounds of the "line" drawn by her husband.

Supari: Sweet betel nut, sold in small packets and chewed like gum.

Sigri: Brazier with coals.

Tuck: Boarding school word for snacks.